continued . . .

THE
BLACK SHIP

A NOVEL OF CROSSPOINTE

Diana Pharaoh Francis

A ROC BOOK

ROC
Published by New American Library, a division of
Penguin Group (USA) Inc., 375 Hudson Street,
New York, New York 10014, USA
Penguin Group (Canada), 90 Eglinton Avenue East, Suite 700, Toronto,
Ontario M4P 2Y3, Canada (a division of Pearson Penguin Canada Inc.)
Penguin Books Ltd., 80 Strand, London WC2R 0RL, England
Penguin Ireland, 25 St. Stephen's Green, Dublin 2,
Ireland (a division of Penguin Books Ltd.)
Penguin Group (Australia), 250 Camberwell Road, Camberwell, Victoria 3124,
Australia (a division of Pearson Australia Group Pty. Ltd.)
Penguin Books India Pvt. Ltd., 11 Community Centre, Panchsheel Park,
New Delhi - 110 017, India
Penguin Group (NZ), 67 Apollo Drive, Rosedale, North Shore 0632,
New Zealand (a division of Pearson New Zealand Ltd.)
Penguin Books (South Africa) (Pty.) Ltd., 24 Sturdee Avenue,
Rosebank, Johannesburg 2196, South Africa

Penguin Books Ltd., Registered Offices:
80 Strand, London WC2R 0RL, England

First published by Roc, an imprint of New American Library,
a division of Penguin Group (USA) Inc.

First Printing, November 2008
10 9 8 7 6 5 4 3 2 1

ROC REGISTERED TRADEMARK—MARCA REGISTRADA

Printed in the United States of America

This book is dedicated to Tony, Quentin, and Sydney

Acknowledgments

I want to thank a number of people for all the help they gave me in putting this book together and making it the best it could be: Kenna, Megan Glasscock, Christy Keyes, Melissa Sawmiller, and Rhona West-brook. Special thanks to Lucienne Diver, Jessica Wade, and Liz Scheier.

I had to learn a lot about ships to write this book, and many books and people helped in that endeavor. They include Miah Gempler, James Fraylor, Alex Zecha, the crew of the *Lady Washington*, and the Tall Ships group on MySpace.

Additionally, I want to give a huge thanks to Cortney Skinner for the map and Michele Alpern for the wonderful copy edit and Paul Youll for a fabulous cover.

I couldn't write without the support of my family and friends and especially my readers. To my family—there aren't words enough for how glad I am I have you. For my friends—you are all made out of awesome and your support means everything. To my readers—you are the best readers anywhere and I thank you so much for letting me tell you my stories.

There will be some whom I've forgotten to thank and even though I do not do it here, please know that I am very grateful. As usual, all mistakes or liberties taken in this text are to be laid at my door. For more information about me or my books or expanded information on Crosspointe, please visit my Web site at www.dianapfrancis.com.

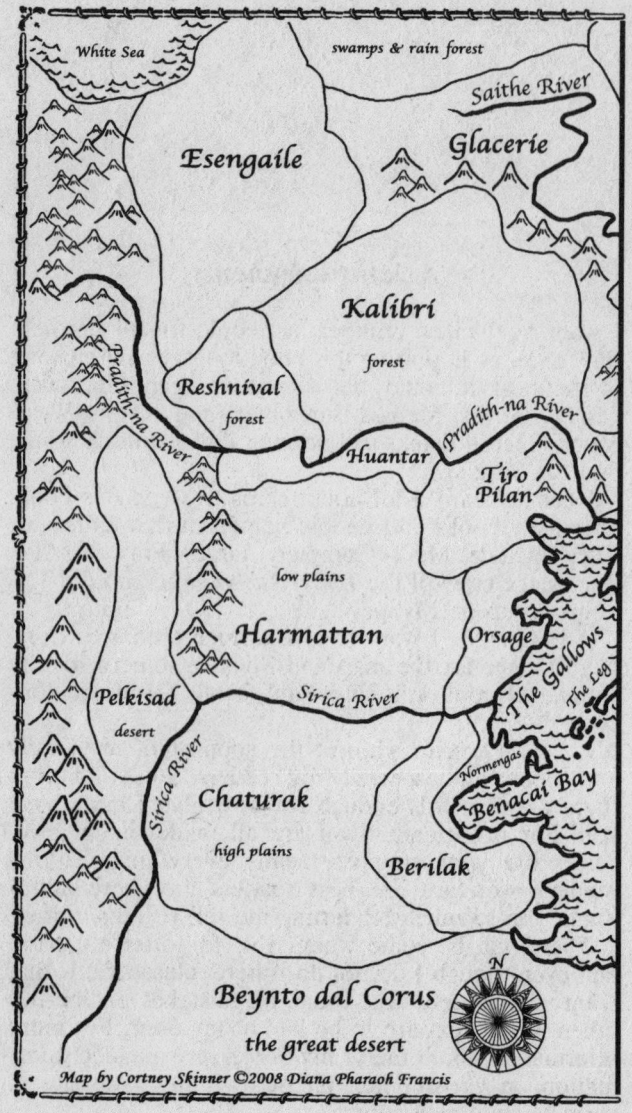

White Sea

swamps & rain forest

Saithe River

Esengaile

Glacerie

Kalibri

forest

Pradith-na River

Reshnival

forest

Pradith-na River

Huantar

Tiro
Pilan

low plains

Harmattan

Orsage

The Gallows

The Leg

Pelkisad

desert

Sirica River

Normengas

Sirica River

Chaturak

Benacai Bay

high plains

Berilak

Beynto dal Corus

the great desert

N

Map by Cortney Skinner ©2008 Diana Pharaoh Francis

Chapter 1

The day began with none of the usual portents sentimental novelists always deem necessary to make their
drivel interesting to mawkish readers. Thus it was that
Sylbrac was not forewarned of his impending doom:
the upcoming murder of his spirit, the stupid sacrifice
of his soul, the end of his life as he knew it. And it
was to be his own fault.

Sylbrac rose early. It mattered not that he'd been
out late the previous night at the Blood Oak, his favorite tavern on the docks. It was a place no other
Pilot would ever set foot inside, which was the at-
traction for Sylbrac. Nor did it matter that he'd put
away the better part of three bottles of wine all on his
own. He disliked slovenly habits and kept a disciplined
schedule regardless of his indulgences. He dressed
with the aid of his valet and ate a sturdy breakfast of
eggs, bacon, buttered potatoes, and strong cream tea.

As he ate, Fitch purred in his lap, gleefully kneading
sharp claws into his thigh with the smug superiority
that came with knowing there would be no retaliation.
Sylbrac manfully ignored the pain. Interfering with the
black cat's fun would only result in a snarling bite or
bloody scratch across the back of his hand. Nor was
that the worst of it. Fitch would then compound her
revenge by shredding Sylbrac's favorite waistcoat. Or
more than one.

After breakfast, he went for his usual ramble along
the headland, leaving Fitch curled up on a cashmere

blanket before the fire. He walked quickly, nearly running at times up the steep path and along the edge of the cliffs. He loved the briny smell of the sea, the whisper of the wind in the twisted pines along the shore, and the sibilant siren song of the water.

The sun was a glowing lemon peel, gilding the black waves gold. He climbed up onto a jutting tor. The wind cleared the last vestiges of his headache. He breathed deeply, gazing out at the horizon. Frustrated anticipation coiled in his intestines. The excruciatingly long month of Chance was over, and riggers were scrambling to get ships ready for sailing. He'd get his assignment within a few days and would lay on deck before the month of Forgiveness was half over.

His fingers flexed. It couldn't come soon enough. He squatted on the jut of rock, his gaze flicking to the Pale. The string of wards protecting Crosspointe hung like fairy lights a quarter of a league offshore. They were entirely green now, the color of new grass, the color of safety. Not too long ago, they and the identical string of tide wards beneath the waves had burned bitter blue. The twin strands of wards protected the island from *sylveth*, a majickal substance that unraveled in tangled knots throughout the black waters of the Inland Sea. The smallest drop of *sylveth* could turn anybody or anything into spawn. From rope to children's toys to spoons—anything could transform into hideous creatures culled from the nightmares of the insane. They were alike in only their mindless hunger. Hordes of spawn had been known to raven through the waves and forge onto the land like seething masses of maggots picking clean a carcass. And they'd keep eating right up until a knacker gang wearing special protective gear was sent to kill or capture them, or until they were eaten by the even more frightening monsters inhabiting the depths of the sea.

But the kiss of *sylveth* was not always a curse. Some lucky few were granted gifts, as slight as beauty and as vast as . . . as vast as stepping out among the stars.

He drew a deep breath, smelling the brine, the wet

of the clouds and a faint biting *tang* of wild majick. The wards stifled his ability to feel waves, the ever-shifting landscape below the waters, the senseless twisted currents, the massive Koreions and the gluttonous vescies, and the tantalizing curls of *sylveth*.

Sylbrac rubbed his calloused hand hard over his jaw. He'd been too long ashore, watching the Pale fade from green to blue and back to green. During Chance, the violent winter storms whipped the *sylveth* out of the waves and into the air, turning the wards blue. The only safe place was inside the Pale. Everyone took refuge on Crosspointe until Chance passed and the *sylveth* settled back down into the water in thick, heavy skeins, making the sea once again navigable. For a special few, anyhow.

Though the Inland Sea was still incredibly dangerous to sail the rest of the year, a good Pilot evened out the odds considerably, able to sense the rise of hull-ripping knucklebone weirs, the opening of boreholes, and the sudden uprisings of mountains from the depths. With a hand on the majickal compass installed on every ship, a good Pilot could read every chaotic change in the seabed and the waters and direct his ship on more healthy headings. Sylbrac was an exceptionally talented Pilot. But he was still dirt-bound, and with each passing moment, his hunger to be free of the obdurate island and return to the sea where he belonged intensified. The need was becoming painful. Given the choice, he'd gladly spend his entire life on the waves and never set foot on the ground again.

The craving swelled and became blinding. For a moment he swayed forward. He caught himself with one hand and then pushed to his feet and climbed down off the tor.

He was too restless to return home, and instead walked down into Blacksea.

The town girdled a forested cove. It was picturesque, with exclusive shops and quaint whitewashed houses made of brick and timber. Large manor houses shouldered through the trees in rising ranks along the low ridge surrounding the town. Pilot homes. Below, a dozen coastal ketches lay at anchor in the harbor. They were painted white with crimson striping down the rails and wales. Banners floated from the tops of the masts, while crews bustled on deck, readying for sail. Smaller pleasure boats filled the marina. None had compasses or Pilots and none of them ever went beyond the Pale.

The air was redolent of woodsmoke and baking bread, and was wet from last night's storm. The scent of pine, tar, and salt overlaid it all. A dog nosed along the edge of the road and a pair of squirrels squabbled beneath a leafless lilac bush. Sylbrac strode briskly. His gaze slid over the shadowy hollows in the doorways and between the storefronts with their white window frames, blue shutters, and gingerbread trim. Nothing seemed out of place. His gaze darted up alleys. He zigzagged slightly to allow himself to glance obliquely back along the street behind him. No one followed. Not that he expected it. But the habits of survival were not soon forgotten.

Just beyond the Exchange, Sylbrac turned up Petal Avenue. At the end was a boxy rust brick building with white shutters and doors. Over the doors hung a wooden cutlass with the words FOR BRAVERY AND HONOR carved deeply into the wooden blade. A brass plate beside the door said merely TORSBY AND SONS. Sylbrac went eagerly inside.

He entered into a wide, shallow foyer. The walls were painted green with a wood wainscoting the color of molasses. Three of them were lined with racks containing several hundred swords of every design. The last contained daggers. Torsby was a master sword maker, the finest in Crosspointe. People came from all parts of the Inland Sea to purchase his blades, and he was eccentrically choosy about whom he allowed to do so. Sylbrac was privileged to own three of Torsby's swords and five of his daggers.

He went through the archway on the far wall, down a wide corridor into the spacious gallery beyond.

Broad windows overlooking the winter skeleton of an overgrown garden ran the length of the back wall. The gallery was divided into three sections by low barriers topped by brass rails. On the far right and left were two small enclosures, each thirty feet across. Within them, three circles of different sizes had been painted on the floor in yellow, each divided into quarters. Round racks of wooden and iron practice swords stood in the corners. Beside them were bins of padded and unpadded cross-staves and a variety of targets. On the walls were rows of hooks holding gambesons of varying sizes. Also hanging on the walls were hobbles, wrist, waist, and ankle weights, and an assortment of other training blocks and tackle. Two pails of powdered clamshells hung on posts on either side of the practice areas and a rack of small towels circled the posts above.

The central section was far larger than the other two, being four times as wide. It also contained a series of concentric practice circles painted different colors, but was otherwise the same in appearance. The place smelled of beeswax, sweat, and leather.

Two women were sparring in one of the smaller enclosures. They'd been at it a while and were breathing heavily. Sweat gleamed on their cheeks and foreheads. Will, Torsby's youngest son, poked one of the women in the thigh with his staff, then rapped the other on the calf, all the while rumbling out instructions.

"Fair morn, young Thorn."

The elder Torsby sat on a bench against the wall, running a soft cloth over the blade lying flat across his thighs. His grizzled hair hung in lank curls to his shoulders, his bald pate covered by a round leather cap. His doughy nose was red, his cheeks rough with stiff gray bristles. He eyed Sylbrac sardonically from beneath his shaggy brows.

"Been expectin' ye."

Sylbrac's black brow lifted. "Were you?"

"Aye. In a foul mood, too. Looks like I was right."

"Been reading tea leaves, have you? Does this mean you'll be putting up a booth at market day and start telling fortunes?"

"None such. 'Tis merely that ye be as predictable as the comin' of Chance. The Ketirvan begins today. Truth be told, I expected ye afore dawn. Grind off a bit of the bitter edge."

Sylbrac's lips pulled flat. At the beginning of each new season, the Pilots' Guild congregated under the guise of conducting the business of the guild. In reality, it was a vast chasm of putridness, with an over-abundance of posturing, backbiting, conspiracy, and scheming. Inevitably, he'd end the session with a fiery pain in his gut and an insatiable urge to kill someone. Usually more than one someone. All told, there was nothing Sylbrac dreaded more—not even being trapped between a gale wind and a knucklebone weir to the lee. At least the latter was a quick death, and far less painful.

He removed his outer wool coat and his frock coat, loosened his collar, and rolled up his sleeves. He stretched his arms over his head and bent from side to side. Torsby continued to polish the blade, chuckling softly.

"I think your hair needs a trimming," Sylbrac said, pretending to be irked at Torsby's amusement. They'd known each other a long time and the other man wasn't put off by Sylbrac's notorious and persistent thorniness. "Perhaps a little off the eyebrows as well, old man."

"Thorn, me boy, ye couldn't scratch me ass if ye had ten swords and I had but one arm."

"In that case, I'd think you'd stop calling me Thorn."

"And call ye by that blasphemous name of yourn? I'd be struck dead. 'Sides, it suits ye better. Never met another such pain in the ass as yerself. Prickly bastard. Thorn in the side, thorn in the foot. But that has nothing to do with how ye swing a sword."

Sylbrac laughed. Most new Pilots swiftly developed inordinately swelled heads that never deflated with time and experience. Their arrogance and hauteur were products of the lack of market competition. No one else could navigate the Inland Sea with any degree of safety. Without Pilots, Crosspointe would wither and die. A fact that made them, quite literally, priceless. But it wasn't as if a person became a Pilot through any innate virtue of his own. It was merely the whim of the gods. Every day Sylbrac gave thanks for the unbelievable luck that had changed his life so abruptly, opening a door on a world of unimaginable beauty and wonder. So instead of selecting an unpronounceable, self-important name from the venerated dead language of the ancestral Ekidey as was Pilot tradition, he'd chosen to borrow the pieces of his name from the sea god Braken and from *sylveth*, the blood of the Moonsinger Meris. Blasphemous it might be, and ironically enough, most of the guild thought it was terribly arrogant as well. But for Sylbrac, it was a gesture of gratitude, a constant prayer of thanksgiving for the gift he'd been given. That his choice infuriated his fellow Pilots was a bonus. He relished every opportunity to prod at their superior smugness.

Still smiling, he unbuckled his sword belt and drew his blade, tossing the scabbard down onto the bench before pacing around to the other side of the circle. He scooped up some of the clamshell powder.

"Shall we see what you have to teach me today, old man?"

Despite his years, Torsby was spry. In fact he was downright quick and nimble. Within minutes Sylbrac was sweating. They went back and forth, swords flashing and clanging in rapid staccato. Torsby kept up a running commentary about Sylbrac's form, jeering at his pupil's growing breathlessness and stiff, jerky moves.

"Gotta give up that soft livin', boy. You're turning into a loblolly. And stop pounding like ye was beating the forge with a hammer. Ye know better. When you're in the circle with a blade in your hand, your head can't be anywhere else."

The reproof stung, the more so because it was true. Sylbrac laid in harder, forcing his mind to focus. Soon all thoughts of the upcoming Ketirvan faded like smoke in the wind and the nettles of tension that had been plaguing him since he'd become dirt-bound unwound from his muscles.

"Aye, there ye go," was Torsby's only comment.

They sparred without pause for well over a glass. At the end, Sylbrac was panting heavily, but relaxed in a way he hadn't been since the beginning of Chance. His body felt fluid, invigorated. He returned Torsby's salute, touching his sword to his forehead before stepping out of the practice circle. He wiped his face with a towel before dipping a tin cup into the water bucket at the end of the bench and drinking deeply. The water was flavored with mint and lemon. He gulped a second cup.

"You'll career yerself if ye keep drinking like that when you're so heated," Torsby commented, sipping from his own cup.

"Better a bellyache from this than the Ketirvan."

"Ye'll regret it when ye have both."

Sylbrac sighed, dropping the cup into the bucket with a splash. "There's no way around it. I am hulled. I shall have to attend and sit through the endless hours of talking and saying less than nothing. By Braken, couldn't they just cut out my eyes and tongue, lop off my legs, and toss me to the dogs like the Jutras? It would be infinitely more merciful."

"Pilots' Guild ain't interested in mercy. Specially to a thorn like you. And whose fault be that? I expect ye'll be takin' the cat again?"

"Most definitely. Fitch wouldn't miss a moment."

Torsby shook his head, his mouth puckering. "Ye invite trouble. Surprised ye never been tossed overboard, what with the cat, not to mention that whistling ye insist on."

"Can't sail the Inland Sea without a Pilot. No matter how much you don't like him. Besides, there's nothing unlucky about Fitch, and whistling is just music, not a summons for the wights of the world."

"Not a sailor on this island as would agree with ye."

"They don't have a choice, do they?"

Torsby eyed him steadily. Sylbrac flushed and looked away.

"It's little wonder you're so much alone."

Sylbrac stiffened. Bleakness suffused him. Torsby was more right than he knew. It was less than two months since Jordan's death. His brother's murder had left Sylbrac completely alone. No family . . . at least none he would willingly claim. He could never forget they were blood, but by the gods how he wanted to. As for friends . . . aside from Fitch, Torsby was the closest thing to a friend he had.

Sylbrac's lip curled in silent scorn. He'd made little effort to see Jordan in the past seventeen seasons. Most of their infrequent encounters happened accidentally when they were both in port over Chance. Sylbrac had made even less effort to make friends. He reaped what he sowed. And yet he couldn't help the ache in his gut at losing Jordan. He felt strangely adrift, as if his brother had been anchoring him through the years without Sylbrac ever realizing it, and now the anchor chain was snapped.

He sheathed his sword and buckled on his belt.

"I choose to be alone. People annoy me."

"Do they, now? And ye bein' such a lapdog. Ye'd think they'd cuddle right on up t' ye."

Sylbrac snorted. "The sea's enough for me."

"Some men like a tickle and a tumble from time to time."

"As do I. But there's no need to worry. I'm a Pilot. It's easy enough to find a skirt to twitch when I want one."

"Then it be a fine life ye got. No naggin' missus, no bawlin' kiddies, nothin' at all to disturb your sleep or aggravate your meals. Come home to peace and ever-lovin' quiet."

"A fine life," Sylbrac agreed, but the burn in his gut intensified.

He bade Torsby farewell and returned home to bathe and dress before the Ketirvan. But he couldn't stop thinking of Jordan, try as he might to shut those thoughts safely away. He couldn't remember the last words they'd spoken to each other. It had been too long ago.

By the time he reached home, his stomach was churning. He was only a bare step away from sinking into the quagmire of his past—a past he'd worked hard to scour forever from his mind. But Jordan's death had ripped open the levees that kept that past at bay. He felt exposed and raw. The fluid relaxation he'd achieved at Torsby's was gone and his mood had turned foul. He dismissed his valet with a snarl, throwing off his clothing and scrubbing himself vigorously in lukewarm water before yanking on his formal clothing.

He donned a close-fitting black suit made of dosken and silk. It was light and easy to move in and bore no embroidery or embellishments. The jet buttons rose up to close tightly around his throat and he wore no cravat. He pulled on a short padded leather coat—a monkey jacket like most sailors wore. The arms were ringed with wide silver bands etched with the serpentine shapes of Koreions. Over that, he wore a sleeveless black robe. It was loose and flowing and shone with a silvery iridescence, like the moon striking the black waves of the Inland Sea. He stamped into his leather boots, tucking a stiletto into the top of the left one, and shoving a dagger into the small of his back. Weapons weren't allowed into the Ketirvan, but Sylbrac had spent years running wild on the docks. He knew better than to trust anyone and never went anywhere without a blade of some sort.

He glanced in the mirror, and yanked a comb through his brown locks. Despite his efforts, they fell over his forehead in an untidy mop, the back of his hair hanging several inches below his collar. He rubbed at the bristles casting a scruffy shadow along his jaw. He'd be damned if he'd shave. He slipped a heavy gold ring on his forefinger. It was shaped like a quatrefoil with a *sylveth* compass rose in the center. It was his official Pilot's signet. He ignored the matching brooch, shoving it to the back of his sock drawer.

When he was ready to go, he poured himself a glass of red brandy and gulped it down in a single swig. He poured another and then went to collect Fitch.

He settled the little black cat on his shoulder. She dug her claws in for balance and wrapped her tail around his neck. Sylbrac scratched her ears. She butted against his hand, purring. The sound made his stomach unclench fractionally. He'd found her almost exactly a year ago. A couple of stray dogs had cornered her on a dock, and though she'd been just a kitten, she'd not given ground. Eventually she'd run them off, coming away with hardly a scratch. From the moment she'd walked away shaking her paws in disgust at the dog drool slicking her fur, Sylbrac had known she was a kindred spirit. He'd kept her with him ever since.

"Are you ready?" he asked her.

Her purr grew louder. He sighed heavily and departed for the Ketirvan.

The guildhall was located on the east side of Blacksea, requiring Sylbrac to cross through town. He took a route along the docks. The air was sharp and the wind slapped hard. Regrettably, the cold cleared the murk of the brandy from his head. Fitch rubbed her cheek against his jaw. He reached up to pet her.

He nodded greetings to the sailors he passed. Most Pilots didn't bother to notice they were even alive, unless and until they were forced to do the job of protecting them at sea. But Sylbrac respected them. He'd *been* them, not all that long ago, before his gift . . . happened. Sailors lived hard, brave lives, most coming to an abrupt end in the black waves of the sea. He liked their rough honesty. He liked that they were too busy surviving to scheme and sell one another out. He liked that they spoke their minds and when they were angry, they told you about it with their fists and shouts. He felt more at home among them than anywhere else.

Home. The idea of it sent a chill trickling down his spine. He remembered that last day, creeping out, a handful of coins in the pouch stuffed down in the toe of his boot, a small bundle on his back. It had all been stolen by nightfall, including every stitch of clothing he wore. He nearly died that night. And almost every night and day after for many seasons to come. But he had counted himself better off than Jordan, whom he'd left behind, knowing what must happen to him.

Guilt assailed Sylbrac, his stomach lurching as bile burned his throat. He had not let himself think about it, not since he'd run away, and not since Jordan's death. But now he couldn't seem to stop himself.

A little over five sennights ago, Sylbrac had returned to Crosspointe. He arrived just a few days before the Chance storms rose, before the Pale vanished and the majicars—despite years of saying they couldn't possibly fix a broken Pale—rebuilt it in the blink of an eye. The pre-Chance storms had been terrible, and he had been so exhausted by the effort of getting the ship back in one piece that he'd slept several days away before he picked up a paper and learned of Jordan's death. By then his brother had been dead for nearly two sennights.

The story was murky. Murdered for certain—there was no doubt about that. At first it had been blamed on Lucy Trenton. She was a royal brat—a niece of the king or some such—who had been working as a customs officer, thanks to the Chancery suit that had tied up all the royal family's finances and forced most of the royal family to find their own means of support. She had been accused of smuggling blood oak, which was high treason. The newspapers claimed she'd killed Jordan because he was going to expose her. But when Captain Marten Thorpe had been convicted as an accomplice, Sylbrac knew there was at least as much falsehood in the story as truth. He'd sailed once with

Thorpe. The man was a gambler and a rogue, but from the stories he'd told aboard ship and the few times Sylbrac had spoken to Jordan in recent seasons, he knew that the two were friends. It just wasn't possible.

And then the story shifted again. A Jutras plot against the crown, and Jordan caught up in it. Lucy Trenton and Marten Thorpe framed and too late to save them from the Bramble. That story didn't seem believable either, though some said the snapping of the Pale was evidence. And then too, a storm-broken Jutras warship had limped into the harbor only days before the Pale fell. The story was *possible*. But there was no way to get to the truth. That's what chewed his innards. How had Jordan become involved? Sylbrac was certain their parents had something to do with it. They had their fingers in everything on Crosspointe. Had one of their vicious little schemes gotten Jordan killed?

Murderous hate rose up in him. His fingers flexed. From the moment he'd read the newspaper accounts, he'd wanted to go confront them. Demand the truth. But years of running and hiding from them made him hesitate. They didn't know he was a Pilot. His parents were devious and ruthless. They wanted him back, and if they couldn't have him, they wanted to ruin him. No one escaped them. They'd found him twice before; he knew well enough what they might do. When it came to protecting their reputation, when it came to their family pride, they were willing to go to great lengths. Horrific lengths. Sylbrac couldn't bring himself to risk it. Enough of the terrified boy who'd run from them still existed inside him to keep him silent.

Besides, even if he could go ask his father, even if he was willing to stand in front of that goat-cracking bastard again, it would be pointless; the lord chancellor was a skilled liar. And his mother—Sylbrac would sooner trust a Chance storm than a viper like her.

He turned off the road, climbing up along the headland, taking the cliff path through the trees. Below,

the tide was rolling in, the strand thinning with every
wash of waves. He broke into a jog, though whether
to outrun his impotent rage or exorcise his depthless
guilt, he wasn't sure. Fitch hissed her protest in his
ear and dug her claws deep into the padding of his
jacket. He left the path, pushing up the hill through
the rhododendron bracken and broom bushes that
cluttered the trees.

He emerged just below the knob of a grassy hill,
upon which perched the Dabloute. As always, he
stopped, awe filling him. Carved from obsidian and
alabaster, it looked like storm-whipped waves, rising
high and falling, frozen in a timeless plunge. Sylbrac
could almost believe that he would blink and the
waves would finish dropping and be gathered back
into the Inland Sea. There were no windows. The
walls were cut so thin they were translucent. Seeing
its magnificent beauty was enough to dispel his tangle
of emotions about Jordan, at least for the moment.

He skirted around to the front of the Dabloute,
feeling the tide rising higher. The Ketirvan would
begin at the moment of high tide and the doors would
be closed against latecomers. Much as he didn't want
to be here, neither did Sylbrac want to be locked out.
Guild law bound him and too much idiocy was likely
to be written into the books if he wasn't there to lend
a voice of reason. Or at least one of mulish obstruction.

The entrance of the guildhall was in the upper half
of a spectacular *sylveth* compass rose. The rays rose
like a sunburst fifty feet in the air. The edges of each
were gilded and a fine filigree overlaid the diamond
glitter of worked *sylveth*. Ironically, as dangerous as
raw *sylveth* was, once worked into solid form by a
majicar, it was safe to touch. Above the compass
points, twined in an erotic embrace, was a sculpture
of Meris and Braken, white on black. Their naked
limbs grappled together, though Sylbrac was never
sure if they were cleaving lovingly to each other, or if
Braken was clutching at Meris to prevent her from
running off to Hurn, her lover. On the inside rim of

the compass, etched deeply in flowing ancient Ekidey, was the phrase "The path to becoming a Pilot is through the blood of Meris and breath of Braken."

The entry into the Dabloute was through the center of the half compass. Pilots walked beneath in pairs and clusters, heads bent together, some laughing, some arguing passionately, others silent and stern. Sylbrac ignored them, striding ahead. No one called out a greeting, but several saw Fitch and made angry exclamations. Sylbrac's lips curved in a scythe-sharp smile.

The inside of the Dabloute was as fantastical as without. The corridors were sinuous, the rooms oddly shaped. The ceilings disappeared into skurls and ripples, the floors rising and falling in soft undulations. There were no carpets or tapestries, no paintings or curtains. Rather, every surface was carved into undersea shapes: knucklebones, Koreions, vada-eels, celesties, and more. The sunlight from outside made everything seem to waver and move as if pushed by waves. Softly glowing *sylveth* lights set in the floors brightened the shadows. As soon as he passed inside, Sylbrac felt a soothing wash of peace. The Dabloute was the next-best thing to actually being at sea.

He turned off from the main corridor, wanting a few minutes' peace and quiet as he made his way to the Ketirvan. High tide was nearly fixed. The feeling was a fullness in the beat of his heart. He didn't have much time. He hurried along, turning sideways at one point where the passage narrowed and then opened up widely. The walls were heavily rippled here, with clefts and nooks like undersea grottoes. Someone in a long blue cloak slid through the narrowed opening ahead of him. She didn't look at him, merely brushing by with quick, hurried steps. He caught a glimpse of a tumble of red hair beneath the folds of her hood and smelled something that reminded him of wind and majick. He wondered where she was going with the Ketirvan about to begin, then promptly dismissed her, the rising tide pushing him to hurry.

He turned sideways and edged through the narrowed passage and began striding along. He halted abruptly when up ahead he heard the sound of raised voices. He took a step forward, and then there was a shark *crack!* and quick, angry footsteps.

The woman who stormed around the corner was short and heavy-boned. Her face was square, her skin coarse and tanned with years of exposure to weather. Her nostrils flared and red spotted her cheeks above a mouth made white by fury. The cuffs of her sleeves and the hem of her robe were edged with small silver compass roses with *sylveth*-drop centers. She was Eyvresia, the Pirena-elect. When she saw Sylbrac, she stopped short, her gaze flattening. Then more footsteps sounded behind her and she gathered her robe, darting past Sylbrac into one of the grotto nooks. She ground one white-knuckled fist against her lips, glaring back at him as if daring him to expose her.

Grains later a man appeared around the corner. He hardly came to Sylbrac's chin. His short, curly gray hair was wild-looking as if he'd been running his fingers through it. His still-black mustache and beard were clipped close, his brows set in a furious scowl. Black gossamer lines like cracks in fine porcelain crisscrossed his eyes, only a few straying across the whites. Those marking Sylbrac's eyes were heavier and more numerous, filling the whites of his eyes like a mass of tangled thread. The shorter man's black robes were ridiculously ornate, weighted by compass roses stitched in gold thread, one covering each side of his chest from collarbone to hip, another on his back. *Sylveth* disks gleamed at the centers.

He stopped short when he saw Sylbrac, his mouth twisting. On his cheek was a scarlet imprint of a hand. Sylbrac grinned. What had Pirena Wildreveh said to make the Pirena-elect hit him?

"What are you doing here?"

As if he were manure someone had tracked in on his shoe. Sylbrac's eyes narrowed as he reached up to stroke Fitch. Wildreveh's gaze followed his hand and his mouth puckered as though he'd eaten a mouthful of salt. It was that snide expression that made Sylbrac step to block Eyvresia from view. She had hit the bilge-sucking bastard, and so she'd earned a reward. Not that he ever needed an excuse to antagonize Wildreveh. He'd disliked him from the moment he'd first met him. Wildreveh was pompous, self-serving, and spiteful. He reminded Sylbrac of his father, and everything he'd learned about Wildreveh over the years had only confirmed Sylbrac's opinion. Their antagonism was mutual.

"I'm on my way to the Ketirvan," Sylbrac drawled, aware that his slow answer goaded the other man's fury.

"Not with that cat, you aren't."

"Oh, but I am. She's such a quiet thing, I doubt anyone will even notice her."

It was a bald-faced lie. Everyone would notice her. Her presence would be like a scream in the night, like smoke in a darkened room. Little he could do would antagonize them more.

"I forbid it. I want her out of the Dabloute before her bad luck pollutes it completely. Now!"

One of Sylbrac's brows flicked up. "I don't believe you have such authority, Wildreveh."

The other man's jaw knotted. "I am Pirena of the guild. That's all the authority I need."

"I don't think so," Sylbrac said. He looked pointedly to Wildreveh's cheek where Eyvresia's handprint remained. "And anyway, you're only Pirena until the end of Ketirvan. You've got no fangs to hurt me."

The other man jerked back. Then his lips slid slowly apart in a death's-head grin. His square, horsey teeth were stained brown and yellow. "Haven't I? We shall see."

With that, he turned and marched away, his shoulders rigid. Eyvresia stepped out of the grotto, watching him disappear.

"I know you enjoy antagonizing your fellow Pilots, but was that wise?"

Sylbrac glanced down at her. "What can he do?"

She shook her head, frowning. "I think it would have been better to know the answer to that question before you pushed pins into him. But it is certain that whatever it is he *can* do, he will." Her brow furrowed as she looked at Sylbrac. "Watch yourself. You've no friends here to cushion the blow."

Sylbrac only shrugged. He wasn't worried. He should have been.

Chapter 2

Sylbrac followed Pirena-elect Eyvresia as she hurried away up the passage. The two slipped inside the Ketirvan just as the chime sounded and the doors swung silently and decisively shut. They would not open again for three days.

The Ketirvan was held in an improbable room. Not even a room. An amphitheater, an inn, a tavern, a hall. Black wave walls towered hundreds of feet in the air, bunching and billowing in static fury. The seats were situated between rolling folds and rising whorls with plush black cushions made of crushed velvet and stuffed with goose down. In the corners were several odd-shaped entries like gaps in waterfalls. These led into the dining hall and from there a variety of sleep cells. Down below, in the front of the cavernous expanse, were three massive thrones sitting high up in a shallow niche in the wall: the largest of ebony in the middle, one of alabaster to the left, and one of heavy timbers to the right. Each was empty in anticipation of a visit by the gods.

Below the thrones and set on a platform was a single black chair. It rose from the floor in a frozen obsidian wave, the arms and back smooth and rolling like cresting water, the pedestal a billowing flow. This was where the Pirena sat to conduct the Ketirvan. Not that Wildreveh sat much. He tended to stomp about and shout.

The room bustled with Pilots, the low rumble of

their voices like the threat of a summer storm. Sylbrac
glanced around, looking for an empty seat. There were
always too many. Each year, dozens of ships and too
many Pilots fell prey to the sea they loved. Few lived
long enough to die of old age.

He climbed up a sinuous stair to a place at the top
where he could have his back to the wall and see the
rest of the room. Hostile eyes followed his progress.
Fitch yawned widely, her tongue curling. She stretched
out a paw and licked it with a studied lack of concern.
The flutter of angry mutters and accusations that followed behind him made Sylbrac smile. They called
cats bad luck, and mixed-gender crews and whistling
and an endless list of other taboos. They just didn't
want to point at their own stupidity or the whim of
the gods, where the blame really belonged.

He settled into a seat, lifting Fitch down onto his
lap. All round him Pilots stood and moved away as if
from a bad smell, leaving him surrounded by a moat
of empty chairs.

A series of chimes sounded. Each note lingered,
growing, echoing. They grew together, turning first to
chords, then weaving together into song. It burgeoned,
filling the cavernous hall and resonating from the
walls. The vibrations made Sylbrac's breath tremble
in his chest and his limbs shake. Fitch dug her claws
into his thigh, her fur standing on end. For Sylbrac,
the pain was hardly noticeable, immersed as he was
in the majick of the music.

The pressure on his flesh and bones increased. His
teeth chattered together and his eyes felt as if they
were about to explode from his skull. He couldn't hear
Fitch's frantic meows as she crawled up to press
against his neck and jaw. Just when he thought his
body couldn't stand it anymore, the sound ceased. The
air quaked with the silence. Sylbrac stroked Fitch with
trembling fingers. She huddled beneath his chin, her
claws digging deep into his jacket, her body rigid. All
around was the rustle of clothing and soft sighs. Syl-

brac scanned the gathered Pilots. A few were pale and
clammy, some red-faced, others sagging in on themselves, others poker-straight and stiff. He forced his
own tense muscles to relax, taking a deep, steadying
breath and letting it out quietly. Fitch's tail continued
to whip back and forth.

Sylbrac never got used to the beginning of the Ketirvan. Those moments of powerlessness were a reminder that they were inside Braken's house, that they
thrived or died at his pleasure, here and on the sea.

The hush lingered until Pirena Wildreveh stepped
up onto the dais. He turned, lifting his face to the
thrones, spreading his arms, and loudly intoning a
summons in Ekidey. It was a dead language from a
dead land no one even remembered now. For centu-
ries, it had been spoken only among majicars and Pilots, and only in ritual. Sylbrac found it pointless. Just
another example of Pilot self-importance.

The Pirena finished his prayers and waited. Sylbrac
snorted softly. Not one of the gods had ever appeared
in guild memory. He eyed the thrones. Only a fool
would think the gods could be so easily summoned.

After a few moments, Wildreveh turned majestically
back to face the gathering and began the ritual opening of the Ketirvan. Sylbrac let the words flow around
him. Despite his hostility, he felt the real power of the
Dabloute coming alive. This was a place designed for
worship and giving thanks to the gods for the gifts
they had given Pilots. He bent his head, sending prayers to Braken, Meris, and Chayos. He prayed for
strength, for luck, for mercy, finishing with a silent
thanks. The prayers were simple but heartfelt. No
matter how much he complained, no matter how much
the ceremony and endless speeches and arguments
went on, he would never have missed Ketirvan, would
not have missed this sacred moment. He came here
each year to give thanks, to beg for clemency from
the endless dangers of the Inland Sea, to pray for luck,
and to give his life over yet again to being Pilot—to

protecting the men and women who sailed the sea. The rest was . . . meaningless. An easy enough sacrifice to show the gods his gratitude.

He jerked back to himself as the roll call began. First the names of those present, then the names of those lost in the last year, then the names of every Pilot lost since the founding of Crosspointe. There was a general murmur when his own name was called. He bared his teeth in snide challenge at Wildreveh, who only nodded his head with a kind of smug serenity that made Sylbrac frown. Like the other man was confident he'd have his revenge and could comfortably bide his time until then. He shook his head slowly. But there wasn't anything Wildreveh could do. He was toothless. Even if he wasn't stepping down as Pirena, the worst he could do was kill some change Sylbrac might want to make to guild law or policy. But the only thing Sylbrac really wanted was to get his ship assignment. There was no way Wildreveh could interfere with that, unless Sylbrac suddenly went mad and killed another Pilot or committed treason. Sylbrac shrugged, dismissing the other man.

The roll call of the dead went on for hours. The slow, sonorous listing of names deeply moved Sylbrac in a way it hadn't before. He couldn't help but feel the weight of so many lives over so many years, all sacrificed to the sea. He knew that none of the dead Pilots would have exchanged the dangers of the black waves for a long quiet life ashore. Doing so would be like chopping out your own heart with a hatchet. He stared at the crevices in the whorled ceiling, suddenly struck. All these names represented men and women who had once been just like the people he shared this room with—the pompous, the inane, the smug, and the condescending. And as their names went by, he realized that tangling with the anger and annoyance he felt for them was a profound . . . respect.

The notion astonished him and instantly he ridiculed himself for even considering the idea. Sylbrac's gaze dropped and raked across the Pilots sitting in the hall. Respect *them*? But as he looked at them, he realized they were not as cold, nor as obliviously disdainful, as he'd expected. Tears ran down the cheeks of many. Some sat with fixed stares, while others hunched into themselves, hands covering their faces. They *cared*. Sylbrac's breath caught. Then he shook his head. No. They merely feared for themselves. Their sorrow grew from their own self-serving terrors.

But doubt niggled. It made him restless. He was glad when the roll call came to an end. Then came the rest of the opening ritual, and then a break to dine. Sylbrac ate alone, sitting with his back in a corner. He set Fitch on the table, feeding her bits of pork from his plate. Just as inside the meeting hall, no one sat near or approached him.

"Which makes you very good luck for me," he told Fitch in a tone that carried to the nearby tables and resulted in angry mutters and stares that would have incinerated him if they could.

He stared back, feeling malevolent. He refused to see the scars, the weariness, the lines of laughter in the weathered faces. He didn't want them to be *people*. Just cold, pretentious, power-bloated leeches, feeding on the desperate need of anyone in Crosspointe who lived or died by ship commerce. Which was the entire population. He wanted them all to be Wildreveh. But then he pictured Eyvresia. He heard the concern in her warning: *Watch yourself. You've no friends here to cushion the blow*. As if he mattered to her.

He closed his eyes, his mouth screwing into a grimace as he felt the relentless memories of his childhood sliding fingers along his mind, looking for cracks—a way back into his consciousness. It was as if they sensed the weakening of his hatred, the doubt sending spiderweb cracks across the mental dam that kept him safe. Safe from guilt, and from the accusations of his own conscience. Deliberately he thought of Wildreveh, snatching at the bitterness of their exchange and wrapping it around himself like a cloak. The memories retreated.

The afternoon proceeded with business. The first order of which was the confirmation of the new Pirena-elect—the one who would replace Eyvresia upon her taking the mantle of Pirena. The ornamental speeches eulogizing the accomplishments and skills of both Wildreveh and Eyvresia went until dinner, leaving Sylbrac with a throbbing headache. After, people split into groups, some playing cards and games or reading books, others taking baths in the large bathing rooms below the Dabloute, others retiring to their sleeping rooms for more salacious activities.

Sylbrac wasn't tired, nor was he interested in joining in any activities—not that he was invited. Nor did he want to watch them. He didn't want to hear their jokes and laughter, hear their stories of children and homes and foibles.

He returned to the silence of the main meeting hall, sitting in a first-row seat and staring up at the thrones and the rippling obsidian wave-walls behind. There was no concrete explanation of how the Dabloute had come to be. Some said that it had really been formed out of the waves by Braken. Others argued it was Errol Cipher, the first majicar. It didn't really matter. This place was a union of the three things that ruled the lives of all Pilots. There were the black waters of the sea, mysterious, treacherous, seductive. There was the moon and Meris, who ruled the tides and spilled her heart's blood into the waters in the form of *sylveth*. From their tempestuous love came all things chance. And then there was Chayos, the mother of earth and all things green, the giver of life. From her came the trees for ships. From her came solidity and truth and from her came Hurn, the stranger god, the third corner of the dreadful lovers' triangle comprising Braken, Meris, and Hurn. And from that triangle came killing storms.

He started from his reverie when someone slid into the seat next to him. He was surprised and irritated to see Eyvresia. She did not look at him, but fixed her gaze on the thrones as he had done.

"One might wonder if you had the sense Chayos gave termites," she said at last.

Sylbrac snorted. "I have been known to wonder that very thing."

She sniffed and stood, crossing to the bottom of the platform containing Wildreveh's chair—soon to be hers—and retrieved Fitch, who was testing the stone leg with her claws. She settled the little cat in the crook of her arm, stroking her. Sylbrac stared. There was more to her than it appeared.

"If it weren't against every law to harm a Pilot, I think you might have been murdered today. If looks could kill and all that. Not that an adventurous soul wouldn't have tried a knife or a poker up against the side of your skull, given the opportunity. So much more satisfactory than merely staring daggers. Someone still might, if they caught you letting this little pretty climb about in here."

He watched her stroking sure fingers down Fitch's back. "What would they think of the Pirena-elect consorting with a cat?"

Her lips tightened in a thin smile. "Consorting?" She lifted Fitch up, holding her so that they nearly touched noses. "Bad luck." Eyvresia stepped closer and set the cat on Sylbrac's lap. "I think you're going to have a lot more of it than you'd like, and it's going to be entirely of your own making. I don't think I'll be able to block whatever Wildreveh is up to—especially not after I slapped him—and you may trust that he is up to something."

"Why would you want to help me?"

Her nose wrinkled in a curiously childlike gesture. "Perhaps I just don't like him."

"I don't doubt that, but people usually don't like me more than they don't like anybody else."

She shrugged. "Apparently Wildreveh has you beaten in that contest. But there's still time, if you'd like to try harder."

The corner of his mouth curled up. "I'll do my best."

"Somehow I doubt your best will match his, but certainly don't let me discourage you. One Pilot making my life truly disagreeable is not nearly enough." She turned, then paused, looking back over her shoulder. "Don't let that cat get away from you. You might find yourself eating it for breakfast. I wouldn't like to see such a fate for her."

"I'll keep that in mind."

Eyvresia met his gaze for a long moment. The black lines tangling her eyes were heavy. She had a powerful connection to the sea. Her square, sturdy presence was comforting, like an anchor hooking deep in the seabed in a storm. She would be a good Pirena. She would be a good friend. If he wanted one. Not that she would want him.

"From the moment you joined the guild, you set out to antagonize your fellow Pilots in every way you knew how. You've made yourself an outsider. Wildreveh knows that whatever he chooses to do to you, no one will stop him. I would, if only to annoy him, but I won't have the necessary support to interfere. He's powerful. If there's something you can do to placate him, I suggest that you do it."

She didn't wait for his reply. Sylbrac sat back and stared unseeing up at the ceiling. Placate Wildreveh? His entire body revolted at the idea. He laughed, the sound echoing eerily in the chamber. Then he thought of what else Eyvresia had said.

It was true he didn't fit. More than that, he made it his mission to be difficult and annoying to his fellow Pilots—a thorn in the ass, as Torsby would say. He dragged his fingers through his hair. The Pilots reminded him too much of his father and mother, of their political machinations in the social theater, of the way they were willing to sacrifice everything on the altar of their ambition. He'd left when he realized what they would do, what they would ask him and his brother to do. . . .

The memories crashed over him, shattering the dam that kept them at bay. They flooded his mind with the bitter acid of pain, betrayal, and rage undulled by time. He sat rigid, caught in the torrent, unable to do anything to escape.

There were things no boy ought to be asked to do, not for love nor money. His parents pretended to be so upright, so moral, so superior. But scratch the lord chancellor and his wife and you found their careful, dignified shells contained a seething quagmire of bottomless ambition. They craved more money, more power, more prestige. There was little they'd not do to attain their desires, stopping just short of crossing the line of the law. Unless they could do so without getting caught. After all, it wouldn't do for the lord chancellor to be found breaking the law. Imagine the scandal. However, some things could be done in the dark where no one could see. And there were plenty more things that were ethically and morally revolting that the law did not regulate. And these things his parents embraced as brilliant tactics and clever strategy.

He was nine seasons old when his parents had called him into the evening salon shortly before a dinner party. The room was gilded on every surface and stuffed with expensive ornaments and knickknacks. A *sylveth* chandelier overhung it all. His mother took great pride in her refinement of taste and believed her home—which shared the salon's crass opulence and suffocating ornamentation—to be a showcase of elegance and style to rival even the palace.

She was tall and slender with blond hair and dark eyes. She would have been striking if her expression weren't so haughty and calculating. She wore rings on every finger, each heavy band set with large, exotic, expensive jewels: dawnstars, a rare Braken's heart, bloodstone, *sylveth*—a rainbow of glittering gems. Chains draped her neck and bracelets circled her arms so that she jingled, and Sylbrac remembered wondering how she could hold herself upright. Her touch was gelid, her eyes hot with eagerness. She looked at him and he felt foreboding hook his intestines.

His father stood with his hands clasped behind his

back, looking out the window. He was dressed in dark blue dosken cut in severe lines, with his chain of office around his neck. Silver embroidery decorated his high collar and the fashionably wide, turned-back sleeves of his coat. Sparkling *sylveth* dotted his coat and waistcoat like stars. Like Sylbrac's, his hair was dark and curly, his skin pale. He stood rigidly upright with a chilly restraint born of careful attention to outside perception. He was known to be congenial with a dry wit and also a brilliant conversationalist. All of it was a role he played. But Sylbrac knew him better. At home, he was a dark, brooding presence, often angry and always demanding. Jordan and Sylbrac could rarely satisfactorily meet his expectations. Their shirts would be untucked, their boots scuffed, their eyes too curious, their voices too loud, their answers to questions too vague or too flip. It was a rare day that he didn't discipline his sons with a stiffly pointed woven leather whip as long as his arm.

Those punishments were hard. The boys learned to take them silently or they paid a higher price. But that was all nothing to what his parents asked now.

Jordan stood behind Sylbrac, chin lifted, staring straight ahead as was expected. The boys were dressed with impeccable care. But surprisingly, their parents did not inspect them, twitching clothing and pinching cheeks. Instead they explained what they required. They had invited a prominent gentleman to the party, a man with whom they wished to do business. Except that he wasn't interested. He had refused them repeatedly. So they had little choice. The Truehelm name and fortune depended on taking action. They had arrived at a plan to force his hand.

In the course of his duties as lord chancellor, Sylbrac's father had discovered this gentleman to be a man of dubious appetites. That in itself was nothing, but with Sylbrac's help, the situation could be turned in their favor. At the party, Sylbrac would allow the gentleman to lure him into a private room and permit himself to be seduced. Oh, certainly nothing terrible would happen. The lord chancellor and his wife would burst in before things progressed too far, but the man would be compromised. He would have no choice but to succumb or a lawsuit would be tendered. The scheme kept just to the right side of blackmail. If the gentleman succeeded in ruining the lord chancellor's eldest son and heir, the expense of it to the family would be worth great recompense. The laws were very clear and a lawsuit was well within their right to recover damages. However, if the man chose to make that recompense without a public trial and to the satisfaction of the family, then it was not blackmail. It was business.

Sylbrac couldn't refuse. If he didn't serve as bait, Jordan would have to. He couldn't let that happen.

Even now, more than seventeen seasons later, Sylbrac's stomach churned at the hate he felt for the man and woman who'd birthed him and then served him up to their guest as a boy whore.

In the end, little of real importance had happened in that quiet room. The removal of his clothing, some fondling, a few thrusting, hot kisses—nothing to forever scar him. Except the triumph on his parents' faces, the feigned concern, the knowledge that in time he'd be asked to do far worse.

He left the next morning before the sun came up. He'd left his parents and his home and he'd left Jordan. He'd not stopped running since.

Guilt bloomed inside him, shredding him like knucklebones. He'd walked away, never looking back. If he hadn't run from home, would his brother have gotten mixed up in whatever scheme had gotten him killed? *Had* his parents' intrigues had something to do with it? And if he'd sought out Jordan as he should have, if they'd seen each other more often than here and there during Chance, would Sylbrac have been there to help him?

The questions, the doubts, they swarmed him like *sylveth* spawn. They chewed at him until he felt as if he couldn't ever escape. He couldn't breathe. Sud-

denly he began to struggle, levering himself out of the
chair, Fitch dropping to the floor with a sharp protest.
Sylbrac stood with his feet braced wide, hands on his
knees, his panting breaths ragged. All he could see
was Jordan's face, so like his own.

He shook himself, pulling himself stiffly upright.
There were no answers. There was no way to make
this right. If Jordan had lived . . . But he hadn't. Regret filled his chest with cold lead. He could only
promise himself not to be such a cowardly fool again.
But the sooner he returned to the sea, the better. He
wouldn't be able to think about anything else then.
The compass would absorb all his attention. It was
only a couple of days away.

He rubbed his hands over his face, thinking of Eyvresia's cautions. He sighed. Maybe Eyvresia was
right. He should have tried harder. He shouldn't have
let his hatred for his parents blind him to the good in
his fellow Pilots. They weren't perfect. Wildreveh was
proof enough of that. But neither was he. And they
all shared an abiding love of the sea.

He straightened. He could change. It would take
time, but he had time. His throat knotted. It was too
late to make things right for Jordan, but he could do
better here in the guild. And he would.

The next day the Ketirvan continued with discus-
sions of price adjustments for piloting services, priori-
ties for crown missions, the projected numbers of new
compasses to be made during the year, the training of
"points," as those newly discovered to have Pilot gifts
were called, the amount of payments to be made to
the families of incapacitated and killed Pilots, the per-
centage of personal cargo space allowed to Pilots on
the ships they guided, and many other items of
business.

Sylbrac found himself staying silent on most every
item. Fitch slept in his lap, her belly distended with
the sausage and cream she'd feasted on at breakfast.
He watched the shifting currents of the political ma-

neuverings, reading expressions and body language. It
was a skill he'd acquired as a boy, before he left his
parents' house and after. Survival depended on understanding people quickly, especially strangers. If you
made a mistake, you'd pay for it. Maybe die for it.
Some, like Porenydil, who was whispering behind his
hand to Leevak, were adept at masking themselves.
Only the tight set of his shoulders and the stillness of
his expression told of his fury. He'd been angling for
the guild to establish a seniority ranking system, adjusting individual earnings accordingly. Junior Pilots
would earn less than half of what more senior Pilots
made. He'd managed to garner a fair amount of support, even from a number of the newer Pilots, who'd
no doubt die long before they reaped the benefits of
that sowing. His efforts, however, were hampered by
Jeannota, a thin woman with a wide expanse of forehead, who muttered none too quietly and crossed her
arms and uncrossed them, tapping her toes. Ironically,
though she supported Porenydil, her incessant gabbling and sharp attacks on those opposing the move
had begun to turn the tide against them. Porenydil
was no doubt regretting his choice of allies and planning his next feint.

Suddenly Porenydil rose.

"Pilot Porenydil, do you have something to add?"
Wildreveh asked warmly when the discussion quieted.

Porenydil bowed. "It appears the direction of this
proposal is controversial at best, ill-advised at worst.
I suggest, unless there is objection, that we postpone
further discussion until next Ketirvan, when the guild
may comb through the ledgers and offer answers to
some of the concerns that have been raised today.
There is yet much to attend to this year and we would
not wish to rush such an important decision."

His gaze wandered over the room, his expression
fatherly and regal. Sylbrac was impressed. It was quite
a performance. Porenydil neither ratified nor rejected
his own position, but postponed the discussion until
he could shore up his support. He came off looking

like the voice of reason, munificence, and wisdom, all of which would help generate support for the next bout. Brilliant strategy, really. Sylbrac smiled faintly. If he wanted to interfere in the other man's machinations, all he would have to do was become a vociferous supporter. Braken's balls, why couldn't he have thought of that sooner and done it to Wildreveh?

It was nearly the end of Ketirvan. The last order of business before closing was to install the new Pirena and Pirena-elect into office. It was a moment that Sylbrac was more than delighted to witness.

Eyvresia stepped up onto the platform beside Wildreveh, followed by a slight woman missing one eye, with burn scars running down the side of her face and neck. Her mouth was twisted unnaturally by the fire damage. Delaverdia was to be the new Pirena-elect, replacing Eyvresia in that office. Sylbrac didn't like her. She had a cold, abrupt manner and an off-putting way of talking over people until they succumbed to her arguments.

Wildreveh called the crowd to order.

"My friends, before we continue, I have some grave news to report. Mosevanar has taken ill with a fever and is quite unwell. We have sent for a majicar healer, but for now, I have accepted the honor of interim Beyoshen. Never fear—you will all receive your assignments tonight, nor will there be delays in the payment of your commissions and other earnings. I hope you know that I will serve you to the best of my ability, as I have done in the duties of Pirena. I hope I will do as well as Mosevanar. As always, it is my pleasure to serve you."

He set his hand over his heart and bowed to the assembly. The guild clapped placidly. So long as someone was sitting in the Beyoshen's chair and handing out the letters of commission, they didn't care who it was. Sylbrac especially.

The Ketirvan ended much the same way it had begun. Chimes rang and resonated into a deafening symphony, while the air seemed to drain from the entire building. Sylbrac's vision blurred and his chest felt as if it were collapsing. Fitch hunched down, her back arching, her fur bottle-brushing, and then she burrowed beneath his robe. And then it was over. Pilots fled like children from the schoolroom, each eager to be first in line for an assignment.

Sylbrac trailed behind. Now that it was so close, he could stand waiting a few more grains.

The line diminished rapidly, each Pilot entering the Beyoshen's office and leaving rapidly with a crisp linen envelope. At last it was Sylbrac's turn. He sauntered inside the office where Wildreveh sat waiting, turning an envelope between his fingers. He smiled unpleasantly as Sylbrac filled the doorway.

"I have been looking forward to this. I suspect that you are quite ready to be back to sea."

Sylbrac couldn't help his spurt of eagerness and fervent nod. "That's true."

"Well, that makes this all the harder, then." Again that smile. "Bad luck really. Seems you're going to be at loose ends for a while. The ship you were scheduled for can't use you after all."

He held the letter of assignment up and slowly dropped it into the fireplace. The paper blackened, the edges curling as the flames caught. Sylbrac watched, hardly understanding. He lifted his gaze back to Wildreveh, waiting stupidly for the joke to end, for his commission to be revealed.

"They can't use you," Wildreveh repeated, sitting forward and lacing his fingers together. "No one can. So long as I am Beyoshen, your anchor's in the dirt."

"You can't do this. I'll—I'll take it to the Pirena." Sylbrac's voice was barely a whisper, his throat closing in panic.

"As you wish. But she is barred from interfering with the decisions of the Beyoshen. She must have the backing of the membership, and I doubt there is anybody who would go against me for the likes of you. And even if they would, all of them are even now scattering to their ship berths. In a few days, they'll all be at sea. But perhaps at the next Ketirvan you can convince them. It will certainly be entertaining to see you try." He sat back, folding his hands over his stomach. "Which one of us lacks fangs now?" he said softly, gloating.

Sylbrac could only stand and stare, his hands loose at his sides. This was impossible. Pilots were too needed, too valuable, just to strand on land for petty hatreds. His tongue unlocked, his voice rasping out. "You're a mother-dibbling bastard. What would the Merchants' Commission say? Or the crown?"

"The business of the guild belongs to the guild. They will not interfere. As far as I'm concerned, I am protecting ships by keeping you dirtside." He pointed to Fitch, perched on Sylbrac's shoulder. "You're bad luck and a disgrace—worse than no Pilot at all. Luckily we have some points coming along in their training. I've no doubt they'll be ready by Mercy or Passion, if not before."

Wildreveh stood, his hands flat on the desk as he leaned over it. "You are no longer needed in this guild. You most certainly aren't wanted, and you can bet on Braken's cods that you aren't going to get another ship. Not on my watch." The last was said with a snarl.

Sylbrac flinched, the words striking him like sword blows. He couldn't breathe, couldn't see, couldn't think. Wildreveh could not . . . *would not* . . . do this. It made no sense! The man was surely not this vindictive? How could Sylbrac have missed seeing that? Then reason fled. He felt as if he were dying, his entrails yanked out and spread across the ground. Not go back to the sea? It was inconceivable.

Feral instinct roared up inside him. His vision narrowed on the gloating man who now stood between Sylbrac and everything he lived for, everything he was. He leaped forward, swinging his fists wildly. He heard Fitch's startled howl, then the thud of flesh. Pressure shuddered up his arm, and he felt the satisfying give of bone and the warm spurt of blood. Wildreveh reeled backward, stumbling over his chair and crashing against the mantle. His head bounced off the marble and he slid senselessly to the floor.

Sylbrac came around to stand over him, wanting to beat him. He felt the dagger in the small of his back. He almost reached for it. He could *make* Wildreveh change his mind. Or kill him. Wildreveh dead would mean a new Beyoshen. A taut thread of reason held him in check. Killing another Pilot was the only thing that would get him expelled from the guild. He could still think enough to know he shouldn't do that. If he walked away now, he still had a chance to return to the sea on ship.

Abruptly he turned about and fled. He stumbled down the twisting hallway, hardly knowing where he was going. Fitch rode his shoulder, clutching close to his neck, a growl emerging from deep in her throat. He turned a corner and saw Eyvresia at the far end, her back to him. She was speaking to someone. They turned when they heard his footsteps. Sylbrac caught a glimpse of red hair and pale skin as Eyvresia's companion put a hand on the Pirena's shoulder, pulled her hood up, and strode rapidly away.

Sylbrac ran to Eyvresia. Hope nearly choked him as he slid to a stop before her. His voice was strangled as he struggled to explain.

"Wildreveh has taken my ship. I am grounded. You must help me."

She didn't speak for a moment, her expression taut. Then she gave a slow shake of her head. "I cannot."

"But—won't you speak to him?" Tears were running down his cheeks. Desperately he clutched her arm, begging as he had never begged his parents. *Help me. Save me.*

She looked down at his hand, then gently removed it. "No."

"Why not? I—I don't understand. I am needed. I don't deserve this. It's a waste of me. A ship will sit at anchor if I don't stand the helm. Wildreveh is—

he's insane. He must be. You have to relieve him of duty and put someone else at Beyoshen." The words spilled out, tripping over one another, his voice rising.

"I cannot interfere." She paused. Something flickered over her face and then her countenance stilled. She drew back, smoothing her hands down her robes. "I am sorry for you. But I did warn you. You won't get a ship this year, unless Mosevanar recovers or Wildreveh steps down. Perhaps next . . . if you can convince the membership to support you."

She paused again. She reached out and ran her fingertips gently over Fitch's head. "It appears you have made yourself . . . dispensable." Her voice hardened oddly on the last words, and she dropped her hand, color rising in her cheeks. "I never thought I'd say that about a Pilot. I'm sorry for you," she repeated. "But now I must be about my duties."

She turned and then stopped, looking back at him. "Fair winds and following seas," she said, the traditional farewell among sailors.

With that, she walked away. Sylbrac could only watch her go, heavy, hot pain knotting in his gut. No! This was not possible! But it was. By Braken's heart, it was.

An accusing voice in his mind whispered, *You were wrong. Too late for Jordan. Too late for you.*

Chapter 3

Sylbrac found himself standing on the headland over-looking the sea with no idea of how he'd gotten there. He stood stiff as a wire, his toes jutting over the edge. The wind rasped over his skin like sandpaper. Fitch butted his jaw with her head, meowing commandingly. Absently Sylbrac put a chill hand up to scratch her ears. The moment he touched her, she began to purr and bump harder.

The sea pulled at him. He felt it through every infinitesimal speck of himself. He eyed the Pale balefully. It muffled the vibrancy of the connection, making him feel like he was wrapped in wet wool blankets. He longed to be on the other side of the wards, where the sea felt like it was caressing him skin to skin, tongue to tongue.

And with a ship's compass—

He sobbed, twisting around and sinking to his knees. He clutched at his chest as if to gouge his heart from the cage of his ribs. With a ship's compass, he *was* the sea. The wash of its waves was the flow of his blood in his veins. Its underwater mountains and valleys, its deserts and shoals—they were his bones, his muscles, his brain—they were his very breath. But now he was suffocating, dying a slow, agonizing death.

I should have killed Wildreveh.

But no. A silver satin ribbon of reason still anchored him to reality. Eventually Mosevanar would recover. Or Wildreveh would step down. Sooner or later. It could be a matter of a mere sennight or perhaps two.

Sylbrac grasped at the idea like a lifeline in a tossing sea. Yes! A sennight. He could wait so long. Or even two. He wasn't banned forever from the sea, from a compass. He just had to be patient. And if Wildreveh didn't step down as Beyoshen . . . there were ways to kill without leaving a trail to his own door.

But already the waiting was pulling his nerves to shreds. Fear clawed up his throat. He climbed to his feet and began walking, lifting Fitch down to hold her against his chest. He stumbled down the path, back toward Blacksea. But he didn't return home. Instead he followed the docks around to the west side and climbed up along the far headland. He walked for hours along the broken rim, unable to stop himself. If he kept moving, the vanguard of pain and loss couldn't catch him.

A squall blew up, soaking him to the skin. His Ketirvan clothing was not majicked against weather. Fitch protested, scratching and biting his fingers and cheek, but he hardly noticed. He fell, tearing rents in his trousers, digging bloody scrapes into his shins. Still he kept going, chased by desolation, helplessness, and unrelenting fear. What if he never got another ship? What if he never again was allowed to touch a ship's compass? What if he was destined to end his days with his soul torn in half?

On through the night and into the next day he fled. His legs trembled and his eyes blurred. He stopped when he came to a jut along a beach where he could neither climb the cliffs nor go around without swimming. If not for Fitch, he'd have struck out toward the open sea and swum beyond the Pale. Instead he sat on a rocky spur watching the tide rise and then fall again. Spray drenched him with nearly every wave. And though Fitch protested wretchedly, she refused to release her fierce grip, not even to allow him to adjust her in his arms.

The tide rolled in again. Fitch had begun meowing

insistently, batting at Sylbrac's face and licking his cold
fingers. He felt nothing. His mind quaked, his thoughts
fracturing and collapsing in on one another. He hardly
knew who he was. The truth was, he wasn't anybody
anymore. He'd stopped being a Truehelm long before
his Pilot gifts had ever emerged, and now he couldn't
be Sylbrac either, because if he couldn't man a compass, he could no longer be that man. He was nothing.

So lost was he in the contemplation of his endlessly
bleak future that he did not see the crimpers coming.
A fist slammed into his ear, sending him sprawling
into the shallow black water surrounding his perch.
He sucked a breath and choked on salty waves. He
coughed and gagged as hands dragged him up. His
head reeled and he staggered, his knees buckling.
They pulled him up again. Vaguely he heard Fitch's
yowl and felt her claws as she clambered up his leg
and belly, over his chest, and up to his neck. She was
wet, her fur standing on end. She continued to growl
low in her throat.

Sylbrac looked blearily at his captors. There were
four of them, dressed roughly in wool monkey jackets,
canvas shirts and trousers. They wore heavy boots and
they had wool caps pulled down low. Two held him
by the arms while a third lashed his hands loosely and
put a rope around his neck. Their hands were rough
and horny with calluses, and their faces were chapped
and red. They were sailors.

"C'mon with ye, then. Halford, get rid of that
cursed cat."

"No!"

Sylbrac struggled violently, wrenching himself from
side to side and kicking out at his captors. His legs
fouled in his drenched robes and he staggered heavily.
Fitch clung to him, screeching fury. He splashed into
the ocean. Instantly he found himself hardly able to
move. He hadn't eaten in two days, the sand was deep,
and the waves dragged heavily against him. The ropes
binding him hindered him further and the men caught
him quickly and dragged him back to the shingle.

"Won't have a cat comin' w' us. May as well wring th' damned thing's neck now as let it run wild spreading bad luck," the leader said, reaching for Fitch.

"Do it and you'll never get what you want from me," Sylbrac grated.

"Really, now? And what do ye suppose we want from ye that's worth the curse of a cat?"

Sylbrac glanced ponderously down the shoreline, scrambling to collect his addled wits. "You mean a cat is a worse curse than the one you get for kidnapping a Pilot? The way I see it, you're crimpers and you followed me from Blacksea. You came for me, presumably because I'm a Pilot. I'm useless if I don't cooperate. So leave Fitch alone."

The other man grinned. He had a round face that was deceptively young-looking. His hair was long and pulled back in a tail, his eyes bracketed with crow's-feet.

"You're right enough. We came lookin' for ye. All right, then. Keep the beast. Leastways for now. Ye can stand off w' th' cap'n about it."

"Captain?" Despite himself, Sylbrac couldn't help the eagerness and hope boiling up inside.

"Aye. Let's be on our way. We've a ways t' go and not much time."

His captors prodded him up the steep path and onto the coast road, where a mule cart waited. They shoved Sylbrac into the bed and propped him against the side, relieving him of his two knives in the course of it. The leader swung in to sit beside him, while two others sprawled opposite on a pile of sacks and duffels stacked along the opposite side. Both closed their eyes, falling instantly asleep. It was a survival skill acquired by mariners after the rotating four-hour sleep shifts vanished with the advent of poor weather and sea dangers. Swiftly bound in chains of exhaustion, sailors learned to snatch rest whenever any was offered. And Sylbrac had no doubt these four men were sailors. From their clothing to the scars on their hands and faces and their weathered skin, they couldn't be anything else. He watched the man called Halford climb up on the driver's seat and pick up the reins.

They headed west, away from Blacksea. The cart jerked and bumped over the ruts, making Sylbrac's head ache and his bones grate together. The North-coast Road was not a well-traveled road—the inland Trunk Line was far smoother and better cared for. Had the crimpers deliberately chosen this route just to torture him? He snorted derisively. If so, Wildreveh had chosen a much better method. They trundled league after league. Sylbrac's spine felt as though it were crumbling to powder. The rope around his neck chafed and though it was loose enough, it constantly felt as if it were strangling him. His damp clothing made him shiver so that he had to clamp his teeth to keep them from chattering. Fitch squirmed, her ears flat, her green eyes staring.

As the day wore on, Sylbrac made a conscious effort to pull himself together. He needed to think. But his head spun like a waterspout and his stomach cramped with hunger and thirst. The cold seeped through him, turning the marrow of his bones to ice and numbing his face and hands. It was all he could do to push aside the demands of his body and try to focus his thoughts. Slowly his mind settled.

It was no dream, no nightmare. He hadn't been given a ship. *He hadn't been given a Chayos-cursed ship.* And he'd been crimped. As impossible as they seemed, those two things were undeniable facts.

But why? He let his head fall forward onto his tied hands, braced by his bent knees. He squeezed his eyes shut, concentrating. *Why* had Wildreveh grounded him? It made no sense. Even as angry as Wildreveh had been, it just wasn't in his character to treat any Pilot so shabbily. It set a terrible precedent. And yet . . . that's exactly what he'd done. And Eyvresia hadn't tried to stop him.

Sylbrac went still. *Why* didn't she try to stop him? And how had the crimpers found him?

The two questions collided in his mind, and he

stopped breathing. *Braken's cods*. It was no coincidence. Wildreveh had *sold* him to the crimpers. And Eyvresia had let him. Or maybe she had helped him. *It appears you have made yourself . . . dispensable*. She'd not been talking about the low regard his fellow Pilots had for him; she was talking about this. He was so dispensable he could be sold to crimpers without worry of detection. Who'd miss such a thorn in the ass? Wildreveh could say he gave Sylbrac a ship and that he'd been lost at sea. Just another tragic death. Who would challenge him? Who would care enough to try? The guild members would merely be grateful to finally be rid of him.

He went rigid as a torrent of emotion crashed over him like a tidal wave. For an instant he was back in his parents' home. He smelled the cloying perfume his mother wore, felt her hands pressed against his cheeks, her fingernails biting into his skin as she bent close to him. Above her, he could see his father's face. His brows were raised disdainfully. Sylbrac could still taste the horror and panic rushing through him as they explained what they wanted, what he must do. Betrayal and guilt smothered him. A voice whispered. *This is your fault*. For not being a better son. For not being clean enough, quiet enough . . . for bringing a cat to the Ketirvan, for insulting Wildreveh, for being so full of himself . . .

The memories of his boyhood swirled together with his memories of the guild. His muscles twitched as if he would run. He held himself tightly bound, letting a rising tide of anger sear away the old hurt. No. This was not his fault, any more than his parents' corruption had been his fault. Wildreveh and Eyvresia had broken both guild law and Crosspointe law. For what? Money? If they'd fixed a bounty on Sylbrac's head, it was no doubt for more money than either would make in a lifetime. And the guild wouldn't have to put up with him anymore.

He began to swear, a slow, vicious litany of curses aimed at Wildreveh and Eyvresia.

"So ye've figured it, have ye?"

It was the leader. He sounded tired rather than smug.

Sylbrac's lips pinched together. He lifted his head. The two men on the sacks blinked up at him watchfully.

"Who are you?" he asked, looking at the round-faced man beside him.

"We be your escorts. That there at th' reins be Halford, th' ugly one wi' th' flat nose and scar across his forehead be Wragg, and that with th' baby face be Blot."

"And you?"

"Crabbel."

"You're risking a lot, crimping a Pilot. If you're caught, they'll send you to the Bramble. Either way, the gods know what you've done. Braken counts Pilots as his own. The sea may be unkind to you."

The man called Crabbel grinned, but his eyes remained hard. "Aye. We know th' risks."

Sylbrac's eyes narrowed. Sailors never tempted the ire of the gods. And they feared the Bramble more than anyone else. They lived their entire lives in fear of *sylveth*. To risk being stranded on the prison island during Chance meant they'd be exposed to *sylveth* and turn into spawn. There was no Pale circling the Bramble to protect them from the Chance storms. To be cursed by the gods or sent to the Bramble . . . there wasn't a sailor alive who wouldn't do just about anything to avoid either destiny. And these four courted both. What could possibly be worth taking such a risk?

Sylbrac dropped his bound hands into his lap, cupping his arms around Fitch. "At least you know the cat won't be the cause of your misfortune."

There was no more conversation the rest of the day, despite Sylbrac's repeated attempts at drawing Crabbel out. He gave up at last and fell into a doze, despite the bumps and jolts. He was still, after all, a sailor too.

They finally stopped two hours after sundown, halfway to Northglen. Halford pulled off into a small clearing. Wragg and Blot jumped down and pulled

Sylbrac out of the wagon bed. They left him standing, not bothering to tie him to anything. He walked about to stretch the kinks from his back and legs, setting Fitch on the ground.

As he watched his four captors work to set up the camp, he quickly recognized a pecking order. Crabbel was a first mate. He ordered Wragg and Blot to see to the mules and then started unloading the night's supplies from the wagon. He said little to Halford, who had set about checking every inch of harness, then crawled under the wagon to examine the wheels and axles. Sylbrac was sure he was a bosun. On board ship, his job was rigging and spars—making sure everything was in working order and no wear on a line or a block and tackle endangered the ship or crew. He took the same care with the wagon.

Their movements had an easy cadence, like they'd berthed together a long time. But Sylbrac had even more questions than he'd had before. A good mate and bosun were worth their weight in gold. And watching Halford's careful examination and the way the other men obeyed Crabbel without question, he was certain they were good. So why had they crimped him? Why weren't they aboard a ship now?

Blot built a fire and cooked a stew using dried meat, grain, withered potatoes, and carrots. He sang as he worked, one quiet chantey after another. The familiarity of the songs was soothing and Sylbrac found himself oddly comforted. Halford sat on the back of the wagon cleaning the harness. He watched Sylbrac darkly, as if expecting him to try to escape at any moment. Wragg and Crabbel sat near the fire and played cards.

As soon as they ate, they rolled up in blankets, but not before Halford tied Sylbrac to one of the wagon's wheels. He glared at Sylbrac.

"Ye ought t' keep that cat close. We got enough bad luck without beggin' for more. Might find it in th' morn w' its neck broke."

"Is that so? Think the bad luck ends with Fitch?"

Sylbrac smiled spitefully, then pursed his lips and began to whistle. Halford tensed, a shiver visibly quivering through him. He thrust to his feet, his hands clenching and unclenching.

"Problem?"

"Stupid t' ask for more bad luck."

"Seems I can hardly have worse luck, don't you think?"

"Can always be worse."

"Ah. Well, maybe if what's bad for me is worse for you, I can live with it. Have my revenge, as it were."

Sylbrac was surprised when the other man chuckled, rubbing his mouth with the back of his hand.

"Not me ye want revenge on. It's them as told us t' come get ye. Them's th' ones t' hate."

"I think I can manage to hate the whole bilge-sucking lot of you." There was no force behind his words.

The corners of Halford's mouth twitched. He nodded, tossing Sylbrac a blanket. "Get in line."

Blot stood the first watch. Wragg snored so loud he shook the branches of the trees. Sylbrac slept awkwardly with his arms extended and twisted before him, the blanket providing little protection against the damp that rolled off the Inland Sea and soaked up from the ground. Fitch returned in the middle of the night to curl against his stomach, licking her fur and then settling down to sleep.

Crabbel shook him awake before dawn, handing him a slab of cheese with a hunk of bread. He washed it down with a tin cup of hot sweet tea. As the other men hitched the mules and loaded the wagon, Crabbel squatted down beside him.

"Ye gotta name ye want us t' call ye?"

Sylbrac stared. Didn't they already *know* his name? Surely they must have been given it in order to crimp him?

"Seems odd to take a man without even knowing his name," Sylbrac said finally.

"I know you're a Pilot. Not much more I need."

Which meant . . . what? Realization struck like a hammer between Sylbrac's eyes, rocking him back.

"Braken's cods," he muttered.

Whoever was behind this wanted a Pilot. Any Pilot. Wildreveh had chosen which to sacrifice. Or maybe it had been Wildreveh and Eyvresia both. *Dispensable.* Sylbrac was dispensable.

His lips pulled away from his teeth in a silent snarl. Then let him die. Let Sylbrac rot in the ground with Geoffrey Truehelm, the son of the lord chancellor who'd run away from home when he was only nine seasons old. Let him die with Fish, the feral boy he'd been forced to become in order to survive alone on the docks of Sylmont, clawing and fighting for five seasons, living a life of constant fear and threat. Fish had at last found a way out of that labyrinth of violence. He'd won a berth aboard a ship as a snottie when he was nearly fifteen seasons old, and then he'd worked his way up to bosun in just six more seasons. But then a miracle happened; he'd become a Pilot. And when he did, he'd let Fish die a quiet death and in his place Sylbrac was born, a Pilot with no past, no roots, no ties.

But now it was time for Sylbrac to die too.

The people he'd been, the lives he'd led—they were dead. *His guild had sold him.* When he went back—and he would, somehow—he'd be someone new. Someone less expendable. He wouldn't be so easy to get rid of twice. If they hadn't liked Sylbrac, they surely wouldn't like the man he was about to become.

He glanced back at Crabbel, cold rage condensing in his bones. "Thorn. Call me Thorn."

And just like that, Sylbrac vanished like smoke in the wind and in his place the rootless Pilot Thorn was born.

Chapter 4

The day passed much the same as the last, except that the freshly christened Thorn grew more sore and exhausted with every jolting league. Midmorning, he was allowed out of the cart to relieve himself. When he did, he found himself stumbling like a cripple, his muscles knotted from his cramped seat in the cart and his night on the bare ground.

"I'll walk awhile," Thorn said when Crabbel ordered him back into the wagon.

"Pilots don't walk," Wragg said, sounding faintly affronted.

Thorn flicked an eyebrow up. "We certainly don't fly. Besides, as I recall, Pilots don't get crimped either." He held up his bound hands. "It appears these are trailblazing days for all of us."

Blot laughed, a boisterous, contagious sound, and his three companions smiled as if they couldn't help themselves. But none of the four offered to release Thorn from his bindings. Not that he expected it. Halford urged the mules to begin again and Thorn paced along behind the wagon. Fitch coiled in a ball on a duffel, her nose tucked beneath her tail, watching him.

Few people passed them on the road; it was not a time of year for traders. Occasionally they saw Corbies patrolling, the private police force paid by the crown to seek out any *sylveth* spawn that had made their way ashore, but otherwise it was desolate. The mule cart trundled along beneath coastal forest trees contorted into eerie shapes by storm winds, their shadows menacing. The wind caught in their branches, making a keening sound. In those times that the road emerged from the trees, Thorn found himself staring out to sea. Every so often he could see the spiky masts of departing ships. His stomach churned at the sight.

They didn't stop in Northglen. They trundled past at a slow, lurching pace with little variation on the routine. Wragg and Blot switched out the driving with Halford every so often, and at Swilden, Crabbel and Blot disappeared into a tavern, returning with a sack of sour wine, bread, and a package of roasted chicken. Thorn was almost too tired and too sore to stay awake to eat the feast. He'd walked much of the day, his bound hands making his gait jerky and strained. As soon as he finished, he curled on his side beside the cart wheel and fell into a hard, dreamless sleep. Late in the night, he woke to Fitch burrowing beneath his blanket. Her fur was damp from the mist off the sea.

Sometime in the night the rain started. A slow, dripping rain that turned into a thundering downpour near dawn. Soon the road was a quagmire. They hadn't gone more than half a league before the cart bogged down and the four crimpers were forced to dig it out. When they had, the travelers withdrew beneath the uncertain shelter of trees and waited for the storm to pass.

The storm slowed and faded just after sundown. Thorn squatted against the bole of an ancient pine, its branches twisted and bent like tortured limbs. He was soaked to the skin, and water squelched in his boots when he walked. Fitch had gone off again, no doubt to find someplace reasonably dry to wait for the storm to clear. As the rain eased, an eerie stillness fell. Thorn tensed and stood. Then a thick, fibrous fog, like wet cobwebs, began to wind through the trees. Soon he could hardly see his bound hands in front of his face. He pulled back against the tree, the rough wood an anchor in the muddled white. A frisson tickled down his spine. Something about the fog felt unnatural, like he'd suddenly stepped into a place between life and death. A land of wights. There was majick here.

"Where's th' Pilot? Where's Thorn?" Crabbel demanded nearby, his voice flattened by the thick fog.

Blot, Halford, and Wragg gabbled out replies. Thorn started to open his mouth to call out a reply, then shut it.

He could escape.

All he had to do was walk away. They'd never hear him. They wouldn't know where to begin looking for him. With a little time and patience, he could slip his ropes and by the time the fog lifted, he'd be well away. But escape to what? There was nothing waiting for him in Blacksea.

"Where did ye see 'im last?"

Crabbel sounded irritated and angry rather than worried. Thorn found himself grinning and shaking his head. A sign of a good first mate. He might shout and bluster, but he was always in control and never alarmed, never nervous, even in the face of catastrophe. Such a mate would bind a crew together through sheer spit and fire, no matter how fierce the storm, no matter how wild the waters.

"Thorn! Answer me, ye fool. Ye don't want t' be lost in this Braken-cursed night. Ye'll fall in a hole and break your neck. Or worse. Ye have no wits t' survive wanderin' alone. What if ye run into stray spawn?"

It was on the tip of Thorn's tongue to answer the challenge, to say something blistering. But before he could speak, the fog swirled. Just in front of him, a hollow opened. He tensed as an apparition appeared in the gauzy mist opposite him, as insubstantial as a ghost. A step forward and then it was inside the hollow with him. With it came silence. Thorn could no longer hear Crabbel or the muttering fury of the three other men as they blindly searched for their captive.

The figure before him wore a dark, hooded cloak, his face hidden deep in the folds. He was shorter than Thorn by a hand or more.

"Who are you? What do you want?"

Pale hands lifted, pushing back the hood. It was a woman. Red hair clung damply to her pale cheeks. Her eyes gleamed silver in the faint light. Majicar eyes. He could make out little else. But he'd seen her before. Twice. At the Dabloute. The second time she'd been talking to Eyvresia.

More pieces of the puzzle clanked into place.

"You . . . ," he growled. "Who are you? Why did you do this?" He jerked forward, lifting his hands up between them.

"I need a Pilot."

Her voice was bright-edged and fierce and something else he couldn't identify, something like resentful. But what did she have to resent?

"What for?"

"I have a ship."

He sneered. "What good is a ship without a compass?"

"But I have a compass."

That caught Thorn up short. His hands dropped. "The guild sold you a Pilot *and* a compass?" he asked, astonished.

"No."

"Then—how?" The guild controlled every ship's compass. Not even he knew how they made them, but he was certain that no one else had the capability of doing so. It was one of the two most closely guarded secrets of the guild.

"Is it not enough I have one?" she countered with a flash of heat, then held up her hand. "Enough. I have come to give you a choice. You can run. The fog will cover your path until you are safely away."

Thorn stared. "Or?"

She looked at the ropes on his wrists and around his throat and suddenly they slithered away like snakes, falling to the ground in a heap. He rubbed his raw skin, watching her.

"Or you can come sail on my ship."

Thorn waited. But she said no more. He scowled.

"What sort of trick is this? You have me where you want me. You have gone to considerable expense to crimp me, and unless you have another Pilot tucked in your pocket, you need me. What is your game?"

She didn't answer for a long moment, examining him like a flawed painting. "The game is you. Because of all the Pilots they could have given me, they chose you. Jordan Truehelm's brother."

Thorn flinched as if burned. "Jordan?" he repeated stupidly.

"Yes."

"How do you—? No one knows he was my brother. He told no one."

"He told me. Jordan was my friend."

The inflection of the last word was strange, as if she didn't really believe it. She looked away a moment, then back. "He wouldn't forgive me if I didn't give you a choice in this."

Forgive. "Do you know what happened to him?" Thorn demanded, unable to contain the need that strained his voice.

She hesitated. "I do." She paused, chewing her lower lip thoughtfully. Then she nodded, coming to a decision. "Here is my promise. If you pilot my ship, I will tell you all you wish to know about Jordan's death." She smiled thinly. "If not"—she shrugged— "then you don't really want to know."

"I want to know," he said sharply. He *had* to know.

"Then I will see you again. But if you choose to escape, the fog will remain until dusk tomorrow. Fair winds and following seas . . . *Thorn.*"

With that, she pulled up her hood and strode away into the fog. The thick, wet shroud closed around her and poured into the empty hollow she'd left behind. Sounds returned. Farther away than before, he heard

Crabbel hollering for quiet and Halford's steady, even-toned cursing. There were the crackles of sticks and the thudding *stump* of footsteps and his own harsh breathing, like he'd been running up a steep hill.

"Braken's cods," Thorn muttered, scraping his fingers through his hair as he leaned back against the tree. What in the depths was going on? *Who is she? Does it matter? She's got a ship and a compass and she has answers about Jordan.*

A sudden movement around his feet made him jump and then Fitch meowed and clawed up his leg in lunging leaps. He caught her, stroking her head.

"What do you think, Fitch? Run or stay?"

But he knew what he was going to do. There wasn't anything to go back to. Wildreveh and Eyvresia weren't going to give him a ship. And they couldn't tell him what had happened to Jordan.

Carefully Thorn made his way through the fog and the trees, following the sound of Crabbel's voice. When he was on top of the searchers, he stopped.

"I'm here." When they didn't hear, he said it louder. "I'm here."

"Where?" Crabbel demanded.

"Here." He pursed his lips and trilled a jaunty tune.

The mate emerged from the fog in front of Thorn. He crossed his arms over his barrel chest. "Ye been busy. Got your ropes off." He cocked his head, his eyebrows shaggy above his dark eyes. "Ye didn't run."

"You have marvelous powers of observation," Thorn said drily.

Halford, Blot, and Wragg converged on them, circling around Thorn to cut off any chance of flight. Crabbel continued to stare a long moment, then turned to Halford.

"Where's the wagon? Better eat and bed down. Keep close." He flicked a glance at Thorn. "Don't want anyone t' get lost."

Halford led them back to the mules with surprising accuracy, given the fog and the darkness. Thorn fell in behind him, the other three bringing up the rear.

Their bread was gluey and wet from the rain, and the cheese was splotchy with mold. Still, they all ate without complaint and then rolled into their blankets, except Blot, who took the first watch. Thorn found a patch of grass that was merely soft instead of muddy, and bedded down there. Halford and Wragg slotted in on either side of him. Thorn smiled to himself. He might have won some trust by not running, but they were still going to guard him carefully. As usual, Fitch burrowed beneath his blanket and snuggled against his chest. Despite the chill and the questions that gnawed his mind, he soon fell asleep.

The next day they slogged along through the white silence. The fog was so thick that they blundered back and forth on the road, guided by the twisting trees hemming each side. The mules struggled to pull the cart through the mire of the road. The men walked to ease the burden, Halford leading the beleaguered animals.

Mud caked Thorn's robes and clumped on his boots, and his legs burned with the effort of walking. Fitch rode on his shoulder, hunching down against his neck. The squeak and rattle of the cart and the labored breathing of both men and mules sounded uncanny in the blind stillness. Thorn found it soothing, like being out at sea, isolated from the ship's crew by the walls of mist. If it weren't for the squelching mud pulling at his every step, he might have been able to imagine the roll of the deck, the popping flap of the wind in the sails, and the wash of the waves against the hull.

Six more long days passed before they came to the village of Horndean beetling along the coast just east of Grimsby Harbor. The fog cleared by the second day, but in its place a steady rain moved in. They hadn't had a fire in a sennight and the bulk of their supplies had spoiled, leaving only a handful of shriveled sausages to divide between them the last two days. So it was that on the sixth day when at last they saw the lights of Horndean, they were exhausted, soaked to the skin, and ravenous.

But the last six days of misery had taught Thorn a great deal about his companions. They were good men. Despite the onerous conditions, they neither frayed nor snapped. Crabbel set the tone with an infinite patience for the mud and the rain and the hunger. But he didn't tolerate the slightest indolence or loafing. The lack of bickering among the men made Thorn wonder how long they'd served together. None ever challenged Crabbel's rule. They fit together like well-oiled gears. Halford muttered under his breath almost constantly, but never turned his wrath on the mules or his companions. Blot slogged along, singing chantey after chantey, his voice growing raspier with every passing hour until the tunes were hardly recognizable. Still, he kept singing and no one snapped at him to stop. Wragg was nearly as silent as Crabbel, but he was there with a hand to help Halford with the mules, to help Thorn up when he slipped in the mud, and to work tirelessly for hours every night trying to spark a flame to wet wood without success.

All of Thorn's questions about where they were going or the ship that was waiting went unanswered. But he noticed that a peculiar tension wrapped each of his companions whenever he broached the subject. It made him wonder—he'd been crimped. How had they been coerced into serving aboard a black ship? They were clearly capable, skilled men. If he'd been outfitting a ship, they'd have been clear choices for mate, bosun, and midshipmen. So why choose a black ship unless they were forced? But he couldn't imagine what would compel all four of them.

It was just after dusk and the black waters of the Inland Sea glowed brilliant purple and pink in the fading sunset. Crabbel called a halt just as they crested the hill above Horndean.

"Been a fair good walk and I be so hungry m' belly is chewing at me own ribs. And I'd be lyin' if I said m' skin wasn't fair sloughing off with this wet. But we've a job, boys, and it be no time t' relax th' watch. Wragg, ye and Halford go get rid of th' cart and snare us what ye can carry from th' tavern. We'll meet ye below at Clark's Cove and roll up on th' beach."

The three mud-caked men looked disappointed, but they didn't argue. Thorn's own frustration was keen. Not that he could argue the point. Between the black filaments spreading across his eyes and the heavy compass-rose signet on his forefinger—there was no mistaking him as anything but a Pilot. And there wasn't a Pilot alive who'd be in such wretched condition in such a place with such men. All he'd have to do was cry once for help and the crimping plot would be ruined. Crabbel was entirely right not to risk it. It was one thing for Thorn to stick close in the middle of nowhere with no food and blinded by fog, and another thing entirely to trust he wouldn't try to escape with help so close.

But Thorn wasn't interested in escaping, nor was he willing to forgo a hot meal and a bath.

"And if I promise not to bolt?" he said quietly.

Wragg, Blot, and Halford all looked up, but Crabbel shook his head. "Nay, sir. Can't trust your word, ye understand. Bein' in such dire circumstances as ye are."

It was fair enough—why should he trust Thorn's word? But somehow the words struck Thorn like quick, hard slaps. He straightened, his face hardening into austere lines as he looked off into the distance. That night in the fog he'd made his choice. Which meant that whether they knew it or not, as soon as they set foot on the deck of their ship, these men would be his crew. His crew belonged to him; he'd give his life to them. This attitude had not made him any more popular in the guild. Pilots, after all, were far more precious than the lives of a few sailors or even a ship. Everyone knew it. Sailors believed it most of all. But not Thorn.

"Of course. It would be ill-advised." His words were haughty and clipped, exactly as a Pilot's ought to sound.

Blot and Crabbel collected their duffels from the

cart. Thorn slung a canvas bag over his shoulder and fell in behind as they followed the road, the mule cart angling off onto the track leading down into Horndean. The town was nestled in a small forested bowl, the far side sloping steeply down to a broken shoreline. It sat just east of the mouth of Grimsby Bay. Most of the shoreline along the bay was inhospitable, though a handful of towns and villages along its lip provided enough reason for coasters to drop anchor, trading for foodstuffs, wood, coal, and metals mined in the Kearnoc Mountains to the south, wool from Datchworth, and glass from Lawley. Even using the necessary host of lighter boats to load the cargo was cheaper than porting the goods across the mountains to Tilman.

Thorn nearly bumped into Blot as Crabbel pulled to a halt. Fitch growled and dug her claws into his shoulder at the sudden jolt.

"Noticed it th' day we took ye, that ye've got calluses on your hands," Crabbel said, turning to face Thorn. "Scars too. Like ye've worked hard."

"Aye, so I do," he said shortly.

"Never seen another Pilot w' hands th' like of yers."

"No, likely you haven't."

Crabbel didn't say anything else and Thorn started to shoulder past him. He was exhausted, sore, and hungry, and he was ready to be done with this Hurn-cursed journey.

"Hard t' trust a man who never hoisted a sail or climbed a mast," Crabbel went on, not moving.

Thorn halted, anger tightening his voice. "Is it?"

"Fact is, most Pilots wouldn't ken th' difference 'tween an anchor chain and a clew line. Still, they hold th' lives of th' crew in their snow-white hands. Have t' trust 'em. Them and th' cap'n is all that stands 'tween them and th' depths. E'en then, too often it ain't enough t' keep body and soul together."

"Fascinating. Really. But I'd just as soon find a dry spot to bunk down, maybe hunt up some wood for a fire. Mind finishing your maunderings as we walk?"

Crabbel ignored him, continuing on in his thoughtful tone, scratching at his ragged new-grown beard. "Thing is, can't trust a man who's got th' hands of a Pilot; can't not trust a Pilot. But ye are a creature of a different stripe. Got th' right kind o' hands, but ye carry bad luck on your back, and what fool would trust a man he'd crimped?"

"You aren't exactly lacking in back luck, having crimped a Pilot," Thorn pointed out acidly. "Do you have a point?"

"I believe I may be a fool, Master Thorn. It appears that Blot here has suddenly busted his leg and we're gonna carry him t' th' inn. He's gonna put his arm over your shoulder and you're gonna keep your eyes down and your mouth shut. Any luck, no one will notice you're a Pilot. We'll get us a private room w' nice soft beds and have a run at th' baths and a hot meal."

Thorn eyed Crabbel a long moment. The other man didn't ask for promises, and Thorn didn't offer again. It was a leap of faith. A gift of trust. Thorn nodded without smiling and shifted the duffel he carried, pushing an annoyed Fitch to the other side of his shoulders. He pulled off his compass signet and tucked it into his pocket. The silver bands on the sleeves of his jacket were tarnished and muddy, the rest of his clothing too torn and ragged to give him away.

"You must be in a lot of pain with that leg, Blot. Give me your arm and I'll help you."

"Eh, damned clumsy o' me," Blot agreed with a toothy grin. He slung his arm over Thorn's shoulder, leaning heavily, settling his hand along the side of Thorn's face to help screen his telltale eyes.

Crabbel took his other arm, then booted him none too gently in the left leg. "That's your broken pin. Don't forget."

The tavern was the first building they encountered as they limped into Horndean. It was a sprawling two-story building. Its clapboard siding was faded and cracked by the salt winds off the Inland Sea, and if it

had ever been painted, there was no color left to show
it. Cracks of welcoming light gleamed around the shutters. A heavy wood sign swung creakily between two
posts out front. The image of an anchor tangled in
knucklebones was carved into the heavy planking. The
colors were brilliant and fresh in the darkness, as was
the red lettering across the top: SAILOR'S LAST
DRAUGHT. Now Thorn could see a couple of hands
and feet drifting through the knucklebones. They were
one of the dangers of the Inland Sea. Weirs of knucklebones appeared and vanished without rhyme or reason. They looked like their namesakes—skeletal white
fingerlike protrusions that rose out of the waves. They
appeared soft like river reeds, but they were sharp
and hard and could tear the belly out of a ship. He
shook his head. The owner clearly had a morbid sense
of humor.

The trio hobbled to the door and pushed inside.
Despite the tavern's foreboding name, the taproom
was crowded and blessedly warm. Pipe smoke drifted
in a blue haze near the ceiling, and a fire crackled in
the massive fireplace on the far wall, where a cauldron
of soup the size of a pony dangled from an iron hook.
Every table was besieged with bodies and boisterous
laughter rattled the windows. The delectable scent of
hot food made Thorn's stomach cramp.

"Hey! Ye can't bring no blighted cats in here!"

The woman's shrill voice cut across the laughter and
the room fell quiet. She pushed away from the nearest
table, her hands fisted on her hips, her long jaw jutting. Her blond hair was cut short on the sides, the
long ends of the top caught in a pigtail behind. She
wore a loose cotton shirt that had once been white,
but now was a dishwater gray. It had been oft-patched
with small careful stitches—there wasn't a sailor anywhere who couldn't sew. She was eyeing Fitch with
flat fury and all around her in spreading ripples, the
rest of the patrons turned to look at the commotion,
their expressions going tight at the sight of the cat.

Thorn swore silently. As a Pilot, no one could gainsay his right to do anything. But an ordinary man . . . how maggot-headed could he be not to have tried to hide Fitch?

He lifted Blot's arm off his shoulder. "Get cleaned up and fed," he said quietly. "Looks like I'll be rolling up on the beach after all."

Thorn spun and pushed back out into the chill night, keeping his head ducked low, his matted hair hanging over his eyes to disguise their telltale coloring.

Outside, the chill air was a sharp slap. He pushed his hair out of his face and fondled Fitch's head. She bumped her head hard against his palm, meowing plaintively. She was as hungry as he was.

"Where d'ye think you're goin'? Where's Crabbel and Blot?"

It was Halford with Wragg. The two men blocked his path, having dispensed with the mules and cart. Thorn couldn't see their faces in the darkness, but the set of Halford's shoulders was menacing.

"They're inside. Go in and join them. I'll be on the beach."

Thorn began to shoulder between them, but Halford grabbed his arm in a meaty grip.

"I'm not allowin' ye outta me sight."

"Then I suppose you should forgo the bath and bed and join me on the beach."

"You just wait. Wragg, go sight Crabbel and measure th' cut of his jib."

Wragg nodded and disappeared inside. The door opened and a wedge of light cut the night. Laughter and boisterous voices spilled out and then the door swung shut. Thorn shook off Halford's hand and went to sit on an upturned stump that served as a chopping block. He pulled Fitch down and snuggled her against his chest, stroking her.

"Bad luck," Halford muttered.

Thorn lifted his brows and then pursed his lips, whistling a merry chantey. Halford swore.

"Don't th' sea and gods send enough damned luck but ye gotta invite more?"

"As if crimping me was a lucky thing," Thorn reminded him. "Besides, I'd think you'd be more worried about my getting revenge by driving us up onto a knucklebone weir."

Halford snorted. "Ye be a Pilot. Ye wouldn't do any such thing."

"Are you sure?"

The sailor just shook his head, crossing his arms, his head tipped back defiantly.

Thorn grinned. He *liked* Halford. Well, he liked that being friendly to the other man grated on him. "As it happens, you are right. But you're wrong about luck. It's all whim of the gods. Nothing we do changes what they throw at us."

"Mebbe so. But then agin, mebbe not. Best t' keep th' lines coiled and neat than take a chance they tangle when ye gotta shift canvas quick."

"Very wise, no doubt. But I'll take my chances."

"And bring your bad luck down on th' entire crew."

"Maybe you should have crimped another Pilot, then."

"Now, that's a right true thing."

They both fell silent, the breeze picking at them. Thorn had suffered much worse cold on deck, drenched in seawater and riding a storm out. But it annoyed him that just a few paces away was a perfectly good tavern with a perfectly good fire and delightfully hot food. He gritted his teeth.

A quarter of a glass went by before Wragg returned. He came around the building, stepping out of the shadows.

"Halford, get inside and find th' rooms proper-like. Pilot, follow me. Keep it quiet."

He led the way around to the rear of the building where a rope dangled down out of the second-story window. Crabbel and Blot held the other end.

"Quiet-like. Up ye go."

Wragg prodded Thorn in the ribs. For a sailor, the climb was a simple scramble. For a pampered Pilot, it would have been a far more difficult production. Except that Thorn was no ordinary Pilot. He'd become a snottie by the time he was fifteen and six seasons later he'd made bosun. Even running the compass, he'd never sailed a ship for which he wasn't willing to lend a hand hauling the sheets or trimming a sail. He'd come by the calluses and scars on his hands through honest labor.

He put Fitch back up onto his shoulder and grasped the rope. The men above began to haul in the line, but he nimbly pulled himself up hand over hand, walking up the clapboard wall until Crabbel could hand him inside. Wragg climbed through a few grains after.

"Halford?"

"Comin' through th' common room," Wragg answered.

"Good."

Crabbel looked at Thorn. "Bathin' room down th' stairs at th' end of th' hall. Better not let 'em see ye. Have t' leave th' cat here."

Thorn considered. A test of trust. He nodded. "But Halford has to come with me. I'd not like to see Fitch claw his eyes out."

"Fair enough." He grabbed a duffel from the floor and held it out. "Here. Some o' your clothes."

Thorn reached for it slowly. "*My* clothes?"

The corners of Crabbel's lips tightened. "Aye. They was given t' us."

"I see."

Thorn set the duffel against the wall, untying it and pulling out clean clothes. His hands fumbled as he worked. He'd figured out that Wildreveh and Eyvresia had turned him over to the crimpers. The redheaded woman in the fog had confirmed it. But the clothing made it real in a way that shook him to the core. He'd been *sold*. When he'd fled his parents' home, he'd sworn he'd never let it happen again. And yet here he was.

He bit the tip of his tongue until it bled. There was no running this time. He doubted he could scrape a life as deckhand or go back to being a bosun; one look at his eyes and no captain would have him, no crew trust him. Not if his own guild wouldn't. Thorn *needed* a compass. Which meant he was trapped. He drew a harsh breath. But he wasn't helpless. The red-headed woman needed him as much he needed her ship and compass. This time he was going to stay and fight.

He straightened up, turning as Halford clumped into the room.

"Go clean up," Crabbel ordered. "Take th' Pilot w' ye."

Halford's chin jerked and his eyes widened; then he nodded and went to his duffel and dug through it. If Thorn hadn't been watching, he'd have missed the short exchange. His gaze narrowed. Something was amiss.

He followed the bosun into the passage and down the stairs. The bathing room was a small shed built over a hot spring at the end of the building. Steam filled the small room, swirled by the drafts that fingered through the cracks in the plank walls. There was a pool large enough to hold half a dozen people, with benches lining one wall and a stack of towels on a shelf near the door. The towels were strips of threadbare cotton sheets and squares of canvas. They didn't look like they'd been washed recently. Several tin pans holding bars of soft yellow soap and washrags sat on the rim of the pool.

Hot water flowed into the chamber from a channel beneath the south wall and out through an opening in the northern side. Thorn had worn the same clothing for a sennight—he was filthy and smelly and stiff with mud. He set his fresh clothes on the bench and began stripping, leaving the dirty garments in a heap alongside the pool to rinse out later. He found his Pilot ring in his pocket and slid it back on his finger.

The water felt glorious. He sank under, rubbing at his hair. He came up, grabbing a scoop of soap and a washrag, and began scrubbing at the dirt that seemed to have embedded itself in every crease and pore.

"You smell like carrion," he said to Halford, who was still standing near the door. "You won't have a chance to bathe again for some time, and in hot water. Or maybe you're feeling prissish about the size of your prick. I can turn my back if you like."

"Why don't ye knob off," Halford said, but he began to remove his clothes.

Thorn watched him obliquely, wondering at the other man's sudden prudery. Halford's skin was pale except for his face and hands. Scars hashed his broad back and stout legs. Working the rigging was dangerous work. The last thing he removed was the wool cap that all the crimpers wore pulled low over their ears. Beneath it he had a full head of dark hair that matted to his skull. He tossed the cap onto the pile of his clothing and turned, standing defiantly.

Thorn stared. Suddenly, a lot of things made sense. "All of you?" he asked.

Halford ran his tongue along the edge of his teeth, his nostrils flaring. He nodded.

Thorn rubbed a hand over his face, scratching at his newly grown beard. Then he laughed. Halford scowled.

"Ain't funny."

"Isn't it? You wear two wreck earrings and a charm on your chest and you crimp a Pilot, and then you have the balls to accuse *me* of bringing bad luck down on you with my cat and my whistling?"

"Ye think it's funny?" He tapped the ebony anchor pendant tangled in silver wire that hung on a silver chain against his chest. "Be a death sentence for us."

No one wanted a charmer. Sailors wore disaster charms so that any ship they sought to serve on would be forewarned about how *lucky* they were and be able to turn them away. When a sailor survived a shipwreck, the Water Guild required him to put an earring in his left ear. It was a common enough piece of jewelry in any ship's company. The second time gave him another earring, this one in the right ear. The third time put the unremovable charm around his neck and he became a pariah. Cursed. No one wanted to sail with a man whose ships kept wrecking. If it wasn't just as unlucky to kill charmers, likely the four of them would have had their throats slit long ago. Charms were a death sentence for someone whose veins were filled with seawater, who'd waste away dirtside. Unless someone gave them a chance to sail on a black ship.

Thorn sobered. "The four of you—you've worked three wrecks . . . together?"

Halford nodded.

It was on the tip of Thorn's tongue to ask what had happened. He could hardly imagine how the same four men had crewed three different wrecks together. But it didn't matter. None of it would have been their fault. He knew better than they did how treacherous and changeable the sea could be. Still, they paid the price. There wasn't anybody more superstitious than sailors. If they could hang the bad luck on some cause, then they would. In this case, it was the four charmers.

"Then it appears your luck has changed. I hope it holds."

Halford's head jerked back, surprise softening the graven lines of his face. Then his lips curved with bleak humor. "Aye."

Thorn's gaze narrowed as he watched Halford step down into the water. "There are more surprises, aren't there?"

"There always are." Halford would say no more.

Chapter 5

Clean, with a bellyful of hot food and ale, Thorn slept well. A paw batting his face woke him up. He opened his eyes. Fitch sat on his chest. The moment she saw he was awake, she began to meow, bumping her forehead insistently against his jaw.

"All right," he muttered, sitting up.

The other bed was empty, the bedclothes rucked up in a knot at the foot. Halford had not liked sleeping in the same room with Fitch, but had apparently drawn the short straw. Clearly he'd made his escape to breakfast as soon as it was acceptable. He'd probably been awake the entire night waiting for the walls to collapse or the moon to drop through the roof.

Thorn opened the shutters to let Fitch out, shivering at the chill. She walked out along a ledge and leaped to a leafless tree and crawled back down to the ground, disappearing with a flirt of her tail around the corner of the building. The sky was pewter and snowflakes spun through the air, dusting the world white. He yawned and stretched, starting when the door opened. A sour-faced Halford came in, carrying a trencher with spiced sausages, a hot loaf of bread under his arm, and a pot of sweet cream tea.

"Ye gotta eat quick. We'll be laying on soon as you're ready."

Leaving the window open, Thorn tore off a hunk of bread and folded it around a sausage. As he ate, he dressed. He stamped into his boots and reached

for his monkey jacket. Beneath it were his stiletto and
dagger. Another gift of trust. He tucked his stiletto
back in his boot and slid the dagger in his waistband,
then donned his jacket and shook out his mud-stained
sleeveless surcoat, wishing Crabbel had thought to
steal one of his heavy winter coats. The clothes he'd
washed had dried in front of the fire and he stuffed
them into his duffel.

He'd shaved the night before, but there was little
to be done about his mop of unruly hair. He dipped
his fingers into the frigid water filling the washbasin
and dragged them through his locks, pulling the tangles free.

He settled onto the bed and drank his lukewarm
tea. Halford prowled the room impatiently.

"Ready?"

"Soon as Fitch comes back."

"You're a blighted thorn in the ass."

Thorn grinned, thinking of Torsby. "That's a true
thing."

Halford snorted, but didn't say anything more as he
sat on his bed. It wasn't long until a black shadow
slunk back inside, her fur spotted white with snow.
Thorn broke up a sausage and offered it to her. She
ate the meat daintily. Halford watched impatiently, his
feet tapping. He shifted on the bed, then stomped
across the room to slam the shutters closed. When
Fitch was finally finished, he grabbed his duffel and
slung it over his shoulder.

"Keep that thing hidden, if'n ye don't want a
brawl," he growled. "Landlord'll be in a high fettle if
he sees ye."

Thorn held Fitch beneath his elbow, his surcoat
shrouding her from sight. Halford led the way down
to the common room, where Crabbel, Wragg, and Blot
waited. Only Crabbel met his gaze, the others looking
at anything else. He smiled to himself. He was probably the only person in Crosspointe who didn't care
about their charms. There was only a handful of other

people eating breakfast and they hardly looked up as the five of them trooped past.

The muddy road had frozen into ripples and ruts beneath the snow, making the footing treacherous. They soon took to the shoulder, following an animal track. The hill dropped away sharply down a narrow ridge. The coastline here was broken, with deep sly clefts and mysterious folds full of shadow and silence.

Clark's Cove was a narrow, black-sanded shingle scooped out of the forbidding shoreline. The hills rose steeply on either side, jutting out into the black waters to offer some protection from the wind. A waterfall careened down the side of the southern escarpment and splashed into a stream that meandered out to bisect the beach. The tide was rolling in, the waves choppy. The wind had begun to pick up, moaning eerily through the trees and driving the snow sideways.

A jolly boat was waiting for them above the high-tide mark. Wragg and Blot untied it and pulled away the screen of evergreen limbs hiding it from sight. Together, the crimpers dragged it down onto the beach, brushing off Thorn's attempts to help. On the shingle, the four sailors unstowed the two masts and set them in place, one near the bow, the other in the stern. Once they set the rigging, they shoved out into the waves. Thorn's boots were majicked against the wet, but that did him little good as the waves drenched his legs and frigid water overflowed the tops. He pulled himself aboard, dropping his duffel into the bottom of the boat and setting Fitch down on the center thwart. Her fur was bottle-brushed and she instantly crawled underneath to wedge herself between the two water casks, growling furiously all the while. Halford and Crabbel set the rudder and lugsail while Wragg and Blot hoisted the mainsail.

Thorn helped haul in the sheets and then unshipped the oars while the other men set the sails. The wind was blowing from the northwest, pushing them back toward the beach. He dug sharply against his oar while beside him, Halford did the same, casting Thorn a startled look, which was quickly replaced by his usual dour expression. Wragg and Blot luffed the mainsail at Crabbel's shouted order, while Halford and Thorn pulled against the chop. They made slow headway, and Thorn's palms began to burn, even as his fingers felt frozen.

When they'd gained enough sailing water, Crabbel called "Hard-a-lee!" and swung the rudder while Wragg and Blot braced the yard hard. The sail bellied and suddenly they were skimming along, close-hauled. Crabbel adjusted the luff and the jolly boat heeled. Black water lipped over the starboard rail and swirled in the bottom of the boat.

They were forced to tack several more times before they narrowly cleared the headland, and then they were scudding ahead of the wind into Grimsby Bay.

Thorn pulled the oar out of the lock and stowed it again, then reached down and pulled Fitch out, cradling her to his chest. She was wet and stiff, pushing away from him and biting at his hands. He stroked her, trying to soothe her, at last letting her go. She settled gingerly on his knee, not so irritated that she was willing to go wading in the water sloshing in the bottom of the boat again.

Wragg and Blot continued to adjust the mainsail at Crabbel's direction, while Halford manned the lugsail. Spray and snow clung to Thorn's hair and icy water trickled down his neck. He turned his hands over. There was a blister on his left palm and another on his right forefinger where his compass ring had rubbed when he rowed. Seven weeks away from the sea and only a little swordplay to occupy him had made his hands soften. He clenched them and crossed his arms, shivering at the chill. It was always this way after Chance. Off the sea he lived too softly and had to be re-inured to the unrelenting cold, wet, and wind.

He grimaced. No, that wasn't true. He didn't *have* to be. He could be like every other Pilot. He could never touch a line, never grasp an oar, never lift a hand but to caress the ship's compass. In fact, most captains and crews would prefer it. They hardly knew what to do with a Pilot who was as much one of them as not. Some it angered—without a Pilot out on the sea, they were almost certainly doomed. If he hurt himself, fell overboard, or became in any way incapacitated—he had no right. And yet Thorn could not suffer to let himself sit and watch the crew work while he did nothing to help. He might have been born to wealth and decadence, but he'd be damned if he'd follow in his parents' parasitic footsteps and live a life of ease and luxury while good men and women struggled to survive around him. No, he wasn't going to be that kind of man.

He stroked a hand down Fitch's back. She swiveled her head, glaring at him, her claws biting sharply into his thigh. When he would have petted her again, she snatched his forefinger in her teeth, clamping hard, her eyes narrowing. When he only waited patiently, she let go and turned away with avid indifference, bending to lick her paw. And then when he stroked her again, he felt the rumble of her purr vibrating into his thigh. He smiled.

Just then Crabbel stepped over the thwart and sat down beside him. Thorn glanced behind. Halford had taken over the rudder.

"Ye been a lighter load t' haul than we had a right t' expect," Crabbel said abruptly. "So it only be fittin' that ye know what be over th' horizon. As ye've guessed, your pilotin' skills be wanted. For a black ship. Every one of us been crimped or scraped up outta th' gutter."

"You're the mate," Thorn said. "And Halford—bosun?"

"Aye on both counts," Crabbel said. "Ye know what we are." His face hardened. His hat was once again pulled down to hide the earrings in his ears. He shook his head. "So we come t' be berthed on th' *Eidolon*."

"The *Eidolon*? How auspicious. A ship named for

wights. And Halford doesn't like cats. I'm surprised he's not spawning a litter."

Crabbel grinned. "Not th' worst of it either. Mixed crew. With your little beastie, it be bad luck any which way th' wind blows."

Thorn pursed his lips. Mixed crews were worse luck than cats and whistling. Men served with men, women served with women, and never the two should mix on deck or certain catastrophe would follow. Or so superstition said.

"And a crimped Pilot to guide you," he said. "Why not set sail during Chance and go with a perfect hand of bad luck?"

"That's somethin' I wanted t' warn ye about," Crabbel said soberly, his round face set. "Works this way. They'll be offerin' ye th' position of Pilot. Ye can take it or no—ain't no way t' force your hand t' th' compass—but ye'll be shipping out either way. Pays better than fair—ye may be crimped, but you're not workin' for nothin'. Same for th' rest of us. Everybody gets a healthy wage—a good bit more than fair—and bonuses for makin' a run without mishap."

Thorn was silent. He'd been kidnapped to pilot an illegal ship—one courting every stray breath of bad luck—and he was going to be paid to do so. Bizarre was too mild a word to describe it.

"There be another thing ye oughta know. Leighton Plusby is master."

Thorn frowned. "I thought they stripped his ticket and put him ashore." As soon as he said it, he knew how foolish it sounded. A black ship wouldn't require a licensed captain—not that it would be able to obtain one. Or even want one. Not if its owners wanted to avoid notice. Though certainly it would have been comforting to have hired a sane captain.

He gave a mocking salute. "It appears that I was mistaken. You are to be congratulated on achieving a perfect hand of bad luck. Lay your cards on the table and sweep the pot. You've won."

Crabbel laughed harshly. "This be a cursed ship, sure as th' wind blows and th' grass grows."

"And Halford has the nerve to call Fitch unlucky."

Crabbel stood, slapping Thorn's shoulder. "We've not even hoisted anchor. Th' black water is a fickle lady. We may find favor with th' gods yet."

"Or more likely, we'll cross the Pale and find a swarm of starving Koreions and a forest of knuckle-bones," Thorn muttered quietly to Fitch, who only turned her head away disdainfully, though she continued to purr.

Crabbel returned to the rudder, leaving Thorn to stare off into the blowing snow. He shook his head. A ship christened *Eidolon* and Leighton Plusby at the helm. It could hardly get worse.

Like the charmers, Plusby was in no position to re-fuse an offer of employment, not if he wanted to be at sea. Plusby had once been a competent captain, even brilliant, but he'd come unraveled. Now he was erratic and volatile. No crew wanted him at the helm. Most sailors went to sea for love of the water. It was a siren's call they couldn't refuse. Not Plusby. Not anymore. He went for hate.

Thorn remembered hearing the tale. It was like a favorite ghost story told around the fireplace on a Chance night when the storms blew so furiously you didn't know if you'd even survive. Apparently Plusby had fallen desperately in love with a woman from Ta-pisriya shortly before it was overrun by the Jutras. He'd managed to have her smuggled out. The ship she'd been on had gone down somewhere near the Root. There had been a handful of survivors—the Pilot, a few sailors. But Plusby's lover had been lost. No one knew if she'd drowned or been turned to *syl-veth* spawn. The stories said the loss had driven Plusby mad. He hated Pilots, blaming the pilot of his ship for the wreck, and some said he'd even hunted down the surviving sailors and murdered them.

He continued to sail for a season after that. The

stories said he cared little for his cargoes or ship, ra-
bidly searching for his lover, seeking her in every port,
and spending hour after hour scanning the shoreline
with his spyglass. He became vicious with his crews
and often refused to listen to the Pilot—the latter had
resulted in a tribunal and his stripped ticket. It was a
miracle he'd not lost any ships.

Suddenly the irony of being well paid despite being
kidnapped seemed far less bizarre. A Pilot who
courted bad luck and a captain who straddled the border between sanity and madness—for the first time,
Thorn wondered what cargo could be so vital that the
redheaded woman would risk so much on such a venture. They could lose everything, and still they hired
the unluckiest, unlikeliest crew. *What was going on?*

There was little time to ponder the question as
Crabbel began shouting orders and the other three
men pulled the yards around, angling south. The snow
was too thick to see more than a dozen yards before
the bow. Gradually, steep tree-covered spurs humped
from the white curtain of swirling snow, closing
around them like claws. A shiver made Thorn twitch.
It couldn't be far now.

Then suddenly the ship was before them, resolving
out of the blizzard like the deadly phantom it was
named for. It was one of the new three-masted clip-
pers. It could have been built only by Henstridge and
Dwiddle—no one else made such tall, graceful masts,
long, sleek lines, and narrow, sharply raked bows. The
Eidolon was freshly minted, though the upstart ship-
builders had a list of orders they wouldn't be able to
fill for a decade, and more pouring in. The redheaded
woman had a great deal of influence—or her backers
did. And they had a lot of money.

The cost of the ship and outfitting her was beyond
reckoning. The compass had probably cost more than
the vessel itself. To populate it with a misfit crew, a
disturbed captain, and a Pilot who carried bad luck
about with him like a manacle was staggeringly foolish. Thorn dragged his fingers through his snow-damp

hair. But beggars couldn't be choosers, and this was a black ship—a ghost ship. The only kind of crew to buy was a dispensable one. Which meant misfits and insanity and bad luck. But why? What was the rush? And there was a rush. Otherwise they would have taken more time in choosing the crew, if only to better ensure the success of the venture. But they'd been willing to take the dregs.

As his companions hauled in the sails of the jolly boat, Thorn realized the *Eidolon* was a black ship in more ways than one. It was painted ebony from stem to stern and its furled sails were charcoal gray. It would blend on the black waves like the ghost it was named for.

He stared upward at her as the watch hailed them. The sound was hushed and disembodied in the snow. He felt his stomach tense. He didn't know if it was from fear or excitement. Then suddenly he grinned, picking up an annoyed Fitch and lifting her to his shoulder. Wildreveh would have given both eyes to pilot such a ship. If only he knew what his betrayal of Thorn had wrought.

Chapter 6

Blot grappled the jolly boat close to the ship with a boat hook while Halford and Wragg worked at removing its mainmast. A thick casing of ice around the fittings made freeing it difficult. Halford reached under the forward thwart, removing a short heavy hammer. He struck at the ice, cracking it away. At last they pulled it free and laid it down in a tangle of ice-stiffened sail and lines that bent like heavy wire. They followed suit with the lugsail, rolling the two into an unwieldy package that they fastened down with loops of rope. Lastly they removed the rudder, settling it on top of the bound rigging.

"Permission to lay aboard!" Crabbel bellowed upward as they completed their task.

An inarticulate answer floated down through the thick snow, and grains later a rope ladder unrolled to flop against the ship. It was followed more slowly by two ropes with tackles swinging pendant on the ends. Wragg and Halford caught hold of them and hooked them to the brass loops set in the bow and stern of the jolly boat. In the meantime, Blot hooked the ladder and was holding it ready.

"Lay on deck, Pilot," Crabbel said to Thorn with a careless salute. Neither he nor the other men offered any of the usual sly grins and officious suggestions for managing the difficult climb up the ladder that most civilians received. Thorn had already proved himself to them. The offer to board first was given as a courtesy rather than as an opportunity to entertain the men as they watched him struggle up.

He settled Fitch on his shoulder, brushing the snow from her back. She shook herself and made a mournful sound deep in her throat, digging her claws deeply into the leather of his jacket and whipping her tail back and forth. This was not her first trip up a rope ladder.

"Hold on tight," he told her, and then reached for the ladder.

The difficult thing about climbing up to the deck from a rope ladder is that the curving hull of the ship offers absolutely no support and the ladder twists and swings. Adding to the difficulty was the snow clogging Thorn's eyelashes, the burn of his blistered hands as he gripped the icy rope, and the swift rise and fall of the ship on the chop. But despite the handicaps, he climbed swiftly and was up and over the rail in a matter of a minute or two, followed closely by Crabbel and Halford.

He was home.

The first thing Thorn noticed was that the *Eidolon*'s deck was narrower than he'd expected, even for a clipper, making the scurrying confusion of the crew seem more frenetic. The second thing he noticed was that the chaos was not the ordinary organized turmoil of a crew preparing to sail. Sailors ran into one another, tripping and shoving and shouting rancorously. They worked in anything but harmony, their discord and dissension reminding Thorn of a pack of wild dogs jockeying for dominance.

The men and women crewing the falls yanked in uneven jerks so that Thorn was certain they'd upend the jolly boat and dump Wragg and Blot into the water. Crabbel shoved between and started calling out a heavy cadence. The six sailors ignored him, growing considerably more clumsy with every tug. Crabbel didn't hesitate. He clobbered one of the women behind the ear with his meaty fist; she dropped like a stone to the snowy deck. The sailor behind her on the fall swore and grabbed for Crabbel, the man's mouth pulled wide in a rictus of hate. Crabbel moved so fast that his hand was a blur. He snatched the sailor by the throat, pushing him up on tiptoe.

"Ye'll haul when I says haul and ye'll stop when I says stop. Or I'll drop ye where ye stand and toss ye in th' briny. Understand?"

The sailor's face was turning red and his eyes watered. He could neither speak nor move to make an answer. But Crabbel wasn't paying attention to him. His gaze raked the other four sailors on the falls. They looked sour and angry, but they nodded, murmuring grudging assent.

"Good, then," he said, letting go. "Halford, take th' bitter end."

Halford stepped up behind the staggering man, who returned to the line. Now their hand-over-hand movements were smooth and synchronized as they hauled the ropes in time to Crabbel's cadence.

Wragg and Blot were spitting with fury when at last the boat cleared the rail. Both were holding their boat hooks as if anticipating a fight, but a word from Crabbel made them set the poles aside and help secure the jolly boat in the davits.

When they were through, Halford, Blot, and Wragg collected behind Crabbel. Once again they appeared like they were expecting a fight. And maybe they were.

Thorn realized suddenly that an eerie stillness had fallen over the ship. The rest of the crew gathered in a silent, menacing half circle around the new arrivals. The thick curtain of snow hid their expressions, but there could be no doubt that they did not welcome the four charmers. They didn't pay any attention to Thorn.

Crabbel ignored the threat, bending to pull the groggy female sailor to her feet. He shoved her at her defender. Her legs wouldn't hold her and the man grappled her to keep her upright.

"Put her in her hammock until she comes to," Crabbel ordered.

"Aye, aye, sir," was the sullen response as the sailor swung her over his shoulder and carried her forward to the crew cabin.

It wasn't until that moment that it occurred to Thorn to wonder where the captain was. He ought to have been waiting to welcome his new Pilot aboard— it was an insult not to. Likely that was the point. And to let the crew handle the charmers.

Thorn gave a mental shrug. It didn't matter. Even if Leighton Plusby didn't hate Pilots, the relationship between a Pilot and a captain was often prickly and difficult. No captain liked to depend so much on a Pilot to guide his ship around the perils of the sea, and no Pilot liked having to trust a captain to listen and act promptly. It was a tenuous balance of power, neither having real ascendance over the other, though the captain was ostensibly the superior authority. Plusby's discourtesy was merely a reminder of that fact, a way to make sure Thorn knew his place.

Despite the lack of welcome, a thin smile curved Thorn's lips with genuine pleasure. The deck lifted and fell beneath his feet and even with the ice and snow, it felt more solid than the rock and dirt of land. He was home at last.

"Perhaps we should report to the captain now," he said to the four charmers, flicking a glance at the rest of the crew. His crew now. Whether they liked it or not. They were angry and it wouldn't take much before they'd attack Crabbel, Halford, Wragg, and Blot. Clearly the crew already knew the four men were charmers, and they didn't mean to let them infect the ship with bad luck. Thorn snorted softly. As if the ship wasn't already carrying more than its own share of it. But he couldn't let them start brawling. Crabbel and Halford were too valuable to lose, and a rebellious crew was dangerous in the open waters. He needed to distract them, become the focus of their hate, before they started killing one another. If he united them in anger against him, then there was a chance they'd forget about the charmers for the time

being. Once they were out on open waters, they'd be
too busy and too tired to cause trouble.

Making a show of it, Thorn lifted Fitch from his
shoulder, stroking away the snow dampening her fur
and settling her into the crook of his arm. She settled
in with an air of annoyance and disdain. Thorn pulled
a fold of his cloak over her to keep the snow off, but
not until he was sure that the watchers had all seen
her. He then set off for the poop deck, pushing imperi-
ously through the glowering crew, not waiting to see
if his companions would follow.

He whistled as he went, trilling the notes loudly.
Each member of the crew flinched away from him,
gesturing to ward away bad luck. He smiled grimly.
The ploy was working. Their ire was focused on him
now.

Ice and snow slicked every surface of the *Eidolon*.
The snow continued to fall, muffling sound. The decks
were thick with it, drifts building in the lee of the
ship's furniture. The weight of the ice could careen a
ship and sink her.

Thorn stepped up onto the quarterdeck, pausing to
stare longingly at the silver compass post. He could
feel the compass inside the hatch just before the post.
Its power reached for him, unraveling golden threads
in his blood, wrapping his heart in a brilliant cocoon.
Thorn shuddered, closing his eyes. Elation filled him.
A joy and desire that made him want to claw through
the decking with his bare hands.

He drew a breath, steadying himself. It was here.
He could wait.

He made himself walk, pulling himself lightly up the
companion ladder onto the poop deck.

Plusby was alone at the wheel. He stood with his
legs spread as if braced against a stiff wind, his hands
plunged deep inside the pockets of his overcoat. The
snow dampened his blond hair and crusted his neatly
trimmed beard. When at last he turned to look at
Thorn, his eyes glinted gray and hard as steel marbles.

His gaze flicked past to the four charmers and then back.

"You're late," he said, though Thorn wasn't certain to whom he was speaking. "It was my fond hope that you'd been killed by brigands or spawn. The lot of you."

His words were uninflected and lacked any force, making their meaning all the more chilling.

"You can't take her out without a Pilot. You wouldn't survive," Thorn said, pointing out the obvious. Or at least, what should have been obvious common sense. But reason didn't apply to the insane.

Plusby's eyes narrowed and he pivoted. "Wouldn't? I think you underestimate me. Just to be clear, as far as I'm concerned, you're a coward and a parasite—a maggot. I'll suffer you for the sake of the shipowners and the crew. They'd never set a sail without a Pilot on the compass. But you—"

He broke off, his upper body jerking forward, though he took no steps. His expression twisted with hatred, entirely beyond reason. But he was no longer talking to Thorn; he was staring at Crabbel, Halford, Wragg, and Blot. "You four I'm glad to have aboard," he said softly. "Maybe Braken will offer the justice that the lord chancellor did not see fit to give. And if he won't, you can be certain I *will*."

"Aye, aye, Cap'n," was Crabbel's only response.

Thorn frowned. What was this about? Leighton Plusby despised Pilots—that was a well-known fact. He blamed them all for the ship that went down, taking his lover with it. But what had the four sailors done to meet with such vitriol? The charms didn't warrant it. But then, Plusby's mind was cracked.

"You stay out of my way. You want something from me, you tell my steward, Bess, and she'll give me the message. You make sure this crew draws together or I'll have each of you flogged until your skins drop off and then pitch you overboard. Then we'll see if your luck holds."

"Aye, aye, Cap'n," Crabbel repeated woodenly. "Is there anything else, sir?"

"Oh, most certainly. I want to see them. Now. Show me."

The four seamen stood very still; then Crabbel slowly reached inside his collar, pulling free the ebony wreck charm. Halford, Wragg, and Blot followed suit, their expressions stoic.

Plusby's nostrils flared as he stared at the charms, his lips compressing so that they were bracketed with white dents. "You will wear those outside your clothing. I will not permit you to hide what you are. Understand?"

Crabbel's throat worked and at last he gave a strangled, "Aye, aye, sir."

"Then get out of my sight. We set sail when the tide turns."

The four descended from the poop deck slowly, as if they'd suddenly aged.

Now Plusby turned his full attention on Thorn. "What are you called?"

Thorn hesitated, still watching the retreat of his four kidnappers, fury kindling inside him. They deserved better. He shook his head. As if this ship wasn't cursed enough. "Thorn. I am Thorn."

The captain scowled. "Never heard of you. Thorn doesn't sound like a Pilot name."

"Doesn't it? Well, it must be. Because I am your new Pilot."

If there was one thing the newly christened Thorn had learned from his parents before he'd escaped them, it was a tone of voice that was both contemptuous and mocking, while at the same time wearing every appearance of civility. Now he turned it on Plusby, to the same grating effect it had always had on him.

"How many ships have you wrecked, Thorn?" the other man snapped back.

"None that I'm aware of. And you?"

Plusby didn't answer, his teeth baring. He was

caught between the wind and a lee shore; there was no good answer to the question. An affirmative said that as captain he'd been responsible for any wrecks he'd endured, even though he firmly believed that Pilots were always culpable. But neither could he say no, because in fact the captain was always the party given responsibility on the paperwork, and Thorn knew that Plusby had captained at least one downed ship.

"I should have hoisted anchor days ago."

"But you didn't. Please the gods, I hope it's because you still have some shred of reason left in you. You knew the crew would have mutinied before you crossed the Pale. They still may. It's one thing to know your mate and bosun are charmers, another to be reminded every waking moment. Seeing those charms on their chests will dash morale to bits and we'll have a mob on our hands."

"And what about your cat?" the captain countered, flicking a pointed glance at Fitch. "They'll take none too well to having it aboard. Perhaps you should feed it to the depths. Or the crew may do it for you." His gaze narrowed, returning to Thorn's face. "I had heard of a Pilot who sails with a cat. . . . A boil on the ass is what I heard. Surely there can't be two of you."

"Surely not."

"Tell me, Pilot Thorn, don't you think their ire would be soothed if we wrung the cat's neck right now and hung it from a yardarm?"

Thorn's expression flattened. "Possibly. But they might take it amiss when I ripped your throat out. Or then again, perhaps they might be grateful."

"Do you think you could?" Plusby's voice dropped. There was a taut hunger in his tone, as if Thorn had just offered him his heart's desire.

"I have not a single doubt. But *I* am not insane enough to want to try the Inland Sea without both a Pilot and a captain aboard. Even one like you."

"Of course not. A *captain* is always necessary. And

balls. But you Pilots all have shriveled little raisins between your thighs, don't you?"

Thorn's neck stiffened, his face flushing with stinging heat. Inside him, the feral boy who'd scrabbled and scratched to survive all alone on the docks for five years before finding a berth on a ship balled up his fists and crouched to fight. It was a visceral reaction—instinct took over and though his head told him *no*, his tongue continued to form words. "Want me to rip yours off and shove them down your throat?"

Plusby's brows rose and a reluctant smile twitched the corners of his mouth and then vanished. "Look at you. You've got the accent of a gentleman and the mouth of bilge scum. Scrape a little of the Pilot away and we see a new man entirely. Who are you really? I wonder."

"I wonder the same about you. How bent is your mind?"

Before Plusby could respond, a rumble of shouts from the forecastle interrupted him. He swung around, scowling. Then he swore and dashed to the companion ladder, vaulting down to the quarterdeck. He skidded and slipped as he pelted down the length of the ship. He fumbled at his hip for his cutlass as he went, shouting orders. Thorn hesitated only a grain. From the poop deck, he could see the *Eidolon* was being swarmed by invaders. They swung swords and boat hooks as they clambered up over the rails. Thorn flung himself after Plusby. He slipped when he landed on the deck, falling heavily to his left knee. Fire burst in his joint. Fitch leaped down from his shoulder and ran for cover. He staggered upright as the *Eidolon*'s crew scrambled up onto the railing. They clung to the shrouds trying to beat back the swarm of raiders. Thorn pulled the dagger out of his waistband, wincing at it before plunging into the fray.

The raiders were dressed from head to fingertip in knacker clothing. Majick made the close-fitting black material impervious to the blows the defending sailors hammered down. Two dozen raiders had rowed quietly up beneath the bow, hidden by the storm. Then it was a matter of a few scurrying up the anchor chain and throwing down boarding lines to their companions.

Thorn had only taken a few steps when a hand on his arm stopped him. He wrenched around. But when he saw who stood there, the angry words dried on his lips.

The redheaded majicar stood beside him. Her eyes gleamed silver, the pupils a brilliant crimson to match the ring circling the iris. She was watching the battle. Her eyes slid sideways at Thorn, and then back to the fighting.

"Not an auspicious beginning," she said.

"What are you going to do about it?" Thorn demanded.

The *Eidolon*'s crew was beginning to fall back under the onslaught. The sailors were ill equipped to defend themselves against skilled swordsmen, and the knacker suits skewed the odds even more. Scarlet flowered across pale shirts as blood spurted and ran. There were agonized screams amid the fury of the fight and now the invaders had cleared the rails and the battle was raging on the deck. He saw Wragg grapple a snottie around the waist and toss the girl aside, out of the way of a deadly downward cut. The raider whipped his sword back around and Wragg battered at the blade with the belaying pin in his right hand. The deflected blade missed chopping down through his collar and neck. Instead it cleaved into his arm. Wragg staggered and turned and Thorn could see his arm was hanging uselessly, blood ribboning over his hand as it dangled.

"Do something!" he urged, starting to step forward again.

The redheaded majicar jerked him back. "No, Pilot. That dagger will do little against knacker gear and you can't be risked."

He yanked out of her grip. "Do you think I'll stand here and watch them be slaughtered?"

"You won't have to."

When she didn't immediately move, Thorn started to walk away again.

"Wait. It's almost . . . now."

The deck jolted and bucked as something enormous knocked hard against the hull. There was a deep resonant *boom* and the *Eidolon* shivered and rocked. Then a black wave thrust up beside the ship and rolled almost silently across the deck, drenching Thorn in icy water. It closed over his head before he could brace himself. Water filled his mouth. He pushed back against the expected thrust of it. But there was none. The wave softened around him, curling away as gently as a sigh. Then it was gone. Froth swirled around his legs and water sluiced out the scuppers. He sputtered and coughed, already starting to shiver, the cold sinking into his bones like water into sand.

Thorn swiped his wet hair from his eyes and spun about. The raiders were gone.

Just . . .

Gone.

The *Eidolon*'s crew looked dazedly about, boat hooks and belaying pins clutched tightly in their hands. A few lay crumpled on the deck; others clung to the shrouds. No one spoke. Then suddenly Plusby was in the middle of them. Blood ran down his forehead and cheek, and his coat and trousers were torn, revealing bleeding rents in his skin. He seemed impervious to the pain, striding about shouting orders and sparking life back into the crew. They began to shuffle about, responding to Plusby's vigor. Moments later, Crabbel's bellow joined the captain's, and the crew reacted as if whipped.

"We feared this. You may rest assured, they won't be back."

"Who were they?"

Thorn twisted to look at the redheaded woman. She was frowning as she watched the activity on the forecastle. Flakes of snow still spotted her cloak. The wave had not touched her. Thorn's skin prickled. She looked at him, the weight of her regard settling like an anchor. He shifted uneasily.

"There are those who would go to almost any lengths to see this ship stopped. Be wary, Pilot. This ship is hunted. They will not give up. Too much is at stake. And once you set sail, I won't be able to help. At least . . . not in time." She paused. "I hope I see you again. Until then . . . fair winds and following seas."

And with no more farewell than that, she went to the rail and swung herself over the side. Thorn lunged after her, staring down at the churning black water, but there was no sign of her. It was as if she'd sunk forever beneath the waves. The same waves that had taken the raiders and left her dry. His stomach clenched. What had he gotten himself into? But there was no time for brooding on it. He put her out of his mind as he went to help the wounded.

Crabbel had the injured crew members hauled inside the crew cabin beneath the forecastle. He was helped by a tall, angular woman with a beaky nose and broad shoulders. Thorn learned she was Bess, the captain's steward. She spoke quietly, in a rich voice that belied her forbidding appearance. She and Thorn examined the wounded, who'd been slung in their hammocks. Many of the injuries were painful but superficial. A number of cuts needed stitching, and there were several broken bones. Four were more severe. One crew member had fallen from the shrouds and cracked the bones in her shoulder and ribs. Another had taken a thrust to the gut. Black blood leaked from the hole in his side. The leg of the third had been sliced nearly through at the knee joint. Her leg had been splinted on the deck before she was carried into the cabin.

And then there was Wragg. The blade that had cut him had nearly sliced away his bicep. He'd gone deathly white and he was shivering. From cold, blood loss, or reaction, Thorn didn't know. Blot knelt beside the other man's hammock and pressed a makeshift bandage over the wound. He spoke quietly against Wragg's ear.

The minor wounds would be easy enough to stitch up. Thorn sent a snottie named Gerry to fetch the cook and a chest of medical supplies. The other four . . . they needed a majicar's healing touch. But the redheaded woman was gone. Thorn guessed she hadn't wanted to be seen. He doubted anyone else had even noticed her. His lips peeled from his teeth in a silent snarl. She should have stayed and helped. He wagered she could heal, and it would have cost her little, with what she was clearly capable of. But leaving could mean the deaths of four sailors.

Plusby strode inside the cabin. "What's your report?" he asked Bess, his gaze raking over the scene.

"Eight can be stitched up. Three of the rest stand a chance, but they'll be crippled. Fourth"—she shrugged—"got stuck in the gut. He's as good as dead." She made no effort to lower her voice, wiping the blood fastidiously from her hands with a canvas rag.

The captain's lips pinched together. "Do what you can. We can't stay here any longer. We're getting under way." He looked at Thorn. "We'll want to set the compass as soon as we cross the Pale. Get out of those clothes. Last thing we need is you catching a fever."

His words were clipped and precise. There was no trace of insanity in the steely determination in his eyes, nor did he seem nervous and unsettled. Thorn wanted to make a snide comment about his flip-flopping about whether he thought Thorn was necessary. He bit it back. Now was not the time.

"Captain!"

A bulky woman bustled in with a small chest under her arm. She was perhaps twenty seasons old, with a square face and a gap between her front teeth. Behind her came Gerry, the snottie, his face tense with fear.

"What is it, Degby?"

"Someone's been at th' water. Knocked out th' bungs of every cask. Have t' go ashore and fill up."

Plusby's expression tightened. White rimmed his lips. He swung about abruptly, turning to his steward. "Take the bosun and a midshipman. Search the hold. See if we've got rats. Make sure there's no other sabotage. Be quick."

"Aye, aye, Captain," she said, and disappeared outside.

"Sabotage?" Thorn asked.

"What else? Someone doesn't mean for this ship to break the Pale." Plusby jerked his chin at the wounded. "Degby is ship's cook. She'll help you sew. That is, if you're inclined to be more than decoration?"

Thorn ignored the dig, peeling off his wet jacket and rolling up his sleeves.

"What do you plan to do?"

"Get under way. We're too easy a target here. We'll make for Eadhere Point and put in somewhere along the highland coast. Snow will hide our passage. We won't be safe until we hit open water."

Thorn thought of the red-haired woman's warning. "And maybe not then," he muttered.

Plusby stiffened, his gaze sharpening. "What does that mean?"

Thorn wasn't sure Plusby knew about the woman and if not, he wasn't sure he wanted to tell him. The captain seemed sane enough just now, but that could change in a heartbeat. At the moment, they both shared the same goal: getting free of Crosspointe.

"It means half the crew is in this cabin unable to work. The sea is not a safe place with a full ship's complement. When you put in for water, you might want to collect a few more seamen."

Plusby scowled and shook his head, a look of annoyance chasing away his suspicion. "Can't. Orders say we go as is. But that wave that took the raiders . . . that was Braken's blessing. I expect the waves will be equally benevolent to us once we've breached the Pale."

Braken's blessing. So much for bad luck and a

cursed ship. Thorn didn't know if he should laugh or
cry at Plusby's ignorance of the truth. Still, it wouldn't
hurt crew morale to think Braken had saved them.
But his throat tightened as he thought of the wave.
He'd never heard of a majicar who had the power to
control the sea. Not even the infamous Errol Cipher,
who'd created the Pale four hundred seasons ago.
There'd never been a majicar since to equal his power.
Or so it was said. But the redheaded majicar had made
a wave rise over the deck of a ship sitting at calm
anchor, and with it she'd snatched away their enemies,
leaving the crew unharmed. If she could do that, what
else could she do? He couldn't imagine. Had Plusby
seen her? He didn't show any signs of having done
so. Thorn decided not to enlighten the captain about
her. Plusby was walking the right side of sanity at the
moment, and Thorn wasn't going to do anything to
push him across.

"We'd better start seeing to the injured," he said.
"See if we can get some of them back on their feet
sooner rather than later. Can you leave the snotties?"

"You can have them for now," Plusby said. "Everyone else lay on deck."

"One thing more, Captain," Thorn said before
Plusby could depart. He went to stand close to the
captain where they could not be overheard.

"What is it?"

"The raiders—any idea who they were or what
they wanted?"

Plusby shook his head. "No. But they were well
prepared for us. The faster we get to open water, the
better off we'll be. Unless you want to stand about
gabbing while they sink us?"

He didn't wait for a reply, but strode out. The sailors who'd been tending their wounded brethren reluctantly followed. Thorn hesitated, then went to stand
by Blot, who still knelt beside Wragg. There was nothing to do about the raiders now, whoever they were.
He put his hand on Blot's shoulder.

"He's gonna lose th' arm," Blot said, rubbing his knuckles against his nose.

"No."

The other man thrust to his feet, spinning around and shoving Thorn in the chest. Thorn staggered back against the bulkhead.

"Ain't nothin' but a majicar can fix it. Wragg finally finds his way back t' th' sea and now he's useless for it. He'll be dirt-bound." His face was creased with fear and rage.

"He won't lose it. I won't let him. I promise."

For a moment Blot looked hopeful. But then his lip curled. "Ye can hull yerself. Ye can't help 'im." He touched the pendant around his neck and then thudded out.

Thorn looked for the cook. "Degby is it? Is that the medical chest?"

"Aye, sir," she said with a deferential bob, passing him the chest. She was careful to neither look him in the eyes nor touch him.

He took the box, setting it on a sea chest and opening it. Rolls of bandages filled the bottom. There were healing salves, syrups, and tisanes, and a tray of fine thread and needles. None of it was majicked. None of it would save Wragg's arm.

"Gerry, you help Mistress Degby. Start with the worst of the minor cuts. Moth," he said to the other snottie, the one Wragg had tossed aside before he was wounded. She was scrawny, the bones of her face protruding sharply. Her blond hair clung wetly to her head where it had escaped its tie. "Build a fire in the stove and when you're done, come help me."

Taking a handful of bandages, he went down the line, wrapping the leaking wounds to reduce the bleeding. The sailor with the gut wound was breathing in shallow gasps, his shirt and coat soaked with black blood, a puddle pooling below him. Thorn dressed his wound, knowing he'd be dead within a glass. He stroked the hair from the man's clammy forehead and murmured softly. The sailor watched him, though Thorn wasn't sure if he was aware or no.

When he and Moth had done what they could to stanch the bleeding, they went to help with the stitching. It was slow, careful work, with the snotties alternately holding the patients still and fetching boiling water from the galley, dabbing away blood, and threading needles.

Thorn heard the capstan turning and the anchor chain sliding through the hawse. Then the creak of straining lines, the pop of canvas, and the odd hush of the crew as they worked in silence. The *Eidolon* rose and fell and then Thorn felt her beginning to push forward through the water. They were under way.

Methodically, they treated each of the eight less-wounded patients. When they were through, he wiped the blood from his hands. The blisters on his palms from pulling the oars of the jolly boat stung. It was little enough compared with the injuries the crew had taken.

"Do what you can for the others," he told Degby. "I'll be back."

He glanced at the body in the third hammock. The gut-wounded sailor had died sometime in the last quarter glass. Moth had draped a cloth over his face and was weeping silently as she went about her work. Thorn's jaw knotted. Abruptly he stalked out of the cabin.

The deck was eerily quiet. Plusby stood the helm. Crabbel paced back and forth, forward and aft. Bess stood on the quarterdeck, relaying the captain's orders to him, and he passed them to the crew who hauled on the halyards. It was all done in hushed voices. Without thinking, Thorn reached out to the water. His ability to sense things was severely curtailed by the Pale, but he could tell there were no immediate obstacles in their way and that if they stuck to their heading, they would clear the sheer, hooked headlands guarding the mouth of Grimsby Bay.

Thorn strode swiftly across the deck to his cabin

beneath the poop deck beside the captain's quarters. The cold wiped away his exhaustion. He thrust open the door and kicked it shut behind him. He had the impression of elegant furnishing, thick rugs, and polished wood. His gaze settled on a tall set of cabinets atop a scrolled chest against the bulkhead. Three strides took him across the cabin. He yanked on the pulls, but the cabinet doors did not open. He scrubbed his hands over his face and pushed his hair out of his eyes. His hands trembled. He was shivering. He'd been working for nearly two glasses in wet clothing. His stomach felt hollow and his mouth was parched. Still, he had little time for comfort.

He examined the wide, filigreed brass work that chased the outer edges of the cabinets. He found what he was looking for in the lower left corner of the upper cabinet. There was a small indentation in the brass. It was shaped like a compass surrounded by a quatrefoil. Thorn slipped off his Pilot's ring and fit it into the lock and pressed. A flickering ripple spread across the wood of the cabinet. There was no sound, but one of the doors popped open a finger's breadth. He swallowed, replacing his ring on his finger before yanking the doors wide. He closed his eyes in relief.

It was normal practice on every ship to provide the captain and Pilot with a personal cache of majicked healing supplies against the possibility that they suffered catastrophic injuries. The crew was largely expendable; their lives weren't worth the expense—at least as far as ships' owners were concerned. Pilots and captains, on the other hand, were vital. Thus, they were always provided with a generous supply of the expensive healing provisions. It was far cheaper than losing the ship.

Thorn reached in, taking out a box of amulets. There were more than two dozen of them in varying colors and fantastic shapes, all made from worked *sylveth*. The colors signaled their purpose and the shapes helped anchor the spells, or so Thorn had been told. He rifled through them, picking out three yellow amu-

lets for pain, three black for general healing, and three
blue for sleeping. He thrust the box back inside the
cabinet. On the second shelf was a collection of clay
jars. Three of them had green seals. He took two of
them and pushed the cupboard shut. Using all this
now put a hard dent in the supplies and if he or Plusby
got hurt, it could mean trouble. Especially if the captain was unwilling to share his. The amulets grew less
effective with each use and the worse the injuries, the
quicker they were spent. Thorn didn't care. His crews
weren't expendable under any circumstances, but at
the moment, the *Eidolon* could ill afford to lose three
more sailors.

He hurried out with his booty and returned to the
forecastle cabin. The *Eidolon* had left the protection
of the headlands and the wind was blowing the snow
sideways. He could hardly see where he walked. He
skidded on ice as the ship pitched. His knee twinged
from his earlier fall. He slowed, picking his way carefully, holding the jars close against his chest. Breaking
them would be unthinkable.

He pushed inside the crew cabin, where Degby was
kneeling beside Wragg. She'd cut away his shirt and
coat. The wound was ugly. It ran from the top of his
shoulder to his elbow. Thorn could see eight inches
of bone through the seeping blood. A flap of skin was
all that kept it attached. Degby looked up as Thorn
entered, her face smudged with dried blood where
she'd brushed the hair out of her face, her eyes dark
and sunken. She held a needle in her hand. Despair
made her shoulders slump.

Moth and Gerry were holding Wragg's shoulders as
he twisted and moaned. Thorn set the jars in the
crease between the hammock and Wragg's hip and
sorted out the amulets. Three sets of blue, yellow, and
black. All three of his companions stared open-
mouthed. He handed a set to each of the two snotties.

"Put these on the others. Make sure they touch
skin."

He jerked his chin at the two other severely injured

sailors and then bent over Wragg, sliding the amulets over his head and tucking them under his collar. Instantly the big man slumped into sleep.

"That should make this easier. Here."

He opened one of the jars. Inside was a clear green ointment. He scooped a dollop onto two fingers. It was cold and it did not warm at his touch. At his nod, Degby turned the chunk of muscle from Wragg's arm. With gentle fingers, Thorn rubbed the ointment over the exposed flesh of both the arm and the carved-away meat. Then Degby pushed the two back together and began to sew. While she did, Thorn carried the jars around to each of the rest of the wounded, soothing the ointment over each wound.

The sailors watched him silently as he worked. Some were grateful. Most were angry, enough even to flinch away from him when he came to treat their wounds.

"Sit still," he ordered one with lacerations along his ribs and hands.

The seaman tried to roll out his hammock to escape and Thorn pulled him back down. He was wiry, his muscles like wood. But he'd lost a lot of blood and his struggles were clumsy.

"Ain't fittin'. That's meant for ye and not th' likes of us. What if ye get hurt or take ill? What if ye die and we be without a Pilot in open waters?"

"What if you die and we don't have enough crew to sail the ship? We'll find ourselves running up on a knucklebone weir or chewed apart by Koreions. We'll be just as dead."

"Ain't fittin'," was the dogged answer, the man still squirming to get up. "You're wastin' th' medicine. And spendin' so much on a *charmer*." His voice roughened in disgust. "Captain'll have your balls for it."

"The captain doesn't think my balls are worth taking," Thorn murmured.

"Then he'll have your head," the other man answered defiantly. But his breath had caught, the pain of his wounds and the loss of blood making him dizzy. He sagged back down into the hammock. "Blighted Pilot," he said weakly.

"My job is to keep you safe—what are you called?"

"Alby Sark. You're s'posed t' keep th' ship safe. Keep us on a safe headin'. Not this. Too risky."

"You've got a much more limited notion of what it means to keep the ship safe than I do," Thorn said, swiping the ointment onto Sark's wounds and retying the dressings. "And I've risked worse. No sense getting to the end of a voyage and having a full stock of supplies and a dead or crippled crew. Not that we'll make the end of the voyage if you don't get back on your feet. Anyhow, it's not like you have a choice. I'm your Pilot. What I say goes. Captain can't gainsay me."

"Our captain would."

"He could try." Thorn stood. "Rest now."

He made his rounds to the rest of the wounded. By the time he was done, he'd used up both jars of ointment. The silence was thick. He smiled grimly. Trust sailors to resent the gift of majicked healing and think it bad luck. He shook his head. He needed a drink. And warm clothing.

He turned to Mistress Degby, who was packing up the unused bandages. Her chin trembled, but her hands were steady. Tentatively, Thorn put a gentle hand on her shoulder, dropping it nearly instantly.

"You did well. I don't think we'll lose anyone else. They'll need food. Bread and soup would be best. You'll have to remove the blue amulets from the three to let them wake up and eat and piss. Don't let them get up. They won't feel any pain and they'll do more damage if they move about too soon. They shouldn't wear them long. A sennight at most. But the healing amulets work faster when the patients are asleep."

She nodded understanding. He scanned the room one more time, feeling the simmering anger. His mouth tightened. He picked up his coat and left without another word.

It was full dark outside. The snow had turned to sleet. It stung Thorn's skin, the wind whipping it. He pulled on his jacket and went to the starboard rail. The deck was thick with ice and snow and he skidded, grasping the stays for balance. The ship had given up any pretense at silence. He could hear Crabbel bellowing. Half the healthy crew were banging staves, hooks, and mallets against the ice to crack it off, Crabbel shouting for them to clear the top-heavy upper yards. The racket echoed like a frantic heartbeat, despite the muffling storm.

Thorn leaned his arms on the rail, closing his eyes and breathing deeply. Momentary contentment washed over him. He turned his head at the crunch of snow and ice as someone approached.

"Master Pilot, sir. Captain Plusby asks for you."

Thorn nodded at Bess, running a hand through his half-frozen hair and turning to follow her.

At the bottom of the companion ladder, he heard a *meow* and saw the green shine of Fitch's eyes. He squatted down, catching her as she leaped into his arms. She was damp, but not wet, and she instantly began to purr as he snuggled her against his chest. He carried her up onto the poop deck as he joined the captain.

"What's your report?" Plusby asked, keeping his eyes on the sails.

They were running on a close reach, tacking to keep on their heading.

"One dead."

"And the rest?"

"Eight with minor enough wounds. The other three . . ." He lifted one shoulder. "We wait and see."

Plusby grimaced, chewing his bottom lip. "We're already working on a thin crew."

"You did say we had Braken's blessing," Thorn said drily.

"The sea god doesn't suffer fools lightly."

"It would be a simple matter to find able bodies in a village along the Craven Dells," Bess suggested.

The captain gave a firm shake of his head. "No."

"But—"

Her lips snapped shut when he gave her a blistering look.

"No." He looked back down the length of the ship. He nodded. "Furl the sails and drop anchor. We'll wait out the night and put in to shore tomorrow. We'll head for open water the day after. That should put a few of our injured back on the falls. In the meantime, we'll clear the ship of ice. See to it, Bess."

She looked like she wanted to argue, but she strode away and soon Crabbel was calling out orders.

"Best get some rest. Have someone bring you some food from the galley. And I thought I told you to put on dry clothes."

"I don't take orders from you," Thorn said, unmoving.

Plusby stiffened, his hands slowly clenching. "Get off my deck before I take you off."

There was no doubting he meant what he said. The corner of Thorn's mouth twitched up grimly. The muscles across his stomach tightened. If Plusby wanted a fight, he could have it.

"You think a brawl between us will help matters?"

"No."

Thorn's brows furrowed; he was taken aback. He'd expected Plusby to bluster. But the deadly rage in that one word told him the captain had again drifted close to the edge of sanity. It caught Thorn up short. If he pushed now, Plusby might snap. And that would be the end of this voyage.

"Very well. As I am cold and hungry, I will retire. So long as someone sees to those." He pointed at the bloody rents in the captain's shirt and coat.

He didn't wait for a reply, but went back down the companion ladder into his cabin. He stripped off his wet clothing. There were smears of crimson down the front of his shirt. None of the blood was his own. He unbuttoned it and dropped it over a chair, followed by his trousers and smallclothes. He found clothing in his duffel and dressed quickly, shivering in the cold. He glanced at the stove, thinking he should light a fire, and instead began searching through the cupboards for something to drink.

He found a decanter of brandy and poured himself a full glass. He drank it in a single gulp, the fire hitting his belly and spreading heat through his chilled limbs. He poured another and drank it down as quickly, setting the glass on the tray on the sideboard with a hard *thunk*. He sighed and went to sprawl on the chaise, laying his head back and closing his eyes. Fitch curled up against his hip. He should feed her. He should go down to the galley and get both of them something to eat. He didn't move.

In the last two months he'd lost his brother, lost his guild, lost his life. In the last few days, he'd gained a black ship with an insane captain, unknown enemies who were willing to kill to take the ship, a majicar shipowner with astonishing powers, and a bitter and divided crew with nearly a dozen wounded crewmen. How could he think the *Eidolon* was anything *but* a cursed ship?

He pressed his knuckles against his eyes. There was no way to go back to being Sylbrac, to being a guild Pilot. He wasn't sure he wanted to. Not after they'd sold him. He swallowed his rage, feeling it harden in his gut. That life was done. But this new life offered far more than he'd ever expected. The four charmers had become friends—brothers-in-arms. The *Eidolon* was a beautiful ship and it had a compass. But it was all so very fragile. A spark could set off a conflagration that would destroy everything. He had to figure out how to settle Plusby down and get him to accept Thorn and the charmers, not to mention Fitch. If they could forge a bond, it would anchor the rest of the crew and keep them from a mutiny. But how he was going to get the captain to relinquish his hatred, he didn't know. It would take something extraordinary. He fell asleep without any answers.

Chapter 7

The thudding crash of the door being flung open woke Thorn. He staggered groggily to his feet, his head spinning with brandy and exhaustion as he slapped his hip. His cutlass was not there. He swung to face the intruders. Plusby barreled across the room, trailed slowly by Bess and Crabbel. The latter two wore deeply grooved expressions of anxiety and doubt as they hung back, helpless to interfere.

"What in the black depths have you done?" Plusby demanded, snatching Thorn's collar in his fists and yanking him close, his bearded jaw jutting, snow melting on his hair and coat, his gray eyes mere slits. "Do you think you can buy loyalty with your healing supplies? Are you stupid? Do you want them to mutiny? They won't cross the Pale with a mad Pilot—and you are most certainly mad to waste your healing supplies on them."

Thorn didn't hear the meaning of the words. Later he would remember them and find bitter humor in the irony of Plusby's accusation. As if the captain hadn't done far more to fragment the crew.

But in this moment, with Plusby's hands on his neck, his fury scorching, the feral boy that still lived inside Thorn's skin screamed to wakefulness. Thorn punched Plusby in the gut with both fists. Then in a fluid motion, he slammed his forearms into Plusby's, breaking the captain's grip on his collar. The captain grunted and let go, his face twisting in fury. His reason

gone, and driven only by instinct, Thorn didn't let
up. He punched Plusby in the jaw, leaping forward
to grab his collar and hold him still as he struck
again. The captain staggered back. Before he could
land another blow, Crabbel snatched Thorn around
the chest, carrying him backward until they crashed
into the cabinets. Bess grappled Plusby, who'd recovered and launched himself at Thorn. She tackled him
onto the chaise. He was swearing loudly as he tried
to shove her off, a sharp contrast to Thorn's unrelenting silence.

Thorn kicked and clawed. Crabbel's weight held
him pinned. His attention snagged on the mate's florid
face. Thorn dug his fingers into Crabbel's windpipe,
hooking his thumb, intending to jam it into the mate's
brown eye. Crabbel's face contorted with pain.

"Pilot!" Crabbel rasped out, unable to say more as
he twisted his head, trying to avoid Thorn's gouging
thumb.

The word struck Thorn like a hammer. He remembered himself. He froze, then let his hands drop
slowly.

"Get off me," he said rigidly.

Crabbel gasped for breath, then slowly rolled away.
"Best if ye don't kill the captain," he advised finally
as Thorn slowly stood and straightened his clothing,
wiping his mouth with the back of his hand.

His knuckles were tender from the blows he'd landed
on Plusby's jaw. He eyed the captain. Every muscle
in his body was twisted tight in readiness. He flicked
a glance at the table and found his dagger and stiletto,
cursing himself for leaving himself unarmed. A part
of him asked why he should care. He was a Pilot. A
voice in his head laughed. Being a Pilot didn't make
him safe. No more than being the son of the lord
chancellor had made him safe. Being wary, being
deadly . . . that was how to be safe. Lessons learned
in the gutter. He shifted so he could watch all three
of his companions at once.

Plusby wrestled free of Bess and sprang back to his

feet. Thorn tensed. But the captain only dabbed at the blood running down his chin. His lips were swollen and a bruise was already blossoming. He licked the corner of his mouth.

"You hit like you know what you're doing," he observed. "And you waste majick on the dregs of the crew. Never met a Pilot who could do either. But what will you do when you need the supplies? I won't give you mine."

Thorn shrugged. "I'll remember not to ask. And I didn't waste anything."

"No?"

"Can you sail this tub with half a crew?"

"Maybe not," Plusby conceded. "But I wouldn't have bothered with the charmer."

Thorn's chin went up and he eyed the captain from head to toe, disdain and disgust thick in his voice. "Then you're a worse captain than I thought. But understand this: the *Eidolon* is *my* ship and while I breathe, I'll do everything in my power to protect her and the crew. Even if it means *wasting* precious majick on a charmer."

The captain's jaw flexed and then his expression became inscrutable as he stared back at Thorn. "You just tried to kill the captain and the mate. Well done."

"Get out."

Plusby touched the bruise on his face, not moving. Grains sifted by. Thorn got the message: Plusby didn't take orders from anyone. Then at last the captain nodded. "I have work to do."

Slowly he went to the door. Bess followed after. When they'd gone, Thorn twisted his head around to glare at Crabbel. Plusby's words stung, but Thorn could not apologize.

"What are you waiting for? Lay off."

"Aye, aye, sir."

Crabbel turned back just as he reached the door, but Thorn's simmering gaze was enough to kill whatever he intended to say. He nodded and left, shutting the door behind him.

When he was alone, Thorn let his shoulders slump, leaning against the cabinets.

"Braken's bloody balls," he muttered. He'd thought all those instincts were dead. He didn't need them any more. He was a Pilot. But he'd almost crushed Crabbel's windpipe and gouged out his eye. His head sagged forward and he drew an unsteady breath. His heart pounded. He might have left the gutter long behind, but not the wild fury that had saved him again and again. It was a mindless willingness to rend flesh and break bones—a killing edge. Even at nine seasons of age, he'd been terrifying when swept up in the frenzy of desperation and need: he *would not* be used; he *would not* be touched, not for any reason. He would die first.

By the time he was two seasons on his own, he'd founded his own little gang, the others drawn to the shelter of his ferocity. He'd killed and maimed more times than he could count, for himself and for those who belonged to him. But that was long ago. When he'd left that life behind, he'd done all he could to forget the names and faces of every last one of them. He tried to hold himself in check, never letting the rage inside him out of its cage. He even kept himself from slicing Wildreveh open from stem to stern. But the instant Plusby had grabbed him, his body had taken over, his conscious mind flattened beneath the onslaught of instinct. He had to do better.

He flexed his fingers and reached for the decanter of brandy. He swigged a glass. A knock on the door made him start and he spun around. He went to open it, pausing on the way to slide his knives into his waistband.

Degby stood outside holding a tray. "Cap'n said ye needed t' eat," she said in a rush, ducking her head and avoiding his eyes.

Thorn opened the door wide. "Thank you."

She stamped her feet to knock off the snow and came inside. She set the tray on the table and scurried wordlessly out.

The food she'd brought was simple and plain: cold sausages wrapped in bread with grainy mustard, steaming cabbage and potato soup, and a dish of stewed fruit. There was also a mug of ale. He sat down and chopped up half a sausage for Fitch. She ate from the edge of his plate.

He polished off the food, tasting nothing, and then retired to his bedchamber. He crawled under the bedclothes fully dressed and fell instantly asleep. But the dreams that came to him that night were not of ships and seas, but of hard fists and snarling mouths, broken bodies and unending screams.

When he woke the next morning, his head hurt and his eyes were gritty. His body ached. Fitch was curled on his chest. He stroked her and she purred, the resonance soothing him. But he could not stay there forever. At last he got out of bed, leaving Fitch snuggled in the warm blankets. His breath furled white in the air. He'd not bothered to build a fire the previous night and Plusby hadn't sent anybody to do it. Not that the crew didn't have plenty to do. Outside he could hear the sounds of hammering and scraping as the few members of the crew fought a battle against the ice.

He stamped into his boots and shrugged into his jacket, buttoning it up. Then he went out on deck. Dawn had just broken and the ship was once again under way. The sleet had turned to a freezing rain. The deck was a sheet of ice. Crew members pushed scrapers along the planking, and beat on the yards and rails to crack off the ice, but their diminished ranks couldn't keep up with the falling rain.

They were under light sail running ahead of a freshening breeze. That was lucky. Or, Thorn thought with a thin smile, perhaps it was Braken's blessing. He glanced forward to the crew cabin, wondering how Wragg and Sark were improving. He blew out a breath and jammed his hands into his pockets. He'd find out soon enough. And he didn't need anyone else glowering at him like he was a child killer just because he'd had the gall to use his healing supplies on them. He wandered over to the starboard beam and leaned his elbows on the rail. The rain stung his face and hands, clogging his eyelashes with ice. His neck prickled and he was certain Plusby had noted him. He scrubbed his hands over his face, groaning softly. He wasn't sure another confrontation with the captain wouldn't lead to another brangle. It was better if he stayed out of the way, at least until they breached the Pale.

After a while he grew cold and went belowdecks to the galley. Degby gave him a steaming bowl of porridge with nuts, butter, and molasses sugar with a small pile of crisp bacon.

"How are our patients?" he asked her as he ate.

She continued to fold and knead the dough she was making and at first he thought she hadn't heard him. He swallowed and started to ask again when she spoke.

"There's some as will be back to workin' today."

Thorn was beginning to get annoyed at the way she avoided looking at him. He wasn't sure if it was deference or dislike. "And the three I gave the amulets to?"

She flinched. Thorn gritted his teeth. How was it possible that the men and women who were Crosspointe's lifeblood could think so little of themselves? How was it possible that he valued their lives more than they did?

"They begin t' mend." She paused, her hands falling still. "You were generous." It sounded like an accusation.

"No, I wasn't," Thorn said shortly, and then stalked out, leaving his breakfast on the table. He returned to his cabin, where he paced back and forth and then removed the deadlight from one of the windows and watched the wake of the ship unfurl across the waves. He wondered if Plusby was right. Did the crew think his mind was bent? Was it so completely inconceivable to them that he might care enough about their welfare to spend his precious healing supplies on them? He shook his head. He'd wanted to unite the crew. Had he instead done exactly the opposite?

The *Eidolon* rounded Eadhere Point just before midday. Two glasses later they put in to a tree-covered cove along the Arreton Highland coast and hove to. A narrow river spilled over the verdant top ledge and fell down the steep, broken slope in a twisting white ribbon. It splashed into a pool at the top of the black sand shingle and overflowed into the sea. The temperature had dropped and it was snowing again. Thorn stood at the rail amidships, Fitch perched on his shoulder, watching as the two longboats were lowered from the port and starboard quarter davits. Each was loaded with twelve empty water casks.

The lowering of the first boat went smoothly enough. The boat tipped stern down halfway along, but Crabbel righted things and the boat was soon in the water, its three-sailor crew rowing for shore through the chop. The tide was coming in and they were soon well away. The lowering of the second boat was another matter. Blot was among the three sailors assigned to its crew. He climbed up on the rail to step aboard the longboat. The rail was slick and the lowering ropes he used to firm his balance were stiff with ice.

Between one blink and the next, Blot vanished. Thorn heard a sharp yell and a splash. He skidded across the deck, ramming hard into the opposite rail. Fitch yowled, clawing, as she was jolted loose. Blot bobbed in the frigid water, cursing loudly.

"Send 'im a lifeline!" Crabbel shouted.

No one moved. Thorn turned. Four sailors faced off against Crabbel. The leader was a whip-thin woman with leathery skin and eyes like shards of glass.

"I gave ye an order," Crabbel growled.

"After I took th' trouble t' shove 'im off?" she asked, her lip curling. "Better he drowns. Better every blighted one of ye drown and take your curse wi' ye." She pointed at the anchor charm on his chest.

"Better I break your neck for ye, Ricker, than stand

a mutiny," Crabbel said in a low, iron-hard voice as he started forward, his fists balled. Ricker braced herself to meet him, raising her own fists.

Out of the corner of his eye, Thorn saw Halford crawling down the shrouds at breakneck speed. There was going to be a brawl. None of them could afford it, especially Blot. Another minute or two in the water and he'd die. Thinking quickly, he grabbed Crabbel's arm.

"Pull him out, or I'll jump in after him and rescue him myself," he said to Ricker. He was taking a stupid chance. This would probably just confirm to them that he was as Pale-blasted as they had begun to believe. But he couldn't let Blot drown.

Ricker's eye twitched as she stared at Thorn, gauging the truth of his words. Fury erupted in him. With one last look at Ricker, he pivoted, reaching for the rail.

"Pale-blasted fool!" Ricker spat, and then brushed past him, leaping up onto the rail and stepping into the boat. Halford followed a heartbeat behind.

"Lower away!" Crabbel hollered as the three remaining mutineers snatched up the falls. He grasped the line behind the single sailor and called out a cadence. "Heave! Heave!"

The boat dropped. Thorn watched over the rail as Halford and Ricker dragged Blot into the bottom of the boat. He lay there panting and shivering, his teeth chattering. Crabbel ordered the longboat hauled back up. They lifted Blot out and Halford carried him off to the crew cabin.

"I'd put ye in irons, Ricker, and take ye past the Pale and feed ye t' th' Koreions," Crabbel said. "But there's work yet t' be done and we got too many wounded. But so much as sneeze th' wrong way, and I'll send ye t' th' depths afore ye can beg th' gods for mercy."

She met his gaze, her face stony. He waited. At last she jerked her head in understanding.

"Good. Then get this boat in th' waves and go finish your job."

She glanced at the three other sailors who'd stood with her. Without Crabbel and Blot, they'd have to lower the boat and climb down into it, risking a swim. Thorn nodded. A good lesson. He turned, intending to follow Halford and Blot. Crabbel put an arm out in front of him, barring the way.

"Ye stand clear. You're makin' things worse," he said in a strained voice. "We don't need ye wipin' our asses. You're a Pilot. Act like it afore ye get us killed."

Thorn watched him go, his belly rolling in a slow churn. The crew was disintegrating. And the more he tried to stop it, the worse it got. His lips pinched together as he looked up at Plusby, who was standing at the binnacle having witnessed the entire exchange. He caught Thorn looking at him. He stared a moment, then turned his back, returning to the helm.

Anger flared again. Ruthlessly he suppressed it. Fighting changed nothing. But something had to be done. Plusby was the key. As long as his poison fed the crew's fears, things would keep getting worse. Cold determination wrapped Thorn as an idea took form in his mind. It was a risky plan. Even if it worked, he would probably make the crew more angry with him. But it was a time-honored way for sailors to settle disputes aboard ship. Maybe they'd see that Thorn was more one of them than not. Maybe they'd see how far he was willing to go for the health of the ship, and realize that spending his healing supplies on them was a sane act. It was the only thing he could think of to do. It would solve several problems at once. If it worked. All he could do was try. Otherwise, the *Eidolon* was as good as dead in the water anyhow. Besides, he and Plusby had their own problems to resolve. Eagerness rushed through him. *Yes.*

"May as well settle things before we cross the Pale, eh, Fitch?" he said, bending to pick up the cat, who was standing on his foot, meowing plaintively. He tucked her into the crook of his arm and headed for the poop deck before he could think about how much sense this course of action really made.

The snow had thickened. The shore was no longer visible. Plusby stood at the taffrail as if waiting for Thorn. A dark bruise spread beneath the captain's beard at the left corner of his mouth, and his lips were swollen. Bess stood nearby, like a guard. Her deep-set eyes smoldered as she watched Thorn's approach.

"A private word, if I may, Captain," Thorn said.

Plusby considered Thorn. After a few grains, he turned to Bess. "Check the injured," he ordered. "Tell the mate to get back to breaking ice."

The steward nodded reluctantly and withdrew with a warning look at Thorn.

"What kind of captain stands by while his crew mutinies against the first mate?" Thorn demanded. "Do you think it will stop with just Crabbel?"

"As I see it, the crew is merely protecting itself. Those Braken-cursed charmers are dangerous. Let them all drown."

"As dangerous as a mad captain? As dangerous as crossing the Pale without a seasoned mate or a bosun?"

"As dangerous as a Pilot who doesn't know his place," Plusby said softly, his gray eyes hardening with contempt. "You've done more to unravel this crew than I have. I'm tempted to lock you in your cabin until we set the compass, and then shackle you to the post with a gag in your mouth. I expect the crew would make no objections. They would likely thank me."

"It's one way to settle things between us," Thorn said. "But perhaps you might be interested in something a little more certain."

"What do you have in mind?"

"A Squall Solution." He glanced meaningfully toward the mainmast.

The captain laughed outright. Then sobered as he saw that Thorn was serious. "You want to run up the mast?" His head cocked, his eyes narrowing. He studied Thorn, his brows furrowed.

The mainmast was the tallest on a ship, and the truck was the very topmost point. To get there, a sailor had to climb up the lattice of ratlines and shrouds. All the while the ship would be pitching and rolling on the chop, the motion growing more exaggerated the higher up the masts the sailor climbed. Just over a third of the way up he'd have to pass the futtock plate, through which a tangle of rigging passed to secure the topmast. There was a hole in it, called the lubber's hole, and no sailor worth his spit would ever think of using it. No, courage required him to climb up around the outside like a spider, with his legs dangling seventy feet above the deck while he pulled himself up over the edge by the strength of his arms alone.

After that, it was another hundred feet up the topmast, then the topgallant mast. The holes in the ratlines would now be too small for anything better than a toehold, and his hands and arms would be burning. But things would get even harder. He'd be weaving between the ropes, blocks, and tackles, scrabbling up the twisting, wobbling lines, past each of the yards and trestletrees to finally arrive at the royal yard. This was about eight feet below the final goal of the mainmast truck, and for those last eight feet, the climb was a shimmy up bare mast. There was nothing left to hold on to. It took brute strength to inch upward to the top, arms and legs clamped about the wood like a frigid, unrelenting lover. And that was on a fair-weather day. Which today was not.

Many a dispute had been settled with a race up the mainmast—a Squall Solution, it was called. It was a time-honored tradition. None of the crew would interfere, much as they might want to.

"Exactly what prize are you offering?" Plusby asked, rubbing a thoughtful hand over his beard.

"Surely if I fall to my death, that would be enough. After all, I am just a soft Pilot. I probably won't make it up to the futtock plate."

Plusby snorted, touching the bruise on his face made

by Thorn's fists. "I think perhaps you might go a little further. Your death would certainly be a reason to celebrate, but what if, gods forbid, you don't die? What do I win then?"

"Name your heart's desire."

"Very well. Two things. I want the cat to do with whatever I choose, and you will also submit to my command. You won't challenge me or undermine my authority in any way or for any reason. You will do nothing without asking my permission."

Thorn shook his head. "Not Fitch."

Plusby's brows rose. "Lost your confidence?"

Thorn's lips tightened. He didn't mean to lose. Fitch would be in no danger. "Agreed, to both."

"Then let us not waste any more time."

"Just a moment. I, too, shall want something if I win."

Plusby smirked. "Certainly. Anything you please."

"Most generous of you, I'm sure," Thorn said. "First—if I win, no one harms Fitch. Anybody who even thinks about it gets tossed in the briny. And second, the charmers wear their pendants hidden and you stop giving them bilge about it."

The captain's lip curled, but he shrugged. "As you wish. Though no one will forget what they are."

"They certainly won't if the charms are shoved in their faces every moment. But maybe the crew will work easier if they aren't reminded constantly. Whether you like it or not, you need the charmers. They are good at their jobs and they have more reason than anyone else to keep this ship afloat and the crew in order. Exposing them that way only adds to the fear and mistrust. It was a mistake."

"Those charms are the price they pay."

"For what? Being lucky enough to escape three wrecks alive?"

"That's right. For escaping and—" Plusby broke off.

"And?" Thorn asked sharply.

"And so let's get to it. I want you to stop fouling my anchor every time I turn around. As soon as we're done, I want you back in your cabin until we cross the Pale. Consider it an order."

He clearly didn't fear losing. The feral boy inside Thorn snarled. He'd taught Plusby one lesson already. He'd teach him another.

Thorn followed Plusby down off the poop deck, across the quarterdeck, and around the main hatch. Crabbel and Halford had emerged from the crew quarters, followed by Bess, Blot, and Alby Sark. Blot was pale and shivering, but he grabbed a hammer and began hammering at the ice. The wind was picking up and the ship rocked on the chop. The thick snow was swirling like mad moths.

Thorn stroked a hand over Fitch's head, scratching behind her ears. She leaned into the caress, purring. It was a foul thing he was doing, risking her life. But he didn't have a choice.

He came to a halt beside the captain at the foot of the mainmast. Their determined progress had not gone unnoticed. Plusby removed his cloak and coat, waving over Bess and handing them to her.

"Have the mate clear the rigging, Bess. It seems Master Thorn and I are going aloft. Unless," he drawled, turning to Thorn, "you wish to concede now and save yourself from disgrace?"

"I think not. But perhaps it is you who wishes to forfeit?"

"Not today, Pilot. Though I could wish for a more worthy rival," Plusby said with an exaggerated yawn.

"I'll do my best to amuse you, Captain."

Thorn turned to find Halford glowering beside him.

"What in the depths do ye think you're about?" he rumbled, his glance flicking to Plusby.

"Ah, good. I need you. Here, hold Fitch, won't you?"

Halford took the cat without thinking, glaring down at Thorn, who was unfastening his jacket. "What's goin' on?"

"I should have thought it obvious, even for you. The captain and I are going aloft. A Squall Solution."

"What for? You're lobcocked. Sure as th' waves be black, ye'll splat yerself on th' deck and we can't afford t' lose either one of ye."

"The captain seems to differ. And consider the bright side—we're still at anchor within the protection of the Pale. But of course you did go to all that trouble to crimp me and haul me here. It would be a shame to waste such an arduous effort. I'll try very hard not to die, if it will soothe you."

"I said it afore, you're a thorn in the ass," Halford growled.

"I am indeed," Thorn said, then paused. He frowned up at the bosun. Halford was holding Fitch like she was blown glass, and his eyes were smoky with a churn of volcanic emotions. Fury burned brightest, but bubbling within was a blend of desperation, hopelessness, fear . . . and defeat. Like he was facing certain death and there was nothing he could do to save himself.

Thorn went rigid. Halford was a charmer. He'd never get another ship. He was beached without this chance, but the *Eidolon* wasn't going anywhere if she was missing a captain or a Pilot. This race jeopardized everything for Halford—everything he breathed for. And not just him—Crabbel, Wragg, and Blot too. And yet, it might be the only chance to unify the crew. Thorn couldn't stop now. But he promised himself that he wasn't going to fail. Fitch's wasn't the only life on the line.

Thorn slowly slid off his jacket. Snow was falling so thick now that it was no longer possible to make out anything above the main yard. He didn't doubt that taking his time and with great care, he could make the climb and return unscathed. But this was a race—he couldn't afford to take his time and be careful. Plusby wasn't going to be restrained by any sense of personal safety. He was unstable. He wouldn't think twice about taking suicidal risks in order to win. His willingness to allow a mutiny aboard spoke volumes for his lack of reason. Which meant Thorn could not allow himself to be hampered by caution. He grimaced. If the crew resented him for using the majicked medical supplies on their wounded, they were really going to hate him for this. They'd hang him from a yardarm. The charmers would gut him and feed him to the Koreions. Halford would personally cut off his balls.

He handed Halford his jacket. "The thing about thorns, my friend, is that they are notoriously hard to kill. As I plan to be—dying is a luxury I can ill afford at the moment. In the meantime, I'd consider it a personal favor if you'd watch Fitch for me. Strange as it might seem, there might be some who want to hurt her."

Halford looked down at the small cat. He looked faintly poleaxed, as if he hadn't realized he was holding her. She stared up at him unblinking, her tail winding slowly back and forth. Her ears were slightly flattened. She reached up a forepaw and batted gently at his disaster charm as if taunting him. The big sailor scowled and grunted a wordless assent.

Thorn turned his back, flexing his fingers to limber them. They were stiff with the cold. He glanced at them. He'd forgotten the blisters he'd earned while rowing the jolly boat. He closed his fingers slowly over them.

"Ready, Captain?"

"Let us lose not a tide—Bess, ring the bell and we'll begin."

When the captain's personal steward yanked the pull, the brassy clang made Thorn start. He leaped quickly to the shrouds, Plusby just grains ahead of him. The ice on the rigging razored the flesh of his palms, though his hands were soon so numb that he hardly felt the pain. He kept up easily with Plusby, making no effort to overtake him. The captain seemed unaffected by the cuts he'd suffered from the raiders or their fight the night before.

By the time he levered himself over the main yard and arrived at the futtock shrouds, Thorn was feeling the strain of the climb in his thighs and shoulders. His hands were clumsy from the cold, leaving behind him a trail of red splotches. He paused to catch his breath. Opposite Plusby did the same, his face flushed, his breath steaming white curls in the falling snow.

"You've done this before. And you throw a decent punch." His voice was faintly admiring. "Tell me, what were you before you turned Pilot?"

"Bilge scum, to hear my parents tell it," was Thorn's dismissive reply.

"Ah, a close-knit family always warms the heart. Shall we proceed?"

"By all means."

Those few moments of conversation had stiffened Thorn's hands into iron. He loosened them with an effort, leaving behind skin and blood. He strained upward, grasping the lip of the futtock plate. It was an act of faith to push off, letting his legs swing free, depending entirely on the uncertain strength of his grip. Plusby was already disappearing over the edge. Thorn was losing ground quickly. He jumped, his shoulders and wrists popping with the strain. He kicked, pushing one foot against the stays and pulling himself up. His foot slipped from its precarious hold on the rim of the plate. He lurched downward. His legs flailed. He kicked, swinging himself back and forth until he caught a heel on the lip of the plate and rolled himself up to safety, his back against the mast.

He sat up, his heart pounding. Plusby hadn't stopped to rest, but was continuing his climb. Thorn followed, molten lead flowing thickly through his intestines—*he could lose*.

Climbing was harder now; the rigging wobbled wildly. He wove in and out of the cocooning tangle of halyards, ratlines, falls, trusses, stays, backstays, lifts, girtlines, and fancy lines. He struggled up past the crosstrees and topgallant yard. The sway of the *Eidolon*'s mainmast was growing loose and drunken as waves buffeted the ship more than a hundred feet below. The snow had turned into a blinding curtain and the only sounds he could hear were his own panting and the creak of the rigging.

The mast swiveled and bobbed in an erratic dance, then suddenly plunged deeply downward as if the ship had been swept up by a large wave. Thorn snatched at a line with his free hand. He missed. Two of his fingernails tore away. Pain screamed up his nerves. He swung outward, his arm windmilling wildly before he caught a handhold. His head hung upside down, his feet thrusting hard against the icy ropes as he hung nearly parallel with the water. His heart pounded, his balls shriveling into marbles.

For a crystal moment, he hung there swamped by paralyzing fear. But braiding through the fear was the fierce heat of exultation. *He'd not fallen.* The ship rocked back the other direction. Thorn lay flat against the ropes on the downward swoop. Exhilaration raced through him like flames and he laughed out loud. He bounded upward like a cat up a tree, no longer daunted by the unsteady weaving of the mast and the pain in his hands and muscles.

A few minutes later, he reached the royal yard and found Plusby sitting astride it. The captain's cheeks were flushed with the cold, a cap of white snow crowning his head. He watched Thorn pull himself up on the other side of the spar.

"Took your time."

"And you waited for me. How kind."

The captain shook his head, his mouth twisting in disgust. "Can't make it. Lost my grip when the ship wallowed. Twisted my arm right around. It's broken."

Now Thorn could see that Plusby was cradling his left arm awkwardly across his thighs. His clothes were smeared with blood from his torn hands, and his face was pale beneath his beard. His eyes and jaw were taut with pain. Tremors quivered through his torso. Thorn frowned. If he fainted, that would be the end of him, and it looked like he might do so at any moment. Plusby had to get down quickly, but how that might be accomplished was the problem.

"Don't wait on my account. The race is yours," the captain rasped.

"You don't mind if I sit a moment and rest, do you? Since I have plenty of time."

"By all means."

The anger behind Plusby's words was palpable. Thorn smiled, wiping the snow from his forehead and eyes.

"How do you plan to get down? Perhaps you mean to fly? Or would you prefer me to send up a couple of hands to lower you down?"

The captain licked his lips. "You're a knobbing bastard. Why don't you go crack yourself?"

"And in the meantime you'll do what? Freeze to death? Fall off your own ship? Ah, you will be a legend. The stories they'll tell of you . . . the captain who splatted off his own ship anchored and calm. You will be the best joke ever told."

Plusby snarled. "You're a bastard."

"Unfortunately not. How bad off are you?"

The captain took a deep breath. "Arm's useless. But I can manage otherwise."

A lie. But one that Thorn was grateful for. It meant that Plusby was willing to try.

"Any suggestions?"

Plusby's steel gaze was considering as he examined Thorn. Finally he shook his head slowly as if confused by something. "Cut the footrope loose and we'll stair step down using it as a safety line."

It wasn't as easy as it sounded. The footrope was attached at intervals along the royal yard by vertical lines called stirrups. Holding his stiletto in his hand, Thorn stretched out along the spar, inching out until he reached the end of the yard. The footrope was fastened to the yard with an eye splice and lashings. Thorn sawed through the rope just below the eye, the frozen wet strands parting reluctantly. At last he was through. The end fell away and he pushed himself backward, cutting through each of the stirrups until he found himself pressing back up against the mast.

Carefully he sawed through the last fastening, making sure to wrap a loop around his wrist so that the freed line couldn't fall.

His hands were shaking when he settled back on the yard. Carefully Thorn began to saw away the thimbles that fastened the stirrups to the footrope, his bloody hands staining the rope red. The trembling in his hands traveled up his arms into his shoulders and spread down into his legs. He swore his aggravation as he finished removing the thimbles and slid the stiletto into his boot. He hauled in the loose rope and maneuvered back around to face Plusby, the mast between them.

He wasn't aware he was still cursing until the captain asked, "Something wrong?"

"I hope Degby has a hot meal on the table when we lay on deck," Thorn growled. "Or I may chew off your legs and stew them for dinner."

The captain chuckled. "I'll make sure you get a bellyful."

"If not you, then the crew. They'll want me roasting on a spit for this," Thorn muttered.

"You do keep trying to endanger their Pilot," Plusby said. "Not to mention their captain."

"You could have said no."

"But they all know I'm insane. You're the one they'll blame," he said through chattering teeth.

Tremors shuddered through Plusby in increasing waves. He could barely keep his balance. Thorn considered lashing him to the mast and descending for help, but dismissed the idea. The captain wouldn't soon forgive him the humiliation of having to be rescued by the charmers; his hatred of them might even make him jump to his death just for spite. Thorn didn't trust anyone else in the crew to get Plusby down safely. It was up to him.

He bent the end of the rope in a circle, tying a rolling hitch to create a loop large enough to circle Plusby's chest. Thorn's fingers were as stiff as the rope, and the resulting knot was looser than he liked.

Still, there was little to be done. He wordlessly passed the noose over Plusby's head and shoulders, helping the other man pull his injured arm through. When he was done, the captain was swaying, his face gray, his eyes squinting with pain. From his movements, it was clear he'd done far more than merely break his arm. He'd torn muscle and ligaments at the very least.

"Are you ready?"

"Better get to the truck or you don't win," Plusby wheezed. "Those bastards will wear their charms for all to see, and I'll eat your cat for breakfast."

"Why do you hate them so much? They've had the bad luck to survive three wrecks, but they are good sailors. You can depend on them."

Plusby laughed, a harsh, barking sound. "Those four bastards are as dependable as spawn."

"What do you mean? You aren't stupid and I'm beginning to think that you aren't as bent as you pretend. You know what you're doing. Why risk your ship to humiliate them?"

Plusby's face went completely blank, all emotion smoothing away. "They killed my wife."

"Wife? But—"

None of the rumors said Plusby had married his lover. Not that it mattered. She was still dead.

"I heard her ship went down escaping Tapisriya when the Jutras came, so how . . . ?" Thorn trailed off, realization dawning. "They were crewing the ship; they survived the wreck."

"Aye, and the cursed Pilot too." Plusby's gaze was hot and accusing.

"Of course he did," Thorn said absently, rubbing a hand over his jaw and pinching his upper lip thoughtfully.

"No 'of course' about it," the captain snarled, his eyes red and bulging with the force of his fury. "They swam off and left her to the mercy of the waves. They saved their own skins and left her to die. Or worse."

His voice broke, bitter tears sliding down his cheeks as he looked away. His face was graven with lines of inconsolable loss. It was a depth of feeling Thorn had little acquaintance with. Even Jordan's death hadn't struck him so deeply.

"These men . . . they would not have just let her die or be eaten by *sylveth*," he argued.

"No? Did they tell you that?"

"They have not spoken of it. But they would not have left."

Plusby's only reply was an angry exclamation of disbelief.

Thorn bent forward. "Cowardice is as unforgivable aboard ship as harming the captain or Pilot. I don't need to be told that if they had seen her, they would have tried to rescue her. Even at the cost of touching *sylveth*. You know it too, though you refuse to admit it."

The captain was shaking his head adamantly. "They survived—she should have, too. She was strong; she shouldn't have been lost. The only explanation is that they abandoned her to save their own yellow skins."

"Think about it. You know sailors never leave anybody behind. Never. And those four? Third time's a charm. They'd have rather died than survive that wreck—better to die than live the life they live now. You've been a sailor too long not to know it. They had every reason not to abandon anyone.

"As for the Pilot—"

He stopped, chewing his lip. "What was the Pilot's name?"

"Remirabel."

Thorn knew him. He was young. This was only his third season as a Pilot. Which meant that he'd been as green as grass that season when Plusby's wife's vessel had gone down. Remirabel had a strong sense of the sea, but it was easy to misunderstand the waves, and to make the wrong choices. But even more likely was that the danger had come up too quickly and too close to avoid. He shook his head.

"Remirabel is a good Pilot. I'm the first to admit that my former brethren rarely get their hands dirty, and then usually only by accident. But no matter how much I despise the politics and the posturing of the guild, most Pilots are decent enough. They wouldn't watch a helpless woman come to harm if they could stop it. I truly believe that. You know there are dozens of possibilities for what might have happened to her in that wreck—have you asked Crabbel or Halford? Any of them? What did Remirabel say?"

Something rippled across Plusby's expression, too quick for Thorn to read. The captain looked away, staring blindly into the fluttering white silence. When he turned back, his expression was a mask of basalt, revealing nothing. Plusby's next words didn't lend any insight into what he was thinking. The subject was clearly off-limits.

"Best course is for you to anchor the line around the mast and release the fall as I descend, then climb down to me and do it again."

Thorn nodded. "I won't be able to brace you while I'm climbing down. Can you hold?"

"We'll soon find out. But I suggest you go sprightly, and pray Braken doesn't toss the ship about unnecessarily."

"Aye, aye, Cap'n," Thorn said sardonically with a mocking salute, and snubbed the rope around the mast. "Shall I give you a push to get you started, then?"

Plusby only smiled, slinging his leg over the mast and sliding off. His weight hit the end of the rope and he grappled for a hold on the shrouds with his good hand, pulling himself around so he could find his footing on the ropes. He clung there, his right arm thrust through the webbing, the left dangling uselessly from his shoulder. His face was deeply lined, blood trickling from where he'd bit through his lip. His ragged breathing sounded loud.

"Looks like that hurt a fair bit," Thorn observed.

Plusby lifted his head, glaring. "Are you trying to be funny?"

"What could I find amusing about you dangling

from your own mainmast, your only safety line held by a Pilot you'd just as soon see dead as not? Best hope I'm not clumsy."

The captain's lips bared in what Thorn imagined was supposed to be a grin, but pain contorted it. "Promise me you'll tell me who you really are when we get down."

"I am your Pilot."

"You're a damned sight more than that. I want to know what sort of man has the compass of my ship."

Thorn shrugged noncommittally. "Perhaps. If you survive. Are you ready, then?"

"Let's go."

And with that, they began the 160-foot crawl down to the deck.

Chapter 8

At first the descent off the royal yard was only agonizing, but it soon turned excruciating and then finally past all bearing. Still, they had no choice. The skin grated from Thorn's hands as he slowly lowered Plusby, freeing the line inch by inch. His arms and shoulders ached with the strain, and the cold sank into him like icy talons. He shook with fatigue and pain, hardly able to keep a safe perch on the shrouds.

They paused to rest on the yards and crosstrees, but dared not delay much—the race was against becoming so cold and exhausted that they simply fell.

Plusby allowed himself to be lowered through the lubber's hole on the futtock plate. His face was the color of pewter and just as hard. He sagged against his safety rope, his strength nearly gone. With every foot closer to the deck, Thorn absorbed more of Plusby's weight, until he feared that in the time it took him to climb down to the next level and shift the safety line down, Plusby would faint and fall.

But then suddenly there was jerking on the end. The line was yanked from his cramped hands and he let go; truth be told, he couldn't have held against the force if he wanted to. Then he struggled the rest of the way down, falling the last several feet to land heavily on the snow-covered deck in the midst of a riot of noise.

His head spun with blurry black-and-white splotches and he could make no sense of the shouting. His eyes felt too heavy to open. His landing had knocked the breath from his lungs and he coughed and gasped. Hands turned him roughly over and lifted him into the air. Fiery pain streaked through him, at odds with the cold that was shaking his body like a baby's rattle. He groaned, earning himself a litany of curses from Halford, who appeared to be supporting his shoulders.

The snow fell on his face, though he was nearly too numb to feel it. His hands burned like he was holding them in a fire. They carried him up onto the quarter-deck and through the narrow door of his cabin, laying him on the velvet chaise.

"How's . . . Plusby?" he croaked.

"Shoutin' orders and bleedin' more than ye. Missin' a fair bit of skin too, but ye'd know as much about it," Halford replied, holding Thorn down when he would have struggled to sit up. "Where's th' healin' supplies?" he asked someone over Thorn's head. "If there be any left."

"If there be any, they be locked up." Blot's voice was thick with anger.

"My ring," Thorn said, trying to fish for it in his pocket. He'd put it there before the race.

"What about it?" Halford asked, pushing away Thorn's torn hands and finding the compass-rose signet.

"Opens the lock. In the corner . . . compass shaped."

Halford tossed it to Blot, who could be heard rummaging. He gave an exclamation of triumph. There was a sound of shuffling and the clunk of something wooden set down hard, then the clanking, thudding sound of an assortment of things being swept together into a bin. Then a blurry-edged Blot reappeared, carrying a deep crate filled with a jumble of healing supplies. He set it down on the floor and stood over it, arms crossed.

"What do I do?" Halford demanded.

"Black amulet . . . for healing. Yellow . . . for pain. You'll want the ring too."

Blot passed over the ring wordlessly. Halford turned it in his fingers.

"Put it on. Doesn't bite."

The bosun did as told, though with a dainty wariness that reminded Thorn of a cat trying to wade through water without getting wet. Which reminded him . . .

"Where's Fitch?"

Halford flicked a glance at him and returned to rifling through the crate. "Blot, make a fire in th' stove and then go be sure th' cap'n's is lit. They'll not survive if they don't get warm. And fetch some Meris's Tears, quick-like."

The bosun's refusal to answer his question made Thorn begin to struggle again, but to no avail. He hardly did more than twitch from side to side.

"Damn it . . . Halford—where's Fitch?"

"If ye wasn't such a damned fool, ye wouldn't have t' ask. Beastie's barnacled t' your ribs."

"What?"

Thorn lifted his clumsy hands, feeling for her. He found her knotted into a tiny ball on his hip, her body tense, her claws curling deeply into his clothing. And perhaps his flesh—he couldn't tell. She nudged against his hand with a worried mew. The tiny movement sent a spray of fiery cinders over his hand and whirling up the length of his arm. He swallowed the pain, knowing Halford would only say it was his own damned fault. Which it was.

Halford fished the amulets out of the bin like they were poisonous snakes. Like most sailors, he didn't like even worked *sylveth*—he didn't really believe it wouldn't come alive and transform him into spawn.

"Hope these be enough. Ye haven't any spares."

His unspoken accusation hung in the air. Thorn had wasted the other amulets.

From the corner by the stove, Blot muttered. "Damned stupid, cocksucking, Pale-blasted Pilots . . . no business . . . can't be trusted . . ."

"Pipe down," Halford ordered before settling the amulets around Thorn's neck.

Instantly the pain evaporated. "Thank the gods," he breathed, pushing himself upright.

"Careful. Ye could make things worse. Likely ye will."

"There should be one or two jars left with green seals. Yes, that one. Open it and put the salve on my hands."

Halford did as told. Thorn gasped as he looked at his hands for the first time and realized the extent of the damage. Only a few bits of muscle and sinew yet clung to them, the flesh worn away by the loop of the safety line. Wrapping the rope around his hands had been stupid—if the captain fell, Thorn's bones could have been crushed, his fingers ripped off. Nothing in the healing stores could regrow them. But he'd been more afraid of losing his hold on the line altogether. He'd rather lose fingers than lose Plusby. But as he looked at the bone shining through the bloody shreds of flesh, at the bruises where skin remained, it broke on him that he could have lost the use of both his hands. Without the majickal healing stores, he surely would have. The realization twisted and coiled in his stomach like a mass of baby Koreions.

He remained silent until Halford was done, then in a subdued voice directed him to wrap his hands with the rolled bandages from the kit. They were made of a soft, clingy black material.

By the time he was neatly wrapped, Blot had finished stoking the stove and fetched a bottle of Meris's Tears.

"How be th' cap'n?" Halford asked, unstoppering the bottle with his teeth and holding it out to let Thorn drink from it.

The Pilot shook his head and took it instead, bracing it between the heels of his trembling hands, and drank. He guzzled fully a quarter of the bottle before he passed it back, wiping a trickle away from his chin with a swipe of his arm. The powerful liquor hit his stomach and exploded. His vision blurred and his body went slack. In a few minutes his head would clear and he'd feel more focused. Such was the power of Meris's Tears. But it did nothing to help his shivering, the cold sunk deep into the marrow of his bones.

"Old man is foul tempered," said Blot tersely, answering Halford's question. "Steward of his be fixin' 'im up."

"Help me get Pilot Thorn nearer th' fire," Halford said, noticing Thorn's palsied shaking. "And fetch 'im dry clothes."

As the two men would have lifted the chaise, Thorn stopped them.

"Give me a blanket and take me to the captain."

"Are ye stupid? Ye need t' rest." Blot spat the words like nails.

Exhaustion and building irritation made Thorn snap. Maybe Blot had a right, but Thorn was done catering to the crew's unhappiness. He was trying to get them out on the water; he was trying to keep them safe. He was tired of the accusing looks and haranguing.

"It's an order from your Pilot. You can damn well get off my ship if you can't obey."

Both men recoiled.

"Fetch a blanket," Halford said finally, breaking the brittle silence.

Blot clomped off to the bedchamber. Sluggishly a memory wormed up to the surface of Thorn's mind. "There should be a hot-blanket. It's thin, like silk. It might be in a very small carton."

Halford awkwardly pawed through the supplies. At last he found a flat, egg-shaped container, hinged on one side, no bigger than a fist. It was enameled orange.

"This it?" Halford asked doubtfully as Blot returned holding a counterpane.

"Aye. Open it."

The bosun sprang the catch and the finely hammered egg popped open. Its copper interior gleamed around a folded bundle of material. He lifted it gingerly and shook it out. It was as fine as spun cobwebs and large enough to wrap a man in. Halford proceeded to do just that, tucking it around Thorn, his hands surprisingly gentle. Instantly warmth began to seep through him.

"Thank the depths," he murmured. "Very well, then. Let's go call on the captain."

Fitch didn't like Halford slinging Thorn's arm around his neck and lifting him to his feet. She hissed, her ears flattening, her tail lashing from side to side. She stalked after them, leaping up to Thorn's shoulder and scratching fiercely at Halford.

"Cursed beast," he gritted through his teeth as her claws hooked his flesh and three welts appeared, running from the side of his mouth to his chin.

Thorn smiled, rubbing his cheek against her fur. "She's just a cat protecting her own, Halford."

The other man grunted, baring his teeth at Fitch. It worked. She desisted from her attack, though she continued to growl and hiss as she settled down against Thorn's neck.

The Meris's Tears were beginning to firm Thorn's rubbery limbs and clear the muzziness from his head. It wouldn't last. The Tears were only a temporary measure. As bad as his wounds were, he doubted he had more than a glass or two of clarity. But he and Plusby had forged a delicate link and he wanted to strengthen it before it snapped. Plus it would do ship morale a lot of good to see him upright and meeting with the captain.

Halford helped him out of the cabin, while Blot went to the galley for hot food and tea. Thorn stumbled and lurched like a man deep in his cups. If not for Halford, he didn't think he'd be able to stand or walk. The yellow amulet had suppressed his pain, but Thorn still felt an odd, disconnected throbbing in his hands; it was a feeling of swelling tightness followed by a fading to slackness. Looking down at them, he gritted his teeth, feeling his face flush in anticipation of the humiliation of being unable to use them. Eating, going to the head—was Halford going to have to pull his pants down for him too? He couldn't help the burst of harsh laughter that exploded from his chest.

"What's so funny?"

"What's the bonus for nursemaiding a Pilot who can't eat, piss, or shit without help?"

Halford was silent a long moment, before letting go a string of blistering curses that cut across the activity on the deck, bringing the crew to a staring halt. Many offered up warding signs to deflect any bad luck. Crabbel stomped over from where he'd been tearing a strip off a trio of very sluggish sailors, his round face wet and ruddy, his eyes snapping.

"Meris's tits! What in th' black depths has tangled your anchor?"

The bosun's teeth clamped on the flow of his fury, his mouth pursing as he spit. "Worthless, crackin' Pilot," he muttered.

"Ah, ye been makin' friends. How sweet. Mebbe ye lovers can get off my deck so th' crew can get back t' knockin' away th' ice. Unless ye want t' careen afore we get under way?"

This was the foulest temper Thorn had ever witnessed from Crabbel. He looked like he could chew the mainmast in half.

"My fault. My incapacity has unsettled our friend." He lifted his hands meaningfully.

The mate made the connections instantly, and a pitiless smile slowly widened his lips. He scratched at his beard. "How long afore ye heal enough t' sail?"

"I can stand the compass now. But I expect—I hope—the captain may wait an extra tide or two. Once we cross the Pale, I'll need to be sharp. Just at the moment, I am . . . tired."

Crabbel sobered. "Not too long or I can't answer for th' crew. Faster this tub gets under way, th' less likely they'll mutiny. Best see th' cap'n, now. Tell 'im how 'tis, if ye don't mind. He'll not like me makin' th' report. Meantime I'll keep this lot busy. Ye help our Pilot, Halford. Stay w' 'im so long as he wants ye."

He laughed at this last, returning to the three recalcitrant sailors.

Halford spit again. "I be no crackin' nursemaid."

"You are today," Thorn said mildly, and then nudged the other man toward the captain's cabin. Halford pounded on the captain's door like he was trying to break it down. It was yanked open by Bess. She stood in the doorway, her head tipped back, her eyelids heavy over her deep-set eyes.

"Pilot wants t' see the cap'n," Halford growled, and began pushing inside.

With him bracing Thorn, Bess had little choice but to back away.

The captain's cabin was much the same as Thorn's, with polished oak cabinets, a broad desk, deeply piled rugs, a scattering of chairs and chaises, oil paintings of seascapes and ships, and various and sundry other bric-a-brac and oddments. There were three wide windows, two on the stern and one on the starboard, each shuttered with deadlights and covered in crisp brocade curtains. A potbellied stove stood in the corner. There was also a separate chamber for sleeping and a small, private head. Plusby was sitting near the stove swaddled in a dozen wool blankets, lines grooving the corners of his mouth and eyes, his face pale and clammy. He was shivering, his teeth chattering.

"Pilot Thorn," he rasped. "Sit, though I daresay you may be warmer on deck."

Thorn scowled. "I thought you were being tended. You look like you've been keelhauled bow to stern and left for dead."

Plusby started to laugh and then it turned into deep, racking coughs. Tears ran down his cheeks as he clutched his chest. "Gods be damned," he choked, his color fading even more, if it was possible.

Thorn's gaze raked the steward. "What have you done for him? Why hasn't he been given amulets for the healing and pain?"

She straightened, her cheeks sucking in to give her

already gaunt face a skeletal aspect. Her dark, sunken eyes smoldered. "I haven't yet located the healing stores."

Thorn bit back his frustration. "Give him my amulets, Halford. And the blanket."

"Belay that," Plusby whispered.

His head had fallen back and his eyes had lost focus. His breathing was fast and erratic.

"Do it, Halford."

The bosun hesitated, but did as told. The moment he removed the amulets, the pain crashed over Thorn like a rogue wave and he staggered, groaning. Bess caught him and helped him to a chair beside the fire. He collapsed, his legs and feet knotting with cramps and his hands flaming like lit torches.

Halford ignored Plusby's weak protests and settled the talismans around his neck. He then gently pulled the warming blanket from Thorn and wrapped it around the captain, his face as expressionless as water.

Halford stormed into the bedchamber and returned with the captain's counterpane, snugging it close around Thorn, ignoring Fitch's hissing anger as she jumped to the floor and then climbed back up to curl in a ball on Thorn's lap.

"Damn," Plusby muttered, relief cracking his voice. "I didn't realize . . ." He trailed off, closing his eyes with a sigh. After a moment, he lifted his head.

Thorn huddled inside himself, the pounding of the pain in his nerves sending jolts of agony screaming through him. He clenched his teeth, unwilling to release the whimpers that crowded his mouth. Tears slid silently from the corners of his eyes as he sat there trying to endure.

"Braken's bloody cods! Bosun—where are the other healing amulets?"

"No more . . . gave them . . . crew . . . ," Thorn choked out before Halford could respond.

"Bess, find the damned supplies. Now!" Plusby barked, his voice gaining strength.

"I've searched everywhere but the locked personal compartments. You have no seal," she said tonelessly, her hands hanging at her sides, her chin jutting.

It took a moment for Thorn to understand what she was saying. Plusby's ticket had been stripped, which meant his seal had been confiscated. As with the Pilot, generally the captain's personal locks were keyed to his seal.

He looked toward Plusby, his vision clouding. The effect of the Meris's Tears couldn't hold against the razoring pain. "What else could they use?"

"Something personal," Bess suggested. "A family crest. Or—" She broke off with a little gasp.

Plusby went stiff, looking like he'd been struck. "They wouldn't have," he whispered.

His gray eyes turned molten, his jaw knotting so tightly Thorn wondered if his teeth might crumble from the pressure. Then he was flailing out of his wrappings, sending his chair crashing as he lurched to his feet. Linen bandages circled his ribs up to his armpits. They were blotched red from seeping blood. Black bruises fingered above the bandages, striping his shoulders, collarbone, and neck from where the lifeline had rubbed him. His hands were bundled like Thorn's, his left arm dangling like a limp rag.

He staggered across the cabin, knocking Bess away with his good arm when he sagged to one knee and she tried to help him up. With a grunt he pushed himself upright, reaching out to brace himself against the wall. His ragged panting turned to harsh coughing. Still he wasn't to be deterred. He struggled to a tall set of cabinets atop a chest of shallow drawers. They matched those in Thorn's cabin, with brass filigree banding the edges. He rattled the doors, but they did not open.

"Lock is in the brass," Halford said, righting the captain's chair.

Plusby examined the filigree, and then he leaned his forehead against the wood, taking slow, deliberate breaths.

Then he lifted his useless left arm with his right hand and pushed down the bandage that rode up over his wrist. Beneath was a bracelet woven of fine wires of gold, silver, and some sort of black metal. The wires crisscrossed in a complex diamond pattern with small blue, red, and green beads strewn on at intervals. Thorn could see no evidence of a catch—if anyone wanted to remove it, he would have to cut it off. Plusby stared down at the band with such a look of naked agony that Thorn averted his eyes. When he looked up again, the captain was pressing his shackled wrist against a strip of brass just below the handles. Then he swung the door open.

He stood staring at the contents and then made a low, guttural sound and stumbled back to the fire. He collapsed onto his chair, his chest heaving.

"Gods damn them. Gods damn them all. May Meris turn them to spawn, may Braken tear out their guts and feed them to the Koreions, may Chayos shrivel their cocks, and Hurn—may Hurn flay them until they scream and may they never die."

"Halford, the blanket," Thorn ordered quietly, once again struck by the depth of the captain's pain.

When the bosun had wrapped up Plusby, he brushed past the silent Bess and rifled through the cabinet. Grains later he strode over to forcefully push the two amulets over Thorn's head, like he would rather have used them to strangle him.

The sudden release from the pain made Thorn cry out. He drew a deep breath, his lips moving in a silent prayer of thanks. A few grains later, Halford tucked another of the hot blankets around him, and on top of that the counterpane.

"Thanks," Thorn said.

Halford made a disparaging grunt and straightened up.

"You'd better go. Both of you."

Bess was still standing near the captain, her expression carefully bland. She hesitated, then followed Halford out. The door closed behind them, leaving

Thorn alone with Plusby. The Pilot sat quietly, still shivering, though the heat of the majicked blanket had taken the edge off the worst of the cold and now the fire and counterpane were beginning to have a beneficial effect. He let his eyes drift shut, not wanting to intrude on Plusby's anguish more than he had to.

The rocking of the ship, his own exhaustion, and the Meris's Tears he'd drunk on an empty stomach contrived to make him drowse. He jerked awake when Plusby began to speak, his voice thinned and tattered. He talked as if he couldn't stop himself.

"The *jeras*—Tapisriyan divine women—can read portents. They said Sherenya's future held terrible danger. We thought they meant the Jutras invasion. At that point, they'd already overrun the northern farmlands and were marching over the mountains. It was only a matter of time. . . . All I wanted was to get Sherenya away safely. I was desperate. You don't know. . . ."

He rubbed his bandaged right hand over his eyes. "The *jeras* insisted that we marry by Tapisriyan high ritual; when I met her, Sherenya had been an *efiole*—a kind of priestess in training. She . . . stopped . . . when we fell in love."

The matter-of-factness of the statement made Thorn strangely uncomfortable. There had been little enough love in his parents' home, and he'd never given more than a few nights affection to any woman. Even his love for Jordan was something he had kept at arm's length and never thought much about. For Plusby to wear his deepest emotions so openly was difficult to witness. He wondered if he'd ever feel such dreadful love. He hoped not.

"With the Jutras coming, the *jeras* were happy enough to let me have Sherenya, to get her to safety, but they insisted on the high ritual. I didn't care; as far as I was concerned, I was married to her the moment I saw her. The weaving of this bracelet is part of the ceremony—one for each of us. It took an exhausting three days all told—we were not permitted to sleep or eat or speak other than the ritual words."

He shifted, letting the blankets fall from his shoulders and lifting his arm into his lap, rubbing a finger over the bracelet cuff. "It is majicked so that it doesn't come off. We are bound together until well after death—whatever may become of us. Not even a grave robber could steal it. And those mother-dibbling bastards used it to key the spells on the cracking cabinets."

The last was pregnant with quiet loathing. Thorn didn't know what to say, but Plusby continued, evidently not expecting a response.

"It changes, you know. The patterns, the colors. They shift. I don't know if they are supposed to tell me she's alive or dead or spawn—"

His voice choked to a halt. After a moment he drew a deep breath and continued. It was as if he were flushing his system of a particularly virulent venom—he needed to speak to rid himself of it.

"She refused to come back with me aboard the *Snowswan*. She was so frightened of the Jutras, and I still had to make a run to Relsea. That was just a year before they were swallowed by the Empire, just months after Tapisriya fell. She begged me to let her sail straight to Crosspointe instead. The *Sesio* was available. It had just taken on cargo and was headed for Chance refitting. It was early yet, but they couldn't afford to wait."

Thorn nodded. The *Sesio* was a Pelk ship and run by a smaller consortium. They didn't have deep enough pockets to run the ship right up to Chance when Crosspointe ships had priority and the prices for refitting scraped the heavens. Thorn could almost hear Plusby's thinking that day—it was well before Chance; his wife would be safe within the Pale before the storms hit.

"I agreed. I knew Shatford. He was a fine captain and careful. I wanted her with me, but Sherenya was

so very frightened of the Jutras—I couldn't tell her
no. I wish to the gods I had. But I put her aboard
and the waters turned vicious. They ended up running
up on a knucklebone weir near the Root. All lives
lost save your four charmers and the Pilot."

"I'm sorry," Thorn said, knowing that saying it
sounded so paltry as to be nearly meaningless. But he
was sorry. Losing Jordan had taught him something
of the pain Plusby felt and he didn't wish it on anyone.
"Why are you telling me all this?"

"Because I owe you something for bringing me
down off the mast. You paid a high price for my clum-
siness and pride."

He fell silent. Thorn scrabbled for something to say,
but he came up empty. Then Plusby spoke again.

"My mind is not bent. I still search for Sherenya—
she is my heart and my soul. I will continue seeking
her so long as my marriage bracelet suggests she's
alive. I will admit that I have let my feelings color my
actions. But I promise you that I will do so no more."
His gaze narrowed. "But you set a high standard. I've
never met a Pilot as selfless as you seem to be."

Thorn snorted.

"Since laying aboard, you've done everything in
your power to protect this crew . . . especially the
charmers. You gave up your healing supplies and you
sacrificed your body and your pain for them. No Pilot
I've heard of has ever taken the oath to guide and
protect a ship quite so seriously. I would like to know
who you are. Who you really are."

"I am Thorn, the *Eidolon*'s Pilot."

Thorn spoke automatically, realizing as he did how
petty he sounded. Plusby had let Thorn see all the
way into the bleakest pit of his soul; he deserved a
better return on that investment.

"In another life, I was Geoffrey Truehelm, and after
I became a Pilot, I went by 'Sylbrac.' And now that
my guild has sold me to crimpers, I am Thorn, Pilot
in service to a black ship."

Plusby looked as if he'd been struck on the head. His mouth pursed in a silent whistle.

"Truehelm. Same family as the lord chancellor?"

"My esteemed father."

"Odd that they'd have sold the son of the lord chancellor to crimpers."

"Not at all. He'd have encouraged it, had he known."

"Ah, you two are close, then."

"As two men who wouldn't mind killing each other can be."

Before the captain could ask any more questions, a knock sounded. He glanced at the door and then to Thorn. "You can keep your damned cat. And the charmers. I'll even let the mate and bosun sit at my table. After all, you won our wager."

"I didn't touch the truck."

"You didn't drop me on my head on the deck either. I should show my gratitude for that."

"I won't refuse." Thorn drew a breath and blew it out. He felt a certain friendship burgeoning between them. It was fragile and he wanted to protect it. Which meant . . . candor. "But surely you know my guild sold me to you. They will not give me a ship. I'm as desperate to be here as you are, as the charmers are. You need not court me. I have no intention of letting you weigh anchor without me."

A slow grin spread across Plusby's face. "So you are saying that the reason you didn't let me fall was because you didn't want to lose the chance to sail? And I need not grovel for your cooperation, is that about it?"

"Aye. That's about it."

Plusby tipped his head to examine Thorn, who shifted uneasily under the scrutiny. Another more insistent knock on the cabin door prompted Plusby to blink, ending his reverie. "I thank you for your frankness, Pilot Thorn, but I see no reason to change my mind. Though I would prefer that you stop putting yourself in danger. I will endeavor to make sure it is not necessary. It gives me some . . . comfort . . . to know that there is a Pilot alive who would sacrifice so much for the men and women in his care."

A flicker of pain swept across his expression and Thorn knew Plusby thought of his wife and her last voyage. The other man's expression smoothed, a thin—but genuine—smile touching his lips.

"And now if you don't mind, I am hungry." And he called for the meal to be brought in.

Chapter 9

Halford and Bess served their meal and remained to
help Plusby and Thorn with their eating of it. Thorn
was able to drink the soup from a pewter mug by
bracing it between the heels of his hands, but couldn't
manage the rest of the meal without Halford, who fed
him bites of roast pork, potatoes, fruit tart, pickled
vegetables, and the dessert custard. The expressionless
bosun worked methodically, as if by efficiency he
could be done with his task sooner. Thorn was astonished when Halford set a bowl of meat on the floor
for Fitch without any prompting. The cat blinked at
him, then dropped lightly to the floor, rubbing against
the bosun's ankles. Halford watched her, his mouth
tightening. Thorn chuckled.

In the meantime, Bess set about re-dressing the captain's wounds using the majicked bandages and salve
from his cache of healing supplies. Plusby accepted
her care with ill grace, snarling at her impatiently
when she rewrapped his chest.

"Would you rather I wait and prolong the healing?"
she asked frostily, standing over him with her hands
crossed over her chest. "Perhaps you want to sit at
anchor for another week while you mend?"

Plusby subsided without further argument, his gaze
narrowing at Thorn's unsuccessful attempt to hide a smirk.

"My predicament amuses you?"

Thorn shrugged, opening his mouth for Halford to
fill it again.

"Yet I am not the one who is being fed like a baby. Nor will I require aid for pissing." Plusby lifted a brow at Halford. "I wonder, bosun, if that is part of your *luck*." He nodded at the wreck charm still hanging in full view.

Halford didn't answer, his face darkening, the tops of his ears turning fiery. The sound of his teeth gritting together was audible.

"I don't believe you've been introduced to my steward. Bess has been with me since I got my ticket."

She snorted at that, still working on the wrappings around Plusby's right hand. It wasn't nearly as ravaged as Thorn's, and still allowed him to eat and tend his necessaries on his own.

"What Bess means by that rude noise is that she and I grew up together. She fostered in my family's holding. Bess hails from Esengaile. She wanted to earn her captain's ticket and so her family fostered her with us. But then the family's fortunes took a bad turn. Bess was stranded and since she lacked the continuing fosterage fee, my parents terminated the contract. Without it, she had no legal basis to stay or work in Crosspointe, nor did she have the fare to leave. She was sold into indentured servitude and my father purchased her contract, placing her with me as my steward. I, however, am luckier than you. My father had the grace to die recently, thus allowing me, as his heir, to release her from that contract. Strangely enough, Bess has chosen to remain with me. I believe she thinks my mind bent, and fears the harm I might do to myself."

"And rightly so," she said, tightening the final knot on the bandage. "What kind of captain and Pilot go haring off up into the rigging in a snowstorm? If you ask me, you're both of you bent as hairpins."

"Yes," Plusby agreed thoughtfully, turning a penetrating look on Thorn. "What kind of Pilot can even make that climb? I asked you who you really are, but I don't think your answer was complete. You are like no other Pilot I've met. Most couldn't find their own asses with both hands. Like they lost all their brains and sense when they touched their first compass. But you run the rigging like you've worked a ship, and recently at that. You throw a decent punch, too." He touched the bruise on his mouth.

"There was a time, between leaving my father's house and joining the Pilots' Guild, that I ran wild in Tideswell."

"Gutter rat?" Plusby's forehead wrinkled as his brows rose. "Rough life."

"Aye, it was." Harder than anyone who hadn't lived it could imagine. "I eventually earned a berth on a ship as a snottie. After a few years, I made bosun of the *Pommern*. But then my parents took an interest in me again. They thought I should return to the family fold, earn my captain's ticket, and serve on the family ships. When I refused—" He broke off, shrugging. "A year later I qualified to join the Pilot's Guild. But I have not forgotten how to be useful aboard ship, even without a compass."

"Indeed not," the captain said, giving Thorn a shrewd look. He didn't ask any more questions, though it was clear he sensed there was more to the story. Instead he pushed his empty plate back. "Unless you require the bosun's immediate assistance to relieve yourself, I would adjourn to the comfort of the fireside with a bottle of brandy and speak privately with you."

Thorn afforded Halford a sideways glance. In fact his bladder *was* full and he needed to use the head. The bosun helped Thorn up and out of the cabin, maintaining a grim silence throughout the process. When he had returned Thorn to Plusby, he started to beat a hasty retreat. But the captain stopped him.

"Bring me the mate, bosun."

Halford stiffened and nodded, leaving the cabin door ajar.

"I don't think your charmer likes me much," Plusby said.

"He feels your fingers around his heart. No man likes to have another's hands in his chest."

"Very poetic. Are you a scribbler in your spare time as well?"

Thorn chuckled. "Put no idler pen in my hand. I've no talent for it, nor the patience."

Just then, there was a knock on the doorjamb and Crabbel entered, pulling his hat off, followed closely by Halford. The two stood stiffly before the captain, staring over his head at the deadlight covering the window behind him. Crabbel was wet, his shoulders, back, and chest dusted with snow. His round face was ruddy, and his brown eyes glittered. Thorn considered how long it had been since the charmers had had a billet. The *Sesio* had gone down more than two years before, just before Chance. That wreck had given the four sailors their charms. Likely they hadn't set foot on deck since. He tried to imagine it. His stomach churned. He'd faced the threat for mere days and nearly gone mad.

"How fares the ship and crew, Crabbel?"

Crabbel started at the sound of his name from the captain's lips. "They be riffraff and bilge scum, sir. The riggin' and masts be heavy with th' ice and snow. Be a long night for th' crew, scrapin' us clean."

"And the wounded?"

Crabbel flicked a glance at Thorn, his fleshy jaw knotting. Thorn could almost hear what he was thinking. *Wasting majick . . .*

"Th' three worst be mending well. Five o' th' others are on light duty. Th' other three will be ready in th' morn."

Plusby nodded. "Good. And you, first mate? How do you do?"

Crabbel's brows rose and then he scowled. "Well enough, sir."

"No complaints? Not even that charm on your chest?"

"No, sir, Cap'n." Crabbel could hardly get the words out through the fence of his teeth.

"Really? It seems the good Pilot here does. He's worried that the crew might respond unfavorably to the sight of your charms. Your authority might be undermined. Do you agree?"

The mate met the captain's eyes, his nostrils flaring. "Aye, sir."

"And you—Halford. Do you also think I've made a mistake in having you wear the charm on your chest for all to see?"

"Ye have your reasons, sir."

"Aye, that I do. But it may please you to know I've changed my mind. The four of you may hide them again, if only to please Pilot Thorn, who apparently is willing to trade his hands for you."

The two sailors lost their composure then, looking uncertainly first at the captain, then to Thorn, then at each other.

"You are dismissed."

"Aye, aye, Cap'n," they both murmured together, retreating to the door, where Crabbel paused.

"Cap'n, sir," he said hesitantly.

"Yes?"

"Thank ye, sir." His mouth opened as if he wanted to say something else; then his lips compressed together and he nodded before stepping out.

"Thank you," Thorn said quietly, stroking Fitch, who was curled up on his lap, her stomach tight and round, purring.

Plusby shrugged. "It *was* stupid. We've got a sufficient headwind already without flaunting the charmers—I'd rather not have a mutiny, despite appearances that may suggest I am courting one." He drew a breath and shook his head as if to shake away clinging cobwebs.

"But now we must speak about our voyage. I shall not keep you long. Both of us should be in bed so the healing majick can do its work."

"A night of sleep won't cure us."

"No, but it is all we're getting. We'll weigh anchor on the afternoon tide, and we shouldn't wait that long."

Thorn raised his brows in a silent question. It was

verging on madness to take a new crew—and such a crew—out on a ship's maiden voyage with a crippled captain *and* Pilot. Plusby read his expression and laughed, shaking his head.

"Aye, it is foolish and insane, but this time it is not my insanity." He sobered, drawing a deep breath. "I have been instructed to tell you that although you have been crimped, you will be compensated—generously—for your service to the ship, as will the crew. The particulars of your wages are sealed in your desk and keyed to you personally. You may of course refuse to serve, but even so, the ship will hoist anchor and you will sail with us."

Thorn nodded. Crabbel had told him this much in the jolly boat.

"Perhaps I should add that I was given a similar offer—I need not captain the ship, but I would be sailing regardless. The crew were likewise hired."

"A fancy ship to turn over to such a motley crew as we seem to be," Thorn observed, struggling against the exhaustion weighing on him. His head felt thick and heavy and it was difficult to keep his eyes open. The effect of Meris's Tears was rapidly fading.

"Aye. And we're carrying expensive cargo."

"What is it?"

"There are jewels, perfumes, precious metals. But they are merely a camouflage, I believe."

"You believe?"

"I have been given a manifest—which I've been ordered to keep locked in my desk and destroy if necessary. It lists everything in the hold, including a vague entry titled 'mercantile goods.' I had the opportunity to tour the hold and found that a small portion in the forward compartment has been set off in a majicked bulwark."

Thorn frowned, waking up a little. "Majicked? Against you? That makes no sense. How will you off-load it?"

"A question I don't have the answer to, although I have my suspicions."

"Which are?"

"I currently have no idea where we are headed, though I have been informed that time is of the essence—the delivery of our goods must be made before the beginning of Mercy, and we're more than halfway through Forgiveness. It's been a rough storm season—with just six sennights, we'll be cutting it close, and that's if our destination is nearby."

The captain paused to sip from his glass and then continued.

"The rest of my instructions are sealed in a packet that I won't be able to open until we cross the Pale. I imagine our unknown cargo to be nearly priceless—what else justifies the expense of this ship, an unauthorized ship's compass, a crimped Pilot, and the attack at Grimsby Bay? Not to mention the majicked bulkhead . . . that's no mean majick. I'm guessing it took at least four majicars working together to even have a hope of getting it to stick on the open water."

Or one majicar who could control the waves. Thorn licked his lips, wondering if he should tell Plusby about the redheaded majicar. No, not yet. Plusby was focused now. Thorn didn't want to do anything to distract him, especially with something that didn't really matter at the moment.

Plusby sucked his teeth, his brows furrowing. He shook his head. "I can't figure it. And I don't mind telling you it makes my balls shrivel. I want it offloaded as soon as possible. I'd rather not end up on the Bramble quite so soon into my new captain's posting—not that merely being in possession of a black ship wouldn't be enough to send us all there."

"That's true enough. But if you're right, then we're more likely to end up somewhere with our throats cut than on the Bramble. No one involved in this will want word getting out."

"What could possibly be so valuable and so secret or illegal that they go to this much trouble and expense?"

"Blood oak is the only thing I can imagine, but the

crown recovered the piece that went missing during the storms just before Chance. There haven't been any other discoveries that I know of, though it's possible some was found and not reported," Thorn said.

Thorn lifted one of his bound hands as if to run it through his hair. He caught himself before he did, lowering it back to his lap. "But if that's the case, where would it be going? Smuggling it in—that's perfectly understandable. You avoid customs and fees and taxes. But smuggling it out? Who would want it? The only people who can make any use of it are our majicars."

"What if the Jutras could?"

The idea sent a chill rolling through Thorn's gut. The Jutras couldn't cross the Inland Sea. They had no Pilots and no compasses. Until two months ago, that had been the truth for several hundred years. Then a crippled Jutras warship limped into Blackwater Harbor, making the crossing despite the terrible, erratic dangers of the sea. They claimed that they had come so far into the sea by accident, chased by *sylveth* tides, Koreions, and wild winds. But as it turned out, they were invaders.

They had been fended off, though the queen had been killed and the Pale had been temporarily snapped. There were few enough details given to the papers. But the fact remained—the Jutras *could* cross the sea. Somehow. And if they could do that, then wasn't it also possible they had found a way to use the blood oak in their majicks? If the one was no longer impossible, why should the other still be?

Which meant that the *Eidolon* could be about to commit the highest possible treason.

Thorn stroked his bandaged hand over Fitch, feeling suddenly trapped. His lungs constricted and his dinner rolled uncertainly in his stomach. But then a realization began to dawn. He met Plusby's waiting gaze.

"You mean to sail anyway."

"I do."

"What if this cargo *is* blood oak? What if this allows the Jutras to invade Crosspointe?"

"What if it's ladies' undergarments? There's no way to tell and I'll not abort without proof. I've been off the waves for a season. I'll not miss another."

"And if the king sends ships after us? Or whoever sent the raiders and sabotaged the water supply. Whatever our cargo is, they don't mean for us to succeed," Thorn said.

"Have you heard of river pyrates?"

Thorn frowned. "What are you talking about? What does that have to do with this?"

"River pyrates. Small boats—schooners and ketches mostly—that run the rivers and the coasts. They steal from seagoing ships when they come into port, or more often steal from the towns themselves. They don't have compasses, so they don't risk the open seas, and during Chance they scurry up to the other side of the Verge to wait out the weather. Surely you've heard of them?"

"Of course. But I still don't see—"

But then Thorn did see, all too well.

"If it comes to it, we'll steal the ship and be the first sea pyrates." Plusby leaned forward. "When I lost Sherenya, I went a little mad. I admit that. I didn't think I could hurt worse, like I'd been flayed and disemboweled. But I was wrong. That next season, they pulled me before a captain's board and stripped my ticket. I died for the second time. I hardly remember what happened since. I've never been to such a dark place. But when I stepped onto the deck of this ship, suddenly I could draw breath again. I'm not going to end up dirt-bound again. I'll never get my ticket back, any more than your four charmers are ever going to get another legal berth. This is truly our last chance and I'm going to fight for it with all I've got."

He drew a careful breath, speaking slowly. "But you—you're another story. You're a Pilot, and you've been crimped. You have no reason but money to stay. There's a lot of money in standing on the legal side of the fence, and you have more to lose by piloting this ship than not."

He lifted a hand to stop Thorn's quick protest. "I heard what you said. You didn't get a ship assignment; you're as desperate to be here as we are. But that isn't true. If you go back, eventually they'll give you an assignment; they'll have to. There aren't enough Pilots to go around as it is. At least, that's what will happen so long as no one finds out you're piloting a black ship. Once that gets out, every door slams shut and you end up exposed on the Bramble like every other treasonous bastard who steals from the crown. By staying with us, you're giving up Crosspointe and your life there. Your friends, your family, your lovers. You give up your home, your possessions—and for what? Something you never really lost. Going back makes sense. Staying doesn't."

"Are you trying to talk me out of piloting the *Eidolon*? Are you sure you're not mad?"

"Maybe I am. But here's how I see it. There's nothing keeping you here and a powerful reason to escape. When you figure that out, when you realize what you've given up, you're going to step over the rail when we're close to shore and vanish, leaving us marooned." Plusby's lips twisted in a sardonic smile. "And there's not a damned thing I can do about it except shackle you to the post."

"I am not going anywhere."

"I'd like to believe that."

Thorn ran the tip of his tongue around the sharp edge of his teeth. "There's nothing in Crosspointe I care about." He smiled at Plusby's snort of disbelief. "All right. Would it make you feel any better to learn there's more than one reason for me to be here?"

"Like what?"

Thorn's gaze slipped to Plusby's bracelet. As he watched, the pattern shifted. He blinked, but the change remained. He tipped his chin at the bracelet. "Let's just say that you aren't the only one looking for answers about someone you lost."

Plusby jerked alert. "And you think you'll find the answers on this ship?"

"That's the promise," Thorn said quietly. He didn't want to talk about it anymore. "I'm tired. Best call Halford in. If we're to set sail tomorrow, I'd better rest while I can."

The captain's sunken eyes were turbulent with questions, but he said nothing as he yanked the bell. Bess and Halford swept inside as if they'd been waiting just beyond the door. The charm had disappeared from Halford's chest, though his expression remained as grim and forbidding as usual.

Thorn lifted Fitch back up onto his shoulder and allowed Halford to pull him to his feet. He sagged and the bosun caught him around the waist, pulling the Pilot's arm over his broad shoulder. At the door, Thorn paused and glanced back at Plusby, who had poured another full brandy, despite Bess's protests.

"You don't know me very well yet, Captain, but there are two things you ought to have realized by now. First, I'm a sailor as much as I am a Pilot, and second, I know how to hold a lifeline without letting go. This is my ship; this is my crew. The only way I'll abandon you is tits up."

He waited for Plusby's slow nod before nudging Halford out the door.

Back in his cabin, Halford set him on the chaise and began tugging off his clothing to check his dressings. He pulled a nightshirt over Thorn's head, then tugged off his boots.

"Leave the trousers," Thorn said, his eyes closing. His mind was foggy and he could hardly keep his head erect.

"Aye?"

Thorn grinned at Halford's doubtful tone. "I was a sailor before I was a Pilot. I've softened enough to take my boots off when I sleep, but not my trousers."

Before either could say more, there was a knock at the door. Halford answered, and Crabbel and Blot trailed in, leaving wet, snowy footprints in their wake. Thorn eyed them warily. He knew they were going to have something to say about the race up the mast and the damage he'd done himself. He gave a silent sigh. Better let them get it out of their systems.

"Something wrong?"

"Be it true ye climbed that mast for us?" Crabbel asked bluntly. "So we wouldn't have t' wear th' charms for all t' see?"

Thorn shrugged. "It wasn't the only reason."

"Be ye mad? Riskin' yerself that way and for us? You're a Pilot!"

As if that made him more important than the four of them. For a moment Thorn heard his father's voice lecturing him to behave better, to learn his proper place as a Truehelm. He felt his face stiffen and saw his three companions recoil from the expression.

"If there's one man left on a sinking ship and four of you are safely away—do you go back and try to save him, though you know it likely means you all die? Or do you save yourselves and let him suffer his fate?"

"What kind o' thing be that t' ask?" Blot demanded resentfully. "We'd never leave anyone behind!"

They glowered down at Thorn, their shoulders set as if for a fight. It was exactly what the captain believed they'd done to his wife, and they knew it.

"Exactly. There is your answer. Now, as I am very tired and we sail tomorrow, I'll ask you to kindly let yourselves out."

They didn't move.

"Something else?" Thorn asked with a sigh, tipping his head back to stare up at the ceiling. Fitch was sprawled on the back of the chaise and nuzzled against his cheek, licking his ear.

"Ye oughtn't have done it. Ye risked th' cap'n and yerself. It was foolish and selfish. Ye put th' whole ship in danger," Crabbel said.

Thorn twisted his head, glaring. "Yes. It was and I did. But it was also necessary."

"For us?"

"For the ship. And you are of this ship."

Crabbel was silent a long minute and then nodded. "We thank ye."

"You'd have done the same or worse."

Another thoughtful hesitation, another nod. "Good night, then," Crabbel said, heading for the door. Blot fell in behind.

"Good night."

But if the other two were satisfied, Halford was not. He helped Thorn into the private head, bristling with hard-held fury, then settled him none too gently onto the bed. He then wrestled the Pilot's ring off his pinkie finger and held it out.

"Here."

"Do you mind holding on to it? I'd hate to lose it." Thorn held up his bandaged hands. "Can't wear it."

Halford's jaw knotted, his lip curling. Clearly he did mind.

"What're ye about? Ye came close t' cripplin' yerself up on th' mast. Ye don't have a right! You're th' Pilot and this ship don't sail unless you're at th' compass. You're supposed t' keep yerself safe."

"Your concern is overwhelming," Thorn said drily. "But you are mistaken and this is the very last time I'm going to say it." His voice hardened into stone. "My job is to keep this ship and crew safe. If it costs a little pain and lost flesh, then I'm not going to quibble about it. Now, I want you to explain that to the rest of the crew. I'll consider it mutiny if anybody harangues me about it again."

Halford's mouth pursed like he wanted to spit, but he contained himself, holding the ring out. "This be yers. Ye take it back."

Thorn shook his head. "I can't wear it at the moment. And it opens nearly every lock in this room. If we lose it, we won't have access to the healing supplies and whatever other provisions are locked up here. Hold it for me. I trust you."

The last caught Halford up short. He glowered, then jammed the ring back on his finger, turning it so the *sylveth* compass was hidden inside his fist.

"Ye'd be wearin' it yerself if ye hadn't gone up th' mast like a damned fool."

"Careful," Thorn said softly, but then relented. "I'm fairly certain it was worth it."

"What did your pain buy ye? Four cursed sailors who ain't worth bilge."

"You are to me."

"What for? And after we crimped ye? Don't make sense, unless ye be lobcocked after all."

Thorn shrugged and yawned. "Fine. I'm lobcocked. Now will you go away so that I can sleep?"

Halford growled frustration. "You're a gods-damned thorn in me ass. Ye keep riskin' yerself. Givin' away your amulets and now ye'll be needin' 'em. What'll we do for a Pilot if ye die?"

"I suppose it will be your job to make sure I don't, won't it? Now go away or I'll be too damned exhausted to read the sea tomorrow and it'll be about the same for you as if I *had* died."

He turned over, only half-aware that Halford draped the bedclothes over him and settled uncomfortably on the floor—in case Thorn called him in the night.

Chapter 10

By afternoon of the next day, the snow had begun falling in slow, desultory flakes. Crabbel continued to shout orders at the crew as they spidered over the rigging, busting ice and scraping away snow. Crabbel kept them running in two-hour shifts all night and through the day. Most of the wounded were back to work, though he didn't push them as hard. He assigned some of them to guard the replenished water supply. Now he sent topmen up to remove the gaskets from the furled sails in preparation for getting under way. Halford and Blot had spent the morning swarming up and down the shrouds, checking knots, blocks and tackle, clew lines and leech lines—every rope and sheet.

Thorn had slept until Halford had shaken him awake in the midafternoon, a little over a glass before the tide would turn. He woke groggily, his body feeling stiff and unwieldy. His arms, shoulders, and legs were weak and shaky and refused to obey his commands. Halford helped him into the head and then dressed him like a doll, his expression as hostile as on the previous night.

"Where'd you get these?" Thorn asked, startled.

"Wardrobe. Be well provisioned for ye. And ye did give me th' key," Halford said, wiggling his fingers where he wore the compass ring.

Thorn glanced down at himself. The clothes were his own, though they had not been in the duffel that

Crabbel had stolen for him. It was the wardrobe he reserved for sailing, made up of serviceable wool and leather. Much of it was majicked against the wet and cold. He'd had those spells renewed during Chance, and though he found it unnerving to have had someone rifle through his things, he was glad to have them. But they were also a reminder of the fact that he'd been singled out and selected for this mission. Because he was dispensable. No one would miss him. His servants would think he'd been assigned a ship, as would the other Pilots, if they bothered to think about him at all. When he didn't return home at the end of the season, they'd assume he'd been lost at sea.

A numbing cold coalesced inside him. What sort of man lived his life so that no one would notice or care if he vanished?

He didn't resist when Halford finished buttoning his vest and then pushed him into the chair in front of the vanity.

"Cap'n says you're t' dine wi' him," Halford announced tersely as he dragged a comb through Thorn's snarled hair. Strands popped and chunks pulled free.

It was a good thing he wore the healing and pain amulets, Thorn thought, shaking his head no when Halford offered to shave him.

"I don't think I want to give you the chance at my throat."

Halford snorted. When he looked as respectable as Halford could make him, the bosun pulled Thorn upright, helping him into the outer room. Before he could drag his charge to the door, Thorn stopped him.

"Help me to the desk."

Halford muttered but did as he was told, settling Thorn into the chair.

"Wait outside."

When the door clicked shut, Thorn drew a slow breath and reached for the top middle drawer. It slid out easily under the light pressure of his bandaged hands, but he knew it was keyed to his touch. Had anybody else tried it, it wouldn't have budged.

Inside the drawer were an empty logbook, a sheaf of stationery, two sticks of blue sealing wax, a majicked candle flint, four pens, three bottles of ink (black, brown, and green), two orange grease pencils, two sticks of white chalk, and a folded letter sealed with crimson wax and bearing no discernible markings.

Thorn clumsily lifted the thick document between his bandaged hands and dropped it on top of the desk. He scowled at it; then holding it down with one of his hands, he pawed at the seal with the other. It didn't open, and majick closed the edges, preventing prying fingers from sliding inside.

"Braken's balls," he muttered. Then with his teeth he wrestled the bandages from his right hand. It took several minutes of yanking and gnawing to loosen up the wrappings enough to get his fingers out. The sight of them made his stomach lurch, bile spilling across his tongue. He swallowed forcibly, trying not to smell the stench, like rotting entrails. It was normal, he knew. It wasn't putrefaction, but rather a product of the majickal healing. And as bad as the wounds looked—as bad as they *were*—he could see the pink edges of new flesh starting to sprout along the bone.

He looked away. But there was no time for squeamishness. Grimacing, he scraped away the seal, leaving behind smears of the green ointment mixed with blood and bits of skin and tissue. The amulets kept him from feeling the pain, but his gorge rose violently again. He gagged and finally spit into a waste container.

There was no repairing Halford's careful bindings without help, and his hands continued to seep. He unfolded the pages awkwardly, holding the missive flat with his left forearm, letting the right rest out of sight beneath the desk in his lap.

The page was blank. But as he watched, words emerged into being on the page, sharpening into a bold, dark script. The letter was addressed to him—

Pilot Sylbrac, formerly Fish of Tideswell, formerly Geoffrey Radick Robert Truehelm, eldest son of the lord chancellor. The salutation shook him. Until he'd encountered the red-haired majicar in the fog, he'd thought barely anyone alive knew who he'd been; that no one but Jordan could connect Sylbrac to Fish or Geoffrey Truehelm. He'd thought his life was his own. He was wrong.

The letter jumped right to business. Of the two paragraphs that had shimmered into being, the first reiterated what Crabbel and Plusby had already told him. He could serve or not as he chose, but he would be sailing with the *Eidolon* into the open sea. The offered wages doubled the guild wage for a season of piloting. Added to that were cargo safe-delivery bonuses that amounted to a staggering five percent of the cargo's value on every run.

Thorn sat back, dumbfounded. Five percent . . . it was too much—like using a club to kill chicks. They wanted him badly enough to pay through the nose. And more than that. They wanted his swift, unquestioning cooperation. He snorted. The majicar might know his parentage and birth name, but she certainly did not know *him.* He wondered if Plusby had the same offer.

Just then there was a knock at the door. It opened before he could answer, and the captain entered, followed by Bess and Halford carrying platters of food and tea.

"I'm too hungry to wait for you." The captain's gaze sharpened on the open document. "Put those down and wait outside," he said to Bess and Halford without looking at them. "We'll call you when we need you."

He sat in a chair, kicking his feet out before him. "You've a look like someone bashed a belaying pin against your head. Let me guess. Five percent?"

Thorn nodded.

"Now you know why I wonder what's hiding in the hold. To spend the money they have, and to promise us ten percent, the mate, bosun, and steward a full percent each, and the rest of the crew a quarter of a percent per head—they want us to be dedicated to delivering this cargo, if only to line our own pockets. And handsomely too. But make no mistake, the bounty is really hazard pay. Does yours say anything else?"

"Only that I have to wait until we cross the Pale for further information."

"And the rest of the drawers? Do any open?"

Thorn tried the left side with no success and then awkwardly reached across himself to try the right.

"What's the matter with you?" Plusby asked. Then when Thorn lifted his right arm out of his lap and held it up, the captain swore. "Braken's cods, what have you done? Halford!" he bellowed.

The bosun flung the door open and thundered inside. His gaze skipped from the captain to Thorn's ravaged hand. He snarled.

"Do ye want t' be a cripple, then? Is that what you're after?"

"You don't have to worry. I don't need hands to run a compass."

Halford's head jerked up and he met Thorn's mocking gaze with a searing one of his own.

"If you're goin' t' have th' privilege of callin' us your crew, then your high and mightiness better get used t' us callin' ye ours," he said stonily. "And we don't like ye riskin' what's ours."

Plusby chuckled and Halford's head whipped around, his voice growing softer. "Funny, is it? Then ye'll be rollin' on th' floor t' know we figure as how ye belong t' us now, too. We couldn't save your missus. We won't be lettin' nothin' happen t' ye."

That caught Plusby up short. His face turned red, then white, and red again. Thorn laughed at his discomfort, earning a look of bitter wrath. His voice was guttural when he spoke.

"I'll thank you not to take your amusement at my wife's expense."

"Oh, but I am enjoying myself at *your* expense. It seems, my Dearest Captain Plusby, that *my* charmers have adopted *you*. Whether you like it or not. And I find that to be very amusing indeed."

Plusby sat back in his chair looking faintly poleaxed, watching with a hollow stare as Halford finished redressing Thorn's hand. When the big man was through, he hoisted Thorn up and lugged him to table, where he set about feeding him. The captain came to sit and a shroud of silence fell heavily over them as they ate.

Thorn studied his companion, but the captain's face was an inscrutable mask, his gray eyes reflecting like mirrors. He attacked his meal quickly and methodically, his silverware scraping and clicking with cold precision. Halford was equally dour as he forked food inside Thorn's mouth. Bess stood behind the captain's chair, her dark eyes crackling, though with anger or amusement, the Pilot couldn't tell. She caught him looking at her through the turgid silence and the corner of her mouth quirked. Ah, humor, then. Thorn winked at her, not minding in the least that he was the source of her entertainment, and then he obediently opened his mouth again, feeling quite certain Halford would jab him in the lips if he wasn't quick enough.

After the interminable meal was done, Halford and Bess cleared away the remains, leaving Plusby and Thorn alone. Cupping his bandaged hands around his tea and sipping it, the Pilot waited for the captain to explode. At last, when Plusby continued to stare at the tabletop saying nothing, Thorn spoke.

"Perhaps we both need mother hens to keep us under a wing. Apparently we've done a piss-poor job caring for ourselves. We must have set some sort of record, breaking out the healing provisions before we even hoisted anchor."

Plusby looked up, his gray eyes softening slightly. "Aye. You tore yourself up worse than I knew. I—" He broke off, grimacing.

"You're terribly sorry for damaging yourself on our

expedition up the mast and for being such a limp bag of guts on the climb down?" Thorn suggested helpfully. "And you feel dreadful that I tore my hands to bits because you were so weak and helpless."

"You really are a thorn in the ass, aren't you?"

"I doubt I'm any more painful to a dainty ass than you are. And now, joy of joys, we are both the adopted pets of the four charmers. I suppose you are to be congratulated for not strangling Halford right here on my rug."

Plusby looked away, his jaw jutting. The austere line of his silhouette reminded Thorn of the harsh, hooked features of a rock-eagle. Then the captain turned back, a shadow of a smile on his lips.

"I don't envy them the job of herding us about. But they are welcome to try."

"And of course we have no choice in the matter, so we ought to accept it gracefully or chance losing what dignity we have left."

"Aye."

Thorn awkwardly lifted his teacup. "A toast, then. Fair winds and following seas."

Plusby lifted his cup and drank, setting it down in the saucer with a click. "Tide's about to turn. Care to join me at the wheel?"

"If you think Halford will permit me to go outside in this weather." He pretended to shiver. "I might catch my death."

The captain smirked and stood. His gaze snagged on the letter still sitting on top of the desk.

"Should you put that away?"

Thorn glanced at it. The ink had faded again. He shook his head. "I don't see any reason to. No one else can read it. And even if they could, those aren't my secrets to keep."

Plusby nodded. "Fair enough. I'll fetch your lady's maid, then, shall I?"

As he was about to open the door, he turned.

"I just realized—Jordan Truehelm was your brother."

Thorn stared, taken aback. He had not expected to

hear Jordan's name spoken here. But he should have. His brother had been a ship captain. It was not strange that he and Plusby might have known each other. "Were you friendly with Jordan?"

"Aye. Not that we saw much of each other. He'll be missed."

"Aye."

The captain exited, sending Halford to help Thorn dress for the outside. Fitch trotted in beside the bosun, jumping up into Thorn's lap. She braced her forepaws against his chest and stood on her hind legs to sniff his face, her whiskers tickling over his skin. She purred loudly, unmindful of her damp fur.

"Ready to head for deep water?" he asked, stroking her clumsily.

"If she ain't, I be more than ready," came Halford's deep reply as he brought Thorn's boots, cloak, and hood from the bedchamber. "I'd be content t' not set foot on land again till Chance."

Thorn thought of their mysterious cargo. By Chance they might be prisoners of the crown and on their way to the Bramble for treason. The only thing valuable enough to merit the expense of this venture would also merit execution if they were caught. He was as sure of it as the sun.

"So we won't get caught," he muttered.

"What?"

"Tide's going slack," Thorn said loudly, snuggling Fitch into the crook of his arm and lurching to his feet. "Let's get on deck."

Chapter 11

The *Eidolon* cut sleekly through the waves, responding nimbly to the shift of the sails. Plusby stood at the wheel, his face tight with something akin to pain. Crabbel relayed the captain's orders with a carrying bellow that no one could ignore. The crew responded with alacrity. They raised the yards, lowered the sails, hauled the braces, and belayed the lines with an increasingly smooth and efficient rhythm.

But Thorn worried. They were working for the promise of riches and because Crabbel had run them ragged all night and all day. He'd hardly let them breathe on their own, much less shirk their duties or plot together. It couldn't last. Once the crew had a chance to settle and rest, there was a good chance they'd revolt against the discipline and against taking orders from charmers and a mad captain. It could get ugly fast.

Thorn's bandaged hand fell to his hip where his cutlass was conspicuously *not* hanging. It hadn't been included in the collection of belongings fetched from his home. His jaw tightened. He'd better find one.

They headed north, skirting west of the Caris Islands. Plusby was making a beeline toward the Pale, and Thorn knew it was no accident that the heading also took them near the Root, the mass of tangled mountain spines that thrust into the Inland Sea like rocky tentacles. They were a haven to spawn and difficult to navigate, because the channels that wove

through them were unpredictable and dangerous. Plusby's wife's ship, the *Sesio*, had gone down on the
northwest side of the Root's Upper Jaw, a far cry from
where the *Eidolon* was now. Still, it was a sensible
choice; they were running before the wind, the courses
and topsails drawing hard.

The breeze was stiff and the *Eidolon* dipped and
rose on the chop, spume breaking over her bow and
splashing across the deck. The snow stung Thorn's exposed skin and eyes. Blot and Ricker were overseeing
a gang assigned to busting ice on the forecastle and
foremast rigging. She was clearly furious at having
been paired with Blot. Thorn imagined that every time
she smashed at the ice, she was delivering a killing
blow in her mind's eye. But she was too busy to do
anything more rebellious—every geyser of spray over
the bow added another layer to the ice. Another gang
was scraping the deck with thin, dull blades attached
to long handles. They pushed the blades along the
wood, slush and ice curling up before them before
they pitched it over the side. The rest of the crew
manned the sails.

All in all, it was not, Thorn decided, an auspicious
beginning. The thought caught him up short. It was
what the redheaded majicar had said when the raiders
had attacked.

It was near to dusk when they finally crossed the
Pale. The necklace of tide and weather wards circled
Crosspointe, protecting it from *sylveth* tides and the
powerful Chance storms that spun *sylveth* into the air.
The only safe place on the Inland Sea during Chance
was within the Pale, or beyond the Verge—a twenty-
league-wide belt circling the edge of the sea.

The wards marking the Pale were green now, a sign
of safety. Crossing them would not be pleasant. It was
like being struck by lightning and battered by thunder
all at once. Those who'd not experienced it before
were often struck senseless for hours after. Those who
had made the crossing regularly were more inured to
its effects.

Thorn braced himself as they approached, his legs shaking both from the anticipation of being out on open waters and from weakness. As they drew closer, he felt the power of the wards pressing against his lungs and heart. He stiffened his spine, taking a breath and holding it.

When he woke, he was lying on the chaise in his quarters, Bess squatting beside him, waving smelling salts under his nose. Fitch lay on his chest, staring at him fiercely, her claws pricking through his clothing. When she saw his eyes open, she meowed and then began licking one of her paws nonchalantly. Thorn sniffed the acrid smelling salts and then coughed, rolling away. Fitch jumped for the back of the couch with an annoyed flick of her tail. Thorn's muscles refused to hold and he slumped back, eyeing the steward balefully.

"What happened?"

"You were Pale-blasted like a green snottie," Bess said, fetching a cup of tea liberally dosed with brandy and honey. She held it to Thorn's lips. "Drink."

The Pilot did as ordered, the liquor streaking through his stomach with searing warmth.

"What about the captain?"

"He did better than you. He didn't drop half-dead."

"How long have I been out? Where are we?"

"Half a glass. And we are holding our heading. The captain wants you. I'll fetch him."

Bess disappeared and Thorn closed his eyes, breathing slowly. He pressed the heels of his bandaged hands against his eyes; they felt like they were going to pop out of his skull. The brandy that had felt so comforting and warm only grains ago now bubbled in his stomach like acid. He groaned and let his arms flop heavily down. He lay there feeling like a child's discarded doll.

But in that quiet moment as he lay limp and spent, he became slowly aware of a *change. How could he have not realized it before?* His heart thudded, his entire body flooding with a pleasure and relief that were

beyond words. Tears trickled from the corners of his
eyes. Thank the gods. He could *feel* the realm of the
water again. Even without the compass, which would
extend his senses much further, he could feel the shifting terrain far beneath the hull, the delicious push and
twist of the currents, the pressure of the air against
the waves, the brush of the wind—

It was like waking from death.

"You told the bosun you can work the compass
without hands. Do you also plan to do it on your
back?" Plusby asked as he shouldered inside the
cabin, bringing with him a cold wash of salt air.

"If need be. The ship's in danger every moment I'm
not at the post."

The captain sat on the corner of the desk. "Crew's
wild. Seeing you drop like a stone upset them a bit.
They didn't like being in open water without a Pilot.
They seem to think you're to blame. They're getting
a mite angry."

"How much worse could they get after our Squall
Solution and my using the healing supplies on them?"

"Enough to make your charmers chew nails."

"They aren't just mine anymore. They claimed you
as well, remember?"

Plusby's smile was pained. "Aye. I remember. But
to business. If you are quite done napping?"

"For the moment."

"And there's no trouble on the horizon?"

Thorn shook his head. "Without the compass, I
can't sense far. But, no, at the moment there's nothing
that requires us to change course."

"Then let's see what our orders are."

The captain reached into his coat pocket and withdrew a thick, folded parchment—a twin to the one in
Thorn's desk. He unfolded it, waiting as the words
materialized. He nodded satisfaction. "As promised,
there is more."

"What does it say?"

"It says—" Plusby broke off, frowning. "No, this
can't be right."

"What?"

"It says they want us to make for Roche Bay and go up the Saithe River to Calenfor."

Thorn stared, taken aback. "Take the *Eidolon* all the way to Calenfor? Is it even possible?"

"I've done it with other vessels, and this ship is narrower than most, with nimble lines. We'll have to use poles or kedge her through some of it. We can always hire locals to help, use mules to haul us up."

Thorn eyed the captain doubtfully. The Saithe River emptied into Roche Bay just east of the base of the Root. It was dangerous enough to sail those waters—the Jutras ran raids on ships headed up the Saithe. Not to mention the fact that sailing anywhere near the Root was a dangerous proposition—the currents were always worse there, the winds more unpredictable, and the shore was rocky and unforgiving. But once safely in the bay, there was the problem of getting up the river. Going as far as Lalant Uly, Azaire's capital city, was hard enough. It was the gateway to Glacerie, Esengaile, and Avreshar, which made the effort worthwhile. But Calenfor was nearly a hundred leagues farther north. They'd have to use light sail, if any at all. It was too easy to get blown up on the banks. And then there was the ever-present danger of a Jutras attack.

"Why all the way to Calenfor? Why not trade it off at Lalant Uly and use a mule tug or river barge to move it the rest of the way?"

Plusby pinched his lip. "Likely they wanted to keep the majick protections in place as long as possible."

"The crew is not going to like this."

"The crew is going to cracking well hate this," the captain corrected.

"On the bright side, they'll probably mutiny long before we get there and we'll be dead. Saves us the trouble of getting up the river. What else does it say?"

"There's a warning here not to go haring off in search of Sherenya, but to stay focused on our task. It also warns to be wary of the Jutras. As if I needed to be reminded. They also mention the majicked bulk-head. And that under no circumstances should I allow the ship and cargo to fall into the wrong hands."

"The question is, aside from the Jutras, who would that be? The crown? Or someone else altogether?"

"They aren't specific. But maybe yours says more," Plusby said. "If you aren't too tired to have a look?"

"Give me a hand up."

The captain did as bidden, helping Thorn to the chair at his desk. The letter remained on top of the desk and unsealed, requiring only that Thorn flatten it back out. At his touch, the words slowly appeared, but now the page was full.

Thorn scanned through it.

"They warn me first about you—that you are unstable and may ignore me or take the *Eidolon* into danger. That I should beware that the charmers were part of the crew that survived your wife's shipwreck and you may take revenge on them."

Plusby swore, his face flushing as he strode across the room, coming to a halt in front of the bulkhead and standing stiff, his legs spread. He stared at the wall a moment before turning around. His nostrils flared white. "I'm getting sick of these people knowing so much about me."

"There's more; do you want to hear it?"

"I'd better. Forewarned and all that bilge."

"It cautions me to be careful, since the crew may be nervous and defiant and are 'slightly disreputable.' Imagine that, they are disreputable. On a black ship."

"Hard to believe. Are there any more revelations?"

Thorn smiled and pawed at the top page with his ungainly hands and read the paragraph on the second page. "Same as you. Don't let the cargo fall into the wrong hands, but no specifics. Watch out for the Jutras. We'll receive more instructions once we near Calenfor."

He folded the letter back and it sealed itself. He opened the drawer to put it away and froze. On top sat two more letters. They hadn't been there before.

There was only one person he could imagine who could have picked the majickal lock and put them there—the red-haired majicar. He drew a slow breath.

"What's wrong?" Plusby asked, coming to stand over him.

Wordlessly Thorn groped the note with Plusby's name between his hands and dropped it on the top of the desk.

"These weren't here before."

Plusby's lips pinched together and slowly he reached for the letter. It was a single page. He opened it. His face went white. A spasm flickered over it. Pain. Hope. Loss. He sank to his knees, crushing the page as his hands tightened.

"What is it?" Thorn tried to stand up, but was still too weak. He fell back into his chair.

The captain's mouth opened, but no words issued forth. Jerkily, he tossed the page onto the desk.

On top, side by side, were two images in brilliant color. They looked like Plusby's marriage bracelet, though as Thorn looked closer, he realized the two were different. As he watched, the pattern in the weaving shifted. He started and drew back, staring at the captain, who was sitting on his heels, his hands loose on his knees, his head drooping to his chest. The pose was one of utter desolation and helplessness.

"Is it—?"

"The left one is mine."

"The other one—?"

"Sherenya's."

"How can you be certain?"

"Look at the ruby beads. They never move. Any more than the emeralds on mine move."

Thorn bent close over the page. Plusby was right. The patterns continued to shift like water over the sand. Then he noticed the writing below. "*By the gods* . . . ," he said softly.

"What?"

Thorn shook his head. "Read it."

Plusby reached for the page, his hands trembling.

He stared at the three words there for more than a minute. At last he looked up. "She is alive." He swallowed hard. "I always thought . . . the bracelet kept changing so . . . But if she were alive, Sherenya would have come to me. She would let me know how to find her." His voice broke on the last.

Thorn put a hand on the captain's shaking shoulder. "Maybe she couldn't. Or—" He stopped abruptly.

"Or?"

"Or someone has been keeping her from you."

He wondered if the red-haired majicar could be so cold-blooded. She was affected by Jordan's death, enough to offer Thorn a chance to escape. But he remembered her eyes as she watched the fighting on the ship. There had been regret there certainly, but there had also been unflinching resolve. She might have offered him the chance to escape, but he would still have been without a ship. A meaningless gesture.

He looked at the other letter on the desk, reluctant to see what it might contain. Slowly he reached for it. This time the seal sprang open easily. He unfolded the paper with trepidation and read:

> *Beware the recall contingency.*
> *Jordan would have willingly sailed this ship.*
> *I will have answers for you.*

And it was signed:

> *Lucy Trenton*

Now it was Thorn's turn to stare in blank shock. Lucy Trenton. The very same woman who'd been accused of Jordan's murder and then exonerated of it. His attention moved to the first two lines. He began shaking his head, his mouth going dry.

"You've gone gray," Plusby said. "What do they have to say to you?"

Thorn turned his head, feeling as if he'd fallen down a deep hole with water rushing in.

"There are some things you need to know," he said in a hollow voice.

Plusby's expression was wary. "Do tell."

"You know of the Jutras attempt to invade Crosspointe?"

The captain nodded slowly, his eyes narrowing. "It was all the papers wrote about for sennights."

"You know too that because of that plot, my brother, Jordan, was murdered. He was the only member of my family who was worth a damn. They accused Lucy Trenton—"

Plusby was nodding. "She was the niece of the king, and a customs official. If I remember, they accused her of smuggling and treason. They said she started the fire that burned most of Salford Terrace. She ended up on the Bramble—they didn't discover she was innocent until after Chance had begun and it was too late to save her or the rest of her family and friends who were convicted with her. Some say it was all a plot against the throne. A tragedy."

"Not really. It turns out she didn't die on the Bramble and she didn't become spawn. At least, not exactly."

"Not exactly? What does that mean? And how do you know this?"

Thorn brushed the hair out of his eyes, slouching in his chair and looking up at the ceiling. "I saw her a couple of times at the Dabloute—the Pilots' Guild headquarters. I didn't know who she was. Then after I was crimped, she visited me. Offered me the chance to escape. She said it was because of Jordan. That they'd been friends and he wouldn't have forgiven her if she didn't give me a choice. I had no idea that anybody knew Jordan and I were brothers. I still didn't know who she was, but then she offered me answers. If I sailed for her, she'd tell me what really happened to my brother. I *have* to know. So I did not run."

He took a deep breath. Plusby wasn't going to like the rest of it. "I saw her once more. She was there

that day when the raiders came. That wave wasn't
Braken's blessing. It was her. She's a majicar and a
powerful one."

Thorn watched as Plusby pushed to his feet and
paced slowly back and forth in front of the desk. The
captain frowned, the lines of grief still carved deeply
into his face.

"You said . . . she didn't exactly become spawn.
What does that mean?"

Trust the man to hook right into the one thing that
Thorn hadn't meant to say. But he didn't have a
choice now. Lying would undo all the trust they'd built
between them. Not that he was breaking any oaths by
telling Plusby. The secrets weren't his. Not since the
guild had sold him. He didn't owe them anything anymore. But he did owe this ship and this captain and
this crew. He'd signed on as their Pilot and he wasn't
going to risk them. The trouble was, telling was as
much a risk as not. He licked his dry lips, wishing for
a drink.

"How do you suppose I became a Pilot?" he asked.

Plusby was taken aback. "What does that have to
do with this?"

"Indulge me. How do you suppose I became a
Pilot? How do you suppose any of us do?"

The other man shrugged. "You're born with a talent. They say that when it wakes, you all head to
water like foxes to henhouses. The guild trolls the
harbors and beaches, looking for you."

"It's true enough, as far as it goes. Something in
the water sings to us." He hesitated. "*Sylveth* sings to
us. It calls us and we can't refuse. Sometimes we board
a ship, sometimes we row, sometimes we just swim.
But we go to the water and we keep going, out beyond
the Pale. We keep going until we touch *sylveth*. 'The
path to becoming a Pilot is through the blood of Meris
and breath of Braken,' " Thorn quoted softly. "If
you're meant to be a Pilot, you are." He tapped a
finger against the corner of one eye, calling attention
to the black filaments unwinding through his eyes. "If

not . . ." He shrugged, dropping his hand. "If not, then you become something else."

Plusby had jerked to a halt. His eyes were wide; his mouth hung slack.

"That's right. I'm *sylveth* spawn. Every Pilot is. And not just us. Majicars too."

The captain sagged down onto the chaise. "Spawn," he repeated stupidly. "You aren't joking, are you?"

"Is it funny?"

Plusby opened his mouth and then shut it, shaking his head.

"Well, you've not tried to stick me in the heart yet or bash me in the skull," Thorn said. "That's hopeful."

"What are you blathering about?"

"What else do you do with spawn?"

"Don't be an ass."

"I must say, you're taking this rather well."

"I need a drink." And suiting action to words, Plusby went to the sideboard and sloshed brandy into a couple of glasses and set one on the desk in front of Thorn.

"Thank you."

Plusby drank deeply, and began wandering aimlessly around the cabin. Thorn watched him. His revelation had distracted the other man from his own letter and drawn him out of his desolation.

"There's more."

"More than Pilots and majicars being spawn? I can't wait."

"Trenton's note mentions the recall contingency."

"The what?"

"Another Pilot secret. If Crosspointe is in danger, it is possible to send a signal to every ship to recall it home for defense or evacuation."

"How?"

"Through the compass."

Plusby eyed Thorn narrowly. "I've never heard of it."

"In four hundred years it's never been necessary. Why would you know about it?"

"And our compass?"

"It will have the capability."

"And if the ship doesn't want to return?"

"Pilots are sworn to guide their ships back home and only home when recalled. They may not go anywhere else for any reason. Certainly a captain and crew may refuse to obey the summons, but if so, the Pilot will no longer stand at the post."

"Very tidy."

"Aye. And if I'm understanding the letter correctly, whatever we're carrying in the belly of the *Eidolon* is enough to trigger the recall contingency. It can only be blood oak, which means this is no longer just a smuggling venture. We are most certainly committing treason."

"Technically smuggling is treason."

"Very well, then. We're involved in high treason. What if this is another plot to overthrow the crown? Less than two months ago, the Jutras almost gained a foothold on Crosspointe. They snapped the Pale. The trouble is, Lucy Trenton also says my brother would have willingly helmed this ship. You knew my brother. He was no traitor."

"She might be lying."

"It's possible. Likely, even."

"But you don't think so."

Thorn sighed in frustration. "She gave me the chance to escape. She told me it was because of Jordan. He confided in her about me. She *knew* him. And he trusted her. Can I do less? But then, I wonder. Am I working so hard to talk myself into this because I want the answers she promised me? If she's right and Jordan *would* helm this ship, then it *can't be* treason. But what other explanation can there be for this ship? The expense of it?"

"I don't know. But we only have conjecture that it's treason. There's no proof."

Thorn folded his arms, just looking at him. Plusby tossed one hand in aggravation and began pacing again.

"The question is," said Thorn, "what if we *are* carrying blood oak? What do we do then?"

Plusby came to stand in front of the desk, legs braced defiantly. "We cross that bridge if we come to it. The fact is that we don't know for certain that we are carrying blood oak or if it's kitchen crockery. But this—" He tapped the page with the images of the bracelets on it. "This is proof that your Lucy Trenton knows where my wife is. Are you prepared to give up the answers about Jordan's murder because you *think* we might be carrying blood oak?"

Thorn hesitated. Slowly he shook his head. "No."

"Then let's set the compass and get to Calenfor. We'd better hurry. The trade has to be made by the end of Malevolence. That's less than six sennights."

Chapter 12

The captain gathered the crew for the setting of the compass. It would boost morale, Thorn knew. Not only to have it sitting on its post like a sentinel watching over a castle keep, but also to see Thorn standing beside it, reading the depths. He *was* the ship's guardian and until he stood at the post, they were essentially sailing blind.

They circled him, standing on the deck and up on the shrouds. Their silence was accusing and furious, but their expressions were more than a little hopeful. They ranged in age from snotties to grizzled veterans. There were twenty-four, including the captain and Thorn. Seven were women, and everyone, young to old, was hard-bitten and as unyielding as ice. Ricker stared at Thorn with her fierce eyes, her hands gnarled and red. From those alone he'd have known she was a sailor. Beside her was Alby Sark, who looked no less stern. Wragg and the two wounded women—Mudge with the nearly severed leg, and Dekay with the ribs and collarbone—had been helped out onto the deck. No one missed the setting of the compass. Wragg appeared hale enough, standing without aid. But he glowered at Thorn through bloodshot eyes. The women were wan and abashed, the other members of the crew except the charmers standing apart from them as if they were contagious.

The compass was stowed in a hatch flush with the deck and situated just before the post. As with the desk and letter, Thorn's touch was required to key the majickal lock. He squatted and hooked his bound fingers under the handle and lifted it, thankful for the amulet that kept him from feeling the pain of it. The compass was wrapped in a silk shroud the color of yellow wine. Halford helped him lift it out and settle it on the deck, and then untied the lacings before standing back.

Thorn pushed back the silk. The thirty-two rays of the compass were made of pearly *sylveth* that gleamed like white opal in the bruised light of the sunset. In the center was a crimson *sylveth* cabochon the size of a baby's head. As Thorn finished pulling away the silk wrapping, he heard an audible *ah* from the onlooking sailors.

He eyed the compass with a roiling mixture of longing and dread. Setting it on the post was going to be very difficult and Halford could not help him. It was a Pilot's responsibility and privilege. In his current condition, Thorn wasn't entirely sure he'd be able to do it. Except that there was no choice. They didn't have time to run back to safety behind the Pale until he healed. He just had to move as quickly as possible and not get distracted.

The four cardinal directions extended a handbreadth farther than the ordinal rays, which extended the same length farther from the minor rays. The edges and tips of the four cardinal directions were softly rounded, the rest sickle sharp—the merest touch would split flesh. In lifting the compass, Thorn had to hold it well away from his body or find himself sliced through. He hoped he'd have the strength; he'd rather not disembowel himself on the deck. Halford would be annoyed. The crew would riot.

Thorn drew a steadying breath, clenching his teeth as he reached wide, gripping around the east and west points. Instantly he was spinning inside a euphoric whirlpool of sensations. The sea became an extension of his flesh. Along his fingers he could feel the shift of the seafloor west of the Root by Tiro Pilan. Along his belly he felt the sliding shift of *sylveth*, coiling like a ball of eels in the Hatrine Bay far to the southeast. He could smell Koreions near the Bramble and taste knucklebones off Normengas. Currents rolled along his spine, spreading tentacles around his neck, torso, and limbs. He held still, wonder unfurling inside him. He'd never sensed so far, so clearly. . . .

But tainting the bliss was a heavy, bitter, clawing *want*.

The *sylveth* of the compass . . . *remembered* . . . flowing free through the black waves. It ached to escape the majickal bindings that hardened it and shaped it to use. The tempering hurt it still. It was so *close* to the sea now, so close. . . . All it needed was to slip beneath the black waves. Eventually a tide of raw *sylveth* would find it, engulf it, free it. It hungered to return to what it was, to burst the bonds that held it to rigid purpose. Oh, how it *hungered*!

Thorn gasped, his face twisting with agonized effort. Never had he felt the compass-yearning so strongly. Worse, he empathized with the desperation and longing in a way he never had before. He knew loss intimately now. But he couldn't afford to give in. He held lives in his hands.

He levered himself up, staggering backward under the weight—the compass weighed well over fifty pounds. Halford's hand between Thorn's shoulders steadied him. Carefully he lifted the compass up so that its fiery heart was directly above the post. With shaking arms, he lowered it, settling it gently on the silver column. A sensation like someone was trying to yank his bones from their bed of muscles clutched him, and then the compass settled. There was a brilliant flash of ruby light and silver radiance coruscated out to each of the thirty-two points, and the feeling of *want* muted nearly to silence.

Thorn staggered back, bracing himself on his knees and panting raggedly. The crew continued to wait in a hushed circle. He could see the fear on their faces, in the hunched set of their shoulders and the tight narrowing of their eyes. From the still-open hatch, he withdrew a wide band of hammered silver shaped like the rays of the compass with rolled edges where the cardinal points should have been. Slowly he straightened. He set it over the top of the compass. The pointed bezel fit over the sharp edges of the minor points, the rolled edges sliding gently over the middle of each of the major points. It would protect anyone who accidentally bumped into it, keeping the person from being sliced in half.

He extended his bandaged hand over the ruby cabochon, holding it several inches above. When he spoke, his voice was little better than a rasp. He coughed and began the ceremonial words again.

"Braken, bless our road with fair winds and following seas. Meris, grant your charity. Guide us so that calamity does not overtake us on our journey. Chayos, lend strength to our timbers that our ship does not fail us in our need. Grace of the waters, grace of the skies, grace of the forest, be ours and crown our journey with success that we may safely return home."

Thorn lowered his hand and settled it over the cabochon. Once again his senses exploded outward through the sea—nearly shore to shore. It was dizzying. He locked his knees against the weakness quaking down his legs. He'd never experienced such clarity at such distance. It was almost too much to take in.

"Do you have a report, Pilot?" came Plusby's voice, intoning the traditional query that followed the benison.

"Shoals rising southeast of the Hook and running the length of the Bites. *Sylveth* tide in Hatrine and circling the Bramble. Knucklebones off Normengas and Lanivet . . . another south of the Leg. Chaos current spinning south of Roche Bay. Storm building in the Gallows. It'll drive south-southeast by morning." He paused, his head tilting as if he were listening, but the sounds he heard weren't sounds at all, but more like phantom touches from thousands of fingers. He turned to look at Plusby. "It may bring a swarming."

Plusby sucked his teeth and spun, looking for Crabbel.

"Mate! Split the watch. Lay first and second watch aloft and send third to the mess. Rotate them through quickly while there's time to fill their bellies. Then hang them in their hammocks on two-hour shifts. Put Blot and Ricker second and third mates to head the watches."

Crabbel didn't wait to hear more but started bellowing orders, and the crew scattered quickly to their assigned duties. Plusby stepped close, speaking low so that only Halford and Thorn could hear.

"We'll tack around to the south of Crosspointe, cut around the southern tip of the Bramble, and approach Roche Bay from the southeast. And pray to the gods we don't get swarmed. Halford, I want my Pilot fed and rested—two hours' sleep shift, then a check on the compass, then another two hours. No arguments," he said when Thorn would have protested. "Once that storm drives out of the Gallows, there'll be no chance to stand down and if there's a swarming, we'll need you. Rest now while there's time."

Thorn nodded and allowed Halford to support him as they retreated back into his cabin. They'd gone only two steps when Wragg blocked the way. He said nothing, holding out the three sets of amulets Thorn had given the wounded sailors. Thorn took them, tucking them in his pocket. Wragg walked away without a word. The charmer set to work hauling in lines. He did not appear to favor his arm.

"Well, at least he didn't break my jaw," Thorn said to Halford as they went into his cabin.

"He be grateful," Halford growled. "Ye want him t' lick your boots?"

"No. No, I don't want anything from him."

But he lied. He was tired of the angry glares and silence. He wanted the friendship that had begun to blossom between them on the journey from Blacksea to Grimsby Bay. It was foolish. Pilots didn't have friends. They had duties.

As he lay down on his bed, Thorn thought of the massive storm forming in the Gallows. He hoped it was slow moving.

In two hours, the storm was still churning inside the Gallows, which was a stretch of sea bordered on the east by the Root and on the south by the Leg, a long, thin peninsula ending in a knot of islands, leaving just a narrow forty-league channel between them and the Verge to get into the Gallows. Storms liked to build there, but when they broke across the Leg into the open sea, they were formidable, vicious beasts. Their power churned the *sylveth* in the sea, pulling it in and spitting it back out in spattering globs so that it was much harder to avoid. Waterspouts were not uncommon, and neither were knucklebones and schools of ship-eating vescies. The dangers swarmed, summoned by and driven ahead of such storms. All any ship could do was try to run ahead of them and find a protected cove and beach itself, or else slip inside the safety of the Pale.

By the time Halford woke Thorn, the *Eidolon* had dropped to the southwest of Crosspointe and was making its turn toward the east. But the winds were becoming erratic. The crew shifted the braces, and the sails would suddenly luff and bag empty. The swells were growing taller. The wind whistled through the rigging and spume sprayed over the deck, water running off through the scuppers, which iced up regularly and had to be cleared.

Thorn's second read on the compass brought more bad news. Another storm was building offshore, south of Normengas. It was too far away and on land, so he couldn't touch it the way he could the Gallows storm, which had turned sharp and biting. It made him glad for the pain-deadening amulet.

The second storm was faster, bringing with it warm,

dry air. The Gallows storm was cold and slow. The
two were heading for a collision directly west of Crosspointe. When they met, the resulting storm would be
massive. And the sea would swarm. Thorn wasn't sure
the *Eidolon* could get far enough away to avoid the
danger.

"How long?" Plusby asked tersely when Thorn
made his report.

"They'll merge in two days at best. Things will
speed up then. It will be bad, Captain. I don't think
we'll have seen worse in the last twenty seasons." He
didn't say what else he was thinking. That they ought
to be putting in to Crosspointe until it was over. Or
at least beach the ship until the storm abated. Plusby
knew it as well as he did.

"Let's get up behind the Bramble, and if time and
wind permit, we'll try to make Roche Bay. With luck,
the storm will turn south and spend itself over land."

"That's a sucker bet."

"Aye. But we are a black ship. We can no longer
just sail inside the Pale and drop anchor. No, we make
for Roche Bay and pray the gods smile on us. Go
sleep now. There won't be much rest for any of us
later."

The next two days were tense and the winds fickle.
One moment they followed; the next they sheered
abeam; then suddenly they flip-flopped and came from
the opposite beam. The currents were little better.
Thorn was able to guide the ship away from downstream currents, but the waters shifted constantly. A
shoal would suddenly surge up, blocking their passage
and changing the action of the waves. The captain
called him out to the compass frequently to read the
heading and then sent him back for healing sleep. It
was working, although slowly. By the end of the second day, his hands were sheathed in new muscle and
a delicate layer of skin. The latter was nearly transpar-
ent and looked like it would tear apart like wet paper,

but the healing would need only four or five days more to be complete. Thorn was still weak and groggy, and weariness sapped his strength.

Plusby was healing slightly faster, despite getting less rest. He slept in short three- or four-hour blocks, spending the rest of the time at the helm. The snow let up, but the spray from the waves froze in thick heavy layers on every inch of the ship. The watches hammered away at the ice, even as the current and wind shifted erratically, the ship now rolling, now yawing, now charging ahead over the swells. By the end of the second day, they were twenty leagues off the Bramble and too far north, the wind on the starboard quarter. They were caught in a powerful current that was carrying them on a curving course back around into the jagged shores of the Upper Jaw, one of three long spits of land that jutted far out into the sea from the bottom of the Root.

Thorn stood at the helm as the captain called orders and the crew hauled the braces around, trying to catch a heading that would pull them across the current toward the turbulent tidal waters of the Bramble and keep them from turning sideways into a trough—they'd be swamped. Their goal was a narrower current that was flowing southward along the Bramble's edge. It was risky. They could overshoot the mark and end up driving aground, or else get turned broadside to the breaking waves and capsizing. But cutting back the way they'd come toward Crosspointe would take them into the storm's path, if they didn't get slammed against the rocky jut of the Tongue first. Then their only choice would be to venture across the Pale and wait out the storm. No one was willing to chance getting caught by customs or the Crown Shields.

Halford stood behind Thorn, buttressing him against the erratic pitch and roll of the deck. Waves crashed over the bow and swirled ankle deep around them. The *Eidolon* began to tack again. Thorn ignored the commotion as sails luffed and the braces swung. His focus was on the sea, one hand locked around the south-pointing ray of the compass, the other pressed flat to the crimson cabochon in the center.

The two storms had merged just east of Normengas's Benacai Bay in the last hours. Already Thorn could feel the sea beginning to swarm.

Knucklebone weirs erupted and then vanished in the space between heartbeats. *Sylveth* flowed from nowhere toward the center of the maelstrom, winding and tangling in a mad, twisting, swirling net. Schools of vescies, voracious bottom-feeding creatures from the depths of the Inland Sea, began to rise in swelling, undulating masses. Herds of Koreions stirred from their nests and began to swim. The storm would pull all of them in and then scatter them back out like weapons.

Thorn could see the Bramble rising from the black waves to the east, its snowcapped serrated spine gleaming.

"Hard-a-lee!"

And they tacked again, east now on a direct collision course for the long island. But the current quickly pulled them north and west. Again they tacked. Slowly they zigzagged across the narrow stretch.

"Almost there," Thorn said.

Halford relayed the message to Plusby. Closer. The ship pitched and bucked. *Closer.* Thorn raised his hand in the air. In the moments before they hit the southern current, they had to spill the wind and haul the yards around, or they might find themselves out of control and foundering beneath the towering waves.

His hand dropped. Plusby shouted. Suddenly the sails luffed. The *Eidolon* rode forward, carried by her momentum, the northern current pulling strongly against her. But then they hit the southern current. The ship shuddered, caught between the sheering forces. She gave a twisting roll, the masts swinging ominously downward to the port. A wave caught them astern and the *Eidolon* yawed, rearing out of the water

and crashing down hard even as she slewed drunkenly around.

Plusby was shouting orders and the spanker and jib
sails were deployed, followed quickly by the topsails.
Suddenly the wind caught and the ship seemed to
grind to a halt. Then she surged forward on a southern
heading, heeling sharply to the starboard, the rail
scraping the tops of the waves. Plusby called orders
to trim the sails, and slowly the *Eidolon* straightened,
running swiftly over the waves.

Thorn's knees sagged and he clutched the compass
for balance. Halford gripped him around the waist.

"Can ye stand?"

"Aye. For now."

He straightened, feeling tremors running down his
legs. "Damn."

"Ye look white as milk."

"I'll not faint, if that's what's worrying you."

Halford snorted, saying nothing more. But when
Moth ran by, he sent the girl for hot soup and sweet
cream tea laced with brandy. When she returned,
Thorn accepted them gratefully, continuing to brace
against the bulky bosun as he drank.

Running the current so close to the Bramble was
dangerous. Several times breaking waves and tangled
tidal currents caught them, shoving them inward to
the shore. Plusby ratcheted a constant stream of orders and the watches responded with alacrity. Whatever fears Thorn had had about the crew rebelling
had been laid to rest. The size of the storm and the
unrelenting danger had pulled them together. They
had no time nor energy to consider mutiny.

The current carried them well south of the Bramble
and back into the path of the storm before they could
make the wide turn to the northeast. Their heading
brought them half a league offshore of the Bites, a
long stretch of forbidding coastline running from
Bokal-Dur to the Naz Peninsula. The cliffs rose like
scalloped fortress walls, gray and impenetrable except

for the occasional vee-shaped crack splitting their featureless expanse. Along the base of the cliffs were
protrusions like snaggled teeth—there was no safe
place to make a landing along the Bites. To the southeast was the former Tapisriya, and to the northwest,
the former Relsea—this entire coast now belonged to
the Jutras, which meant Jutras warships. They might
not be able to navigate the open waters, but they were
thick in the coastal waters, the dangers of the sea
being less potent along the shore.

The wind was increasing and the *Eidolon* was running close-hauled, tacking often to make headway.
Thorn was exhausted. He was relatively dry, thanks
to the majickal protections on his cloak and clothing,
and the body-and-soul lashings wrapping his arms and
boots to keep the drenching water out. But his mind
was thick and muzzy and his face and hands were icy
on the compass. His teeth chattered and he was as
weak as a babe. Halford was a silent, stolid presence,
unmoving as a brick wall. Without him, Thorn would
have fallen and likely been swept overboard by one
of the powerful waves sluicing the decks.

Darkness fell over them like a mourning shroud.
Thick, lead clouds obscured the moon and stars, making it impossible to see, and the wind carried snow on
its back. Only Thorn's awareness of the changes along
the seafloor and the waves kept them safe. He concentrated his attention on the closely surrounding sea, no
longer able to focus on the broader reach. He held
on for what seemed like seasons. But exhaustion, his
injuries, and the cold conspired against him. Fractures
threaded across his fragile focus. Dizziness shook his
hands and his head swirled so that he could hardly
hold his thoughts together. And before he could warn
of the powerful surge in the ocean just off the starboard bow, he slumped, unconscious.

Chapter 13

Thorn woke in his bed. Moth stood over him, shaking his shoulders. When she saw he was awake, she retreated to the door to summon the captain. Plusby strode in, eyeing his Pilot with undisguised worry and anger. He was haggard, his gray eyes sunken and looking bruised in his exhaustion. The lines around his mouth were deep and his hair and beard were matted and wild. Thorn blinked at him confusedly, rubbing his gritty eyes and struggling to push himself upright. Panic streaked through him as memory intruded. He thrashed at the bedclothes. "Uprising on the starboard bow!"

"Aye and well enough do we know it," Plusby said tightly. "Rammed it square. Cracked the bowsprit and a couple of ribs and we're taking on water. We need to put in somewhere if we're going to make real repairs. For now we're fishing the bowsprit and hoping it'll hold, and making makeshift repairs on the ribs. In these seas, we'll suffer for not having the jibs and the forestay sail, but there's no time to unreeve the stays and fix them through the hawseholes." He paused, tapping his hand against his thigh. "We've seen Jutras sails southwest of here. There's no more time to waste; we've got to get under way. I am beginning to think we truly are cursed."

Thorn looked away, unable to hold Plusby's gaze. His mouth twisted and he slumped, running his bandaged hands over the top of his head in frustration.

"My apologies, Captain. It seems you have chosen a poor Pilot."

"Meris's tits, man. You fainted."

As if that were an excuse and not a condemnation. "Aye. I should not have."

"I should not have tried to rip my own arm off and made you rescue me off the mast. But recriminations aside, I would welcome you on deck. Are you able?"

Thorn swung his legs over the side of the bed and stood. But the cabin spun and he swayed and staggered, catching himself on the bedpost. "Braken's balls!"

"Can you stand post?"

"I can. I will."

"For how long?"

Thorn hesitated. His body had never failed him so completely. Shouldn't the healing amulet be doing more for him? Perhaps it was depleted. "I don't know."

Plusby made a sound of exasperation and went back to pacing. Finally he stopped. "All right, then. We'll strike north and stick close to the coast. I know of a couple sheltered coves off Relsea—where Relsea used to be," he corrected himself. "Hopefully we'll manage to outrun the Jutras and be able to hide."

"Wouldn't the Bramble be safer?"

Plusby shook his head. "Nowhere to put in on the eastern coast, especially in heavy weather. And if there was, I don't want to risk the open sea in the storm without jibs and the forestay. With any luck, these Jutras ships are stragglers and the rest of their fleet are waiting out the storm in Korbel Bay."

"What about—" Thorn hesitated. "What about Crosspointe ships? Any signs?" Not that they'd provide any help to a black ship. Not that they had any to give. Crosspointe ships had no weapons, depending instead on speed, maneuverability, and their unique ability to navigate on the open sea for their defense. Even the foreign ships making use of Crosspointe's Pilots didn't carry weapons. None were permitted within the Pale, and every sea crossing required putting in to Crosspointe—to pay taxes, customs, and fees.

"No." He licked his lips. "My guess is they've all taken shelter inside the Pale or beached themselves. The crew's unsettled. With you falling down dead, cracking the bowsprit, and the Jutras on their way—the money they've been promised has lost its allure, I'm afraid."

"Did you mention to them I'm not dead yet?"

"They seem to think I might be . . . mistaken."

Thorn's brows rose. "Mistaken?"

"They are worried that you finally managed to off your own self, as it seems you've been trying so hard to do. There is also some concern that I might have lost all reason and strangled you in your bed. Seeing you on deck might help."

"Only some concern?" Thorn gibed as he took a step. He didn't collapse, though neither did he release his grip on the bedpost. "Surely the healing amulet should have had better effect by now."

"It's only been a few days. And your hands are much repaired. It is possible it is weakened too much to help. Which is why I brought you another."

Plusby put the amulet around Thorn's neck, removing the first one and dropping it on the bed.

"And you said you wouldn't share," Thorn said sardonically. But he was grateful. He didn't want to fail the ship because his body was too wasted to let him work.

Plusby ignored him. "That should boost your healing. Though without sufficient sleep, your progress will still be slow. But we cannot afford to let you sleep any longer."

"How long have I been indisposed?"

"Six turns of the glass."

Thorn was taken aback. "So long?"

"It seemed advisable. The question now is, are you rested enough?"

"Aye. Let's go soothe the children, shall we?"

"Not before you eat. But do not dawdle. We don't dare let the Jutras cut us off from the open sea."

Plusby spun and strode out. Thorn watched him, noticing that his left arm swung at his side, no longer bound tight. The captain's posture was stiff with an air of barely suppressed fury. He was not a man who liked being at the mercy of anyone else. And just at the moment, he was subject to the vagaries of the sea, the damage to his ship, and Thorn's continuing weakness.

It took all of Thorn's resolve to move himself out of his bedchamber. He dragged his feet, staggering, gripping the furniture and leaning against the walls for balance. He didn't understand it. He should be getting stronger. But he felt almost as drained and weak as he had when he'd come off the mainmast.

He struggled into the main cabin. Bess was waiting for him. She slid her arm around his waist, helping him to the table, where a trencher of steaming food waited. Fitch leaped up onto his lap and squirmed up onto the table. She rubbed her face against his jaw, making a low, worried sound in her throat.

"I'll be fine," he said, reaching out to stroke her. The bandages on his hands were dirty and unraveling. He eyed them balefully and began ripping them off, using his teeth.

"Halford wouldn't approve," Bess observed, standing over him with her arms folded over her chest.

"Halford can rot in the depths," Thorn growled.

He finished pulling the bandages off and handed them to Bess. "Have them washed. We may need them again."

"Aye, sir," she said with a mocking salute, and then left.

Left alone, Thorn examined his hands. The skin had thickened a bit more, though the bones still protruded sharply. There were no scars and no calluses—his hands were as pale and soft as a newborn's. He flexed his fingers. The skin fit more snugly, like too-small gloves. But at least he no longer needed anyone else to feed him. Or help him with holding his prick while he peed. He grimaced and pulled the trencher close, spearing chunks of stewed vegetables and salt horse.

Fitch batted at his fork.

"Get your own," Thorn remonstrated, but he angled the trencher so that she could get at it better.

She lifted her head haughtily as he made the adjustment, and then settled down and began to pick daintily at his food.

He ate quickly, hunger seizing his belly. He couldn't remember the last time he'd eaten. He snorted. He couldn't remember much of the last day. He dragged his hands through his salt-sticky hair and scratched his scalp before gulping down the pot of strong, sweet tea. Feeling the grains sliding past, he left Fitch to lap up the last of his meal and made his way out on deck. He was still tottering drunkenly and the bottoms of his feet and his toes felt half-numb. And not from the cold.

The deck was swarming with activity as the crew made ready to hoist anchor. The uprising remained on their port side, a finger of knobby black rock well over fifty feet tall and at least as wide. It was covered with a spongy, green-gray growth. The tide was topping and all around them, the waves churned into an angry white froth.

Halford was finishing the fishing on the bowsprit. Two hollowed-out lengths of wood had been set like splints around the break and wound around tightly with cordage. Waves drenched him as he straddled the spar, riding it like a bucking mule. Plusby was standing rigidly on the deck behind, hands clasped tightly behind his back as he waited for the repairs to be completed.

At last the bosun began to back off the spar. The moment he did, Plusby whipped around and headed for the helm. He veered over to Thorn before climbing up onto the poop deck.

"I want to swing wide of Kutranil Bay and get around the Goa Maru's horns before we look for a place to lay to. If the Jutras try to pursue us, we'll head for wide-open water. Are you ready?"

Not that there was any choice. Still, Thorn hesitated. Plusby's face hardened, his gray eyes molten.

Then reluctantly Thorn said, "I could use a sturdy arm to steady me."

The captain jerked around and shouted for Blot, who had just stowed a length of line in a hatch. He latched it shut and hurried over.

"Watch after our Pilot. Try to keep him on his feet, won't you? And Pilot Thorn, if there's a chance of scraping the Jutras off on knucklebones or a swarm of vescies, I want to know." He turned to climb up the steps, pausing a moment to squeeze Thorn's shoulder.

Thorn drew a tired breath in. Blot had remained taciturn and prickly since Thorn had promised to heal Wragg's arm. Doing so had not won him any prizes with either man. He wasn't sure if Blot was more angry with him now than then.

As Blot walked him to the compass post, Thorn became aware of a silent watchfulness among the crew. They stared obliquely, like people fearing a mad dog. Or more accurately, a dead Pilot, Thorn thought mordantly. His appearance was guaranteed not to promote confidence. He looked like a Kyries—one of Chayos's walking dead. His lips twisted into a smirk. The crew could worry either that he'd drop dead and strand them in the middle of the black waters without a Pilot or that he had really become a Kyries and would start hunting them, disemboweling them one by one and eating their entrails while they watched. Either way, it was a doomed ship.

He caught sight of several sailors stroking a splayed hand across their eyes, and a few others balled their left hands into fists and blew across the knuckles. Whether the ward signs were directed at him or merely any bad luck that might cling to the ship, Thorn didn't know, but he wished heartily that it would work. And that the ward signs would drive off the ghostly leeches that continued to sap his strength.

Thorn set an unsteady hand on the heart of the compass, catching his breath. The sweep of the black waters felt more intimate than usual. It was hard to know where he left off. And despite the breathless euphoria of the experience, it alarmed him. He felt so amazingly connected, like he was everywhere at once and filled with throbbing life and nearly limitless power—but he also felt himself blurring and fading, like a drop of milk dispersed into a bucket of water.

"Ye well?" Blot asked, jolting Thorn from his reverie.

They were the first words the other man had spoken to him in nearly a sennight, since the day of the raider attack.

"Aye. Well enough," Thorn murmured, pulling himself back from the mesmerizing glory of his communion. The effort nearly drove him to his knees. His chest felt tight and his heart hammered as if he'd been running up the side of a mountain. He felt a tearing cramping in his thighs that reached up to grip under his ribs. He had no doubt that if he weren't wearing the amulet to stave off pain, he'd be miserable.

A ghostly tentacle of thought whispered across his mind, and for the first time he wondered if the crew was right to worry he might drop dead. A chill quivered down his spine. *No.* His hands were much better. Still, he couldn't lose the feeling that something was dreadfully wrong. He shrugged away the thought. He didn't have time to think about it. The Jutras weren't going to wait.

He focused on the water, considering what was around them. The storm had tightened into a dense mass, swirling in a slow circle over Crosspointe. It pulled on the waves, creating chaotic rip currents. It pressured the malleable seafloor; in the depths, mountains rose and fell, sending tidal ripples across the wide sea. Canyons gaped wide and deep and then snapped shut. Waterspouts danced like malicious fairies on the water, and herds of Koreions hunted and played in the roaring turbulence. Ribbons of *sylveth* gathered at the center, circling the Pale in a shimmering moat. But the storm was starting to move. North and east—the *Eidolon* was about to sail directly into its path.

Thorn thought of the cracked bowsprit. What cracking bad luck it should have happened now. If they were caught in the tempest before they could find a safe place to lie to, the repair wouldn't hold. But that would matter only if the clots of *sylveth* spewed out in front of the storm didn't turn the ship and crew to spawn, or a Koreion didn't bite them in half, or a swarm of vescies didn't eat the *Eidolon* out from under them. . . .

The grin that split Thorn's lips was sharp as a hatchet blade. Maybe whatever was draining the life from him wouldn't have a chance to kill him. Maybe the fury of the gods would finish him first.

He began to rattle off information about the immediate sea to Blot, who relayed it up to the captain. Plusby gave orders to raise the sails. Slowly the *Eidolon* slid away from the uprising and arced around to the west.

They were just inside the mouth of an inlet. They'd anchored on the lee side of the uprising they'd collided with, which had provided them some slight cover from the Jutras as they made repairs. Now they crept carefully around it and struck for open waters.

The Jutras ships were close—less than a quarter of a league south, one point forward the port beam. They were coming on fast, their red and black triangular sails bellied. Their ships were three-masted, but stubbier than the sleek, long lines of the *Eidolon*, with broader beams and high narrow forecastle decks and poop decks that stretched fully half the length of the ship. The bowsprit rose from a beaky protrusion at the forefront of each just below the castle deck, and gaudy yellow stripes ran the length of each ship above the wale and below the waist.

The ships sat high in the water and looked deceptively tottery. But while they would be troubled in open water, they were fast and nimble in the coastal waters. They were on a heading to trap the *Eidolon* in the cove.

Blot was jigging back and forth on the balls of his feet, jostling Thorn.

"Stand still," he said through gritted teeth, his eyes fixed unseeing on the horizon. There was a tantalizing movement near the Bramble. He couldn't identify it yet. The feeling faded and a swarm of vescies well south of the Naz Peninsula caught his attention. But the swarm wasn't moving. His mouth pulled down grimly. Vescie swarms stopped only to feed. He hoped they dined on a Jutras ship.

Plusby was heading them on a starboard tack, angling for the gap between the forbidding headland and the lead Jutras vessel. The water was deep enough, and the tide had turned. The current was pulling them, adding to their speed. The sails popped and filled and the *Eidolon* surged. The wind was on the port beam, which served the Jutras better. But Plusby was on a beam reach and his ship was built for speed. Motivated by fear of the Jutras, the crew leaped to answer every order, shifting braces and trimming sail efficiently.

Thorn felt their skill in the grace of the *Eidolon*'s quick leap. She caught the wind and heeled to leeward. Sailors took in the sheets and she straightened up, skimming over the waves.

The lead Jutras ship closed on them. Thorn could see the faces of the crew. They were a ragged bunch, dressed in motley clothing much like what the *Eidolon*'s crew wore. And they had varying lengths of hair. Thorn frowned. That was odd. He'd seen Jutras sailors in the free ports. They were members of a water caste that had rigid rules. One of them was that they wore their hair cropped very short. And he'd never seen one that wasn't wearing blue.

The tickle from the Bramble flittered along the inside of his skin like a blown breath. He tensed.

Change was coming there. A weir? Or an uprising? He shook his head. It was impossible to know. He'd keep the *Eidolon* moving more north than west.

There were shouts from the Jutras ship and he jerked his head to look. They were waving madly at the *Eidolon* to give way. He snarled. Right. The Jutras would have themselves a beautiful clipper, a Pilot and compass, and nearly two dozen slaves. Or sacrifices. They were a bloody people, and their temples were houses of carnage and torture. It was said that their priests and priestesses knew how to peel all the skin from a man without letting their victim have the relief of unconsciousness, much less death. They'd pare your eyelids off so that you couldn't look away when they slit your stomach open and let your guts spill out over your feet. Then they'd reach inside your chest and pluck out your still-beating heart.

There wasn't a single member of the *Eidolon* who was willing to chance Jutras mercy, or risk handing even one compass and Pilot into the Empire's voracious hands. Only weeks ago they'd been reminded of the danger. A single Jutras ship—crippled by wind and wave—had managed to navigate the dangers of the Inland Sea and sail brazenly into Blackwater Bay. And then its crew had stolen unhindered into the palace— all the way to the throne room—capturing the king and murdering the queen.

Thorn hated to think what worse havoc the Jutras could have wrought if their ship had had a compass. They could have settled in a secluded cove and sneaked into Sylmont with no one the wiser. Or they could have gone hunting Crosspointe ships, kidnapping Pilots and stealing compasses until they outfitted an invading fleet. He swallowed, cold spreading through his gut. The possibilities of what else they could have done seemed limitless.

Wintry fury swept through him. No. The Jutras were not going to get even one compass. Not on his watch.

Chapter 14

The prow of the Jutras ship rammed the *Eidolon*'s stern with a booming thud. The ship shuddered and wood screamed over the whistle of the wind. Blot braced Thorn, who clutched the east and west rays of the compass as he fell forward. The rounded southern point thrust hard into his groin and he gasped at the force of it. His stomach roiled and bits of his meal spurted sourly up onto his tongue. He swallowed hard and panted, glad yet again to be wearing the painkilling amulet.

"Are ye well?" Blot asked, pulling Thorn upright.

"I may never enjoy a woman again," he rasped.

He glanced astern. The *Eidolon* had been knocked cockeyed by the collision with the Jutras ship, falling off the wind as she drifted perilously close to the headland's teeth. But Plusby had already straightened their course and they were pulling away from the danger. The Jutras ship had bounced off their stern and its momentum had carried it much closer to the shore. But the other ship's captain was good—better than good.

Swiftly its sails were doused and raised again in quick time, the braces hauled, and the forestays deployed. The tottery ship swung sharply about, rolling hard on her starboard beam. A sailor dangled from the foremast, his legs kicking wildly. Thorn could not hear his screams, but knew the terrified man's throat would be tearing with the force of his fear. As he watched, the Jutras ship rolled onto her port beam. When she rose again, the sailor was gone. The ship was already starting to haul again and was pulling away from the shore. Blot swore softly.

"He's close to shore. He should make it," Thorn said with feeble reassurance, no longer able to see the man's head bobbing in the churn. If the beach had been forgiving, his words might have been true. But the waves would batter the man to bits on the reef rocks. He was as good as dead, if he wasn't picked up by another ship.

Blot said nothing, his body rigid, his forearms like bars of iron across Thorn's chest. He didn't even breathe as he scanned the water. It didn't matter that the fallen man was Jutras—he was a sailor, and he was in the water. The duty to save him was too ingrained in both Thorn and Blot for the small matter of his race to mean anything.

The two of them were so focused on their futile search that they didn't realize what else was happening until the sea began to explode.

Thorn wrenched about as sounds louder than thunder reverberated through the air, quaking the deck.

"What in the depths are they *doing*?"

The following Jutras ships fired on their wallowing sister. From their high castle decks, the first three launched projectiles using a kind of ballista device. There were two set up on the front corners of each of the castle decks and larger ones behind on the poop deck. The missiles launched in a low arc, landing in the water well off the target ship's starboard bow. The water erupted, sending geysers of water and flame spuming fifty feet up in the air. Noxious pools of an oily yellow substance spread over the black water, resisting the roil of the waves and remaining oddly cohesive, spreading out in wide puddles. A few started burning, giving off a thick, greasy smoke that lay heavily across the water.

Thorn could feel the substance through the compass. It was a corrosive, gnawing feeling that itched unbearably at the soles of his feet and the backs of his thighs. In his mouth he tasted an overwhelming burst of a vile flavor—like burnt cabbage and rancid meat. It was so foul that he barely resisted the urge to vomit.

The ships launched their missiles again. This time their aim was better. They nearly struck their target. But their prey had caught the wind and was angling quickly away on a beam reach. And she was headed unswervingly after the *Eidolon*.

"Where's she think she be goin'? She gonna ram us again?"

Thorn shook his head in reluctant admiration. "She's running for safety into open water. And her captain is planning to use us for her compass. He's got brass balls, that one."

It was more than risky. They couldn't know the *Eidolon* was crippled, but even so, the sleek clipper would likely outrun the bulkier Jutras ship. But its captain had little choice. Their pursuers were too close and too many. But now Thorn understood the raggedy appearance and motley clothing of the fugitive ship's crew. They were undoubtedly some of Plusby's river pyrates who were trying to steal a warship. He smiled and raised a mental toast to their boldness and wished them luck. He was always in favor of Jutras hunting Jutras.

"Hard-a-lee!" Plusby shouted, and the *Eidolon*'s sails luffed as the crew frantically hauled the yards around. There was a moment of coasting without the push of the wind, and then the sails caught and she began to cut through the water again. It put them on a direct course for the southern tip of the Bramble, which was exactly where the captain had not wanted to go, but it was a safer bet than running close to the coastline with the Jutras ships firing their weapons at them. If the *Eidolon* could get far enough away, her pursuers would be left at the mercy of the sea. And if not—they'd have to scrape the bastards off, Thorn thought. He glanced over his shoulder. The renegade ship was five hundred yards off the *Eidolon*'s star-board quarter and tacking to match her course. The other five warships were all following suit.

"Braken's cods," Thorn muttered. "We've got a cracking fleet after us."

"Aye," came Blot's gloomy response as he buttressed Thorn against the pitch of the ship. "We're gonna need th' forestays and jib. Pray Halford's splint holds."

As the hours passed, the waves grew steeper, the troughs deeper. The *Eidolon* rose and it seemed like it would fly up into the sky or pinwheel backward. But each time it slipped over the crest of the wave and slid down in a gut-wrenching drop, the bowsprit spearing into the roiling obsidian walls. Water sluiced the deck in drenching wings; the crew ran safety lines, tying themselves to the relative security of the ship. The wind had picked up and there was a taste of snow in the air. Ice thickened on the rails and lower rigging, where spray froze on contact. The only good news was that they'd gained some distance on the Jutras. But that was in no small thanks to the addition of the jib and one of the forestays. Halford stood on the prow, all his attention fixed on the bowsprit and his repairs.

Thorn was numb. He couldn't feel his feet or his hands. There was a real danger of frostbite, but the healing amulet would take care of that. If it could. The weakness inside him was growing. He could hardly stand, even with Blot's steadfast aid. His bones felt spongy, his muscles like grimy, knotted ribbons. But there was no time to think of why, of what was eating him alive. There was the ship and the crew and the sea and the Jutras. Thorn scrabbled at the edges of his mind. He focused blearily and poured all his waning strength into reading the sea.

The tempest over Crosspointe had begun to grind slowly forward into the Ankerton Strait. As it pulled itself back into open water, its energy burgeoned. Thorn gasped at the hard pull of it. He'd never felt such a storm before, such pressure and distortion in the sea, like it was being dragged in all directions at once. The force of it made his joints ache and he began to shake. Blot said nothing, merely firming his grip.

Then suddenly the storm contracted.

It sucked into itself tightly, as if trying to become something solid—a giant demon made of shadow and cloud, lightning and ice. There was a single shining moment of silence and stillness, like the world took a breath.

The storm exploded, its tightly coiled energy screaming free.

The force of its loosed power shredded through air and water and rock. The changeling sea bucked and the waters thrashed as cracks threaded across the seafloor. Currents fractured and whirled apart, spider-webbing into new, treacherous flows. The silky moat of *sylveth* girdling Crosspointe splattered outward like flung paint. The wind raged across the water, pushing waves higher and driving the *sylveth*-splatter tide.

The tickle he'd been feeling came again and blossomed into an itch, then searing, ripping pain, even with the amulet. Thorn gasped and made a sound halfway between a groan and a scream. It felt like someone was pressing a dull, rusty spear through the middle of his chest. His back arced and his head banged against Blot's. Black mist feathered the edges of his vision. And then fear clamped him in a bony fist.

"Bore!" he croaked. "Hard about! North! Strike north! Now!"

His voice was a creaky rasp that lacked any emphatic force. His body had become too frail to do better. Still, Blot heard him despite the wail of the wind, the crash of the waves, and the haunting song of the rigging. His reaction was immediate. The charmer dropped Thorn like a stone and ran for the helm, shouting the message. A bore. Flee north. *Pray we have enough time to escape.*

Thorn slumped on the deck, hooking his elbow around the base of the compass pedestal and locking his hands around his wrists. Water sluiced over him. It was frigid. He choked on a breath that was as much salt water as air. He coughed and struggled to pull himself up. But he could not make his spent body obey. He was helpless.

He didn't need the compass to feel the bore opening. Thorn shivered as fear whipped spiny tentacles around his bowels. But it wasn't all fear. There was a healthy dose of awe. Wonder. Glory. The gods were at work here, the sea turning terrifying and primal. To be in the middle of it—to *witness* it . . . it was almost worth getting crushed to bits.

Bores outside of the Chance storm season were rare—maybe one in ten seasons. Most were small, with mouths no bigger than a wine barrel. But the throat of the beast—the bore—might go a thousand leagues. When the mouth opened, it gulped the sea, sending it frothing through its rocky gullet to erupt out the other side, wherever the other side was. But this one . . . this one was shockingly big—a gaping, sucking maw. It could swallow the *Eidolon* whole without even cracking a timber. And it was too damned close! Just off the southern tip of the Bramble.

Already Thorn could feel the inexorable, uncompromising drag of the current, slowing them, hauling back against the push of the wind.

Hands gripped him, yanking him up. Blot. And Plusby. The captain's face was strained, white lines bracketing his mouth. Bruised shadows circled his sunken eyes.

"How bad is it?"

"Monstrous. Just southwest of here—sixty or seventy leagues at best."

Blot blanched. "So near?"

"Captain?" came Crabbel's questioning growl.

"Take the helm, charmer," Plusby ordered. "I'll give orders from the compass."

Crabbel nodded and loped away.

"Blot, keep our Pilot on his feet. Don't let him faint." Plusby's gray eyes studied Thorn. "Or die."

"Winds are coming," Thorn said tightly, still unable to draw a steady breath into his constricted lungs. His arm was draped over Blot's shoulder and he sagged against the other man. He couldn't feel his feet. "Gale. Seventy or eighty knots. Maybe more. You might want to hurry."

Plusby spun around and began giving orders to furl sails. Too much canvas would rip the masts up by their roots when the powerful wind hit. But taking them in meant a lessened resistance to the bore's sucking current. And those weren't their only problems.

Thorn grasped again at the compass. His hands fumbled clumsily into place. He couldn't feel them. Nor his feet. It was more than the cold. Thorn chewed the inside of his lip, tasting blood. He had to get the *Eidolon* to safety—at least to the seaboard, where the crew wouldn't be entirely stranded if—when—he collapsed. Not dead, he told himself firmly. Not dead. But he wasn't convinced.

He concentrated on the chaos that was the sea. The bore's current was no longer merely pulling them backward. It had begun to swing them to port as the massive flow of water draining into the bore swirled into a spinning vortex. It was driving them straight into the Bramble.

Plusby accepted the information with a stoicism that would have made a block of granite proud. He ordered a tack to the starboard. Then the unleashed storm winds struck.

The ship surged, yawing wildly. Plusby straightened her out, but the waves had grown into mountains. The deck tilted nearly perpendicular. The masts strained, the sails stretched to splitting. Thorn could no longer hear anything but the whine and howl of the wind. The cacophony was nearly deafening. Pellets of ice rattled down and struck sharp blows on his white-knuckled hands, covering the soft new skin in red welts.

The next hours were grueling. They hardly made any headway in the heavy seas with the bore's current dragging at them like an anchor. Every creak of the

masts had Thorn looking up, waiting for one to snap.
They were running with a dangerous amount of sail
for a ship that *didn't* have a cracked bowsprit. But
they had little choice—they'd certainly be drawn into
the bore if they used any less.

"How long can th' damned thing go on?" Blot
yelled against Thorn's ear.

Thorn could only shake his head. There was no way
to know. Bores were as unpredictable as anything else
in the Inland Sea. It could close as abruptly as it
opened, which would create new problems. Or it could
stay open indefinitely. At some point its throat should
fill up and the draining stop. But as large as this one
was, he feared that could be hours, even days.

Pray we have enough time to escape.

He didn't doubt that every sailor aboard ship hadn't
stopped praying since the bore opened.

He didn't know how much time had passed when
he finally felt a *release*. They had broken free of the
sheering current. He slumped, his head dangling as he
took deep breaths.

"Pilot?" Blot asked, his voice thick with exhaustion.

He shifted and Thorn became aware of how heavy
he must be, especially after leaning on Blot for
hours—or was it days? He shook his head, his mind
fuzzy. He pushed himself upright, the effort costing
him more dearly than he'd ever admit. His skin actually felt gray; he was so weak and the shaking that
had plagued him was in his bones, in his blood. He
couldn't quite see clearly, as if he were looking
through murky water. But he refused to give in. There
was time enough to . . . *rest* . . . when he'd brought
the ship to safety.

"Captain," he called. The wind stole his voice away,
sending it spinning off on a flurry of snowflakes.

Blot repeated it more loudly. Plusby jerked around,
his mouth snapping shut midsentence, and came to
Thorn, standing close so he could be heard over the
wind and the snap of the sails.

"You look like the Koreions have been chewing on you," he said.

"I'm not dead yet."

"Are you sure?"

Thorn shrugged. He wasn't, but saying so aloud was not going to boost morale any.

"What next?"

"The bore is driving vescies and a splatter tide toward us—they're coming fast. We need to beach. Roche Bay down to the Upper Jaw is peppered with knucklebones."

Plusby rocked back on his heels and rubbed his thumb across the sharp edges of his teeth. "What about the Bramble?"

Thorn grimaced. "Seaboard is better."

Plusby's brows drew together as he waited for Thorn to elaborate. The Pilot glanced at Blot and Bess, who was hovering behind the captain, then gave in.

"You won't find a new Pilot on the Bramble."

All three of them went rigid. Bess's lips tightened and she looked away. The captain swore softly.

"My *advice*," Thorn said, emphasizing the second word heavily, "is to run up toward the coast east of Roche Bay. Wait out the storm. Afterward, you can make your way up to the Saithe River to Lalant Uly."

"And start shopping for a new Pilot?" Plusby's lips hardly seemed to move.

"If it comes to that."

"Blot, Bess, stand off."

Plusby's arm snaked around Thorn and the other two scuttled out of hearing, driven by the naked brutality in the captain's voice.

"What in the holy black depths are you saying?"

Thorn shook his head, lurching as the ship rolled. "I'm fading. The healing amulet isn't working."

"But your hands appear to be repaired. . . . I don't understand."

"Neither do I." Thorn shrugged. "But I can feel it.

You don't want to be on the Bramble, Captain. Not without a Pilot."

"You're not dead yet."

Thorn smiled. "All the same, you wanted my advice and I'm telling you to run due north. Beach the *Eidolon* as soon as you can."

"And what about you?"

Thorn turned to look out onto the churning black waters, pewter clouds roiling above in a mirror reflection. "A *sylveth* dunking would cure me." He glanced at Plusby, whose face was a study of consternation and repulsion. "I'm spawn, remember? *Sylveth* is a sure cure. But it's too dangerous to the ship. So run north. And do hurry."

"In these seas with a clear heading, we can be off the coast of Relsea within another day. Two at worst."

Thorn wasn't sure he was going to last that long. He didn't say so. There wasn't any point stirring that pot. But Plusby read it in his silence.

"Tell me directly should you sense *sylveth* on the horizon."

Thorn's eyebrows rose, then furrowed. He shook his head. "No. Besides, it's possible a little rest onshore will put me to rights. Perhaps a warm, willing woman to keep me company."

The captain laughed, a harsh, barking sound. "What would you do with a woman, Pilot? Prod her with your thorn? I think it likes the view of your feet."

"I might surprise you."

"You already have."

With that, Plusby signaled Blot to take back his burden and returned to the wheel.

Chapter 15

Only two of the Jutras ships still pursued them. The renegade ship clung to the *Eidolon* like a barnacle. She was only two hundred yards off the starboard quarter, never gaining, never falling behind. The other Jutras warship was five hundred yards behind her and making steady headway. The other ships must have been wrecked on the Bramble or sucked into the bore. But now how to be rid of the remaining two?

Thorn didn't let himself think about it. His strength was quickly ebbing and his breath was coming in short, gulping gasps. The numb feeling that had started in his feet and hands now claimed his lower legs and forearms. A spidery coldness spread out from his chest, looping strands of iron around his heart and squeezing. He knew without a doubt that he had precious little time to bring the *Eidolon* safely to shore. He just wished he knew what in the depths was happening to him.

He ought to have been frightened. Or perhaps angry—railing at whatever invisible leech was sucking the life from him. But all he could think of were the leagues of water that surrounded them, and the vescies and *sylveth* riding the waves behind them. At least the vescies would feed on the Jutras ships first.

The *Eidolon* passed the northernmost point of the Bramble. It dropped behind them steadily. The winds still raged, blowing above seventy knots, and the waves were towering. Despite the risk of losing the masts or shredding the canvas apart, Plusby called for more sail.

Thorn felt the ship jerk and lunge as more canvas was added. They were on a beam reach and pushing strongly. The ship's timbers shook and shuddered as it rose out of the waves and dropped back down, battered by the wind. The masts creaked ominously, but still Plusby didn't take in any canvas.

They were twenty leagues off the Bramble when a rogue wave rose suddenly up off the port beam. It swept so suddenly out of the sea that Thorn didn't feel it building beforehand. He rasped a warning to Blot, who shouted the information to the captain. Instantly, they began to come about, heading the prow into the wave.

They had less than two minutes. It was not enough.

The black wall of water slammed broad on the port bow, crashing down on top of the forecastle and sweeping across the deck like a giant's hand. The water wrenched Thorn away from the compass and shoved him across the deck. Blot clamped his arms tightly around Thorn's thighs to prevent him from being washed overboard.

They slid over the deck and crashed heavily against the pinrail. Thorn's head bounced off a rail rib, his skull filling with a smothering charcoal mist. He scrabbled to grab at his tattered consciousness as the mist settled heavily over him, pushing him down and down and down. . . .

Water filled his mouth and nose. Another wave rammed him against the rail again. He struggled to find the surface. His heart rattled inside his chest. He thrashed feebly, fighting the black cloud, fighting the flaccid weight of his own body as his muscles refused to answer his need.

Then suddenly the weight on his legs was gone. A fist grappled his collar and yanked him up. His head bobbed above the floodwater and he sucked great gulps of salty air. Blot's hand was inexorable and he pulled Thorn all the way to his feet. Instantly the Pilot bent and began to cough—deep, racking coughs that carved away at his insides until he retched, spewing out nothing more than bile.

Another wave slapped his face and sent him staggering backward. Blot held him tightly, and then another arm wrapped around his waist.

"Get this line over his head!" Ricker shouted over his head to Blot. Together the two worked a loop of rope over Thorn's shoulders and around his chest. Ricker let go of him to scrabble up the steep pitch of the tilted deck to hitch the line about the compass post. The *Eidolon* was lying over at a steep angle. Sailors scrambled to douse the heavy sails to allow her to right herself and to save the bowsprit.

Too late.

A slow, agonizing *crack*! cut through the noise of the storm. The stiff forestay and jib sails luffed and then slowly collapsed as the bowsprit ripped free with a splintering sound that made Thorn's chest ache. The wind swung the heavy spar violently in the air, its loose cordage and sails whipping wildly. Bits of the splintered dog rail rained down on the deck.

The bobbing bowsprit hammered against the foremast and stays, tangling around them, pulling at them with all the weight of the heavy spar and the sodden sails.

A gust of wind burst across the *Eidolon* and there was another ominous cracking sound. The ship shuddered and groaned. Stays whined with a high-pitched keening sound and then separated with loud *pops*. The foremast screamed as it arced downward, raining splinters and shards of wood down onto the deck before smashing against the pinrail and sliding over into the water. The sea caught it, pulling the *Eidolon* onto her beam end. Stays sang again. Sailors on the mainmast sawed madly at the four stays and the four braces attaching it to the foremast, trying to free it from the heavy drag. A flurry of others sawed at the web of lines attaching the mizzen to the main, trying to preserve it if the main went.

Another terrible *crack*ing sound as the maintop splintered halfway up. Thorn could only watch in foggy horror as it toppled. The sailors swinging from its rigging screamed and leaped clear, falling into the waves and thudding heavily onto the deck. The mess of rigging, sails, and cordage swept drunkenly down, landing heavily half in and half out of the water. The rail shattered at the blow. The *Eidolon* listed heavily, the weight of the broken masts, yards, sails, and cordage pulling her over.

Thorn had no time to notice more. Blot and Ricker yanked his safety line free and dragged him up onto the poop deck, fastening him to the fife rail before abandoning him. The fallen debris had to be cut free before the *Eidolon* was dragged down to the depths by its weight.

Sailors swung axes and sawed at the cordage. Others lifted and dragged their companions free of the crushing tangle. Crabbel hauled against the tiller, trying to manhandle the ship out of the trough. Then the *Eidolon* rolled sickeningly, battered hard on the broadside by the high seas. Thorn's feet slid from beneath him as the deck was now nearly perpendicular to the water. Frigid waves battered him. Once again the charcoal mist filled his mind like smothering sand. It was all he could do to push himself to his hands and knees.

Suddenly a shape rose up alongside them on the port side. The renegade Jutras ship. The sea tossed the ships together and the sound of the collision was like thunder. The *Eidolon* shook and trembled, twisting and rolling. Four of the Jutras crawled up on the rail of their ship and leaped onto the *Eidolon*, trailing ropes behind like spiders. They secured them to the clipper, and were quickly followed by a dozen more invaders.

The Jutras swarmed over the deck like ants. Thorn climbed to his feet, struggling to unknot the safety line about his waist. He should fight. But his fingers fumbled uselessly against the wet rope.

The Jutras started first on the masts and the tangle of cordage and canvas. The *Eidolon*'s crew didn't realize at first that there were enemies among them. When they did, they attacked the intruders, swinging scrapers, knives, and belaying pins, but they were too exhausted to have much effect. Blot and Ricker fought back-to-back but were quickly overwhelmed. Thorn saw Plusby and Halford crumple as they were hit from behind. Except for Thorn and Crabbel, the *Eidolon*'s crew was swiftly contained. The Jutras bound their prisoners with lines cut from the tangles of cordage and shoved them into the forward crew cabins.

More Jutras came aboard—Thorn was horrified at how many there were. Behind him Crabbel swore violently, but he could not leave the helm without the *Eidolon* capsizing.

As the two watched, the pack of Jutras set to work hacking apart the wreckage and shoving it overboard. Thorn was torn between an appalling burst of gratitude—*his ship saved!*—and an equal measure of soul-killing dread. Not for himself. He'd draw his last breath long before the Jutras could do anything to him. But he feared for his crew. Cold coiled around his windpipe and filled his lungs with glacial ice. Their fate at the hands of the Jutras would be the sort that gave nightmares to hardened torturers. Ghastly beyond imagining.

Two more Jutras leaped across from their ship, landing with catlike grace. They scuttled up onto the slanted poop deck followed by three more. Three of them dragged Crabbel to the deck and bound him. Another took the helm and the last stood over Thorn. Not that he needed a guard—he had no strength to fight, and he was safely tethered, a dog without teeth.

With so many hands, the debris of the fallen masts was quickly dispensed with, though they remained a serious threat to the ship. Driven by waves, the heavy masts and spars pounded against the *Eidolon* like battering rams. Thorn bit his tongue against urging his captors to try to move away from the wreckage—at any moment one of the massive yards could drive a hole through the hull and sink the ship. He wished for it, prayed for it to the depths of his being, even as his heart ripped in half.

No longer burdened by the wreckage, the *Eidolon* rolled upright. The mizzenmast remained, but most of its stays danced loosely on the wind. With it, they could make some headway scudding before the wind and using poles, but before they could hoist canvas, the mast needed to be secured. That is, if the renegade Jutras wanted to keep their newly won prize.

Thorn caught his breath as realization bubbled up through his murky mind. His captors needed him to get to shore safely.

But he didn't have to do it.

He could ride them up onto a weir, head them into a horde of vescies, or turn them directly into the path of the coming splatter tide. He'd prevent them from having the ship and the compass and save his crew from slavery and sacrifice. He just had to kill everybody to do it. The bitterness of the thought was like eating lye. He'd worked so hard to bind them together, to keep them safe and well. And he'd succeeded. And now the only way to save them from a fate worse than death was to kill them all. He wanted to puke.

His thoughts were interrupted by an explosion. Chunks of wood, burning sail, and cordage hailed down on the *Eidolon* and the Jutras ship. Where they landed, they continued to burn. The smell of charring tar and wood swept the ship, mixed with an eye-blistering stench like burning hair and carrion. Too much of the burning debris fell on the forward cabins where the *Eidolon*'s crew was imprisoned. Jutras sailors did nothing to stamp out the fires that flared to life on the wet wood. Thorn fumbled again at his rope tether, but strong hands closed over his. His head jerked up and he glared at his Jutras guard, his mouth pulled into a snarl. He wrenched himself away, staggering and falling weakly against the end of the rope.

His guard steadied him with firm, relentless hands, standing him up and pushing him back to lean against the fife rail.

Thorn swore virulently at the other man, who merely stared impassively back at him, the corner of his mouth lifting as the Pilot's labored ranting went on.

He was mixed-blood Jutras. That much could be told from the greenish cast of his yellow eyes and the softened lines of his cheekbones and nose. His skin was a deep brown—though whether from the sun or from his heritage, it was impossible to tell. His short-cropped hair was a dark walnut with streaks of gold from the sun. He wore a motley collection of clothing in blues, greens, and browns, liberally strewn with carefully stitched patches, the kind sailors were adept at. He was a few years younger than Thorn, with a seamed face that suggested he smiled often. A close-cut beard edged his jaws, and a wide, patterned band of delicately scribed scars overlaid a series of geometric blue tattoos running down the left side of his neck. He was powerfully built, and clearly capable and resolute.

He was also more than a little amused at Thorn's continuing tirade. His smile widened. Seeing it, Thorn snapped his mouth shut, his jaw flexing as his teeth ground together. He was disgustingly breathless, his lungs pumping with the effort of his blistering torrent of words. He turned his back so his guard couldn't see his deplorable frailty.

The fires lit by the noxious projectiles continued to burn. The wings of water sweeping the decks as the waves crashed over the rails seemed only to spread them.

"Do not have worry. The fire will not sink the ship."

The Jutras guard had stepped up behind Thorn, his lips close to his ear. His accent was oddly musical and guttural at the same time. He spoke Celwysh with a fluency that made Thorn start.

"What about my crew?" Thorn rasped, glaring around at his guard.

The other man was taken aback. "The *Zhala* has crew enough."

"My crew will die if those fires aren't put out," Thorn said, speaking slowly as if to a stupid child.

"It matters not."

"It does if I say it does," he spat. "You think you've won this ship? Think again. It's not yours until you can sail it. And you can't. Not without me. Not unless I pilot it safely to shore. And you can bet your cods that if even one of my crew is killed because you let them burn to death, I'll run her up on a knucklebone weir. And then we'll see how *you* like it when *your* crew dies screaming. Or they're turned to spawn."

The Jutras stiffened in obvious surprise, his mouth falling open. His eyes narrowed.

"But you are the Pilot, yes?"

"Didn't I just say so?"

"Then I understand you not. What does the crew matter?"

Thorn could have wept. It was one thing hearing that bilge from Blot and Halford, another coming from a Jutras soldier. He took a steadying breath, fury crackling through his muscles, giving him a spurt of phantom strength. "Save my crew or die. Do you understand?"

The other man shook his head slowly, his expression regretful, or possibly disbelieving. One shoulder lifted in a shrug.

"First must destroy the Dhucala's wolves. Or all will burn."

"At least free them from the cabin. Put them belowdecks."

"No time. They will wait."

"They will die."

Again that half shrug. Thorn swallowed his fury. Arguing wasn't going to gain him any headway. Instead he returned to working at loosening the knot around his waist. Then he remembered his dagger. He pulled it from his waistband and attacked the hard, wet rope. But he was too weak to do more than part

a few strands. His fingers trembled so much that he
dropped the dagger. The Jutras guard watched, making no effort to stop him. Thorn snarled at his own
helplessness.

He staggered as another blast ripped apart the air.
This time the projectile struck the waters astern.
Water poured over the taffrail and the *Eidolon* rocked
forward with a jerking lurch. The lines holding it to
the Jutras ship stretched and then the warship followed with a jerk. The two ships collided and a shudder ran the length of the beleaguered *Eidolon*. She
bucked in protest and there was a sound of cracking,
like river ice in the spring. Thorn caught the fife rail,
his knees buckling. The wave that smashed into his
back held him upright, pinned in place. It swirled
away, dragging at his legs, and he slid down into the
water. His guard caught him under the arms and lifted
him up, shoving him up against the rail and holding
him there.

He scowled, scrutinizing Thorn's sagging body from
head to foot.

"You are broken, yes?"

The Pilot lifted a shoulder in a half shrug guaranteed to irritate.

"Tell me how you are harmed," the Jutras sailor
said, giving Thorn a little shake.

"I appear to be dying."

The guard's eyes went flat, his nostrils flaring, white
bracketing his lips. "What?"

"I am dying. I probably won't survive long enough
to get you to shore. Even if I wanted to."

It took a few grains for him to process that. Then
the pieces snicked together. He let go of Thorn like
he was made of fire.

"This cannot be," he said. Something wild flickered
over his face. "It must not be!"

"I'll notify the gods," Thorn said sardonically.

Just then the renegade ship launched its weapons.
There was a sharp *twang* and a *pop* and then more
projectiles were whistling in the sky. The air rattled

with the explosions and then two more missiles launched as the ships rode the upswell. There were more detonations, some close by, others farther away. The reverberations made Thorn's teeth ache and his marrow quiver. He couldn't tell if any of the missiles found their mark.

Then there were cheers from the renegade ship. Thorn glanced at his guard, who went to look over the taffrail. He had a sword on his left hip with two daggers tucked into the small of his back and one more in his boot. He swung back around and strode back to Thorn.

"The Dhucala's wolves die."

"What about my crew?"

The guard began to shake his head, then lifted his eyes, his attention snagging on something behind Thorn. The Pilot turned, following his gaze.

More Jutras were leaping onto the *Eidolon*'s deck. Men and women both, and carrying with them heavy duffels that they dragged to the forecastle, where the fires were spreading. Each of the canvas sacks was full of black sand. The Jutras sailors shoveled it out, tossing it over the burning wood. They were methodical, taking on one patch at a time. Thorn watched, twitching with frustration. But he recognized the sense of the strategy. Waves continued to crash over the deck, washing away the sand. Every time that happened, the fires flared up and spread more. The Jutras had to work quickly to smother the fires between each wave flood.

The flames that couldn't be put out with sand— those on the rigging and rails—had to be chopped out. The sailors donned heavy gloves and gauntlets made of leather and soon the racket of chopping wood was added to the noise of the wind and the wreckage.

"What is that stuff?" Thorn asked his guard, not expecting a reply.

"Agun."

The word meant nothing to Thorn. The guard seemed little inclined to elaborate and the Pilot did not push. He had to conserve his strength, such as it was. Relief at the immediate safety of his crew made him breathless. But beneath it was a quagmire of guilt—he ought to have hoped they died and were safe from slavery and sacrifices to the bloodthirsty Jutras gods.

His hands tightened on the fife rail until his knuckles gleamed white. There was still one more chance to protect his crew—but did he have the balls to kill them all to save them from what the Jutras had in store?

Chapter 16

Thorn was so lost in his internal tug-of-war that he didn't notice his guard closing in on him. He grasped Thorn's shoulder, pulling him back from the rail. A dagger flashed in his hand and before Thorn could react, the guard sliced through the safety line. He took the end of the rope still attached to Thorn and tugged him along.

"Come."

Thorn staggered after. He could barely lift his feet, nor could he feel the deck as he stepped. His ankles sagged and his knees knocked together. His bones felt like jelly. Suddenly the deck bucked and the guard windmilled his arms in the air for balance. He jerked Thorn's leash and the Pilot went sprawling on his stomach. The wave that crashed over the poop rail washed him forward, pushing him over the edge of the deck and dropping him down to the quarterdeck like a child's doll.

He managed to wrap his arms around his head, the wave rolling him over as he fell. He landed heavily on his back. Water filled his mouth and ears as he gasped for breath. Ungentle hands grabbed him by his lapels and dragged him upright. Instantly he doubled over, held in place by an iron arm slung quickly around his belly. He coughed and gagged, his head spinning. His feet slipped again and more hands clutched him. He was aware of shouting that seemed very far away and a darkness that closed around him with the numbing cold.

Then he found himself inside Plusby's cabin. They pushed him into a chair and he continued to cough, his head hanging between his knees. He felt his ribs moving oddly as if they'd come unfixed. Something trickled over the back of his ear and he couldn't decide if it was water or blood. He could feel his heart beating too fast, and his spine felt like rotten rope. A worm of something wriggled in his mind. He groped after it. It was elusive. Still he kept trying to bring his whirling mind to bear. And then it came to him.

He was being murdered. If two healing amulets were not working—it could only mean . . . someone was trying to kill him. Someone was succeeding.

The realization rocked him. He caught his breath. There had been the raiders first . . . then the sabotage to the water casks. . . . Why not an assassin? Someone who could be sure the *Eidolon* never made its destination.

And the only thing that could successfully fight the amulet's majick was more majick. Someone had attached a cipher to him. Ciphers were spells woven into some sort of object, often something innocuous like a button or a comb. Their properties varied widely—to help a bald man grow hair, to make a person appear younger, to discourage unwanted attention, or to cure bad breath. But ciphers could also be very dangerous. Four hundred seasons ago, Errol Cipher, Crosspointe's first majicar, had used them to torment his enemies. He'd created powerful ciphers that once attached could not be removed. Thorn was certain now that someone had attached him with a cipher in order to kill him. But when had anyone had an opportunity? He tried to think. And why hadn't he noticed it before?

A hand shook his shoulder. His thoughts swirled apart like autumn leaves in the wind.

"Do you answer, Pilot?"

He blinked, trying to tear his mind from the new certainty that he was being murdered. With a groan, he pushed himself up, resting his elbows on his thighs

and slowly lifting his head, following a pair of bare
feet up a women's legs, braced wide, then up her
thighs curved with muscle, over her slim hips to her
stomach. He paused there, having no strength to sit
up straight and look his captor in the eyes.

"Said I, do you answer?"

The woman's voice was deep and rich, like dark red
wine and fiery peppers. It was difficult to imagine that
such a seductive voice came from the mouth of a vicious Jutras.

"Answer what?" he said, knuckling his eyes.

She squatted down in front of him. Her eyes were
golden topaz. For a moment they locked his gaze to
hers and he felt like she could see inside his head. He
dropped his gaze, feeling his face flush with fear.
Could she see inside?

His heart was pounding, blood throbbing in his temples. He opened his eyes, avoiding her gaze and instead examining her sharp-edged features beneath a
short cap of raven hair. Her mouth was a compressed
slash above a strong chin. Her skin was the color of
walnut. Thorn caught his breath. She was pure-
blooded Jutras. On a renegade ship? It hardly seemed
conceivable.

Like his guard, there was a patterned band of scars
and tattoos running down the left side of her neck.
Caste marks. But they weren't what caught his attention. There was another set along her right cheekbone,
curving from her nose to her hairline. Unlike those
on her neck, these were raised and had a malevolent
look to them. He knew enough about the Jutras to
know it was unusual for any to bear more than one
set of caste marks, and these on her face looked . . .
punishing.

"Malik tells that you are broken. Yes?"

She spoke quietly, but with the weight of command.
Thorn found himself wanting to answer.

He nodded. "Yes."

"How are you harmed?"

"Aside from whatever broke falling off the poop deck? I'm dying."

"From what?"

He smiled. "Something deadly."

She frowned, looking him over from head to foot. He couldn't tell whether she was irritated. Her face was a mask that showed little of what she was thinking.

"You can guide the ship safely over the black waves?"

His eyebrows rose. He thought of his crew inside the burning forecastle. His smile became cold and hard. "I can. And I can sink this ship."

There was a grumble of voices behind him. She glared first in their direction and then back at Thorn, before thrusting to her feet with liquid grace. She rattled off a string of nonsensical words. They were met with silence and then he heard squelching footsteps as several people exited the cabin. Then she put firm hands on Thorn's shoulders and pushed him back to sit upright. He didn't fight her—not that he could—doing his best to appear relaxed, his hands folded in his lap. They were trembling. But now he knew why. Majickal poison.

He tilted his head against the back of his chair. She was standing before him, her arms crossed, her eyes narrowed. Like his guard—Malik—she wore patched motley with a mix of grays and blues. She was small; if he were standing, she would likely not come to higher than his chin. But she was powerful. Her hands were callused and muscular. She wore a curved sword on her right hip, and a dagger with a plain wood handle in her well-worn belt.

Thorn continued to avoid her gaze. The Jutras had a majick of their own, and he didn't want her crawling into his head and poking about.

The ship rose and fell, hit by a powerful wave. The wreckage of the masts slammed against the hull, sending a booming tremor through the ship.

"Ship will crack soon. Or tip."

"She might," Thorn agreed.

"All will die."

"Or be turned to spawn, yes."

Her head tilted. "You wish this?"

He shook his head, looking into her eyes at last. If she did have majick, she'd know the absolute truth of his words. "No. But neither do I wish them to become Jutras slaves. Or be sacrificed to your gods. Better my crew ends here."

"You said not to let them burn."

He shrugged with a nonchalance he did not feel. "Call it sentimental foolishness. I've come to my senses."

Her lips smiled, but her eyes remained sharp and cold as they watched him. "Maybe gut them now. Wash the decks with blood, offer eyes, tongues, hearts, and hands to Uniat and Cresset. The gods will sing glory for us."

Thorn felt himself blanch. He tightened his hands into fists. His throat closed so that he could hardly speak. "You will do what you will do. But no matter how much glory your gods sing you, I doubt they can get you safely to shore, can they? I wonder what *sylveth* will make of you."

She stared at him a moment longer, then turned and paced away. She moved like a cat, her muscles liquid beneath her skin. She ran her fingers through her hair, lacing her hands behind her neck as she stared at the wall. Then she spun about and returned, squatting down and looking up at him. He had a feeling her posture was calculated to make him feel in control. It didn't work. Someone on his own ship was trying to kill him. If he couldn't trust his own crew, how could he trust her?

"Do you not help us, people will die."

"I heard you the first time. Wash the decks with blood—"

She shook her head. "No. I do not speak of such.

People, my people, are to be slaughtered. I must carry them to safety before the Dhucala's wolves hunt them to death."

Thorn's brows furrowed together. "I don't understand. What does that have to do with us?"

She lifted her hands in frustration or supplication; he wasn't sure which. "I will explain. But there is little time. We are pyrates. We live outside the laws of my people, preying on ships and villages along the shore and rivers. We are allowed to be, because it is too troublesome to burrow us out of our warrens. But that no longer is as was.

"Early in Nisacar—the season of Bear—it began. Understand that there are two gods—Uniat and Cresset—who rule in balance. One is giver of all life, the other the harvester. They are not always the same. Do you understand? There is a change that comes. It is called Seir Muta Re. Who was giver of life becomes harvester. Who was harvester becomes giver of life. Do you see? Balance."

Thorn nodded, though he didn't really see, nor did he see what any of her explanation had to do with him or the *Eidolon*. She took a breath and continued.

"Seir Muta Re happened fifty-six days ago. The first in twenty seasons. Cresset turned from giver of life to harvester. But Uniat did not change from harvester to giver of life. Do you understand? There are two harvesters. The balance is broken. It is a sign. The gods are angry and hungry. My people go to war. No—"

She shook her head fiercely at his dismissive shrug. It wasn't anything new. The Jutras had been warring against the countries surrounding the Inland Sea for many years.

"I do not speak of the business of gathering, as we have done for many, many seasons. This will be true war as you have not seen. The gods want sacrifice. Their thirst is greater than the stars in the skies. My people must feed them the blood of our enemies or the gods will drink of us. There will be no slaves taken; there will be no increasing the *shaghis* with adopted peoples. All will die."

Thorn lifted his head off the back of the chair. Her eyes were wide and she looked more than a little frightened. It was not an expression he expected to see on her, and he could tell it was not familiar to her. It did more than anything to convince him that this change among the Jutras gods was truly something to fear. As if the Jutras weren't already terrifying enough.

"I don't see what that has to do with me helping you back to shore."

She grimaced and then her face lost all expression, returning to that impassive coldness he'd first seen on it. But she couldn't mask the flames of anger in her eyes.

"Before the Dhucala's wolves may be unleashed beyond our walls, they must first wipe clean the taint within the people. They will destroy those who have strayed beyond the laws to make our people pure. The gods demand it. My village is no longer safe. We captured the *Zhala* to carry my people to safety. We hoped to go south to Opiloron, but the wolves already lie in wait for us. The only safety for us waits across the Sanam's black waves. When we saw you, we knew it had to be. The gods of your people will shelter us."

Thorn snorted. "Had to be? I remind you that you were going to let my crew burn to death. A moment ago you threatened to butcher them. Are you mad? Why would I agree to help you?"

Her lips bent up in a ghost of a smile and then it faded. "Mad I may be," she agreed. "I could not chance harm from your crew while I was battling Dhucala's wolves. Both the *Zhala* and your ship would have been destroyed." She chewed her upper lip, her brow crimping. "But I believed—"

She stopped, pinching her lower lip as if reconsidering her words. But then she forged ahead. "It is said Pilots do not . . . value . . . the people of their ships. Neither captain nor crew. That is not so?"

Thorn felt himself flushing. "It is not so for me," he said in a brittle voice.

She stared a moment and then smiled, a wide grin that took Thorn aback. The expression made her seem all too . . . not Jutras. She seemed like someone who would enjoy a filthy joke and a frothing ale. But she *was* Jutras, and whatever they might look like, they were all killers and slavers. Even as he told himself so, he wasn't sure he believed it. Her worry for her people seemed real enough.

As quickly as it had appeared, her smile vanished. "There is little time. This is my bargain. We will help you make shore and aid in your repairs. Then you will help save my people from the Dhucala's wolves and lead us across the Sanam's black waves. Do you agree?"

Just like that. As if he had any reason to trust her. But he wanted to; if it was possible, he wanted to save his people. "What about my crew?"

"Do they agree, they will be allowed freedom. Do they not, they remain prisoners until we reach land. Then we will release them, though it will be on Jutras land. Not safe."

It was tempting. If he was able to get the *Eidolon* to safe harbor before he dropped dead. But it would nullify his only trump card—once ashore, the Jutras would no longer need him as a Pilot. They could trade him, the compass, and the *Eidolon* to the Dhucala's warriors in exchange for the safety of the village, amnesty from persecution, and likely a hefty reward on top of that. If there even was a village. Not that he thought he'd survive long enough to see it. But the ship and the compass were a prize worth a great deal.

Thorn studied the Jutras woman. She appeared sincere, her eyes wide and intent, her body tensed with what appeared to be a desperate need for him to believe. But she could be an excellent actor—she was a pyrate and therefore skilled in the arts of trickery and deception.

"This isn't my choice to make," he said finally. "My

captain should hear what you say. And the bosun and mate too." It would take all of them to sell the crew on the idea, if they agreed to it.

She nodded and went to the door. She spoke to someone outside and returned.

"You are wanting spirits? To drink?"

"Gods, yes," Thorn said heavily.

He watched her from between slit eyes as she went to the sideboard and poured brandy into a glass. Her movements were economical and deft.

He took the glass, gripping tightly. His hand quaked so hard he sloshed some onto his legs. He quickly drained the glass before he could drop it or before he'd have to suffer the humiliation of her help. It was one thing to have Halford helping him to piss and eat, but the idea of her witnessing his weakness made him cringe.

"May I have your name?" he asked.

"I am called Savaiu," she said. "I am the captain of the *Zhala*. You are called?"

"Thorn."

She waited a moment, as if expecting something more lofty and imposing. When nothing more was forthcoming, she tilted her head, scrutinizing him.

A sharp knock sounded at the cabin door and then it was thrust open. A rigid and bruised Plusby stalked inside, followed by a glowering Halford and an unsettlingly quiet Crabbel. The bosun had a black eye and a lump on his forehead. His knuckles were raw. Behind them came Malik and two others. Both of the last two were mixed-bloods, with no visible caste markings. Both had shoulder-length hair caught up in a series of intricate braids. Their motley clothing matched both Savaiu's and Malik's, but included brilliant orange embroidery on the collars and cuffs. Each carried his bared sword ready at his side.

The three Crosspointe sailors were lined up opposite Thorn with their guards behind and Savaiu between. Halford paled at the sight of the Pilot and the corner of Thorn's mouth twisted. He must look as bad as he felt. Savaiu looked at Thorn.

"Do you explain."

Thorn's gaze settled on Plusby. "The crew?"

Plusby's lip curled. He glanced at Savaiu and then back to Thorn. "Considering ways to kill themselves before they have to watch Jutras priests feast on their entrails."

Thorn nodded. He drew a breath. His chest was tight and there was a clutching feeling in his right side where he'd landed on the deck.

"This is Savaiu, captain of the Jutras warship *Zhala*."

He gestured at her. She tipped her head, her face expressionless, her topaz eyes glittering.

"She has extended an offer to us. She claims to need a Pilot to help ferry her village from Jutras lands before the Dhucala's soldiers massacre them. It seems the Jutras gods mean to make war—of a different kind than we've seen before. It will be a war of annihilation, if my understanding is correct, and it starts by clearing out the bilge scum at home."

Thorn glanced at Savaiu. She nodded.

"Savaiu is a pyrate and has stolen the warship she captains."

Plusby's brows shot up in surprise and both Halford and Crabbel looked at her with grudging respect.

"In exchange for ferrying her village to safety across the Inland Sea, she has offered to help us repair the *Eidolon* and free any of our crew who chooses to leave once we reach safe harbor."

Thorn hesitated. Should he tell them his conclusions? He had to. It would bear on their decision. And if they intended to deal fairly with Savaiu, she needed to know too. More so if they didn't intend to.

"There's something else. I believe I know now why the healing amulets have not helped me more. I think someone is trying to kill me. And it appears that he is doing so quite successfully."

Chapter 17

"What!"

There was a chorus of undiluted astonishment from Plusby, Halford, Crabbel, and Savaiu. They erupted in a loud clamor of discordant, demanding voices. At last Plusby overrode them all.

"Explain yourself, Pilot," he said grimly.

Thorn's words were slow, almost slurred. Exhaustion was overtaking him, as were hunger and his injuries. The brandy he'd drunk made his head reel. And adding to his infirmity, something else, something sly and deadly, was creeping through his veins, poisoning him.

"It is quite simple. Though I wear the healing amulet, I am growing weaker, more frail. Which is very strange, given that it repaired my hands."

He held them up, their palsy pronounced. There were audible gasps. He let his arms drop weakly into his lap.

"If the amulet works, then something else is chewing on me. Something powerful enough to counter the healing majick. It cannot be natural. It must be . . . contrived."

He could almost laugh at the identical expressions of slack-jawed shock that swept over his listeners.

"I understand not," Savaiu said before anyone else could speak. "Why should anyone wish harm to you? Are not Pilots *viata*—how would you say—sacred?"

"Aye, they are. Even the sorry likes of him."

Plusby met Thorn's gaze. His face was haggard and tense, his gray eyes almost black as they bored into Thorn, who gave a slight shrug. He had no comfort to offer. Only regret. He glanced to Halford and Crabbel and back to Plusby. They were brothers-in-arms. Trenchant, boorish, vulgar brothers, but brothers nonetheless.

"Who would harm him?" Savaiu asked.

"I've annoyed a fair number of folk in my life and many of them on this voyage," Thorn said, rousing himself. "But in this matter, I think it clear that someone wishes to be sure the *Eidolon* never delivers its cargo. Someone has already tried to stop us twice. Kill me and the ship is almost sure to disappear into the sea."

"You think it's some sort of cipher," Plusby guessed suddenly.

Thorn nodded. "Makes sense, doesn't it? Anything else the amulet would have cured, except something particularly catastrophic and dramatic like a knife to my heart or a quick-acting poison."

"But why? Killing you at Grimsby Bay or when we put in for water makes better sense."

Thorn shook his head. "I don't know. He must have his reasons." The corner of Thorn's mouth lifted. "Apologies, Halford. It's pure maliciousness. Not bad luck after all."

The bosun swore, his shoulders bunching as his body clenched. He was like a bull about to charge, except there was nothing to charge at. Behind him, the guards shifted uneasily, lifting their sword tips.

Savaiu snapped at them in Jutras and they settled, though they remained tense.

"What is this cipher? How do you restore the Pilot?"

Thorn admired her quiet control and single-minded focus. If she was telling the truth about her village, she had to be feeling the flames of panic. If she wasn't telling the truth, she and her crew were in dire straits. But she kept herself in check, neither fidgeting nor pacing as he dearly would have liked to do.

"A cipher is a majickal device," Plusby explained.

"A tit-sucking curse," Halford growled.

He glared at the Jutras captain with hot fury and Thorn wasn't sure if his statement referred to the cipher, to the Jutras, or to Savaiu in particular.

Plusby lifted his hand to quiet the interruption and Halford subsided. But his rage continued to roll off him in palpable waves.

"Ciphers carry spells that can provide protections. For instance they might allow the wearer to understand languages he doesn't know, enhance his appearance, allow him to hear over greater distances—any of an endless variety of things. However, they can also carry nasty attacks. They can be attached to anything from the most expensive baubles to the most innocuous."

"Do you not remove it and take away its power over you?" Savaiu asked.

"Ciphers tend to hold on tightly until they've run their course," Thorn said. "And I have no idea what it might be."

"Shouldn't be too hard to discover," Plusby said.

"If it matters," was Thorn's reply.

"There is no way to take off it?" Savaiu asked.

There was grim shaking of heads. Except for Thorn's.

"There's one way."

"How?" Halford demanded, taking a step forward, his fists lifting.

"Don't get too hopeful. It is an unlikely solution. And would endanger the ship—both ships," he said. "I'll only try it if we make landfall first."

Savaiu was staring at him the way a drowning man looks at land. At his words, her mouth compressed into a white line, her topaz eyes flaring. Thorn slid a sideways glance at Plusby. He too wore an expression of desperation and rigidly clamped hope. Thorn could almost see when his captain put the pieces together.

Plusby rocked back on his heels, looking up at the ceiling.

"Blood of Braken, breath of Meris," the captain muttered, answering the question.

Thorn nodded. "Aye."

"What's it mean?" Halford demanded, looking between his captain and his Pilot.

Neither answered. Plusby wouldn't. His men already thought him half-mad; this would only confirm it. Savaiu might believe, but Thorn didn't intend to tell her. She was Jutras. The risk was too great. Besides, if she was sincere, then she might wait for *sylveth* to roll in on the storm waves. Even whole and undamaged and running with full canvas, a swift ship like the *Eidolon* might not be able to outrun a *sylveth* tide, and that with advanced warning from the compass post. To dunk Thorn, they'd have to wait for it to roll in. It was too dangerous.

"It means," Plusby said slowly, "that if Captain Savaiu's offer is still open, and if we accept, then we run at whatever speeds we can manage for the coast, haul the ships out of the water, and pray we're in time to save our Pilot. If so, we will fulfill the rest of our bargain with our new allies. If not—" He broke off and looked at Savaiu.

"If not, we will still help repair your ship and you will be free to do as you wish," she said.

"How can we trust 'em?" Crabbel demanded. "They be Jutras."

Savaiu straightened, her chin jutting. She wasn't pretty by ordinary standards. Her face was bold and stark like a wind-and-sea-carved headland, her body as graceful and dangerous as a *sylveth* tide. She was capable and strong. She stalked over to Plusby, looking up at him.

"I will give you my hand on it."

There was an audible sound from Malik, quickly cut off as Savaiu hammered him with her stony gaze. She turned back to Plusby and something passed between them—captain to captain.

"Bosun, mate—do you say aye or nay?"

Thorn's jaw dropped. Plusby was *asking* the *charmers*? Both Halford and Crabbel were taken aback, neither answering.

"Do not keep me waiting," Plusby said sharply.

Crabbel answered first. "I'll follow your helm."

Halford's reply was slower, grudging. "As ye see fit."

"Then we accept your hand on it," Plusby said, extending his own. "And we thank you for your help."

Savaiu looked at his hand, then slowly clasped it. After a moment, Plusby pulled away and turned to Halford and Crabbel.

"Inform the crew of our bargain. Tell them if they cannot agree, they will remain imprisoned until we make landfall, at which time they will be free to make their own way to safety. Then secure the mizzenmast so that we may use it. I want a report on the repairs and any other damage in a quarter of a glass."

The two men departed, followed by two of the Jutras guards, leaving behind Plusby, Savaiu, and Malik. The latter began stirring up the fire with fierce energy while the two captains closed on Thorn.

"He should be searched to find this cipher. It will be on his skin, yes?" Savaiu said to Plusby.

"Aye. He needs dry clothing anyhow. And rest."

"He should be guarded. In case his enemy believes he will succeed in bringing us to shore. They may try to kill him more surely."

"I agree. My steward will do it. She's been with me a long time. I trust her."

Savaiu shook her head. "My people have every reason to protect the Pilot—"

"The Pilot's name is Thorn and he's not a trinket to be examined and guarded," Thorn said, annoyed.

"You are far more valuable than a mere trinket and you most certainly are to be examined and guarded." Plusby settled his hand on Thorn's shoulder.

"If you are thinking you want to see me bare-skinned, you should know I prefer women, not skinny, ill-tempered captains with scruffy beards and no manners," Thorn retorted, pushing ineffectively at Plusby's hand. His strength failed him and he slumped back into his chair.

"I'll have Degby bring some food up," Plusby said, his voice patronizingly kind, the pitying tone one used for dying invalids. "I'll make sure there's no poison in it."

Thorn listened to his boots thud across the floor. Malik continued to fuss with the stove. The ship rose and fell, the wind howling and the waves crashing. The wreckage continued to scrape and pound against the *Eidolon* with patient fury. Thorn hardly noticed. His eyes drifted shut. He drew a deep breath, smelling the coal of the stove and the brine of the sea. He opened his eyes, meeting Savaiu's concerned gaze.

"Do you hurt?"

He gave a faint shake of his head. "I am merely . . . tired."

"How long before—?" She stopped herself, shaking her head and flushing. "Apologies, Pilot. A rude and foolish thing to speak."

"I take no offense." Though he was feeling a bit like meat going bad. How long before his carcass began to stink up the ship? But she had a right. Her people were in danger. Every grain Thorn clung to life was a grain closer to their rescue.

"To answer your question, I do not know. I've never been murdered before. At least, the last time someone tried to kill me, it was with knives and fists. When the cipher will choose to finish its business is anyone's guess."

She said something in Jutras, the guttural, angry syllables almost smoking with their vehemence. Thorn grinned. If he'd the energy, he'd have been swearing to blister paint.

Just then Malik came up behind her. "All is ready."

Savaiu's face shuddered and Thorn had a sense of

her withdrawing into herself, as if preparing herself for battle. She nodded at Malik to signal she'd heard him and then addressed herself to Thorn.

"You will bear witness for your ship?"

Thorn didn't understand. "Witness?"

But Savaiu had not waited for his reply. She followed Malik, who stood waiting for her beside Plusby's desk. With exaggerated care, he drew a dagger from his belt. He lifted the blade, point up, and pressed it against his lips. Then he flipped it in his hand, swinging his arm and driving the point of the dagger deeply into the top of the desk. It quivered there and then Savaiu drew her dagger, repeated the kiss to the blade, and drove it into the wood.

The two daggers stood like sentries, mirrors of each other.

Thorn watched without understanding as Savaiu rolled up her right sleeve. Her dark skin gleamed in the firelight. Slowly she drew her curved sword and offered it to Malik, resting it across her forearm. He gripped the hilt, but didn't lift it away. Instead he spoke a string of Jutras words that ended on a high, questioning note. His face was stony, the shadows carving his face into a demonic mask. Savaiu replied and he lifted the sword, holding it point up and kissing the blade.

Savaiu dropped to one knee beside the desk and slotted her arm into the channel between the two blades until the inside of her elbow rested against her own dagger, her forearm jutting out the other side. Her left arm hung at her side, the fingers curled into a white-knuckled fist. She looked at Malik and gave a firm nod.

Thorn couldn't believe his eyes when Malik stepped to the side and raised Savaiu's sword over his head. Like an executioner. Except he was about to chop off her hand.

"Stop! What in the cracking depths are you doing?"

The lolling impotence fell away from him as horror and panic drove him upright. He staggered across the narrow floor, latching onto Malik's arm and jerking him around.

"You carrion-loving brice whore! Are you mad?"

Malik said nothing, his mouth pulled tight with strain. He wrenched from Thorn's grip and snatched the Pilot by the throat, his fingers biting deeply.

Savaiu spoke sharply. Malik stared bitterly at Thorn a long moment, then slowly dropped his hand.

"Thorn. Thorn," Savaiu said his name insistently.

He turned, but did not take his eyes off Malik, who was once again holding the sword out before him in both hands.

"You must not interfere. You must witness."

"I'll not watch him chop off your hand. What madness is this?"

"It is as agreed. My hand to prove my words are true. Your captain accepted this. It must be done. There is little time."

Thorn's mouth dropped open. Words failed. She sounded like she was about to sacrifice a pig or a goat, not her own hand.

"No," he whispered.

"All will be well," she assured him, her voice thinning with each word. "Malik will seal the wound with fire."

She nodded at the woodstove, where Thorn saw now that the hilt of Malik's sword protruded, the blade sunk deep into the coals and searingly hot.

Savaiu's lips tightened. "It shall be quickly done."

"No," Thorn said more firmly, his lungs aching for air. His heart thudded in his chest. "You are wrong. Removing your hand will not mean anything more than what you've already done."

He was lying. Of course it would. For her to allow herself to be mutilated, to give her hand—it was a powerful testimonial. One that the entire *Eidolon* crew couldn't help but acknowledge.

"It was agreed," she said with an air of finality. "The bargain is made. Sacrifice is required."

"It is not," he insisted. "Plusby—none of us knew what you were offering. It is unacceptable."

She drew back slightly, her eyes widening. Malik made a strangled sound, lifting the sword so that the tip was suddenly pressed against Thorn's throat.

"Do not!" Savaiu ordered.

Malik didn't move. His expression was a rigid mask of helpless hate and rage. His fingers flexed and knotted more tightly on the hilt and he pressed forward. The sword's point bit into Thorn's throat. Blood tickled as it began to flow from the wound.

Savaiu burst into a furious tirade, though she did not get to her feet, nor did she remove her arm from the brace of knives. Malik ignored her. Thorn stared at the other man, seeing the twitch at the corner of his left eye, and the sharp jut of his chin. He held himself very still. Malik wanted only the slightest excuse to drive the blade through Thorn's neck and damn the consequences.

"I don't want her to lose her hand either," Thorn said quietly.

Malik's jaw moved as if he were about to speak, but he remained silent. The tip of the sword dug deeper.

The cabin door opened. For a moment the only sounds were the crackling of the fire, Thorn's own ragged breathing, and the wail of the wind. Then there was a low exclamation and the singing of metal as a sword was drawn. Footsteps pounded across the floor and another blade sliced across Thorn's line of sight. It jabbed into the base of Malik's throat. Blood ran freely from the cut. The Jutras man drew a sharp breath, but he did not move.

"What is this?" Plusby asked, his voice as cold and black as the depths of the Inland Sea.

Thorn licked his dry lips. "Seems when Savaiu offered you her hand, she meant it literally. I have objected."

Plusby swore. Then he slowly lowered his sword. A moment later he smashed into Malik's chest with both forearms, sending the other man stumbling backward. Thorn staggered and caught himself on the edge of the desk. Malik leaped forward, his blade flashing, his mouth pulled into a rictus. Plusby countered the wild swinging easily on his own sword. He twisted and Savaiu's sword skittered across the floor. Plusby grasped Malik by the collar and pulled him around, laying his blade against the Jutras man's throat.

"I'd like for us to all get out of this alive and in one piece," he said. "Would you mind leashing your hound before I have to put him down?"

Savaiu gave a slight shake of her head, looking sternly at Malik in silent command.

"Forgive my brother, Captain. He is . . . young."

Brother? Thorn glanced between the two. Certainly there was a resemblance, but he'd assumed it was merely shared Jutras heritage. He rubbed his jaw and scraped his fingers through his hair.

"My apologies, Captain Savaiu, but if your brother does not douse his sails, I'll have to cut his stays. I fear the strain it would put on each of our crews. They might mutiny. Think of your people—we'll never save your village if that happens."

Savaiu rattled off a string of sharp-sounding words, her voice rising. Malik went rigid, and then slumped. Plusby felt it and let go. Malik stumbled away, hands braced against the wall, his head dangling. Relief made Thorn dizzy. But they weren't out of danger yet. Savaiu remained on the floor, her face set.

"Captain Savaiu, I would ask you to rise and put a stop to this grisly business," Plusby said.

She gave him a long look. "I offered my hand. You accepted. This is our bargain. The blood must be spilled, the flesh offered."

"No. Not this way. I did not understand what you offered. What I accepted, what my crew accepted, was your word. Removing your hand serves no purpose. Belay that; it serves a dreadful purpose. Certainly Malik is not the only member of your crew who will take the loss of your hand amiss. It will only increase the friction and I couldn't vouch for what would happen."

"It is our bargain," Savaiu insisted. She gestured in

frustration with her free hand, searching for words. "It is our custom. It binds us. My crew understands this. Malik—he is my brother and he is foolish. The ritual is begun. We cannot stop without offending the gods. There must be blood and pain and flesh."

"Very well. Then consider this as well. Suppose your crew does accept your sacrifice without protest or retaliation, and suppose my crew perceives the act as a grand gesture demonstrating the truth of your pledge. What then? What use are you then to us? Removing your hand will endanger both ships. You won't be able to handle a line or save yourself if a wave sweeps you off your feet in these seas. You and your crew are all whip-jacks—you haven't sailed the open waters before. You've done well enough so far, but our ship is crippled and we're being chased by the worst things Braken has to throw at us. We may not survive if you are not at your best. It's enough that our Pilot is dwindling—let us not add to our deficiencies. Hear me well: we cannot afford to lose any able body right now, particularly with what's coming behind us. Thorn?"

He knew what Plusby was asking. Reaching his perceptions out to the water as far as they would go, he began to speak.

"The storm that is driving us now began days ago far west of here. It was a massive coil. As it grew and blew east, it sucked in *sylveth* toward its center from all over the sea. It also churned up vescies—they are small creatures, mostly sharp mouths and stomachs, that live in the coldest, blackest depths. Large storms pull them up to the surface. A swarm can eat a man in a matter of a few grains. They can gobble a ship in less than a glass. Right now, they are ravenous and they are hunting. When they scent us, we'll have trouble outrunning them. For the moment they are hampered by the sheering current of the bore's williwaw. But when the bore closes, as eventually it will, they'll be after us fast."

He paused, waiting for her to indicate her understanding. She nodded slowly, but her expression remained adamant. Thorn continued.

"The vescies are minor compared with our other problem. When the storm let go of Crosspointe, its force exploded the ribbons of *sylveth* it had drawn toward it, creating splatter tides. These are . . ." Thorn searched for the right word. *Dangerous* didn't begin to describe the horrors they could wreak.

"Splatter tides are rarely seen outside of the season of Chance. The *sylveth* disperses over vast stretches, washing willy-nilly. A droplet is enough to transform even something as large as a ship. The bore has not slowed the *sylveth* down. Instead it has spun it out in an even broader casting. We must get the ships out of the water and above the high-tide mark, or they and everything they carry will become spawn. And even then we won't be safe. Where it makes landfall, where it rides the tide up rivers—there will be a massive spawning. I cannot describe the things they will do—" He stopped, lifting his hands as if to signify surrender. "We will want every pair of hands to fend them off."

Savaiu continued to look at him, searching his face as if for signs of lies. Plusby tapped his fingers against his thighs and then spoke.

"Certainly if you still wish to mutilate yourself later, after our ships are repaired and your village is safely removed to free shores, then you may do so with my blessings. I'll even help you, if you wish. But right now we need you whole and we don't have time for frivolous self-indulgence. So please, get up off your ass and help me get these ships moving."

Plusby's cutting attack made Savaiu start and then her cheeks flushed. Her eyes hardened.

"Do you understand? There must be blood; there must be flesh; there must be pain. The ritual is begun. The sacrifice must be worthy."

Plusby snarled and then nodded. "Fine."

He yanked out his dagger and set his hand on top of hers, splaying her fingers. Without hesitation, he sliced down through her little finger just below the fingernail. Thorn watched in horror. It happened so quickly, he did not have time to protest. Savaiu made no sound, her face contorting.

"Give me that damned sword so I can cauterize it," Plusby demanded.

Malik leaped to grab it. The smell was nauseating and worse was the sizzling sound as he touched the hot metal to her bloody flesh. Savaiu gasped, her body going rigid. Then Malik tossed his blade aside. Without a word he pulled his dagger from the desk. He lifted it to his lips point down, and sheathed it again. Savaiu did the same and then stood. On the desk was the tip of her finger and a puddle of blood. Holding her injured hand above them, she murmured words.

Nothing happened. Thorn wasn't sure what he expected. Savaiu looked first perplexed and then a flicker of something like fear raced across her expression before her face settled into a smooth mask.

"The gods do not answer. It is to be expected."

"So it was for nothing," Thorn grated.

She looked at him, her yellow eyes gleaming in the firelight. "Or it was not enough," she said.

"Or," Plusby said, "you are no longer favored by your gods. You said yourself, you and your people are hunted. Is there any sacrifice you could make now that would make them happy?"

He didn't wait for an answer. Instead he went to the door. A few minutes later he returned with a hatchet. Without a word, he chopped away the corner of the desk until a chunk of wood bearing the blood and her finger was free. He picked it up, holding it out to Savaiu.

"If your gods aren't interested, then we'll offer it to the sea. Maybe Braken, Meris, and Chayos will look on you kindly."

He opened one of the deadlights. Spume splashed him and the floor. He gestured. "Feed this sea."

Savaiu stepped up to the opening and pushed the wood through. Whether she spoke or not, Thorn couldn't tell. There was a rushing sound in his head that had nothing to do with the waves or the wind. He gripped a chair to steady himself, but found his legs no longer held. Slowly he sank to the floor. Malik said something sharply in Jutras, and Savaiu and Plusby spun about and came and hoisted him into the chair.

"Let's get him to his cabin," Plusby said. "We've a glass or so before we can get under way. He needs food and rest. With a guard."

"I'll do it."

Bess was inside the door holding a tray of food. She stepped forward, setting the tray on the table near Thorn. Her craggy face was pinched and her hands shook slightly. Savaiu looked skeptically at her, but Plusby nodded. "I've explained the situation. I trust her."

"One of my people will watch also," Savaiu said implacably. "None have reason to murder the Pilot."

But if Thorn was correct about being poisoned by a cipher, then at least one member of the Crosspointe crew did. Savaiu didn't trust any of them. Though she did not say the words, they hung in the air all the same. Bess's face went dark and her mouth curled downward. Her hand slid surreptitiously to the hilt of her sword.

"Then I want Malik," Thorn said, as he snatched up a piece of bread and began to bolt it down. It was stale and smeared with cold drippings. It was the best thing he could remember having tasted in his life.

"Are you mad?" Plusby demanded. "The man just tried to kill you."

Malik's face had gone slack with surprise. Bess looked so outraged that Thorn thought her head might start smoking. Even Savaiu looked unconvinced.

He chewed and swallowed, grasping the mug of sour ale and drinking deeply from it. He glanced up.

"I believe I did give him some cause for wanting me dead, unintended of course," Thorn said. "I think I may have grown on him since then. At any rate,

Captain, it was not so long ago that you also wanted me dead. In trying to kill me, Malik betrayed Savaiu's trust—as a member of her crew and as her brother. He'll do anything to redeem himself, even stop somebody from killing me. He's the one I want."

Grinning slyly, Thorn looked at Plusby. "I've recently had rare good luck trusting those I shouldn't. No sense changing tack now."

"Aye, and someone on this ship has tried to murder you. Doesn't that tell you that you place your trust too easily?"

"Neither you nor any of the charmers did this to me. Of that I am certain. Aren't you?"

Plusby shook his head in exasperation. "Very well. You can have Malik. But if he kills you, I'll buy him a drink and a whore and maybe pay him a fat reward as well. And I will piss on your grave. That's a promise."

Thorn laughed, a shaky, soft sound that soon turned into a hacking cough. It made the others frown, even Malik. Slowly the attack subsided and Thorn wilted sideways against the arm of his chair, wheezing. "And what treasures will you offer him if he keeps me from dying?"

"I'm not sure that actually deserves a reward," Plusby mused. "Perhaps I'll set him on the Bramble."

"I think you just sealed my fate."

"I was thinking *you* did," was Plusby's sardonic reply. "Now eat and let us get under way."

Chapter 18

Thorn refused to allow Bess or Savaiu to witness the search for the cipher. Fitch was nowhere to be found either. He hoped she was just frightened of the storm and too many people crowding his cabin and that she'd emerge from her hidey-hole soon. All the same, who knew how the Jutras might react if they saw a cat? They might think Fitch was a harbinger of doom, which would make them no different from the Cross-pointe crew. Still, he would have liked to hold her.

He put a hand on Plusby's arm as the captain started to peel off his wet cloak.

"Fitch—you'll make sure she's all right if things go . . . badly . . . for me?"

"Don't you think things are already going badly for you? They could hardly go worse."

"Then will you look after her? Make sure Halford doesn't feed her to the sea with me when I'm dead?"

Plusby grimaced and scrubbed his hands over his face. His cheeks were sunken, his eyes bloodshot. He looked as if he'd aged twenty seasons. "If it will make you shut up, then yes. I will."

"Thank you." Thorn let his hand drop.

"It is little enough payment for hauling me down off the mast."

"It wasn't kindness—I wanted to sail."

"I disagree. It was a great kindness and came at a cost. You could have sent the charmers up and saved yourself a great deal of pain and suffering. Mothering your little beast is hardly payment in kind."

"It is to me."

"So my dignity and health are to be measured by one cat's safety, is that it?"

"Don't get greedy. Fitch is worth two of you."

"Then you shall owe me."

"Absolutely. You may remove a pound of flesh before dropping me over the rail."

"I'm not sure there's a pound of flesh left hanging on your bones," Plusby said, and then with Malik's help proceeded to none too gently drag off Thorn's cloak.

"Explain to me how and when you could have been attached with a cipher and not be aware of it."

"I've been thinking about it. The only time it could have been attached was while I was sleeping. As it turns out, I've been . . . sleeping . . . rather heavily of late. As to why I don't feel it?" Thorn grimaced. "If truth be told, my sense of touch has been . . . declining. No doubt a product of the cipher. I might have seen it, but I haven't changed clothes in days."

"You smell like it."

The two men undressed Thorn with ruthless efficiency, tossing the sopping clothing into a heap in the corner. As they pulled off his shirt and trousers, they both turned grim. They refused to meet Thorn's eyes.

He looked down at himself. He *was* rather repulsive. His skin bagged in loose scallops beneath his arms; the bones of his wrists protruded sharply, and his arms looked like sticks. It was as if he'd not eaten in a month. His legs were spindly, his trunk raw with cold and bruises. His stomach was concave and he could count every rib. Except on his left side. Those looked mushy and dented, a purple blotch spreading over the top. He looked like a battered skeleton wearing an ill-fitted suit of skin.

"Ah," he said. "There it is."

The cipher was hardly more than a cobweb. It wrapped his right ankle, a thin seam of white, almost invisible against his pale skin. He wasn't sure he'd have noticed it even if he'd been changing his clothes more regularly. Thorn watched with little expectation or hope as first Plusby and then Malik sawed at the shackle with their daggers.

"Forget it," he said at last, blood trickling down over the top of his foot and heel from numerous small cuts inflicted during the attempts to remove it. "It was made to last until it completes its spell. It will come off easily enough when I'm dead. I'd prefer to be a bit more dignified when I do stop breathing, so if you don't mind, can you fetch me something dry so I can sleep a few grains?"

"What if we removed the leg?" Malik suggested.

Thorn shot him a searing look. "Chances are that the cipher won't permit itself to be defeated so easily."

"Is there not a chance also it might succeed?" Malik pushed, his brows rising as he crossed his arms over his chest.

It was a none-too-subtle reminder of Savaiu's courage and commitment. She would have cut her hand off. Surely the Pilot could do no less if it might mean the safety of the two ships and an entire village of people, not to mention saving Thorn's own worthless life. But he was not so self-sacrificing nor noble. He wasn't going to cut his damned leg off for the slim hope of being rid of the cipher. At least not yet. He had a way to get the cipher off. He just had to survive long enough.

"I very much doubt it," Thorn answered firmly, ending the discussion.

They wrapped his cuts with a bandage, then dressed him. The entire procedure was humiliating. They lifted his arms and legs as if he were a rag doll. Malik managed the whole affair more deftly and gently than Plusby, though he didn't bother to hide his annoyance. When Thorn was bundled up warm again, they helped him settle back on his bed.

"The plan clearly is to kill you," Plusby said, standing over Thorn. "But what I can't figure is if you were helpless enough to attach a cipher, then you would have been easy prey for smothering or a knife in the neck. Why not kill you quickly?"

"I don't know, though the cipher should probably have worked more quickly. I'd likely be dead already if not for the healing amulet I've been wearing. My bet is that it slowed the cipher's majick. And my killer couldn't have predicted the storm. Perhaps he hoped we'd put in to shore somewhere after he attached the cipher and he'd be able to jump ship."

Plusby slapped his forehead. "Damn! The water casks. I forgot about them. What if Degby discovered they'd been tampered with before she was supposed to? If she hadn't found them so soon, we'd have been in open waters and would have had to find a place to put in to port. That would have given the killer a day or two at least to attach the cipher, and then jump ship when we went in for water. But instead he was trapped aboard. I surely would like to know exactly what it is in our hold that is worth a suicide mission and the life of a Pilot."

Thorn's lip curled. "I am not dead yet. There's still a chance for me."

"Yes. Through the breath of Braken, blood of Meris. Is that right?"

"The birth and life of every Pilot," Thorn agreed.

"I hope you're right."

"I hope we're in time."

"I'll see how close we are to getting under way. Bess and Malik will keep watch outside. No one will disturb you. Try to get some sleep."

"Aye, aye, Captain."

Thorn slid into sleep so quickly and deeply that he didn't hear the door shut.

He woke in darkness. Instantly he was alert. Prickles ran over his scalp and down his body. His heart slammed against his ribs. *Someone was in the room.*

"Who's there?"

"Just me, Pilot. I'll fetch a lamp."

Bess.

There were footsteps as she went into the outer cabin. Thorn let go a ragged breath and slowly unclenched his body. A glow illuminated the doorway and he struggled to sit up. At last he slumped against the wall, panting.

Bess entered again, carrying a brass lamp. She stepped carefully over something on the floor just inside the doorway and came to the side of the bed, setting the lamp on the nightstand with a click.

Thorn rubbed his eyes and blinked at Bess, who sat down on the edge of the bed facing him.

"There is very little time. We are nearly ready to be under way," she said.

"I'd better get moving, then. Help me up, if you would," Thorn said.

Bess just looked at him. His stomach curled with foreboding.

"Where's Malik?"

She glanced over her shoulder toward the foot of the bed and then back. "Gone tits up," she said. "As should be."

Thorn went rigid, realizing suddenly that she was turning a dagger in her fingers. He instantly recognized Malik's weapon from the aborted ceremony with Savaiu.

"You put the cipher on me."

"Aye," she agreed thoughtfully. "They paid me well, you see. Not just money. I was going to get my own captain's ticket. And my family would be permitted to immigrate to Crosspointe. They would get a house in Sylmont and twenty thousand dralions. Things have been so bad for them in Esengaile since . . . I couldn't refuse such an offer."

"Most sailors prefer not to be without a Pilot on the open waters," Thorn said, still trying to hitch himself upright to be in a better position to wrestle with her. The only weapons ready to hand were pillows. He clenched a hand on one. It might serve to foul the blade when she came at him. Maybe he could keep

her talking until someone came to check on them.
"How were you going to survive without a Pilot?"

She dug in her pocket and pulled out a chunk of
sylveth. It was smooth and oval with a flat side. It was
the size of a plum. "We weren't supposed to be at
sea. I set off a beacon when we put in at Grimsby
Bay. But they failed to take the ship. Then I tried the
cipher when Degby discovered the water casks too
soon. I have to be on land to activate this." She held
up the oval chunk of *sylveth*. "I thought I got lucky
when the bowsprit cracked. If we'd have beached to
make repairs, I'd have had my chance. But then the
Jutras came."

"And now?"

"I won't be food for the Jutras gods and I'll be
damned to the depths before I'll wear an iron collar
again."

"But we've made a bargain with them. They don't
plan to kill us or capture us." His gaze flicked to the
door. When would someone come?

She smiled, pocketing the *sylveth* stone. "That's the
problem. You're too trusting. They are savage and
brutal. And it isn't just me. I can't let them have you.
I can't let them have the *Eidolon*. You should understand. Think about the danger to Crosspointe. You
wouldn't like to be a slave either," she added in a
calm, sure voice. "It's much better this way." She
lifted the dagger.

"It surprises me that you didn't warn Plusby off. I
thought you had some fondness for him," he said
quickly. He chewed his lips. He had to keep her mind
off the knife in her hand, until someone came to fetch
him to the compass post. Hopefully he didn't anger
her so much she cut out his liver. "Or maybe this is
revenge—getting at the father through the son. His
father sold you into servitude and bought you back.
He's dead now. . . . Why not take vengeance on the
son? Better yet, you'll be able to watch him die, enjoy
the spectacle of it."

She smiled unhappily. The dagger dangled from her

slack fingers. "Leighton is a strong man with a determined mind. I tried to deflect him from taking this berth. I *tried*."

Leighton? Thorn locked in on her use of Plusby's first name and the way her voice softened over it. She did care for him. Maybe that would be the key.

"Did you really? Why didn't you tie him hand and foot until the ship was beyond his reach? But instead you agreed to serve under his command, *knowing* you planned to sink us. You must truly hate him."

"No." She flipped the dagger between her fingers. "But he wanted this. And I could not risk everything just for him. For my own ticket and for my family—I had to take the offer. But none of that matters anymore." She turned to face Thorn, dire purpose hardening her eyes. "It's much better this way."

He was out of time.

He tightened his fist on the pillow and swung it around to strike at the dagger, still loose in her fingers. The weapon clattered to the floor, sliding against the bulwark as the ship rolled on the waves.

Instantly Bess dived after it. Thorn lurched forward, forcing his legs over the bed. He grabbed the lamp on the nightstand. It was made of copper and brass with a squat glass globe for a chimney. He raised it up as Bess surged up from the floor, the dagger ready in her hand. He swung it down with all his might, smashing it against her head. The chimney shattered and droplets of burning oil spattered over the floor, Bess, and the bedclothes.

He had precious little might. She rocked back, falling dazed against the bulkhead, still gripping the dagger.

"Crack it!" he swore.

He glanced at the door behind him. As weak as he was, she'd recover and overtake him before he could get out on deck. He looked back at her. She was already clambering to her feet. She shook her head, firming her grip on the dagger. She lunged again.

Thorn dragged up every ounce of strength he had,

leaning back and lifting his legs to shove her back.
She fell against the wall again. He staggered to his
feet, clutching the base of the lamp. It was him or her.
Even as she began to struggle to her feet, he battered
her head with the lamp. Once. Twice. Three times.
Her head flopped to the side, blood running in weaving strands over her forehead and cheeks. The sight
of her made Thorn's stomach turn. The familiar wild
anger did not rise to bolster him as it had when he'd
attacked Wildreveh and later Plusby. Instead he only
felt bitter sadness for the waste and for Plusby's pain
when he learned of her betrayal.

Malik was sprawled just inside the doorway, Bess's
knife protruding from his chest. Thorn coughed and
drew a hard breath. His lungs filled with smoke. The
oil from the lamp had begun to burn in earnest, filling
the windowless room with acrid smoke. He choked
and stumbled over Malik's body, swallowing bile at
the feel of the Jutras sailor's dead flesh beneath his
bare feet.

He staggered through the main cabin and unlatched
the door. The wind pushed back against him and it
was all he could do to squeeze through. White spume
sloshed around his calves as he waded out onto the
quarterdeck. He clutched his arms around himself,
leaning back against the cabin wall to steady himself.
The cold cut through his shirt. Sailors pounded against
the thick layer of crusted ice clinging to every surface
of the ship, while others stretched towlines between
the *Zhala* and the *Eidolon*.

He looked wildly about for someone in the *Eidolon*'s crew. He coughed again, the cold damp making
his lungs contract. He stumbled forward, his numb feet
skidding on the skin of ice sheathing the decks. The
ship rolled and a wave crashed over the port bow. A
thigh-deep wash of frigid water swept across the fore-
deck, flooding the waist and quarterdeck. It rammed
Thorn and he went down.

He fought to keep from breathing. His lungs were
empty sacks, deflated by his coughing attack. An angry

itch burned in the back of his throat. He clamped his lips together, kicking and paddling for the surface. He rammed into something and scrabbled for a hold. The pinrail. He gripped an empty belaying pin and held on.

The water ran off through the scuppers, though more poured over the rails and white, icy spume plumed upward, falling again in a stinging spray. Thorn sucked deep, wrenching breaths, gasping and gagging. He was on his knees, both hands clenched around the bottom of the belaying pin.

A taste of acrid smoke on the wind drove him to his feet. He lurched about, shaking, this time with the primitive fear living inside every sailor—fire aboard ship. A thin feathering of gray whispered from the banging door of his cabin.

"Fire!" he called, but the wind shredded the puny sound. Thorn tried again. "Fire!"

He let go of the belaying pin and braced himself back against the pinrail, waving his arms above his head, hoping to catch someone's—anyone's—attention. It was Gerry, one of the snotties, who finally noticed him. He came running, a scrawny, pale-skinned young boy—maybe twelve years old. His blond hair was cut close to his head in a bristling style. He was wet to the skin and shivering, his lips blue.

"D'ye want for somethin', sir?"

Thorn dropped his arms heavily to his sides, where they hung like gallows weights.

"Fire," he said.

Gerry looked at him in confusion.

"Fire! Get the captain, the bosun, the mate! Run!"

His sudden intensity jolted the boy and he splashed across the deck to the forecastle. Thorn slumped against the pinrail.

Gerry scrabbled up the ladder, standing at the top and shouting. He jumped aside, dropping back to the deck as mist-blurred bodies leaped over him and came toward Thorn at a skidding run. The first to reach him was Halford, followed quickly by Crabbel, Plusby, and Savaiu.

They all were shouting, trying to be heard above one another. Thorn grabbed Halford, who stood closest to him, and pulled him close.

"Fire . . . my cabin. Malik . . . dead. Bess . . . knocked cold . . . traitor."

The bosun turned his head so fast he knocked his forehead against Thorn's. The Pilot rocked backward, losing his grip on Halford. Crabbel caught him before he could fall.

"Bosun! Report!"

Plusby's powerful voice cut across the wind and the babble.

"Sir! Fire in th' Pilot's cabin. Says Malik be dead—"

He glanced at Savaiu. Her face had gone white, her yellow eyes widening with shock.

"And th' steward—" Halford lifted his chin. "Master Thorn says she be a traitor."

To Thorn's amazement, Plusby took action instantly, without even a moment to express his shock.

"Mate—sound the alarm."

Crabbel was already moving before the captain finished.

"Bosun, with me." He looked at Savaiu, his expression softening slightly. He gripped her elbow a moment. "Mind our Pilot, if you would, Captain."

Then he and Halford were splashing across the deck while Crabbel yanked on the brass bell hanging from the mizzenmast. The clanging sounded muted against the wail of the wind and the noise of the ships. But it was a sound every sailor feared to the deepest marrow of his bones. Fire at sea.

Instantly Crosspointe and Jutras crew members swarmed to the quarterdeck, carrying lengths of wet canvas and buckets of water hastily scooped from the white foam frothing over the deck. A few carried axes.

The mob descended on Thorn's cabin, smoke billowing out of the doorway in earnest now. Thorn watched, helpless to do anything. Savaiu's arm around his waist lit only guilt and pity in him now. He knew all too well what it was to lose a brother. And she and Malik had clearly had a closer bond than he and Jordan had. He wanted to offer comfort, but had neither the words nor the strength.

Grains trickled past. At last Plusby and Halford came staggering out carrying Malik's limp body. Their faces were black with soot, and burnt patches were scattered over their clothing. They carried his body to the main hatch and laid him on top. Two other sailors emerged with Bess. Her clothes were ash and blackened shreds. Only her boots remained intact—they'd been too wet to do more than smolder. There was no place that her skin wasn't charred. It had split in places and pink flesh gaped like hungry mouths. Thorn's stomach jerked and bucked. He gagged, lumbering about to retch over the rail. Bile flooded his nose and mouth, burning like acid.

He'd burned her *alive*.

"Mother Moon, forgive me," he whispered. "Braken, take her to your arms and grant her comfort from her suffering."

The sailors made quick work of the fire, forming a bucket brigade and smothering it with the wet canvas. When they were done, they collected in an uneasy clot on the quarterdeck. And for the first time Thorn noticed that Blot and Wragg were not among them. He scanned the rest of the ship, his gaze settling on the crew quarters. Had they not given their parole? But his eyes were drawn irresistibly to the ragged stumps of the foremast and the mainmast. There had been sailors in the rigging and others on deck who'd been swept overboard or crushed by the massive debris. He couldn't believe that Blot and Wragg wouldn't have followed Crabbel's and Halford's lead with the Jutras bargain. No, they weren't standing here because they couldn't anymore.

A spiral of pain and loss circled Thorn, its barbed coils drawing tighter and tighter. He'd felt this way when he first learned of Jordan's death. He'd never expected to feel it again; never wanted to. Not for anyone.

And it was only then that he thought of Fitch, that she'd probably been hiding in the cabin under a chair or beneath the bed.

His mouth fell open, but no sound emerged. His mind was a seething cauldron of misery, guilt, and loss. He stood like a statue, unable to move, unable to breathe. Savaiu shook him, then reached up and pressed her cold hand against his cheek, drawing his head around. She held his cheeks wedged, not letting him look away. Her eyes were red-rimmed and tears ran down her cheeks, dashed away by the wind and the torn shreds blown from the tops of the high waves.

"The rest must be made safe," she said in a voice as steady as a stone mountain. "We must take them to shore. We must make this sacrifice worth it. We will not lose another soul."

The last was both a vow and a question. Would he dissolve in his own misery or carry on? She stared up at him as if this was a test of who he was. She was right. He was not going to fall apart and abandon his friends, his crew, his ship.

Thorn nodded jerkily and let her help him across the deck, resolve filling him, smothering his agony.

No one else was going to die because of him. Not this voyage. Not on his watch.

Chapter 19

Savaiu helped Thorn across the deck to where the *Eidolon*'s crew gathered. A dozen Jutras sailors gathered in a knot to the side. Thorn's people opened ranks for him. They were tense and watched Savaiu like wolves protecting their young. They didn't like her touching their Pilot, or even breathing the same air. Given the slightest excuse to do so, Thorn thought they would tear her to bits with their bare hands. It wasn't merely hatred of the Jutras or of having been captured. They were zealously protective of their Pilot. Thorn smiled thinly at the irony. Protective of a man who had done nothing but annoy and frighten them since leaving Crosspointe.

He stopped, twisting about as they closed around him. There wasn't one who wasn't bandaged and bleeding from a fresh wound. There wasn't one who wasn't battered and bruised with torn nails and red, swollen knuckles. Their clothes were soaked through and ragged from the violent work of saving the ship. They all wobbled with weariness and hunger, yet still they stood straight, upright, and proud.

This last was the most striking thing about them: that despite the bleak fear and the horror that twisted their faces, they remained silently stoic—resigned to the hazards of sailing on the Inland Sea. None bemoaned their desperate straits; none whimpered at the sight of Bess's charred body. Despite Thorn's ghastly appearance, they watched him with wary faith—he would lead them to safe harbor. At last. The crew was united and he was no longer on the outside. But at such a cost.

He extended his hand. For long moments no one moved to take it. Then Ricker grabbed him, her grip hard with calluses. Another hand—Alby Sark. More hands. A clamping grip, a sliding brush, a ghostly stroke. One after another. A question asked, a pledge made. He'd get them ashore or die trying.

Thorn turned away, feeling himself beginning to shake. He didn't want them to see. He drew deep steadying breaths, gathering all the scraps of his strength.

Halford, Crabbel, and two other sailors were sewing Malik and Bess inside a pair of canvas hammocks. Their stitches were broad and uneven as they worked quickly and methodically, each taking an end and moving toward the center.

Plusby had disappeared inside Thorn's cabin and now emerged. His skin was gray and he walked stiffly and gracelessly like a man hard in the grip of powerful, painful emotions. He stopped in front of Thorn, ignoring the sailors who crowded close.

"What happened in there?"

Every eye bored expectantly into Thorn. He scanned their faces again, feeling their urgency—they *needed* an explanation. He knew what they were thinking: that the *Eidolon* was a cursed ship. And if it was—there was no hope left.

They had seen too much bad luck since boarding. They had measured their entire voyage by escalating instances of bad luck. From the ill-omened name of the ship, to the power of the storm, to smashing up against the uprising and the opening of the bore, then being chased and captured by Jutras, and finally the devastating snapping of the bowsprit and masts and the hands who had been lost to the sea when the great timbers fell. Not to mention that their Pilot was dying, though they did not know it yet. And now this—a fire with two gruesome deaths.

He licked his stiff lips. His tongue was thick and clumsy. He knew now that it was more than mere exhaustion or hunger—it was the work of the cipher Bess had attached to him. He swallowed.

"Well?" Plusby demanded. "An explanation is in order."

Thorn spoke slowly, carefully. Plusby had to lean close to hear his quiet, disjointed words.

"Safe harbor first."

Something moved in Plusby's sunken, bloodshot eyes. Thorn's blood chilled. For all he appeared collected, had Bess's betrayal truly bent Plusby's mind? They'd been close for many years. And then she'd tried to destroy his ship. After losing his wife and his captain's ticket—had this been enough to tip him over the edge of sanity?

Suddenly the captain noticed the gathered crew crowding close, trying to hear the exchange. He snarled.

"Get to your posts, you squibs!" he roared. "Ice breakers, back to work! The rest of you, secure the ship! Prepare to heave to!"

The crew reacted as if lashed with a whip, their years aboard ship ingraining in them an involuntary instant compliance with their captain's commands. That sort of conditioning died hard, requiring time to stop and think and then rebel. But they were aboard a crippled ship in the middle of the Inland Sea. The storm had abated little and there were vescies, Koreions, knucklebones, and *sylveth* in the water. A moment ago they might have mutinied; now habit drove them to survive. Thank the gods.

"She was the one who put the cipher on you? She tried to kill you?" Plusby asked, his gaze still locked to Thorn's.

"Aye. And she hasn't failed yet. There's not much time left."

Plusby hesitated, then nodded his head jerkily, and relief swirled through Thorn. Not bent. Not entirely anyhow.

As they had spoken, the grisly business of stitching the dead inside their cocoons had been completed.

"Get the bitch off my ship," Plusby ordered implacably when Crabbel approached. "Let her feed the sea."

Without a word, Halford and Crabbel lifted Bess's canvas-shrouded body, carrying her to the side of the ship and unceremoniously shoving her over. Sailors expected to be returned to the sea, but usually some sort of ceremony honored their deaths. This was an ignominious ending. When they had finished, Plusby directed them to return Malik's body to Thorn's cabin.

"Unless you wish otherwise?" he asked Savaiu, the question curt.

She shook her head, her own voice clipped. "No. Rites of Forever will be given when we rest ashore."

As the two charmers set about their task, she focused on the business of getting the *Eidolon* off the open sea.

"I will return to my ship. It will be needed that one of your people accompany me—one with high skill and knowledge of your ship. They will relay the Pilot's instructions and weave our efforts as we try to tow you to safety. There are many private coves of deep water east of Roche Bay where the mountains kiss the sea. It is far from Bokal-Dur and with the storm, there will be fewer chances to meet the Dhucala's wolves. It is safest."

"It'll let us run before the wind," Plusby agreed. "That would cut the chances of ramming you too." He looked at Thorn. "What do you say, Pilot?"

"Let me check the compass."

"Your feet," Savaiu said suddenly.

Thorn looked down. His bare feet were mottled blue and purple. He couldn't feel them, though he thought that was as much the cipher as the cold. He was also soaked to the skin, wearing only a shirt and trousers. Plusby swore. He stalked away, disappearing into Thorn's cabin. He returned a few minutes later, carrying boots, socks, and a blanket. Savaiu steadied

Thorn as Plusby wordlessly dressed him. Then the captain lifted Thorn's arm over his neck and he and Savaiu half dragged him across to the compass post. Once there, Thorn shook them off and settled his hands in their customary position. Instantly he was in the sea. It filled him like his own breath. He felt the wind beating across the waves, whipping them into a frenzy; he felt the slowing spin of the bore; he felt the contours of the seafloor a hundred fathoms below. Before he could slip away on the bliss of the contact, he reined himself in firmly and looked for dangers.

"Braken's buggered ass," he murmured, his chest filling with ice. They were blocked on all sides. North of them, a deadly knucklebone weir stretched east to west, from Roche Bay nearly to Goa Maru. From the southeast came a vast swarm of hungry vescies riding the waves. They were moving quickly. The ships might outrun them, but only by running ahead of the wind—straight into the equally deadly knucklebones.

But that was not all. Even as he watched, the bore began to close its enormous maw. A mighty surge vomited from its stone throat as the massive tunnel collapsed in on itself as if it had never been. The resulting thrust of water was more powerful than anything Thorn had ever seen in his life. There were no words to describe its strength and size.

In no more than two turns of the glass they would be hit by a wave of such proportions that he could barely conceive of its possibility. It would tower far above them: a black mountain of water. When it hit them, it would shatter the ships to bits. There could be no surviving it, no avoiding it. And on its back it carried a dazzling tapestry of *sylveth*, like glimmering stars scattered over a moonless sky. Exquisite death. And dreadful birth. The broken bits of the two ships and crews would be turned into spawn.

North, south, east and west—they were completely and utterly hemmed in. Their only hope was to run north with the wind and hope the vast knucklebone weir vanished before they arrived. It was the best of some very bad choices. And there was no time to waste.

"We have to move!" Thorn shouted at his companions, the words tearing his throat. "Run!"

Neither Savaiu nor Plusby asked questions. Thorn's panicked urgency told them all they needed to know. Savaiu ran to the forecastle, followed quickly by Crabbel and Halford. Once there, she swung over the rail, grasping one of the taut lines that ran between the two ships. Swiftly she pulled herself up, hooking her ankles over the rope, and hauled herself across hand over hand. Crabbel hastily followed after.

Plusby shouted orders. The sails on the now-stable mizzen were raised and the long oars they carried for emergencies unstowed and slipped through the oarlocks that were notched out of the sheer strakes. There were four on each side of the ship, each manned by three sailors, half of them Jutras.

The *Zhala*'s canvas ran up her masts and she began to draw. The lines fastening the two ships together sang as the wind played them like harp strings. Thorn clutched the compass with white-knuckled fingers, his knees locked.

Despite his fear and physical weakness, a flower of exhilaration had begun to unfurl inside him. The wet wind whipped his hair and scraped his face like a rusty razor. His blood quickened.

The wave behind was magnificent. It swept across the Ankerton Strait. The Bramble would slow it down, perhaps even deflect it. But he doubted it. Maybe if they were farther east—but tacking that way would take them that much closer to the vescies. Neither was a palatable end. Nor would they make it back to the Bramble, though it was far closer than the coast—not with a sixty-knot headwind.

"Report, Pilot."

Plusby had come up beside him, his face austere. Whatever he felt about Bess, he'd put it away, focusing entirely on his ship.

"We're running straight at the biggest knucklebone weir I've ever seen."

Plusby said nothing for a long moment. Then, "Have you gone completely maggoty?"

Thorn shook his head. "Best choice we've got at the moment."

"Explain."

"Vescies to the east, coming fast. Knucklebones north."

"And south?"

Thorn pursed his lips, whistling a refrain from a bawdy tune. He smiled thinly. "Bore wave. Biggest I've ever heard of. It'll splinter us within two glasses."

Plusby jerked back. After a moment he collected himself. "What are our chances?"

Thorn shook his head again. Fully rigged and running at full speed, they *might* have made it to a safe anchoring before the wave hit. If the knucklebones didn't rip out their hulls first. But in their crippled state, he figured they'd run afoul of the weir right about the same time the wave struck.

"What if we heave to, put our bow into it, and ride it up?"

Thorn hesitated. How to explain just how massive the wave was? "This wave is . . ." He searched for words. "It's a killer wave. Our only chance is to out-run it."

Plusby looked unconvinced, and why wouldn't he be? His Pilot, who was infected by a cipher, had them headed on a direct course for a deadly knucklebone weir and was telling him it was the safest course. It was a mark of the captain's sanity that he *was* doubtful.

"It will be a hundred feet high. Maybe more."

The captain goggled. "You're certain?"

Thorn nodded, his gaze bleak.

"Then we run. And pray." Plusby started to turn away. He caught himself, turning back.

"I want you to know it's been an honor to serve

aboard ship with you," he said. "I apologize for Bess. I don't understand—" He broke off, looking off into the sea as if too shamed to meet Thorn's gaze. "We were like family. Why didn't I see . . . ? Why would she do this?"

Thorn drew a slow breath. There was no sugaring this to make it more palatable. "They paid her well. For what it's worth, she did say she tried to protect you, that she tried to talk you out of taking the helm."

"Paid?" The idea was clearly staggering. Loyalty mattered to sailors. You held the lives of your companions in your hands every moment of every day. And Plusby had trusted her without question.

"Not just money. She was going to be able to bring her family here. Give them a fresh start. She said things were bad for them in Esengaile," Thorn explained, hoping to soften the blow. It didn't help.

Plusby's teeth gritted audibly together and then he nodded. "All right. All right."

But it wasn't. Thorn knew all too well the burn of acid in the soul, the hurt that was worse than having a limb ripped off. It was the agony of betrayal, of feeling so stupid, so used, so helpless. His parents had done that to him; so had the Pilots' Guild. And Plusby had already suffered enough loss in the shape of his wife and his captain's ticket. Bess's betrayal would be like nails hammered into unhealed wounds, wounds freshly opened by the discovery that his wife, Sherenya, was alive, but she had neither come to find him nor contacted him. He had to be drowning in bitterness, loss, and humiliation.

As Plusby turned away, Thorn reached an unsteady hand from beneath his blanket and stopped him.

"Don't—," he began, then stopped. *Don't what? Don't blame yourself? Don't hate her for her betrayal? Don't ache for a beloved wife who has not come seeking you?* Thorn thought of Jordan, of running away and leaving his brother to suffer the diabolical plans of their parents. He imagined how Jordan had felt, finding himself alone and abandoned. He must have been terrified and furious. And yet Thorn knew he hadn't had a choice. He could not have stayed, and he could not have protected his brother on the streets. Sometimes betrayal was just need.

"Don't be too hard on her," he said at last. "Things have a way of getting beyond us all. We have all done things we regret. And she's paid a hard price for it."

Plusby didn't speak a moment, staring off into nothing. Then he looked at Thorn. "I'll think on it. If we get to shore. We've got a few minutes. Go get dry clothing on and a coat. You don't have to freeze to death before the sea kills us."

Chapter 20

Plusby sent Halford to help Thorn. Halford said nothing as he half carried the Pilot back into Thorn's cabin,
but his silence was eloquent. Thorn sighed. There was
no winning with these men. And dying wasn't exactly
his own fault. In fact, his race up the mast had helped
him by necessitating the healing amulet. Without its
countering effects, the cipher would have made much
quicker work of him.

The stench of acrid smoke and burnt wood and fabric met them as they entered. It mixed with a cloud
of ash, and was enough to make them both break into
fits of coughing. Halford went quickly to take down
the deadlights. Thorn sagged into a chair, doubling
over as the coughs ripped through his chest.

Halford returned, offering him a glass of brandy.
Ashes settled into a thin layer on top of the liquor
before Thorn could swallow it, but the fiery liquid
steadied him.

When the coughing fit had subsided, he stood, tottering. He wanted to see the inside of his bedchamber.

The fire had not escaped into the outer cabin. The
bed was a shapeless mass of burnt feathers, fabric, and
wood. The stench of it filled his nose and throat with
a revolting taste like hot tar, burnt hair, and roasted
meat. The walls and ceilings were scorched black, and
the opposite bulkhead held the outline of Bess's body.
When he saw it, Thorn's gorge rose and the contents
of his stomach splattered onto the charred floor,

splashing onto his feet. Halford made no comment, merely stepping out of the room and returning with another glass of brandy. Thorn tossed it back, rinsing his mouth before swallowing, holding it down with an iron will.

When Thorn had steadied himself, he went to his wardrobe. The fire had blackened the doors, but the clothes inside were untouched, though they reeked of smoke and char. He had little choice, however, and drew out a change of clothing. The wind would blow the stink away soon enough. With Halford's help, he stripped and dressed, adding boots and a warm coat.

The generous dose of brandy made him feel light-headed. He hadn't eaten since before—he couldn't imagine ever wanting to eat again, but he had to if he wanted to keep up his strength. He had Halford help him back out on deck, sending him to scrounge for something from the galley. Not waiting for his return, Thorn took hold of the compass, letting his senses drift wide.

The wave was closer now. The hairs on his neck rose. He resisted the urge to turn and glance back on the horizon. He knew all that would be visible was low clouds and mist, which was a relief. No one else would know it was there until it appeared suddenly astern like the hand of Braken rising up from the depths.

As for the weir, if anything, it had drifted farther offshore and closer to the ships. *Damn and damn again!*

Halford returned with a flask of sweet cream tea and a loaf of stale bread. Thorn gnawed on the bread, trying not to think of food, trying not to think of the smell of Bess's roasted remains. As he ate, he took stock of the crew on the oars and up on the forecastle and poop deck. The men and women at the oars were already exhausted—their faces were set in harsh lines of strain as they stretched toward the stern, dipped the oars, pulled the stroke back through the high seas, and began again. None showed signs of stopping or slowing, but they couldn't keep this pace up without food and water.

"Halford, what is there for the crew to eat?"

The bosun looked startled. He glowered. "Lady's maid and now table servant, am I?"

But he went stomping off again. A half a glass later he returned, followed by Degby. Her face was bruised from her being tossed about in the galley, and a bandage wrapped her fleshy arm. It was neatly wrapped and knotted—Halford's handiwork.

The two carried bins of sandwiches, which they passed out to the crew. They were greeted with weak smiles of gratitude. The rowers jammed the food into their mouths, their cheeks puffing out, and then returned to their business. Halford and Degby disappeared again belowdecks and returned a few minutes later. Halford carried a butt of ale under one arm. Degby had a half-dozen pewter mugs hooked on her fingers. They served each sailor a dram. Halford offered one to Thorn, who guzzled the sour ale, wiping his mouth with the back of his hand before handing back the mug.

"Make sure you eat too," he told the bosun, who muttered something about goats and Pilots as he walked away.

Another half a glass passed. The thrust of the wave behind them was beginning to drive them forward faster. They were only twenty leagues off the coast now, and the knucklebones were a scant five leagues away. They showed no signs of vanishing.

Suddenly, a chill ran up Thorn's heels and over his flanks, and wriggled up his spine. His prick curled up between his legs, his balls shriveling. He sucked in a deep breath, bracing his feet wide. The wave had arrived.

His head dipped forward, his chin resting on his chest. "Braken have mercy," he murmured, then straightened. He turned to Halford, who continued to hover, ready to catch Thorn if he fell.

"Cut us loose from the *Zhala*. Now."

His voice brooked no argument. Halford hesitated, then ran forward. Thorn felt the motion of the ship slow as the lines were severed. Their backs to the bow, their eyes fixed on the deck with concentration as they drew on whatever strength they had left, the rowers did not notice. There were shouted questions from the poop deck and the sailors up on the mizzenmast. None had yet seen the wave. Why should they? Their course was dead ahead; the danger was running into the *Zhala* or a weir or an uprising. What did they care about the seas behind?

Halford returned, scowling as usual, his jaw thrust out, his meaty shoulders squared. His hair was slicked to his head. He stopped in front of the compass, saying nothing, waiting. The weight of his trust was excruciating. He'd answered Thorn's unexpected command without question, nor had he stopped to confirm with the captain.

"Have them ship the oars."

Halford's mouth worked as if he wanted to demand why, but he only nodded and did as told. Soon the sailors gathered in a worried knot on the deck. The ten Jutras sailors who had remained on board looked furious and confused, eyeing the *Eidolon*'s crew with undisguised worry and hostility. They gabbled among themselves, their distress growing louder and more angry.

Plusby came down, having struck all but the spanker sail. He came to stand beside Thorn. He began to speak without preamble, not bothering to soften the news. Thorn wasn't sure there was any way to make it less horrifying than it was.

"We've a weir ahead of us, vescies to the east, and behind—well, you can look for yourselves. We'd hoped a hole would open in the weir and we'd get to shore before we were struck. The *Eidolon* is unlikely to survive. With luck, the *Zhala* might get away. See to your safety as best you can. And pray the gods have mercy on us."

The crew only stared uncomprehending, the Jutras

gone silent. Thorn wasn't even sure they understood what knucklebones and vescies were. Then suddenly Ricker gave a strangled shout, pointing. They all turned to look at the sea beyond the stern.

The wave filled the horizon. It rose like a sheer black wall, towering higher than seemed possible. It was perhaps a league away now and coming on fast.

No one moved.

"See to yourselves!" Plusby barked, shattering their frozen immobility.

They scurried, snatching up lines and fastening makeshift safety harnesses.

"I'd like to see it from the poop deck," Thorn said.

Plusby nodded and walked him to the companion ladder. Halford dogged behind, helping to push him up. The three of them went to stand on the taffrail. Awe swept Thorn as he gazed out on the monster wave. It was a hundred feet tall at least and showed no signs of breaking.

"Bad luck," Halford muttered.

Thorn shook his head. "No such thing."

"Ye haven't ridden four wrecked ships. What d'ye know about it?"

"My brother was murdered before Chance. I don't keep lovers, I don't have friends, and my crews change with every ship and season. Before I set foot on the *Eidolon*, I was adrift. But I'd rather stand on this deck with you right now than be safe at home or on any other ship. I belong here. If it's luck, then I call it good luck."

Halford snorted. "Dyin' might change your mind."

Plusby laughed, clapping Halford on the shoulder. The bosun started and stared at the hand.

"You've both gone maggoty."

Thorn leaned over the rail, closing his eyes, feeling the swelling power of the wave. He drew a deep breath. If he was going to die, this was the way. Standing among friends on the deck of the ship. He looked over his shoulder at Halford and Plusby. But whatever he was going to say evaporated on the tip of his tongue. He froze, sensing something in the wave *change*.

"What is it?" Plusby demanded.

Thorn shook his head. "I don't know. Something. Get me to the compass."

They half carried, half dragged him back down onto the quarterdeck and to the compass. He gripped it and was instantly overwhelmed. He sank to his knees, but didn't loosen his hands.

"Pilot, report!" Plusby's voice cracked like thunder.

"It's impossible," Thorn muttered. "She said she couldn't. . . ." Then more loudly. "Lifelines, now! The gods may be smiling after all."

Neither of his companions asked questions. Instantly they began fashioning harnesses. Thorn found himself trussed and fastened to the compass post by Halford. As Plusby finished tying the knots in his own harness, he turned on his Pilot.

"What's going on?"

"Get to the helm. Halford, signal the *Zhala* if you can. Keep the stern to the wave and raise the sails. Be ready. I'm not sure. . . . We may not be done for yet."

He gasped, the air rushing out of him. He held on to the compass weakly, his eyes closed as he concentrated. *What was happening out there?*

The wave was cresting. But it wasn't natural. There was a *pull* in the water, like someone had gripped the top of the massive wall of water and yanked it downward. And it was centered directly behind them. It could only be the work of Lucy Trenton. She was fighting hard against Braken's might.

Thorn felt as if his bones were threaded on wire, like beads on a necklace. The wire pulled taut, winding tighter and tighter. He moaned with the pressure. He had an insane urge to run and jump off the stern and follow the demand of that steady, relentless draw. If he'd had the strength to stand, he might have tried. As it was, he could no longer move. He could not have let go of the compass if he wanted to.

The sea was churning, resisting the pressure dragging the wave down. The *Eidolon* pitched and yawed, rolling all the way onto her port beam and then back onto the starboard rail. She bucked against a mad sea that was suddenly full of baffling currents pulling her every which way.

Suddenly the resistance ended.

The wave crested, curving over in an elegant arc and plunging downward into the sea with crushing force. White spume roared up into the sky as water met water in a horrendous crash. If the ships had been under it—there wouldn't have been a piece of them left bigger than a spoon.

The mountain of water punched down, burrowing deeply below the surface of the black water. Almost instantly, another wave began to form, shoved upward by the impact. It surged, rolling outward faster than the gale winds. As it swept along, Thorn had a sense that the same power that had pulled the great wave into submission was holding this one in check. Or trying to.

"You can do it," he whispered. "Just a little bit more. Don't give up on us."

The new wave jerked and stuttered, galloping along and then rearing back. It was like a wild thing wrestling against despised fetters. Thorn held his breath. *Only a little longer . . . just a little longer.*

And then there was a *ripping* as Lucy Trenton's majick suddenly tore in half like a worn spot in a tightly bellied sale. For a heartbeat the wave seemed to hesitate; then it leaped forward.

Thorn slumped as the majick gave way, his hands falling limply to his sides. He began to shake. He sprawled onto his back, staring up at the storm-tossed pewter clouds. Though he was no longer touching the compass, he could feel the swift, rushing rise of the wave, and, not far ahead, the knucklebone weir. There was nothing left for him to do but wait. And hope. Now there was hope.

He began to laugh when he felt the wave roll under the *Eidolon*. Yes!

The ship rose up in the air, riding the crest. The

deck tilted as the bow rose, the wave growing taller.
It was a monster—perhaps thirty feet high—but nothing like the ship-killing wave caused by the closing of
the bore.

The wind swept frigidly across Thorn's prone body.
They were nearly upon the knucklebones now. He
held his breath, waiting. He pushed his senses out into
the wave, feeling it surge, feeling it meet the edge of
the weir, and then it swept over and past, carrying the
Eidolon with it.

Thorn began to laugh again. Relief and triumph
made him giddy. He had no strength to sit up, to look
to see if the *Zhala* had survived.

A shadow fell across his face. Halford. The bosun
squatted beside him, the bitter end of his safety line
in his hand. He eyed Thorn warily, which only made
Thorn laugh harder.

But he hadn't the breath or strength to continue
his merriment for long. Soon the laughter turned to
coughing. Halford sat him up, pushing his head between his knees and pounding his back until he began
to breathe normally again.

When he was in control, he straightened. "The
Zhala?"

"Off th' port bow."

"Thank the gods." Crabbel was aboard that ship.
And Thorn was surprised to find that he didn't care
for the idea of Savaiu dying either.

Halford shook his head, scrubbing at the bristles
along his jaw. "Don't be so quick. Shore's less than
four leagues off. Wave's fixin' t' crack us like a walnut
on th' headland."

"Then steer us to a softer landing."

"Ye *have* gone maggoty," Halford growled, standing up and reaching down to haul Thorn to his feet.
He swayed, his knees buckling. He felt boneless. The
bosun caught him around the waist with a grunt.
Thorn leaned heavily against him and reached for
the compass.

"There's a river ahead. Two points off the starboard

bow. Deep channel. Savaiu will know it. That's where she'll head. Follow her. And Halford, tell the captain not to miss the mouth or we'll be crushed on the rocks."

Halford glared at him, then marched off, leaving Thorn to clutch the compass for balance.

He grinned.

He was dying; the *Eidolon* was nearly unsteerable and riding atop a tidal wave. To make matters worse, they were less than four leagues off a craggy shore and a splatter tide was closing in behind. They not only had to steer into the river's mouth, but they had to navigate its channel, then get farther up the river than the *sylveth* could reach. It seemed hopeless. Yet Thorn felt hope. Not only that, there wasn't a place in the world he'd rather be. Halford was right. He was barking mad.

Chapter 21

The headland thrust quickly up into menacing relief. The minutes ate the leagues far too quickly, and this time there was no sign that Lucy Trenton intended to interfere with the wave's progress as it barreled toward shore. Or maybe she couldn't. On the poop deck, sailors shoved on the rudder, using lashings to hold it in place while the ship edged to the starboard. It was delicate work—the force of the water could easily snap the rudder off, and if they turned too far, they'd end up broadside to the wave and it would roll them over and sink them.

Even with the aid of her sails, the *Zhala* was having more trouble. She was top-heavy and maneuvered clumsily. Still, Savaiu was a skilled captain. Thorn watched admiringly as the Jutras ship doused every sail but her main course and mizzen sails and began to cut across the wave, lining up with the river's mouth. The *Eidolon* slowly shifted into place behind her.

The river itself was only a quarter of a league wide. Its current ran swift, running downhill from the mountains. That was lucky. Together the current and downhill slope might abate the power of the bore wave, allowing them to slow down and navigate the river. Hopefully it would help prevent them from being slammed into the river's rocky banks. With any luck at all, they'd find a clearing along a low bank to beach on.

The rimrock cliffs of the headland loomed, a tower-ing wall of sheer gray cliffs. A wide, vee-shaped notch drilled down into it, signaling the mouth of the river. Twisted conifer trees beetled along the slope and spread out along the top of the headland.

As they drew closer to shore, the sea turned shal-low, forcing the wave higher into the air. Though he expected it, Thorn's mouth went dry. If they were off even slightly in their aim, they'd end up battered against the escarpment.

The shoals forced the wave to crest. Thorn's hands tightened on the compass and he held his breath. Now the real danger began. They needed to ride the wave until it dissolved. If they tipped over the crest, they'd be cartwheeled end to end until they shattered, or they'd be slammed to the bottom of the trough and crushed by a thousand tons of water. Either way, the end was the same.

Ahead, he could see the black and red-striped sails of the *Zhala*. The top-heavy ship tottered and tipped as she fought to stay on course. Plusby shouted orders to unstow the oars and insert them in the oarlocks. The crew scrambled to obey, unfastening the stirrups holding the oars against the foot of the rails. They nocked the long poles into the locks. At the captain's command, a quick shove would extend them. The sail-ors firmed their grips on the smooth wood handles and settled down to wait. First the *Eidolon* had to make it onto the river.

The ship bobbled, dropping sickeningly, and then steadying. Thorn's balls crawled up into his throat and his heart pounded.

The escarpment seemed so close that he thought they must certainly be about to crash into it. It filled his vision until it seemed there was no longer a sky. Then there was a roar and the air reverberated with grinding thunder. The *Eidolon* shivered, her timbers squealing and creaking as she scraped against a rocky protuberance. On either side, water exploded. The ship was enveloped in a froth of water. It slapped

Thorn, filling his eyes and swarming the deck with a knee-deep wash of water. Then suddenly it was gone. The prow dipped and they were sliding downward in a stomach-turning drop. It felt like they'd plunged off the edge of a cliff.

Much of the bore wave's power had dissipated when it struck the cliffs. They landed bow-end on the river. Wings of water flew up all around them, filling the decks. Thorn fell forward against the compass, his feet skidding from underneath him. He slid across the deck on his back, checked up short by the safety line attached to the post. The ship's nose burrowed into the river; then it wrenched upward and back as the stern splashed down. It hit with a hollow *boom!* If they'd still had a bowsprit, it would have been ripped off.

Behind them, a second wave rolled through, shoving them up the channel. Plusby shouted for the oars and instantly they were deployed and the sailors dug hard into the turbulent water.

Halford stood on the quarterdeck bellowing orders: "Port, dig hard! Dig! Starboard, luff! Dig, ye cock-biting squibs! Now starboard! Haul! Haul!"

Thorn struggled to sit up. His head spun and he shook it to clear it. He felt a trickling warmth along his stomach and glanced down. A dark crimson patch was spreading over the blue cloth across his stomach. In the middle of it was a hole where the southern ray of the compass had drilled through his shirt into his flesh when he'd fallen against it. The wound didn't hurt. He still wore the pain amulet. But every drop of blood he leaked depleted his already severely sapped strength. He grimaced. There was no time at the moment to stanch it with a bandage.

He clambered slowly to his feet, adjusting his safety harness so that it would help hold his hand in place as he pressed it against the wound. He slid his hand beneath the rope, pressing as hard as he could. It would have to do.

When he looked back up, the *Eidolon* had straight-

ened, guided by the oars and rudder. Ahead, the
Zhala slewed sideways in an eddy and drifted near the
left bank. There were shouts and a whir of chain as
her starboard anchor dropped. She caught with a jerk,
swinging about, pulled back toward the middle of the
river by her momentum and the rapid cut of her oars.
Instantly the capstan rumbled and the anchor chain
rattled up through the hawsehole. The anchor was
quickly catted and the *Zhala* continued up the river.
Thorn was more than a little impressed at the demon-
strated skill of Savaiu and her crew.

It seemed almost easy now, with the bore wave
pushing them up despite the swift-flowing current. But
the banks were ominously steep and though there
were trees aplenty to build new masts and yards for
the *Eidolon*, there was no way to get off the river.

They'd gone nearly two leagues up the winding
channel when the bore wave began to abate. Thorn
felt it going and knew they had little time before they
would have to start warping, using the trees and oars
to pull themselves up against the river's fierce current.
All the same, it was a good sign. The *sylveth* would
not be able to follow farther than the bore wave.

They came around a bend in the river, scraping up
against the right bank and having to push off against
the rocks. When they completed the turn, Thorn was
astonished to find the *Zhala* no longer riding the river
ahead of them. He looked wildly about. Where was
the other ship?

Shouts from the starboard caught his attention. The
Jutras ship had slid into a narrow fork off the river's
main artery. There was precious little room for a tall
ship. If the *Eidolon*'s prow were not so raked, if her
lines were not so sleekly narrow—she'd never have
fit. As it was, turning her required that they use ropes
and the trees to forcibly draw her around.

Thorn sat slumped on the deck just in front of the
compass post. Blood continued to trickle through his
fingers. He'd had no idea the side channel was there.
Of course not, he chided himself. His skill was reading

the salt waters of the Inland Sea. Not rivers or lakes. The compass didn't talk to them. He rubbed his free hand over his face and shook his head, trying to clear the murk that clouded his skull. But it closed around his mind like a downy fist and he slid sideways, unconscious.

When he woke, he was no longer aboard ship and more than a little surprised to be alive. He was lying on a pallet, wrapped in blankets. A tight wrapping of bandages circled his waist, making it hard to draw a breath. Above him the branches of the trees tossed. He could see clouds and the glimmer of the moon high above. The storm was passing. They weren't far from the river. He could hear it bubbling and splashing nearby.

Groggy, he turned his head. He was in a clearing, a fire burning beside him. Several other pallets were lined up nearby, containing other injured, he supposed. More fires gleamed in the darkness farther away and he could see shadows moving around them. He smelled the rich scent of pine and woodsmoke and meat cooking. His stomach clenched with hunger. He ignored it. He was too tired to fetch anything. Even if he could stand up and walk, which he doubted.

"You're still alive."

Thorn turned his head to the other side to find Halford watching him. He was sitting on the ground, his back against the trunk of a tree, a boat hook lying on the ground beside him. He was holding something in his arms. He was *petting* it.

Green eyes gleamed at Thorn as Fitch turned her head to look at him.

"Fitch," he whispered, his throat dry and tight, his eyes burning. He hadn't seen her in how long? He'd thought she'd burned in the fire.

He coughed weakly and Halford set Fitch on the ground and rose, crouching down beside Thorn. He dipped a cup into a bucket and held it to the Pilot's lips.

"Easy, now," he admonished as Thorn drank greed-ily of the cold, sweet water.

When he was sated, he slumped again. Fitch leaped up on Halford's shoulder, nuzzling his jaw. The bosun pushed her away with an annoyed grunt, but she ig-nored him, purring as she rubbed his ear.

"I thought she died in the fire," Thorn said, torn between relief and amusement and a little hurt. Imag-ine, Halford with a pet cat. Because Fitch had clearly changed her allegiances.

"Figured she'd be panicked w' th' storm and no company. Put her w' Blot when the Jutras took us."

"Blot? He's alive?"

"Caught under th' mainmast when she toppled."

"How bad?"

Halford's face contorted a moment and then re-turned to its usual scowl. "Legs crushed. Somethin' be wrong inside. Talkin' outta his head."

"What about Wragg?"

"He fed th' sea."

Damn and damn. Thorn looked away. If Halford so much as hinted that helping Wragg had been a waste because he ended up dead anyhow, Thorn would cut the bosun's prick off. He swallowed, sorrow pulling at him.

"You still have my ring?" he asked, his voice thick with emotion.

"Aye."

"Get the healing supplies from my quarters. Give him whatever's there. Anybody else who needs it, too."

Halford rocked back on his heels. Then he shook his head.

"Orders be t' watch over ye," he said. "In case an-other body wants t' kill ye. And ye might need what ye have left."

Thorn could see that Halford was not going to obey. The bosun's jaw jutted mulishly. He lifted Fitch down from his shoulder and set her none too gently on

Thorn's chest and then returned to his station at the tree.

Fitch stretched up, sniffing along Thorn's mouth and up to his ear. She licked his cheek tentatively, her tongue scraping his skin roughly. Then she turned her back, leaping to the ground, and padded back over to Halford, winding lovingly around his legs. The bosun looked appalled, shoving her away gently with his foot. She nuzzled it and then, just as was her habit with Thorn, she leaped up his thigh, climbing up over his hips and chest to end up purring on his shoulder as she rubbed herself against the side of his head.

Halford grunted and cursed as her claws hooked through his flesh. He started to push her off when he caught sight of Thorn and began cursing in earnest. He thrust himself across the narrow space, easily capturing the Pilot's hands and pulling them from where he was trying to remove the amulets around his neck.

"What in th' holy depths do ye think you're doin'?" Halford demanded.

"Blot needs them."

"Crack that! Ye be needin' 'em worse."

"They might save his life. They aren't going to save me."

"Ye said if ye made shore, there'd be a way t' get th' cipher off and heal ye."

"I did say that."

"Then what be ye waitin' for? A love note from th' queen?"

"Bad form, Halford," Thorn chided. "The queen's barely gone off to Chayos's altar."

"Suck bilge," he returned. "Stop twistin' me wick and get t' business."

Thorn's grin was weak. But Halford was right. If he was going to try his cure, he had to do it soon. Before the *sylveth* tide withdrew.

"Fetch the captain." It was an order he had no power to enforce.

"I told ye—"

"I know. You're guarding me. I'm dying whether you guard me or not. Fetch the captain." His voice faded on the last so that it disappeared into nothingness. He didn't have the breath to say more.

Halford hesitated, then stalked off into the darkness, Fitch riding on his shoulder. Thorn smiled at that. It made his heart light to see the cat alive and well, and, more wonderfully still, to see her ruling Halford's affections. Even if he could rid himself of the cipher on his leg and regain his vigor, he didn't think Fitch would return to him. He wondered if Halford counted the little cat as good luck or ill.

It was not long before a tight-lipped Halford returned with a fuming Plusby. The captain had clearly torn a strip off the bosun. He stood over Thorn, a featureless shadow.

"You sent for me?"

"Now or never," Thorn whispered, his chest feeling as if it were weighted with lead. He knew he had to get to *sylveth*-ridden waters or he'd die, sooner rather than later.

Plusby's shoulders slumped. "You're certain? It's the only way?"

"It might not work."

The captain nodded. "We'll get a jolly boat and be back for you. Try to stay alive in the meantime." He turned his head. "Halford! Do something about that damned cat and come with me."

Plusby turned on his heel and marched off. Halford lifted Fitch down and deposited her on a pallet on the opposite side of the fire. She mewed protest at his desertion, but soon curled up to sleep. Thorn watched her. The man must be Blot, he thought. Astonishing. She'd won the charmers over. His lips bent into a thin smile and he slipped into a doze.

He woke when Plusby and Halford returned. The bosun's face was a tight mask. He obeyed as the captain directed him to link hands with him under Thorn's knees and back, though it was clear he had no idea what they had in mind to do and was thinking they were all mad. If they could have managed without him, Thorn would have made him stay at the camp. As it was, he didn't know how Halford was going to take discovering what Thorn's cure actually was. He was most definitely not going to like finding out that Pilots were spawn.

Plusby and Halford carried Thorn silently through the darkness to the edge of the river. Carefully they waded in, firming their steps on the slick stone bed. They lifted him into the jolly boat, laying him in the bottom before the mast and settling a blanket over him. It wasn't until then that Thorn realized he was shivering.

The boat rocked as Plusby climbed aboard. A voice interrupted Halford as he started to hoist himself up.

"Do you go somewhere?"

Savaiu. Thorn grimaced. It was one thing to tell Halford what Pilots were, another to tell a Jutras. But Thorn was reaching the end of his life. If they wanted to save him, they couldn't waste precious grains spinning a story she'd believe.

"We have an errand, Captain Savaiu," Plusby said at last.

"This is to save Pilot Thorn?"

"Aye."

"Then I shall come with you."

No one argued. There was no time. The boat rocked again as Halford and Savaiu climbed aboard. They quietly released the mooring and unshipped the oars. The contrary current wasn't as swift on this fork and though it was not an easy effort, they made good time to the main trunk of the river.

Thorn was aware of the boat picking up speed as they floated out into the river's swift current. Urgency spurred them, and his three companions continued to paddle, pushing the little boat faster.

The tide was beginning to come in. Thorn sank into himself, reaching out to try to touch the thrust of the Inland Sea pushing up into the river's channel. He felt it only vaguely. His breathing continued to be labored.

He tried to relax, to prepare himself for what was to come. It was going to take all the strength he had. It might not be enough.

The closer they drew to the sea, the stronger his senses grew. At last he struggled to sit up.

"Stop now."

Though his words were hardly more than a whisper, Plusby heard. He ordered Halford to drop the anchor, and the jolly boat jerked and bobbled before the anchor flukes caught the stony river bottom.

"Here is where I get out." He panted, forcing out the words he needed to say. "You should get up on the bank. Be careful. You might get visitors."

He clumsily pushed off the blanket and tugged at the laces of his shirt. It was almost more than he could manage.

"What are you doing?" Plusby asked.

Thorn glanced at him and then at Halford and Savaiu. He couldn't hide what he was doing from either of them. His lips twitched. Halford's reaction was going to be interesting.

"Anything I'm wearing will become spawn."

Savaiu sucked a breath, rocking back as if shoved. Her skin was silvered by the moonlight, her startled eyes like dapples of sunlight on a shadowy pool.

"Spawn?" Halford demanded, his voice echoing loudly.

"Yes," Thorn said, managing at last to pull his shirt over his head. His skin pimpled in the cold. In the dark, the blood blotching the bandages around his waist was black as ink. He became all too aware of Savaiu's gaze on him. He felt himself flush. He was nothing but a leaking bag of skin and bones. The idea of Savaiu witnessing the ravages of his body was unexpectedly disturbing. He twisted in an effort to hide himself.

"What are ye sayin'?" Halford was standing up.

Thorn had never seen him so angry. Plusby started to say something and Halford swung around, gripping his throat in one meaty hand.

"Hush, now," he said to Plusby in a quiet voice that sounded like it came from the bleakest depths. Not letting go, he turned slowly to look at Thorn. "Explain."

"Let Captain Plusby go," Thorn said. This was a side of Halford he'd not seen.

"When ye explain." Calm. Cold. Menacing.

"Let go before you kill him."

Halford's face contorted, his nostrils flaring, his jaw flexing. Abruptly he released his grip.

Plusby bent forward, elbows on his knees, head dangling as he gasped for air.

Halford stood over Thorn, his hands clenching and unclenching. He crossed them over his chest, as if it was all he could do not to hit someone. Likely it was.

"What's goin' on?"

"Brace yourself," Thorn said softly. "You're going to hate this."

Halford spit over the side into the river. "Worse than ye dyin'?"

"Maybe."

"Tell him. You're wasting time," Plusby growled.

Still Thorn hesitated. Every so often someone survived *sylveth* whole and gained great gifts. But such people were still considered cursed by *sylveth* and they faced suspicion and hatred. No one trusted them. What if their outward appearance hid dreadful changes? If Halford and the *Eidolon*'s crew learned what he really was, would they still trust him? He felt sick.

"He's spawn. That's how they become Pilots," Plusby announced when Thorn still didn't speak. "He says if he touches *sylveth*, it could take the cipher off and heal him."

Thorn looked up at Halford. The big man said nothing.

"And if it don't?" he asked finally, surprising Thorn with his lack of revulsion and horror.

"Then I'll feed the sea."

"Probably spit ye back out," Halford muttered. He

sucked his teeth. "Meris weeps. All right. I always knew there be somethin' wrong w' ye."

Then he helped Plusby undress Thorn. They cut away the bandages around his stomach. Thorn heard Savaiu swearing at the sight of the wound.

"It is believed among my people that Pilots are soft," she said. "This one is not. Are they all as brave?"

"Brave?" Halford snorted. "Hardly. He ain't nothin' but stupid. Clumsy. Foolhardy."

"Aye. A thorn in the ass. Need to put him in shackles just to keep him from killing himself," Plusby agreed. "And no, I've never met another like him."

"You would prefer a different Pilot, then?" she asked, still watching the proceedings as Halford and Plusby pulled off his boots, socks, and pants, leaving him in his smallclothes.

The captain grinned, meeting Thorn's gaze. "No. This one is . . . exceptional. We'd as soon keep him."

"Aye," Halford agreed.

"Then help me over the side," Thorn said waspishly, annoyed at being discussed as if he weren't even there.

The other two men hesitated.

"Current's strong. Can ye swim?" Halford asked.

"There's no choice. You cannot risk coming closer."

"I don't like this," Plusby said. "You might drown before you get there."

Thorn shrugged. "I might."

The captain swore and then with Halford's help lifted Thorn up on the side. He perched there a moment.

"Get onto the dirt. Watch for spawn."

"When should we expect you?" Plusby demanded.

"I don't know. When you see me." If he survived. Even he could hear the doubt in his voice. "Take the amulets off me. I'd rather not let the *sylveth* destroy them." He paused. "If I don't—" He broke off, wincing as Halford's meaty hands clenched on him, warning him not to say it. "If I'm *late*, see that Blot gets

those. Halford has my ring for opening up any of the
locks in my cabin."

Plusby scowled. "Do not be *late*," he said, then
pulled the amulets over Thorn's head.

The pain was instant and agonizing. He convulsed,
making a keening noise. He'd never felt such agony.
Except in his legs. From just above his knees to his
toes he could feel absolutely nothing. He moaned and
instantly his companions began to pull him back into
the boat.

"No," he said hoarsely. "Put me in."

Reluctantly they lowered him into the water. It was
frigid. His lungs constricted so that he could hardly
breathe. But the pain eased as his flesh numbed. He
clutched the side of the boat, his arm quaking, his
bare legs drifting downstream on the current. He
reached down and pulled off his smallclothes and
lifted them back into the boat. His teeth chattered,
making it even harder to speak. He looked up at their
faces—Plusby's contorted with emotions he couldn't
contain, Halford's tight with helplessness and fury, and
Savaiu's full of pity, horror, and fear. He ought to say
something profound, a proper farewell. But he could
think of nothing.

"Fair winds and following seas," he said at last, then
let the current sweep him away.

He had little fear of battering against submerged
obstacles—the channel was too deep. But that
wouldn't keep an eddy from catching him and swinging him to the bank, where he would be chewed to
bits on the boulders hiding there. He wouldn't be able
to swim free. It was all he could do to keep his head
above water. He rolled onto his back, using his arms
as rudders. The pain in his body had settled, the
numbing effects of the water granting him some re-
prieve. But still he *hurt*. He'd abused himself in the
last sennight or so, knowing that he'd not feel the
painful repercussions while wearing the amulet.

The water was as black as the night, and his sense
of the underwater terrain and the *sylveth* increased as

the river began to meet the rising tidal waters. He reached out, trying to feel the *sylveth*. He'd hoped it would wash up into the throat of the river, but it had not. It floated like stars in the surf beyond, more than a league away yet.

He clenched himself tight, feeling his legs sinking, dragging him down deeper into the water. His arms were leaden. He could no longer guide himself. He could barely keep his mouth and nose above the water. He tried to kick, but his feet didn't respond. They dragged like anchors, already dead.

The incoming tide slowed the rate of his descent to the sea. He gulped water and coughed, sinking below the river's surface. Bands of icy steel coiled around him, twisting tighter. The cold seeped deep inside, curling glacial tentacles around his intestines and heart. But there was salt water reaching into the river water now, and he felt it begin to buoy him, welcoming him. He was spawn. The sea was his father, *sylveth* his mother. Neither would let him drown. He wriggled his body, trying to squirm upward. The brine lifted him. He broke the surface and gasped.

It was easier to float now, but he had to start worrying about spawn. They'd feast on him as quickly as anything else. There was always plenty of debris in the water—driftwood and the rubbish that washed down from inland towns and cities—to create spawn. And if the tangle of yards, masts, and cordage from the *Eidolon* had washed into shore, there would be a mass of hungry spawn searching for food. But they weren't his only worry. The things that lived in the sea and fed on spawn would also come hunting. The Koreions followed the *sylveth* in search of food, as did vada-eels, celesties, and, when they'd been stirred up, vescies.

Touching *sylveth* would hopefully remove the cipher. He'd told the others it would cure him as well. But he didn't truly know. There had been a time when he'd been sorely wounded on a ship that had been ripped apart by a knucklebone weir rising up beneath it. He'd been cut to bits, one arm hanging by a hinge of flesh. The *sylveth* tide that followed the weir had wrapped him in its silken warmth and healed him. But those had been mere flesh wounds. The cipher was majick and had been killing him by inches for more than a sennight. And even if the *sylveth* did reverse the damage, it could not mend his terrible weakness and exhaustion. He'd still have to find his way back up the river with a spent body.

He felt the sea grab him more tightly as he reached the mouth of the river. He washed out into the surf. He let himself drift, swallowing as much water as air. He struggled to lift himself higher from the thundering waves, but he could not. Desperately he felt for *sylveth* and found it. Not far—only a few hundred feet away.

But between him and it was a squirming mass of spawn.

Chapter 22

Every grain brought him closer to the wriggling horde of spawn. He struggled to change his course, to go around, to go back to shore . . . to no avail. His body was limp and useless. He forced himself to relax back on the waves, trying to breathe, trying to gather himself. He didn't have the strength or weapons to fight them off. The terror he'd been fending off clamped razor teeth into his heart. For a moment he was paralyzed. With a superhuman effort, he pushed away the fear. He *could* endure this. He didn't have to fight; he just needed to survive. He just had to stay alive long enough to get through the spawn to the *sylveth*.

And then what? They eat me again?

He refused to think about it. First he had to get through them.

It was then that Thorn felt how alone he was. It ached, worse than the cold. It was a pain that he'd first begun to feel when he learned of Jordan's death. A dull arrow pushed slowly through his flesh. But that pain had become . . . bearable . . . on the *Eidolon*.

He thought, rising and falling in the frigid water like a broken doll, that he should have said something more when he left them, something better, more meaningful. Something to say how much Plusby and Halford, Moth and Ricker, Degby and Alby Sark—all of them, the contentious, angry, resentful bunch—had come to mean to him.

And then it was too late for recriminations.

He was lucky. The current pulled him to the edge of the writhing jumble of spawn instead of right into the middle. He could feel them, could hear them splashing, their squeals and chittering cries, every one different, every one strange. There was a kind of singing too, almost human, but terrible—like the song of fire and metal. There were eyes that glowed like lamps—orange, blue, white. Thorn tried to stay quiet, to be invisible. But they caught his scent or his taste.

The first one grasped his foot, yanking on him, jerking him down. He had no strength to kick or fend it off. It shook its head, its teeth slipping, scraping away skin and flesh. Thorn bobbed back to the surface. Immediately another mouth snatched his heel. Another fastened on his arm. Sharp, shallow, serrated teeth on his foot, a soft, sucking mouth on his arm. Then there were more. Tiny bites that stung, burrowers that tunneled between his ribs, rough, hairy tongues that wrapped his prick and slipped inside his mouth, licking and tasting . . . feasting.

The horror of it was beyond any nightmare, any imagining. He suffered the chewing, the licking, the ripping pain as they nibbled away his flesh and gnawed on his exposed bones. He suffered—he had no choice. He pushed the panic away, far down where he couldn't touch it. He didn't let himself think. If he did, he'd go mad and *sylveth* couldn't cure a broken mind.

It went on for minutes or hours or days. He had no understanding of time, only the tug of teeth, the tearing of flesh, the crack of bones. It was endless. He had no idea that there was so much pain in all the world, no idea he could feel so much and not faint, not die.

He floated on the waves, things butting up beneath him, pushing him to the surface even as they feasted. He kept breathing, choking sounds emitting from his mouth past the *things* that crawled inside, stripping the soft flesh from his tongue and cheeks, and slipping down inside his throat.

But he was already so close to dying. He felt himself

fading, slipping away, following his senses out into the black waters. He let himself go, thrusting out of the horror of his body.

He no longer felt.

The release was like flying. He was skimming through the waves. He sensed everything, every grain of sand, every pebble, every Koreion scale and claw, every current and eddy, the kiss of the wind, the sweet spin of a waterspout. He touched every shore at the same moment, dipped inside Crosspointe's expansive Blackwater Bay, rippled through every tortuous and twisted nook and cranny of the Root, and dropped down into the deepest depths where vescie eggs nestled in the sand, waiting to hatch, and opalescent celesties shimmered like windblown silk in the obsidian darkness.

Death was . . . bliss.

But he wasn't quite dead yet. The pain anchored him still; a slender, fraying thread of agony told him his body still lived. He couldn't last long. He thought of Plusby and the charmers, thought of Savaiu and her village. Regret filled him. And something more. Obligation . . . compulsion. There was something yet he wanted, something he could have only in his body, in his life. A treasure.

Friends. Brothers-in-arms.

Halford would be very angry if he didn't return. Dread. What if they came looking for him?

Remembering them, remembering those new, fragile ties and fearing for his friends running into the spawn—it was enough to make him grasp ahold of his pain, hauling it like a lifeline, pulling himself back into his body.

Instantly the agony was back. It ate his mind, grinding his reason and sanity between rusty metal blades. Blindly, stupidly, he held on, embracing the torture. He *would not* die before his heart stopped beating. But that would not be overlong.

Suspended inside the savage, relentless cloud of pain, his body gnawed, spawn feasting from within and without, Thorn slowly became aware of something else. Something velvet and hot and sweet, like the sound of a single crystal chime singing in the sunlit dawn. Like golden wine and the brush of eagle wings and the rainbow arc of a waterfall.

Sylveth.

It was coming.

Treacherous hope.

His heart beat raggedly, sluggish and uncertain. His mind lost cohesion, fragmenting like shattered glass. Bits of it clung to thought, darting quickly and incisively. Other parts melted into puddles, glutinous and lethargic. His thoughts tangled and bogged down in the quagmire of his mind. But underneath, feral instinct told him to bide a little longer.

He waited, feeling spawn squirming inside his chest and wriggling through his entrails. He felt the wash of cold seawater against the insides of his ribs, felt the scraping grit of teeth on his skull. He waited.

Sylveth.

A single silvery drop. It kissed his hip.

A volcanic explosion erupted through him. It was scorching hot—he did not burn. The fire was comforting. There were screeches and yelps, screams and moans, as the spawn abandoned their feast, slithering out of his stomach and chest and away. A fumbling at his leg as something tenacious returned greedily to its meal. A scorching flash, acrid smoke, charred flesh.

He felt the tight band of seeping blight that wrapped the bone of his thigh. The cipher. It had retreated upward, from the spawn's feeding frenzy, clinging tenaciously to its murderous purpose. So much for Malik's plan to chop off his leg. At the touch of the *sylveth*-born fire, the cipher dissolved into ash, drifting harmlessly away on the waves.

Freed of the poisonous majick and the hungry spawn, Thorn's body repaired itself. Ragged ends of bone lengthened and curved, merged into joints. Tendons, veins, and arteries snaked a net around the bones; muscle thickened, layering over all. New skin skimmed over him, sliding over his head and down-ward over his arms and legs, puckering closed over his fingers and toes. He was reborn from the inside out.

He lay spread-eagled on the waves, rising and falling in the cradle of his rebirth, the spatter tide of *sylveth* washing around him like stars. He curled his toes, feel-ing his legs again. He touched himself, running his hands over his face and down his body, cupping his prick and balls. Whole. The memories of the spawn were all too real, too present. He could still feel them inside him, dragging his entrails into the water and chewing.

He wept. Staring up at the thin wisps of clouds flut-tering across the night sky, he prayed, thanking the gods, his tears adding to the fertile brine of Braken's sea.

After some time, his stomach cramped and he real-ized he was hungry. And his friends waited. Worried for him. Needed him. He eyed the waves, searching for spawn. He didn't sense any. Had they crawled ashore? Swum upriver? As soon as the protection of the *sylveth* dispersed, he feared, they'd come back again. The thought goaded him. His stomach twisted, his heart thumping in his chest, his legs spasming. Never. He began to swim for the dubious safety of the shore. He had no choice.

He was weak. He rolled onto his back often to float and rest, panting heavily. The *sylveth* remained with him. A gift of the Moonsinger.

When he found footing on the sandy seafloor, he stumbled out, falling to his knees on the black sand beach. He slipped into unconsciousness, his feet in the water, *sylveth* washing over them as if to stand watch over him.

It was dawn when he woke. The tide had gone out and returned since he'd reached the shore. The air was bitter. He tried to stand, but found himself too stiff, too cold to even push himself to his knees. In-stead he inched himself backward, returning to the water. It should have been colder than the air, but surprisingly it warmed him. He pushed himself into the waves, kicking only as necessary, swimming along the shore with desultory strokes.

His head throbbed from hunger and thirst, his body quaking with effort and weakness. He kept a sharp eye out for spawn, but saw nothing. Had hunters come in the night and eaten them? Thorn shivered. If they had, what astonishing luck that they'd left him alone. Or was it luck? The gods were smiling on him. He should have been dead many times over on this journey already.

By midafternoon, he arrived at the mouth of the river. The tide was pulling out and he could not battle the river's current. He crawled up onto the beach. He lay there for minutes or glasses—he had no idea. When he could gather his strength, he pushed himself to his feet and stumbled along, following the river. Thirst drove him. With the tide going out, he needn't go far for fresh water.

But the bank was steep and sheer for better than a half league. He stumbled along, the low-growing scrub scraping his new skin. Soon his legs were a patchwork of crisscrossing scratches and welts.

At last he came to a narrow seam in the rocks that crumbled into a natural staircase down to the water's edge. A stream trickled through it and scrub bushes grew thickly inside. Thorn sat on the edge, the stone cutting into his bare thighs and buttocks. He pushed himself down, landing in the middle of the creek, tearing his cheek open as he stumbled on the sharp rocks and scraped against a prominent branch. Blood ran down his face and he tasted copper on his lips. He bent, scooping up the icy water from the creek and cupping it to his mouth. He slurped, licking his fingers. He sighed and scooped again. It wasn't enough. His parched tissues wanted more.

He stumbled and lurched over the rocks to the edge of the river. Kneeling down, he pushed himself full-length along the bank. With both hands he ladled water to his lips, drinking deeply.

The cold liquid cramped his throat and stomach, but he couldn't stop. He drank more and more. Finally the pain was more than his waning thirst and he sat back. His belly was a tight lump and tingling cramps radiated out along his ribs and down into his bladder. He sighed. He couldn't stay here. This shelf would be submerged when the tide rolled in again.

He scrambled back up the seam, scrabbling up over the lip, tearing skin and fingernails. He rolled onto his back, laughing unevenly as he gasped for air. What a waste of a perfectly good healing.

The wind was picking up, turning his skin blue and pimply. He sat up. Not far was a thicket of twisted coastal pines. He crawled up under their low-growing limbs, hardly noticing the pricks of the needles on his bare skin or the scrape from the rough, flaking bark. He shivered, his teeth clattering together. He was so hungry and exhausted that his vision turned blurry. His belly continued to ache. He lay on his side on the thick bed of brown needles damp from the mist off the sea and pulled his knees up to his chest, wrapping his arms around them. He closed his eyes and fell instantly asleep.

He woke in the dark. Again he was so stiff he could hardly move. He slowly pushed himself up, banging his head against a branch. He leaned back against the tree's trunk, his head spinning. His entire body throbbed from the previous day's swim and hike for water. But it was nothing compared with the pain from the spawn. He shuddered, his gorge rising. He swallowed it down forcefully. The memories surrounded him, grasping him with iron hands. He felt again every bite, every awful caress: noses pressing and nudging, tongues that lapped and tickled, reaching into his crevices, into his bleeding wounds, into his mouth and down his throat. . . .

He retched violently, tears streaming down his face. Keening sounds of terror filled his throat and mouth, but he held them chained. He'd learned young not to reveal so much about himself. These were habits his mind *would not* break.

Dawn had brightened the sky by the time he was able to pull himself from the morass of his memories. He sat quietly, listening to the splash and chuckle of the river, the twitter of birds, the sough of the wind in the trees, and . . . voices.

He stiffened, twisting his head.

"—should go back to the ships. Need a captain to—"

Thorn slumped, overwhelmed by a crazy quilt of emotions—gratitude, relief, joy, annoyance, embarrassment.

"Think he even made t' th' sea?"

"To be certain," answered Plusby. "Though whether he was dead or alive when he did, I couldn't say."

Thorn grinned and struggled up onto his knees. The hatching of scabs on his legs cracked and seeped. He bent, crawling out from under his shelter. Outside the arms of the thicket, he crouched, looking about for his friends. He saw them at last, wending toward the riverbank just downstream of his den. They had been forced to go around a towering thrust of granite just behind the knot of coastal pine where he'd spent the night. Otherwise they would have tromped right past him, and doubtless overheard his sniveling and found him. And if he didn't stop them now, he'd have to either wait until they returned or follow after. He didn't relish either choice.

He stood and waved.

"Hey!"

His shout was pitiful and didn't even frighten the jay berating him from the trees. He tried again.

"Hey! Halloo!"

Still nothing. They continued on, Savaiu trailing silently behind. Thorn drew a breath deep into his lungs, his head spinning at the effort.

"Hey!"

Savaiu stopped. Plusby and Halford continued on.

She cocked her head, turning back and forth. Thorn waved again and then bent and put his hands on his knees as he began to cough. Loudly. Or loud enough. Suddenly he heard shouts and then the thump of boots and the snap of branches and twigs.

Then they were standing in front of him in a half circle, just staring. He collected himself and straightened, suddenly very aware of his nakedness as Savaiu scanned him from head to foot. He flushed.

"Well?"

"Ye still dyin'?"

"Freezing to death. Starving to death. Those, most definitely."

Plusby took the hint and stripped off his coat and handed it to Thorn, who pulled it on gratefully. It hung to his knees, bagging loose like a sack. He pulled the edges tight and belted it, the heat remaining from Plusby's body warming him.

"You will live?"

Thorn looked at Savaiu's knees, not meeting her too-observant topaz gaze. Did she see the terror that still clung to his skin like tar? Did she smell the stink of his waking dreams? Did she know he bawled like a baby under the tree?

"Aye. The cipher's gone. I'm healed."

"Ye look like ye been chewed by spawn," Halford said doubtfully.

Thorn flinched, tensing as if to run. He caught himself, his mind fleeing away from the memory crawling up his spine.

"These are nothing," he said, his lips wooden.

There was a long moment of silence.

"We left the jolly boat beached where you left us. It's just short of a league upriver. Halford and I will fetch it back and pick you up."

Thorn shook his head. "I can walk."

"No. It'll cut your feet to ribbons. Wait here. You've been through enough."

Enough? For what? Thorn shied from the thought.

"Waste of time. I've come this far. I'll go the rest of the way."

"You're a goat-cracking fool. Do I have to tie you hand and foot?"

Thorn twisted his head to look at Plusby. He didn't know why he was suddenly so angry, feeling like he needed to break something. Or someone. He was *glad* to see his friends. He was. And yet he was full of molten fury and didn't know what to do with it. He wanted the pain of the hike, wanted to feel something else, anything else, than the rising memories of the spawn feeding on him.

"I'll walk," he said.

Plusby stared back at him and a fleeting expression flickered across his face. Thorn couldn't read it. But the captain finally nodded. "Suit yourself. Don't expect us to coddle or pet you when your feet are so bruised and torn you can't walk."

"I'll still manage the compass."

"Aye, if I have to shove a stick up your ass to stand you upright, you will."

Plusby strode past Thorn and began making his way along a game trail back to the jolly boat. Thorn followed, trailed by the too-silent Halford and Savaiu.

The track was too narrow to allow anyone to walk side by side, making it nearly impossible to talk. This pleased Thorn beyond reason. Plusby's acerbic replies had made him feel better, releasing the tension building in him. He couldn't take gentleness now, nor kindness. He needed the pain, needed the anger.

It wasn't long before he was leaving a trail of bloody footprints. Halford set up a lewd commentary about Thorn's parentage, his sexual predilections and skills, his unborn children, his carnal taste in women, men, beasts, and inanimate objects. He hardly seemed to take a breath, and went on with creative zeal, never once repeating himself. It was almost enough to make Thorn smile.

He was limping when he reached the jolly boat.

Halford forcibly sat him on the ground, putting the two amulets back on his neck before he could object. The two captains launched the boat, and Halford swung Thorn over his shoulder and dumped him into the bottom before climbing aboard.

The journey upriver was a silent one. They set the sails and then Halford and Plusby took the oars and rowed while Savaiu sat in the stern and managed the rudder and the luff sail. Thorn dressed in the clothing he'd shed two nights before. He offered Plusby back his coat, but the captain refused, ordering him to don it again.

Their progress was sluggish. It was nearly sundown when they made the turn onto the side channel. Halford was red and sweating. The entire voyage he'd stared unrelentingly at Thorn, never looking away for an instant. Now he stowed his oar and helped reef the sails. When he sat again, he watched the trees drift past.

Hours of Halford's ceaseless regard had at first made Thorn uneasy. The pain amulet robbed him of the distraction of physical discomfort and he felt pinned in place. Trapped. Slowly he found himself growing angry and resentful. He embraced the feelings, letting them shield him from the waiting bog of his memories. But as the day wore on, he found himself unable to sustain his fury. Slowly he sank down into his memories of being eaten by spawn. He withdrew deep inside himself, reliving each moment again and again. Outwardly he remained stoic; inside he screamed and screamed and screamed.

They came around a sharp bend in the river and were greeted by shouts. Too many of them sounded angry. There were splashes and Halford tossed the mooring line to someone. Quickly they were dragged up onshore.

"Seems they were worried—both captains and their Pilot gone missing," Plusby said, stepping onto the bank. He looked at Thorn, who was struggling to rise. "A right reassuring sight you'll be," he said drily.

Thorn took the hand Plusby stretched out, and stood. His body was tight and he felt feverish and hollow. Like his memories were burning him up from the inside out.

The rich scent of roasting meat made him nauseous and the crowd of gabbling sailors made him cringe. He found himself pressing closer to Plusby.

"Halford, get our Pilot some food and some water and bandages for his feet. If he gives you any trouble, you've my permission to knock some sense into him."

The bosun nodded, grinning maliciously, and then tossed Thorn easily over his shoulder, carrying him to back his pallet, leaving the two captains to calm their crews.

He fetched Thorn a trencher of salt-horse stew made with potatoes, turnips, and barley. While Thorn picked at the food, torn between desperate hunger and nausea, the bosun fetched a bucket of warm water, a jar of green healing ointment, and the majicked bandages from the healing kit. He knelt and silently began washing the grit, pine sap, and blood from Thorn's feet.

Halford's touch was none too gentle. When Thorn would have protested his aid, saying he could manage for himself, Halford waved a fist at him and smiled that taut, angry smile. Thorn subsided.

Fitch appeared beside Halford, winding around him and rubbing against his arm. He ignored her, concentrating on his task. Finally she twitched her tail with supreme indifference and leaped up onto Thorn's cot, curling up against his thigh and closing her eyes. Her claws curled through the fabric of Thorn's trousers, piercing his skin.

The bosun finished his ministrations, tying off the bandages with neat knots, then stood. Thorn had finished eating and had set his trencher where Fitch could nibble the scraps. He'd left the meat. Chewing it brought back the spawn attack all too vividly. He glanced up at Halford as the big man collected up the remnants of his supplies.

"Thank you."

"Cap'n's orders."

"Will you do something for me?" Thorn asked quietly.

Halford hesitated. "What do ye want?"

Thorn reached up to lift the amulets over his head. Halford growled menacingly and his fists came up. Thorn paused, his teeth clamping together.

"Blot needs these more than I do. I would like him to wear them," he said softly.

"You're the Pilot. You're injured. Ye wear th' damned things."

Thorn gave a faint shake of his head. Tears burned in his eyes, and his throat knotted. The memories of teeth and tongues made his hands shake. He lifted off the amulets and held them out to Halford, who made no move to take them.

"They be for ye. Pilot's privilege." The last he sneered.

Thorn sighed and let his head sag forward, resting his elbows on his knees. Then he straightened and stood.

"Do with them what you want, but I'll not wear them."

He tossed them on the ground at Halford's feet and limped away.

Chapter 23

Thorn had no idea where he was going. But he couldn't stand still, couldn't lie down, though his body ached with his exhaustion and he could hardly keep his eyes open. He needed to keep moving, keep his mind distracted.

He kept to the shadows, avoiding the crowded fires where the crews of the two ships had gathered to be soothed by Plusby and Savaiu. He angled toward the river, knowing Halford was not going to let him wander off alone. He walked carefully, not wanting to ruin the careful bandaging on his feet.

At the river, he sat on the bank, tossing stones into the water. He was aware of Halford standing in the trees behind him.

"Where are the ships?" Thorn asked.

"Downstream behind th' crook. River goes wide. Be a clearin' there." Halford's voice was wary.

"Are there trees for masts?"

"The cap'n says so."

Thorn knew he was referring to Savaiu, not Plusby. He fell silent, continuing to toss the stones. His arms and shoulders were rubbery and heavy. Still he didn't return to the camp. He did not want to sleep. He shivered, the cold seeping up from the ground, the wind burrowing under his clothing.

After a little over half a glass, he climbed stiffly to his feet. If he stayed any longer, he'd fall asleep on the ground. He didn't relish the idea of Halford carrying him across the camp again like a bag of rags. Bad enough he was hovering like an angry vulture. His head spun and he wavered in place a moment. Halford twitched as if to grab him, goading Thorn to stagger back to the fire. He went into the trees and relieved himself, then returned to his bed. The amulets were gone.

He lay down. He stared at the fire, trying to stave off sleep, but eventually he slid into darkness.

Again the spawn came for him. It was as if he were back in the water, floating helpless on the waves. He felt the gnawing begin, the tearing, the crunch of bone, and the icy flood of seawater into his chest cavity. He could not escape, could not scream. He could only endure.

He woke with a start. The fire was crackling. Someone had stirred it up and added wood. It was still dark. He was drenched in sweat and his mouth tasted foul. He sucked in deep breaths of the cold night air, his breath like white smoke. Frost covered the ground and it smelled of snow.

He kicked off his blankets and stood swaying, rubbing at the grit filling his eyes. A movement caught his attention and he spun around, staggering. Halford. The bosun was leaning against a tree, his face unreadable in the darkness. Thorn ignored him, stalking away. This time he did not stop at the river, but wandered downstream, picking his way carefully in the dark.

The camp was quiet. Dawn was still a glass or more away. He heard the crackle of twigs snapping and the scrape of Halford's boots, but didn't acknowledge his watchdog.

The terror of his nightmares slowly receded, leaving him feeling limp. Every step he took was a struggle against enervation. But his mind prodded at him to *move*, to keep himself distracted so that he couldn't think, couldn't remember.

He followed the river around the crook and found the *Zhala* and the *Eidolon*. They sat at anchor in the middle of the river, hulking out of the darkness like the spirits the *Eidolon* was named for. The creaking of the ships and the smooth shuffling sound of the water against their sides soothed Thorn.

A low voice near the *Eidolon* questioned their presence.

"Pilot takin' a walk," Halford answered.

"A guard on the ship?" Thorn asked.

"Aye. Might be th' steward weren't workin' alone."

Bess. Thorn had almost forgotten her. He was glad enough to have something else for his mind to stew on. But all he could think of was her blackened body and the smell of roasted meat.

Bile filled his mouth and he spit and walked on. He focused on lifting up each foot and setting it down, on listening to the twitter of the birds coming awake, to the sigh of the wind and the merry slosh of the river.

They'd gone half a league by the time the sun rose. Thorn didn't want to go back. He didn't want to talk to anyone, didn't want to be among people where he had to sit and be still. He wouldn't be able to escape his nightmares.

But he couldn't keep going forever and Halford was beginning to look like he was ready to drag Thorn back by his hair. He sighed and started back the way they'd come.

The camp was in an uproar when they returned, and it soon became clear that they were the cause. Or rather, Thorn was the cause and Halford to blame for letting him wander off.

Plusby treated Halford to a blistering diatribe. Thorn watched Halford's face turn scarlet. The crew that had gathered for the show slunk back a few steps in case Plusby decided he wanted another target. Thorn shook his head and thrust between the two men, putting Halford behind him.

"Perhaps you should direct your invectives at me," he said, crossing his arms and lifting his brows challengingly.

"Oh, I was getting to you. What in the holy black depths were you thinking?"

He was about to say more when he noticed their audience. Grabbing Thorn's arm, he dragged him away, taking him down by the river. No one else dared follow.

Plusby yanked Thorn around to face him. His voice was low and intense with fury. "Bess could have had a partner or more. What if someone came after you again? Do you want to make yourself a target? We already almost lost you. You are the heart and soul of this ship—if we lose you, that's it for us. Is that what you want? And in bandaged feet—haven't you damaged yourself enough this journey to last a lifetime? Or do you like torture?"

Thorn's lips pinched together. He wasn't going to explain himself. He couldn't if he wanted to. Fury lent steel to his voice.

"Very well, Captain. I will not leave the camp again until the *Eidolon* is ready to sail. I will sit on my thumbs and scratch my cods and pick my nose. If you like, I can shit in full view so that you can be comforted that no one will catch me unawares with my pants around my ankles. Does that satisfy?"

Plusby's lip curled, his gray eyes glinting like a knife-edge. "Aye. You do that."

"Then we are agreed. Now, if you will excuse me, I'd better get started on my new duties."

Thorn brushed past and limped back to his pallet, flopping down on it and staring up at the sky. A while later, Savaiu brought him a plate of lumpy porridge with dried fruit and a mug of watered wine. He sat up and took the food, knowing he was being petulant and rude, but too afraid that if he relaxed at all, the memories of the spawn would crash over him and he'd be helpless to fend them off.

She dropped neatly down on the ground, crossing her legs and shifting her sword out of the way. She watched him eat. He was all too aware of her gaze as he scooped up the porridge with the stale piece of bread. He quickly finished, driven equally by hunger and the desire to rid himself of her watchful attention. He set the plate aside and she stood gracefully, picking it up. She soon returned with another plateful. He ate this just as swiftly.

"More?" she asked when he was through.

He shook his head. "No. Thank you."

"You are well?"

"Yes."

Her frown indicated she doubted the truth of that. "Do you wish to sleep?"

"No."

She nodded, making no effort to stand.

"Is there something you want from me?" he asked at last, beginning to twitch under her steady regard. Then a realization struck him. He glanced behind him. Halford was nowhere to be found.

"I take it that you've been assigned to be my nursemaid?" His voice was like broken glass.

"You are to be guarded."

A bitter smile flickered at the corners of his mouth. "By all means," he said mordantly, and lay down again on his back.

Silence fell between them. He did not sleep, though his eyes grew heavy. He felt his memories circling around him like hunting Koreions and braced himself.

At midday, he ate again. This time Savaiu joined him. It was a relief to have her eyes off him, and fascinating to watch her compact, delicate motions.

Periodically Halford or Crabbel wandered through to check on Blot. He was the only one of the injured who remained in their quiet nook outside the main portion of the camp. The others had recovered or died. Blot was languishing somewhere in between. He breathed shallowly and with great effort, his skin cold and clammy with sweat. Both of his visitors looked exhausted. Crabbel was overseeing the repairs to the *Eidolon*, while Halford was readying the rigging and new sails, when he wasn't standing watch over Thorn.

Crabbel's quick visits were a welcome distraction.

His mind was knotted up in the problem of the masts and he muttered on about boots, futtocks, trestle trees, funnels, yards, slings, tackles, and sheers. He rarely noticed Thorn, except when prompted with questions about the repairs. He rarely stayed longer than a few minutes before he was wandering back to his repair duties.

Halford was equally engrossed. His job as bosun was the care of the lines and canvas. The *Eidolon* carried ample stores for repair, but rerigging makeshift masts would be a tedious, difficult job, and if done shoddily, it could result in losing the masts yet again, and quite likely in the middle of another storm. Or while running from enemies.

Most often Halford ignored Thorn, sitting over Blot, watching him, leaning close and muttering things near his ear, and petting Fitch. She'd been completely ignoring Thorn, snuggling with Blot when Halford wasn't available. He didn't blame her. His mood was foul and even her company was unwelcome.

As he had that night in the sea, Thorn felt completely adrift and alone. No matter that he had company, no matter that just days ago he'd counted Plusby and the charmers as friends. Now that seemed another life, another man. He dared not reach out to them. He felt the memories of that night waiting, circling, hunting. He had to be wary and watchful. He had to keep himself leashed and not allow himself to be distracted or they'd overtake him.

But he had to sleep sometimes. It brought him no rest. The nightmares descended on him full force. The days passed, the sounds of hammering and chopping echoing in the air. He forgot to speak, huddling in on himself. He remained at the camp, as he'd promised Plusby, wandering only as far as the riverbank. Someone—Savaiu and Plusby mostly—remained with him always. He didn't look at them, hardly acknowledged them. He sank into himself, like he was retreating from an army, slowly giving ground as his defenses were overwhelmed. Exhaustion and hunger wore him down. He couldn't—wouldn't—eat meat. The feel of it was too evocative of that night in the water, of the beasts that haunted his dreams and stalked his waking moments.

His sanity was slipping away. He clutched at it with all his might, but it squeezed through his fingers like smoke. He felt the others' concern. But distantly, like they were on the other side of a thick wall of glass. Crabbel and Halford had begun to visit him as much as Blot. They spoke to him, but he could not make sense of their words. Savaiu's voice had gone flat and tinny to his ear.

Plusby alone had an effect on him. He had suffered; he had feared. His wife had been torn from him; his foster sister had tried to sink his ship. Thorn remembered the raw emotion on Plusby's face when he talked of his wife. He knew that of anyone, Plusby might begin to understand the horrors of his nightmares.

As if recognizing this, the captain rarely left Thorn's side. He spoke constantly, urgently, his voice growing raspy and thick as his own exhaustion weighed on him. But even that last anchor line was shredding. Thorn felt his attention wandering, the nightmares clawing at his mind. His last defenses were nearly gone. He knew that when they fell, he'd vanish. His body would remain, but his reason would drift away on the wind.

He could do nothing to stop it.

Liar!

A savage voice in his head. A boy, alone, clawing to survive on the docks, fighting off those who would steal his body and his life. He'd dropped the cloak of urbanity and civilization his parents had worked so hard to cultivate, and he had gone feral. In him had risen an animal instinct to fight, to win, to subdue.

He was that boy once. He had been that boy when he attacked Wildreveh and later Plusby and Crabbel on board ship. He was that boy still.

Surely the violence and fury that still burned in him could be used to save himself rather than mindlessly hurt others.

Thorn cupped his hands around that spark of angry, atavistic strength glowing inside him. He nurtured it with his heart and with his need. Slowly it grew stronger, pushing back the terror.

He came to himself slowly. He was sitting on his pallet. His legs were drawn to his forehead and his hands clutched each other around his knees. He was aware of a quiet, furious argument. He lifted his head slightly, looking blearily about. Plusby, Halford, and Savaiu stood in an angry triangle near the end of his cot. The shadows from the fire made their faces appear twisted and hollowed, like Hurn's fabled demons. They gestured toward him and then toward the river and the sea.

"*Sylveth* cured him once—let it do it again!" Plusby grated in a forceful whisper.

"Won't help," Thorn said, his voice cracking.

The three whirled and stared. Plusby lunged forward, stopping inches away and looking him in the eyes. His face was ravaged and haggard.

"How do we help you if the *sylveth* won't?" he demanded, straight to the point, as if he wasn't sure how long Thorn might be able to hold on to sanity.

Thorn shook his head, a slight movement. "Can't."

"Goat piss. I'm not letting you go tits up. What in the holy black depths is wrong with you?"

Thorn breathed a faint laugh. "Fear."

"Of what? Come on. Stay with us. Explain. I've not seen you back down from anything. Not even that blighted wave. How can fear be doing this to you?"

Thorn licked his cracked lips and Halford held a cup of water to them. He sipped gratefully. The cold wet was the best thing he'd ever tasted.

"The other night . . ." How many nights ago? He'd lost time. He closed his eyes, squeezing them shut. But the memories were as fresh as ever, there in the dark of his mind. He'd invited them. He'd opened the

door. He'd decided to fight. *He'd decided to fight.*
"The other night there was spawn in the water."

His three companions gasped and Halford swore,
slowly and methodically. Thorn leaned on the sound—
it was reliable, predictable, just like the bosun.

"In the water?" Savaiu asked. "But . . . that is not
possible, yes? We found you unharmed."

Thorn shook his head again. "No. I was . . .
eaten . . . first."

Utter silence.

"Eaten?" Plusby repeated through teeth that
seemed fused together.

"There was a mass of them between me and the
sylveth tide. I knew . . . if I could just survive long
enough . . . the *sylveth* would heal me. I could not
fight. I had no strength." The last was an apology.

Plusby gripped Thorn's hands tightly. "By the
gods."

"They gnawed and chewed and clawed." Thorn
couldn't stop now. He needed to say it out loud.
"There were so *many* mouths." He shuddered.
"They . . . they crawled inside me."

Savaiu made a sound, one hand covering her mouth,
her eyes wide with revulsion and pity. Thorn looked
away.

"I could feel them squirming and tearing at me."
His voice broke. He drew a breath and kept going.
The words were like poisonous barbs pulled from his
flesh. Though they hurt, they healed as well.

"They chewed off my feet and pried out my eyes
with their tongues. They were in my mouth, down my
throat, in my entrails. I don't know why I didn't die.
But then I was through them and in the *sylveth*. I
was safe."

He stopped, his ribs bellowing rapidly as if he'd
been running. He looked up at Plusby, his brows furrowed in confusion. "I was *safe*. I *am* safe. Why do
they haunt me so?"

The captain's face contorted and then he pulled
Thorn to his chest, wrapping his arms around him.

"By the gods, how could that *not* haunt you? And we were going to go put you back into that mess."

Thorn laughed shakily. "I do not fear the sea—blood of Meris, breath of Braken."

"You're a damned fool."

Thorn pushed himself away, scrubbing his hands over his face. He felt lighter, cleaner. He'd spoken of his torment and fears and he had not run gibbering into the night or curled up into a ball and died. The spawn were gone and he was alive and safe. He took a breath and let it out slowly. He knew he'd still have nightmares, but he knew also that they'd no longer own him, forcing him to their will. Nor did he think he'd ever lose himself in mindless anger again. He wondered if he'd ever eat meat again, or watch a man gnawing on a meaty joint without feeling queasy.

"I want brandy," Plusby declared. "And a lot of it. Halford, will you fetch it from my quarters? And Savaiu, if you wouldn't mind. Some food for our Pilot." He looked at Thorn. "No meat, I think."

The two moved off with alacrity. Thorn reached out and gripped Plusby's arm where his marriage bracelet circled his wrist, easily reading the anguish in the other man's eyes. He squeezed, wanting to offer comfort, but he had none. Any reassurances he might have given would have rung hollow. It was entirely possible that when the *Sesio* wrecked, Sherenya Plusby had been turned to this kind of spawn, eating the bodies of the sailor who'd manned the ship. It was a nightmare to match his own.

"All the note said was that she was alive," Plusby said.

But not in what condition.

Thorn licked his lips. "It would be evil to offer such hope if your wife did not at least know herself. I do not think Lucy Trenton is evil."

It was cold comfort, but comfort nonetheless.

Chapter 24

The repairs on the *Eidolon* proceeded briskly. It had been ten days since they'd made landfall. Thorn had been lost in his mind for at least a sennight. His recovery buoyed the entire camp. Savaiu took on much of the burden of watching over him as well as Blot, whose breathing had become more steady, though he otherwise seemed unchanged under the majick of the amulets. Perhaps their power had been too depleted by Thorn's needs. Fitch lay on the big sailor's chest or in the crook of his neck when she wasn't out hunting. Thorn fed her much of the meat from his meals, though he forced some down, knowing his body needed the nourishment. She was no longer his cat. Even the rest of the crew had begun to offer her a quick petting, most of the time without an accompanying gesture to ward off evil.

The crews had begun working together with surprising companionship. They shared a love of the water and ships, and though they came from far different places, they each recognized the courage and loyalty that the other had displayed in getting to this safe anchorage. While trust was another thing entirely, the crews not only toiled on the repairs together, but also took meals with each other, talking and even laughing.

Meanwhile, Thorn was gaining strength and vigor, but was still quite weak and nightmares still plagued him every time he closed his eyes. Slowly he was gaining control over them. He never woke from them alone. Savaiu or Plusby was always with him. Their constant presence was no longer oppressive. They offered quiet, undemanding comfort, talking when he wanted to talk and sitting in companionable silence when he did not, which was most of the time.

At the end of their second sennight ashore, the *Eidolon*'s mainmast had been raised, and the planking of her hull repaired. Thorn itched to escape the confinement of camp. He felt jittery and trapped. But he'd been enough trouble to his friends, and there was still the possibility that someone was trying to kill him, though Thorn privately thought it unlikely. He'd concluded Bess was working alone. It would be hard enough to sneak one spy and saboteur aboard, much less two. Still he didn't fight against the limits Plusby had set. He forced himself to be content walking along the river between the repair clearing and the camp, soon wearing a path into the dirt.

One evening when he came to relieve Savaiu, Plusby brought Thorn his cutlass and daggers. The cutlass had been given to the captain in case of need. Plusby sat on the end of the cot.

"Can you use this or is it merely decoration?" he asked, turning the plain sword over in his hand.

"Want to try me?"

Plusby chuckled. "After the way you climbed the mast, I think I will take you at your word." He hesitated. "If you are well enough, tomorrow you and Savaiu should take a scramble up along that ridge." He pointed back up behind them. "I understand it's a beautiful view of the sea."

Thorn stiffened, turning his head sharply. "Truly?"

"Aye. The crews are busy enough with the repairs. None will be able to sneak away without notice. Just strap that cutlass on your hip and keep it loose in the scabbard. And do try not to fall off a cliff or slip and crack your head open on a rock."

"Aye, aye, Captain," Thorn said, eagerness surging through him.

The next morning he woke early, gobbling his

breakfast and then waiting impatiently as Savaiu collected provisions for lunch and filled a water flask. Plusby stopped them before they left.

"Be back before sundown or I'll tie a rope around your leg and leash you to a tree until we get under way."

"Aye, aye, Captain," Thorn said, fully aware that Plusby was entirely serious.

The climb up the ridge took most of the morning. Thorn was easily tired and rested often. His thighs and calves burned and he panted with the effort. But he delighted in being free of the confines of the camp and pushed himself up the track. Savaiu followed behind, allowing him to set their pace. When he stopped, she offered him water and then settled to wait. She was not impatient or restless. It surprised him. In her position, saddled with watching over a half-addled invalid and worrying about her village—he'd have been chewing down trees.

"How large is your village?" he asked during one stop.

It startled him that he did not know. In fact, he knew almost nothing about her. Their conversations had been limited to the present—the repairs to the ship, the food, the weather, and Blot. Thorn had not wanted to think about the past or the future. But now his curiosity began to wake again.

"There are one hundred and twenty-nine of us. Less now that Malik, Sukna, and Jamen did die." Her voice cracked on Malik's name and then firmed.

"You said you live on the fringes of Jutras society. You're pyrates. Where did you all come from?"

She shrugged. "Each is born to a caste—there are eight: priests, merchants, dirt workers, warriors, craftsmen, water people, servers, and slaves. Inside each are many *shaghis*—these are . . . special skills, some with more respect and value than others. What you are born to, you remain. It is not possible to change, except to fall." She looked off into the trees, her mouth hardening. "But change did we, and we *did not* fall."

When she did not seem inclined to say more, Thorn rose and began to climb again. At last they reached the top of the ridge. It was steep and unforgiving, but the trail picked through the rocky outcroppings and contorted coastal pines to a pile of boulders that hunched around a small, flat clearing layered liberally with pine needles. The front gave a spectacular view of the Inland Sea.

Thorn scanned the horizon, looking for sails. He saw none. White storm clouds humped up in the southwest. There would be rain or snow soon.

"Where is your village? Is it far?"

She pointed to the east. "A day, perhaps. It is up a narrow river, beyond the *ziyada-had*."

It was one of the few Jutras words that Thorn knew. She was talking about the Verge. When the Chance storms blew, the air and sea filled with *sylveth*. Inside the tide and storm wards, Crosspointe was safe from the warping dangers that the storms brought. The Verge was a twenty-league band of no-man's-land where the storms would often drop *sylveth*. Anybody living there chanced becoming spawn.

He glanced down at the ground beneath his feet, scuffing the needles with his toes. The entire shoreline, where they stood now, had been touched by *sylveth*—cursed by *sylveth*. And though he had become a Pilot through its touch, he might just as easily have become spawn. He thought of Sherenya Plusby and wondered what had become of her. Had she transformed into spawn? Had she been like one of the creatures feeding on him? Or maybe the change had been more positive, as his had been. But he knew if that had been the case, she'd have come looking for Plusby. If she felt for him even a small part of what he felt for her, their bond was too strong for her to stay away unless something was very wrong.

Thorn cleared his throat and sat down on the ground, motioning her to join him. "Shall we eat? I've worked up an appetite."

The food was cold and bland and required a great

deal of the sour wine to wash it down. The food stores were running low and they had little enough means to replace them. There had been efforts to hunt, but most of the wildlife had not yet returned, following the Chance storms.

When they were through, he glanced over at Savaiu as she put the remnants of their meal back into the pack. The white scars on her cheek gleamed in the shadow light. Unthinkingly, Thorn reached out and brushed his fingers across them. She jerked back and slapped his hand away, glaring. Thorn pulled his hand back, curling his fingers into his palm. The marks were raised, with an ugly, malevolent appearance, and he found himself unaccountably angry that someone had done this to her.

"Who made those?" he asked, well aware that he had no right to pry into her secrets.

Her chin came up and she stared at him, her face cold and forbidding. He was surprised when she answered.

"Kiryat," she said shortly.

"Who is that?"

Her mouth quirked and she shook her head. With a sigh, she sat cross-legged, facing him. *"Kiryat* is priest caste."

"The priests did it? Why?"

She shook her head, and Thorn didn't know if she was annoyed at his questions, or if it was something else altogether. Her ability to speak Celwysh had improved considerably in the past two sennights.

"I was born *daxs*—you see?" She pointed to the band of scars and tattoos on her neck. The end of her pinkie finger was a livid pink but healing well. "Water people. I was *daxs maryad*—the *shaghi* of captains— superior among the *daxs*. You see? I served very well. I was one of the Dhucala's wolves."

Which explained her skill with the stolen ship and its weaponry. But how had she become a pyrate after being the captain of a warship? She anticipated his question.

"When Jutras conquer lands, many who are taken

become *neallonya*—slaves. Others are given to *kiryat* to honor the gods. Some may become *picrit*. If so, they are given to *picrit arrai*, the lowest *shaghi* of the warriors. If they serve well, their children are permitted to go in a *thana*—like a farm. They are farmed and the children given to other castes. Jutras grows strong with new blood."

She paused, frowning, tracing her finger in the pine needles. "My mother was a wolf of the Dhucala like me, and was honored above many. She brought great wealth and honor to our people. Because of her prowess and skill, when she had injuries and was no longer able to sail, she was given a *thana*. Do you understand? As Jutras grows and flowers, it must have more people to seed new lands. *Thanas* husband children. The younglings are given to the castes to swell their ranks."

She waited for Thorn's slow nod. This was nothing he'd ever heard of and it was more than a little repulsive, if he understood her correctly. Just as they bred cattle or goats or pigs, the Jutras also bred *people*.

"The *thana* of my mother held more than one hundred head of *hishmali*—those chosen to breed because their mothers and fathers were *picrit arrai*. Also, they were culled from the *neallonya* when they showed great talent, beauty, skill, strength, or courage. Many were captured as Jutras flowered. There were also *kiza*—purebloods who had fallen. All Jutras except *picrit arrai* and *neallonya* may breed to *hishmali*. The masters of the *thana*,—like my mother—make plans for mating of *hishmali* to grow valuable traits within the children."

She paused, giving Thorn a searching glance. He kept his face carefully neutral, though he recoiled from her explanation. His skin prickled with a chill that had nothing to do with the wind or the frosty air. She nodded and continued.

"Mother bargained for a *hishmal* from another *thana*. He was one of your people—a Pilot. He had eyes like knotted black thread."

Thorn started, sitting up straight and staring. Of course ships disappeared all the time, and the Jutras had to have captured some of the survivors. But to hear of it . . . how many others had suffered a like fate? His stomach clenched, but he had to hear the rest. He'd nearly forgotten the question that began this story. He was completely caught up in the unfolding mystery of Jutras culture. He nodded at her to keep going.

"My mother was *daxs*, and he was Pilot. She decided she should mate with him. It seemed a wise breeding to create a *daxs maryad* like she and I. Too, it might unlock the secrets of the black waters for my people. She kept him in her rooms and was often with him. It was not long before she was fat with child. But she had also become attached to Devri, as she named him. This was a breaking of *kiryat* law. If discovered, she and her blood would lose all caste and be given to the *neallonya* or made *kiza* and sent to breed in a *thana*.

"When my brother was born, she feared what she was doing, what could be lost. She sent Devri to live in the *thana*, arranging him to service others. She planned that she would lie with him again when she turned ripe. She did so, but also took herbs so his seed would not take root in her. So long as it did not and she did ripen each month, she kept others from the questioning of her.

"I was seven suns when Malik was born. I loved him as my mother did also. He early showed that my mother planned well. The black water called Malik; it sang to him. He grew strong and proud and my mother did continue with Devri. To mask what she did do, she would at times offer him to those who asked for him. I was twenty-four suns and a blooded captain of a warship when it all broke to pieces. I had luck. I was on my way to Mother's home for the festival of *Yad-Pati* and so I was not taken immediately.

"My mother was taken to the *kiryat* for punishment. They offered her pain to the gods for shaming the sacred laws. It took seven days for her to die. Devri was given to another *thana*—he was worth too much as a *hishmal*, and it was my mother who was tainted, not him. Malik had been made *daxs maryad* when he was thirteen suns. He had accomplished his first four seasons of training and was to be given to my ship for his fifth season. This news I planned to tell him at our *Yad-Pati* celebration. But when he reached home, they waited for him. He was to be made *parastraya*. Do you understand this?"

Savaiu's voice was strained and her hands had begun to shake. Without thinking, Thorn reached out and took one between his. Her skin was icy.

"I do not," he said.

"It is to make a woman of a man—to remove all that is man between his legs."

She made a scraping motion near her crotch with her free hand. Thorn recoiled with a strangled sound. For a moment he felt the tongues and teeth of the spawn on his prick again. He shuddered, swallowing bile. Savaiu saw his reaction and her fingers clamped on his.

"I could not allow it. Not to Malik. He was my heart."

Her voice broke. A single tear ran from the corner of her eye and her expression twisted with pain. He knew that pain. He knew it only too well. His thumb stroked the back of her hand. At his touch, her expression cleared. She gathered herself and the impassive mask she always wore dropped back into place, but she did not pull away.

"With loyal friends who on my ship served and some who served my mother for many seasons, we killed those who had come to take Malik. He escaped. I was taken. It was decided that the *kiryat* would first punish me, and then I would be made *kiza* and be placed in a *thana*. Men of pure blood would mount me. It was thought this would extinguish the taint of my mother's blood in any child I made. I was to be given a season to take seed. If I did not, I would go to the *neallonya* as a *chinai* for the *picrit arrai* who earned reward."

Thorn didn't need to ask what *chinai* was. The idea of Savaiu being raped by an unending string of captured men who had too many reasons to want to take revenge on a Jutras woman made him ill. His hand tightened on hers.

"How did you escape?" he rasped, disconcerted by the anger he felt on her behalf, and the hatred he felt for the men who would have been sent to use her. Men who had been captured, their families torn from them, and who had been made to conquer and kill for their new homeland. He ought to sympathize with whatever vengeance they managed to take. Instead he loathed them.

"The *kiryat* made punishment as was fitting."

There was a haunted look on Savaiu's face and in that moment Thorn knew that she understood all too well the kind of torture he'd suffered in the water with the spawn. She met his gaze and something passed between them. It was . . . acknowledgment. A recognition that neither was alone; the other shared in the same depth of horror, the same depth of pain.

Thorn pulled her hand to his mouth and pressed his lips against her cold skin. He held it against his cheek to comfort himself as much as her as she finished her story.

"After the punishment, they marked me." She touched the scar with the tips of her fingers. "It says I am *kiza*, but when I am no longer able to mother a child, I am to be *chinai* and I will be so until I die.

"But Malik stole me back. It is against the sacred laws to set blood above caste, above our nation. But this is what we did. As I rescued him, so he did take me from the *thana* where I was held. We gathered those who helped us with their families and ran. We built a village, and we turned pyrates."

She fell silent and Thorn did not speak.

"I am sorry about Malik," he said at last. "He should not have died. Not for me."

Her hand tightened on his, and then she pulled away, putting her chin on her knees and wrapping her arms around her legs.

"My brother, Jordan, was murdered just before Chance," he said slowly, wanting her to know he understood. Another dreadful thing they shared.

She turned her head and looked at him. Again that acknowledgment passed between them. Not sympathy—what they had each suffered went too deep for sympathy to touch. But what they shared was the knowledge that someone else had been to the same appalling place of agony and horror and had come away scarred, but alive. Bitter comfort, but comfort nonetheless.

Thorn climbed to his feet. The shadows were growing long.

"We had better return or Plusby will cut our jackstays."

She rose, dusting the needles from her legs. She caught his arm.

"Had Malik touched *sylveth*, would he have become like you? A Pilot?"

"It is not something that is passed from parent to child. But from what you said, how the water sang to him, that is how it was for me. It is very possible."

A flicker of pain rippled over her expression and she shook her head sadly. "He would have been happy. Very much."

All the way back down the ridge to camp, Thorn held her hand warm in his, letting go only when they came within sight of the cook fire. And though he told himself he did it only to ease her, to offer her the same comfort she'd given him these last days, he knew that he lied to himself. He wanted to comfort her, but he was quickly discovering he wanted more than that.

As he sat on his pallet, watching her walk away to check on her crew and the progress of the repairs, he rubbed the heels of his hands against his eyes.

"You're a goat-cracking fool," he muttered to himself.

An unfamiliar feeling had been growing on him since he'd kissed her hand on the ridge. He refused to examine it. But he felt it delving down deep inside, curling iron roots around his spirit.

He was astonished to realize how much he hated watching her leave him. Which was patently ridiculous. He shook his head. Jordan would have told him not to let his little head rule his big head. Have a quick tumble or two and get it out of his system. His father—Thorn's lip curled. The lord chancellor would blather on about the family name, and how could his eldest son have such little regard for his parents and heritage to go chasing after a Jutras woman—one who was a pyrate and a murderer? Not that he was chasing. *But he wanted to.* The thought wouldn't leave him. Halford would call him twenty times a fool and then dunk him in the river until his prick was so withered he couldn't have pleasured a flea. And Plusby . . .

Thorn smiled wryly. Plusby would tell him love is fragile and fleeting. Grab hold of it hard and drink deep of the cup while you can.

Thorn caught his breath. Love? No. He was not in love. He admired her. Respected her. Perhaps even wanted her. But he did not feel the way Plusby did for Sherenya. Though given time, he thought it might be possible. Except that there was not going to be any time.

He groaned, thrusting his fingers through his unruly hair. By the holy black depths, the gods were laughing at him. He was certain of it.

Chapter 25

The next few days were soothing and restful for Thorn. More so than any other time in his life that he could remember. It was almost idyllic. He had no responsibilities. There was little enough he could do to hurry the repair of the *Eidolon*, and Savaiu's company was a pleasure. The sun came out every afternoon and though snow fell at night and ice skimmed the edges of the river, every dawn glowed brilliant pink and yellow. His nightmares had begun to feel less real and he was able to avoid thinking as much about Jordan. He was content merely to let himself drift on the moment.

He and Savaiu walked a great deal and he taught her to play Fedecor, a game of cards using strategy and wit. Each hour he found himself growing more comfortable with her. Though she did not speak again of her life or family except in oblique ways, she asked many questions about Crosspointe and about sailing the Inland Sea. Thorn was happy to talk about his first love and as a result, he talked far more than she did. He did not touch her again except in passing and she did not invite his touch.

It was afternoon and they'd retired to a wide, flat boulder that edged out into the river just above the makeshift shipyard. Thorn lay on his back, his eyes closed, the sun warming him. Savaiu sat beside him watching the repairs. Thorn opened his eyes, watching her. The expression on her face surprised him. It was bleak and hard, like winter ice. There was a certain savagery in the set of her jaw and the twist of her lips. It was as if she had peeled away a mask and what was revealed was . . . Jutras. A shiver of foreboding slid through him. Her entire attention was fixed on the bustle around the ships. Her hands flexed together, her knuckles white.

"What's wrong?" he asked, sitting up.

She started and looked at him. Her expression remained fierce. Wolfish. She did not answer.

"You look like you want to break something. What's the matter?"

Spiders of fear suddenly crawled up his spine and he twisted his head, looking wildly around. No one was near. No Jutras warriors had found their camp; no assassin was lurking to kill him. They were alone. He turned back to her, frowning.

Her grim yellow gaze ran over him, prying, appraising. "Repairs on your ship will finish soon," she said abruptly.

Thorn glanced at the *Eidolon*, the sheers still in place from raising the masts. "Aye. Soon we'll be ready to go after your people. Is that what's bothering you? You are worried we won't get there in time?"

A shadow of a smile flickered across her mouth and vanished. "I worry. Should the Dhucala's wolves find them, my people will be butchered. All depends on you."

The last was inflected up, like a question.

"And you are afraid I'll shatter apart before we can get to them. I assure you that I won't. I am getting stronger every day. I'll be able to handle the compass."

"No. You would not fail." It sounded like an accusation.

Thorn rubbed a hand over his jaw. "Then what is the problem?"

Savaiu opened her mouth and then she snapped her lips shut. Her liquid yellow gaze locked with his. "A man does not walk two directions at the same time," she said.

"What in the depths does that mean?"

She shook her head, looking back at the ships. "My people believe that you of Crosspointe are weak. You have no honor. You are not to be trusted. Pilots care nothing for their crews. You startled Malik that day we boarded your ship. So angry. You have surprised me. You would die for your crew. You did sacrifice your pain for them."

Again, her words didn't sound complimentary. More like proof of a crime. But what crime had he committed? What had turned her so aloof and tense?

She looked at him again. "A man who loves his crew so much can have forgiveness for what he does protecting them."

It took a moment for Thorn to understand. He felt his face harden, his nostrils flaring.

"I gave my word."

"There will be much danger for you to rescue my village. The Dhucala's warships hunt. If you are captured, they will take all your crew as slaves and you will go to serve a *thana* the same as Devri. You are young. You will make many children for the Empire. You will not see the sea again." She smiled, almost kindly. "We are Jutras; we are your enemies. A wise man, a man who loves his crew, he would take them to safety far from here and leave us behind."

Her words painted a terrifying picture. But then understanding started to waken. Thorn's jaw knotted until it felt like his teeth would crumble. "There is nowhere safe on the Inland Sea," he said tightly.

"But those dangers you know. This is a different thing."

"Are you trying to talk me out of helping you?"

Very reluctantly the words fell from her lips. "I want to be sure."

The corners of Thorn's mouth pulled tight with gallows humor. But he didn't feel amused.

He pushed to his feet, his arms crossing over his chest, his fingers curling into fists. Anger uncoiled inside him. She was actually suggesting she would understand if he became a lying bastard and reneged on their deal—something he hadn't even considered doing. But now that her side of the bargain was nearly fulfilled and he'd gotten what he needed, it was time for him to take his ship and run for open waters, abandoning the *Zhala* to fend for itself. All in the name of his crew, of course. It was perfectly reasonable. Even laudable. And completely spineless and despicable. He chewed the insides of his lips, tasting blood.

"You can't be sure," he said at last, biting off each word, his mouth stiff as iron. "You can trust me. Trust us. Or not. Either way, it's your cracking problem." He looked away, his lip curling. "I wonder if Plusby has any of that brandy about."

He stalked off before she could speak again.

He found Plusby standing on the riverbank, watching as the bowsprit was settled into place. Cauldrons of acrid-smelling pitch were hanging over several fires. Sailors with long-handled spoons stirred chopped bits of rope into one of them to form caulking for leaking seams on the ship. Thorn strode between them, coming to a halt beside Plusby. If the captain noticed Thorn's fury, he didn't comment, merely nudging his chin toward the *Eidolon*.

"Take a day to set the stays and raise the standing rigging. Then we'll hoist the yards and string the running rigging. Another day to bend the sails. Everything goes well, in three days we can be under way."

Plusby looked behind Thorn and nodded a greeting to Savaiu. Thorn felt her yellow eyes on him, but didn't look at her.

"We lost six of our crew, including Bess and Blot. We'll want to borrow at least three hands from the *Zhala* to fill our ranks. Can you afford them?" Plusby asked Savaiu.

Her eyes widened. She nodded emphatically. "It is well. I have more hands than I need."

And even if she didn't have spare hands to lend,

she'd have given them anyway, if only to keep the *Eidolon* from running off. Thorn spat on the ground, his mouth tasting of ash.

"While there's light, I'd like to go over the charts for where we'll be sailing," Plusby said, reaching into a basket beneath his worktable and withdrawing two long wooden cylinders.

He unrolled the charts, setting rocks on the corners to hold them flat. He and Savaiu began to pore over them.

"The village is here? Above the Verge?" Plusby asked.

"Yes. But my people began a trek to the sea at the end of the great storms. They await us here." She pointed to a spot on the map.

His fury knotting in his intestines, Thorn wandered away from the sound of their voices, watching the scurry of activity aboard the ships. There were still several hours before the light failed, and Halford meant to finish fixing the bowsprit stays and deploy the shrouds. It was a delicate process to get the tensions correct and even.

He eyed the *Eidolon*. He'd been belowdecks only once, to the galley. He wanted to see her insides. Ordinarily, he made a habit of poking into every nook and cranny of a ship before leaving port. He liked to know every timber of a ship. In many ways, he and the *Eidolon* were strangers. He needed to change that. He needed a distraction.

At last the shadows began to creep over the ground and the work halted. Savaiu and Plusby were still bent over the charts. Thorn glanced at her and then away. Grudgingly he told himself that she had a right to be suspicious. Many lives depended on her. There was a long history of hatred between Crosspointe and the Jutras. Why should she trust him? He expected too much. Still he couldn't shake his anger. Or maybe it was something else. No man likes to discover a woman he cares for believes him capable of such contemptible duplicity. One thing was certain: he no longer relished the prospect of three more days in her constant company.

The next morning dawned gray and cold. Thorn rose early and accompanied Plusby out to the makeshift shipyard. Savaiu was nowhere to be seen.

"I'm of a mind to go aboard and have a poke around. Care to accompany me?" he asked the captain.

"Poke around?"

Thorn lifted one shoulder. "She's a beautiful craft. I'd like to introduce myself more formally. She's been abused. I'd like her to know I appreciate her sacrifices."

Plusby nodded agreement. "She's been a damned fine ship. Best I've ever sailed. Let's go aboard."

There was a wood ladder leaning up against the *Eidolon*'s side. It was made of pole pines hatched with rungs made of uneven pine branches lashed together with rope. The top was fixed to the rail with more rope.

Thorn went up first, the ladder shaking and flexing beneath his weight. It was more difficult than he expected in his weakened condition, and when he climbed over the rail, he was panting, sweat trickling down his back. He'd composed himself by the time Plusby leaped down onto the deck.

"Where do you want to start?"

Thorn's eyes narrowed thoughtfully. "How about the majicked bulkhead?"

"As good a place as any. Follow me."

Plusby grabbed a lantern and struck a flint to the wick and then went to the forward hatch. He lifted it aside. "It's on second deck, just aft of the foremast," he said, leading the way down, the lantern bobbing in his hand. "The rest of our cargo is gold, silver, and copper ingots, wire, a hundred butts of brandy, cloth, embroidery, salt, and the usual sort of odds and ends—glass, jewels and jewelry, sculptures, paintings, and the like. Expensive, but not unusual."

"Nothing to warrant the expense of this ship."

"No."

Plusby lifted the hatch leading down to the second deck and descended. It was full dark here, the lantern providing the only light. Outside Thorn could hear the sounds of the shipyard stirring to life.

He was halfway down the ladder when he stopped dead. He swept his head back and forth, searching for the feeling that had tantalized him a heartbeat before. Nothing. He took another two steps down and froze. A frisson curled up his spine. This time there was no doubting it.

"What's the matter?"

Thorn gritted his teeth together. This wasn't possible. It simply wasn't. But he felt the slide of *hunger* across his mind, an endless, desperate *want*. He recoiled in shock.

They weren't carrying blood oak. They were carrying ships' compasses.

He leaped the rest of way down the ladder, hardly aware of what he was doing. Stooping to keep from hitting his head, he turned to examine the bulkhead. It was made of the matte black stone the majicars used for knacker sheds. Complex silver patterns swirled elegantly across its surface. The compass yearning grew stronger, though it was muted by the majick in the bulkhead. He put his palm on the silver-traced black stone and then yanked it away, shaking it. His hand stung and was turning red as if burned. But the momentary surge in the compass yearning confirmed what he already knew. There were compasses inside. More than one.

He ran his hands through his hair, stepping back. He was too shocked to know what to feel.

"I take it we're in trouble," Plusby said. "Are you going to tell me about it or do I have to guess?"

Thorn licked his lips, still staring in disbelief at the bulkhead. Jordan would have agreed to this? She was lying. Lucy Trenton *had* to be lying. Jordan would never betray Crosspointe.

"Ships' compasses," he said at last, feeling Plusby's impatience. "We're carrying compasses."

The captain's response was immediate. "That's not possible."

"It shouldn't be. But then, how is it possible the *Eidolon* is fitted with a compass at all? If they have one, why not more? Now we know what warrants the expense and secrecy of this ship. If we deliver these, we open a door onto the sea that we can never close. Once that happens, Crosspointe will never be safe. Even if the Jutras aren't the buyers, they'll get them eventually. And Leighton—" Thorn met the captain's gaze. "They are trying to breed Pilots. Savaiu told me."

"Mother-cracking moon," Plusby muttered.

Silence fell as both men considered the situation. Thorn saw the captain twist his marriage bracelet almost violently. Lucy Trenton had chosen her bribes well. For Plusby, the lure of finding his wife, and for Thorn, the story of Jordan's death. But she'd lied. And if she'd lied about one thing, then she could have lied about the rest.

"What do you want to do?" he asked Plusby.

"I want to kill someone."

"What about this?" Thorn jerked his chin at the bulkhead.

"As I see it, we've got three choices. We can sail her out into the sea and scuttle her where no one will find her. We can take her back to Crosspointe and turn her over to the Crown Shields. Or we can steal her."

"And the compasses?" Thorn asked.

"Can't off-load them so long as they're majicked. We can just sail with them."

"Sooner or later Lucy Trenton will find us. She's powerful. And she has power over the waves."

"Then we sail to Crosspointe. We'll off-load the crew and the cargo—they'll never have to worry about money again. And then we'll turn her over to the Crown Shields."

"My father would love that. He'd have to publicly condemn me. Might be worth it just for that," Thorn said slowly. He was more surprised than he liked to hear Plusby's decision. Somehow he'd expected the other man to be ruled more by his desire to find his wife. "What about Sherenya?"

Plusby swallowed jerkily, his mouth twisting down. "If she's alive, I'll find her. Or she'll find me. With or without Lucy Trenton."

But she hadn't tried to find him. If she was alive. Thorn didn't point out the obvious.

"And Savaiu's village?"

"We made a bargain."

Thorn snorted, thinking of Savaiu's doubts. If she only knew. "It's Jutras territory. If we're caught . . . they'll find a way to break through this bulkhead."

"Then we won't get caught."

Plusby spun on his heel and climbed up the ladder. With him went the light. Thorn hesitated, reaching out to brush his fingertips over the bulkhead. *Fire* scorched him again and he pulled away.

He caught up to Plusby on the deck. He stood at the rail, watching the work below.

"What do we tell them?" Thorn asked, coming to stand beside him.

"Do you think any of them will want to deliver the compasses?" Plusby shook his head. "Not likely. Smuggling is one kind of treason. Selling compasses is something else altogether. They're already going to be nervous sailing into Jutras lands. Let's not panic them. We've made our decision. We gain nothing by telling them. At least, not until we have to. Gods willing, they'll walk away with wagons of money and their lives."

Thorn was too edgy to settle. Savaiu's presence only made it worse. At last he approached Plusby.

"Put me to work. Let me help run the rigging."

"You're Pale-blasted. Go. Rest. Take a walk somewhere."

"You cannot actually order me not to," Thorn
pointed out. "I am the Pilot, not a member of your
crew. Asking is just a courtesy. Besides, Savaiu has
her own work to do. She cannot be expected to watchdog me any longer. I shall be perfectly safe sitting
here where you can keep a watchful eye on me. Don't
forget, I made bosun before I became a Pilot. I really
can help. And . . . I need to keep busy."

"Nightmares?" Plusby was alert.

"Something like that," Thorn said tightly.

Plusby was nodding. "Very well. But you *will* rest
if you get tired, and you *will not* strain yourself," he
ordered. "Do you understand?"

Thorn nodded. "Aye, aye, Captain."

The work both invigorated him and distracted him
from thoughts of Savaiu. When he wasn't helping direct the setting of the rigging, he was worming, parcel-
ing, tarring, seizing, knotting, reeving, braiding, and
splicing. By the evening of the first day, he was exhausted, his hands shaking. But it was the first time
he'd felt useful in more than a sennight. That night he
bolted his food, even the salt horse, and slept soundly
without nightmares.

The next day was much the same. He didn't even
mind that his hands were growing raw from manipulating the ropes. The work required concentration, not
permitting him to think about anything else. It was
a relief.

At midday, Plusby dragged him away to rest. Thorn
protested the entire way. They retreated to a hulking,
flat-topped tor overlooking the repairs. The captain
withdrew a flask from his coat pocket and offered it
to Thorn. He unscrewed the cap and drank, expecting
brandy. But inside was Meris's Tears. He took a
deep swallow.

"That is good."

Plusby smiled thinly, taking a sip as he sat down.
"I figured you could use it."

"Yes," Thorn agreed, taking the flask back.

"So what is this business between you and our Jutras captain?" Plusby asked bluntly. "Something I should know about?"

"What are you talking about?" Thorn said warily, offering the flask back.

"Two days ago you turned cold as Braken's prick during Chance. Haven't said a word to her since. I started wondering if it had anything to do with our cargo. So I'm asking you, Pilot. Is something going on that's going to put my ship at risk?"

"You mean other than carrying ships' compasses and kiting off to rescue a Jutras village from Jutras warships?" Thorn asked.

"Other than that," Plusby said drily.

Thorn shook his head, pacing to the edge of the tor. "It was a misunderstanding. Or rather, what was misunderstood is now perfectly clear."

Plusby sat back against an outcropping, kicking his legs out in front of him. He drank again. Slowly he began to chuckle. "You've gone over on your beam end for her."

Thorn's head jerked around, but his words of denial died on his lips. He scowled. "You find that amusing?"

"I take it she does not return your interest?"

"Her opinion of me appears to be not quite as high as the one you had of the charmers when we first met."

"What did you do to earn such a high estimation?"

"Damned if I know," he lied.

"You didn't insult the *Zhala* or get drunk and piss on her boots?"

Thorn laughed, the sound hurting his chest. He took the flask again when Plusby offered, and sat beside him. "She doesn't trust us to keep our end of the bargain."

"She thinks we will sail off and abandon her people?"

"That's the heart of it."

"Ah. I wondered if it would come to that. But you can't blame her. We agreed under dire circumstances.

We were forced to trust her. And now she's forced to trust us and it's chewing her up. She'll find out different soon enough. I don't plan to chop off a hand or finger or any other parts to prove it to her, however."

Thorn smiled without humor, picking up a rock and hurtling it over the edge of the tor. "Indeed. But she's seen enough of me to know I don't break my promises."

Plusby was silent for a long moment. "Aye," he said heavily. "But perhaps it is just as well."

"Oh?"

"I'm not sure but that love is a curse," Plusby said, his hand wrapping around his wrist where his marriage bracelet was obscured beneath his clothing.

Thorn snorted. "I am *not* in love," he said emphatically.

"No?"

"Tell me about Sherenya," Thorn said, changing the subject. "Was she funny? Did she make you laugh?"

Plusby eyed him in surprise. "Most people ask if she was beautiful."

"I expect she was. To you, if no one else."

"This is true. She was beautiful. But she did not often laugh. It was difficult to earn a smile. Her life had been . . . difficult, with the Jutras invading. She put a good face on it. The *jeras* taught her serenity. And then I turned up. From the instant we saw each other, we were . . . at the center of a hurricane. She broke all the rules of her order to be with me. For her, I'd have left my ship standing at anchor and never looked back at the sea."

Plusby scratched at the back of his neck, frowning down at his feet. He shook his head. "I have often wondered if the gods cursed me. To give me such a gift, and then to rip her away. Did I offend them somehow? I would have given my life for hers. I still would. But I can't give Crosspointe."

He drank deeply from his flask, emptying it. He stood unsteadily. "What you experienced with the spawn? I feel that every day, every time I think of my wife. That is what you risk for love. My advice? Run. Fast and far as you can. If it isn't already too late. Now, if you'll excuse me, it appears you have company."

Plusby scrabbled down off the tor, nodding to Savaiu, who climbed up slowly, squatting down beside Thorn, who looked down on the ships, refusing to meet her gaze. His emotions were still roiling and far too close to the surface.

"I must apologize."

Thorn shrugged, trying to ignore the effect her voice had on him. "There is no need."

She knotted her fingers together, her elbows resting on her knees. She looked nervous and more than a little irritated as she sought words. Before she could speak, Thorn held up his hand to stop her.

"Let us speak plainly and put an end to this. We made a bargain with you and we mean to keep it. We will help you rescue your village; we will not abandon you. I realize you have no reason to trust me to keep my word, but you'll just have to live with the uncertainty. Now, since that should cover all we need to discuss, I'll go check on Blot."

He started to stand, but she gripped his arm and shoved him back down. She stood, her legs braced wide, her hands on her hips. She was spitting mad. Thorn looked up at her as she rattled off a litany in Jutras. It didn't sound complimentary.

"Sorry," he said sardonically when she finished. "I didn't catch that."

She crouched down again, her face thrust close to his, her eyes blazing.

"It means your head hides up so far inside your ass that no one can hear words when you speak."

"Ah, is that so? Well, I should tell you. That isn't exactly a secret."

Her fingers flexed and then flattened on her knee like she was trying to resist hitting him.

"I wish to apologize," she said, anger hardening her voice and making her sound anything but sorry.

"I do not wish to hear it."

"Why?"

"Because I don't care to hear you lie to me."

"Lie?" She nearly shouted the word. "I. Do. Not. Lie."

"You would if you apologized. You cannot tell me that you don't think we plan to run off and desert you once the repairs are done."

She reached out and closed her hand over his mouth in a bruising grip. She bent close so that when she spoke, he could feel the wash of her breath brush across his face.

"Do you not speak now." She paused. "There are many stories of Crosspointe's Pilots in my land. You are soulless spirits from the sea. You eat on the fear and blood of your crews. You don't die, you can steal minds, you would sink your own ship for anger, and many more evils are you guilty of. No," she said, tightening her hand when he tried to pull away. "You have spoken. Now I will speak.

"You made the promise to help us when there was little choice for you. You needed us. I wondered, would you not break that promise when you had no more need of us?"

Thorn reached up and grasped her wrist, pulling her hand away from his mouth. It was, he noted absently, the same one she had tried to chop off to seal their bargain. He scowled at the missing end of her little finger before gently pushing her hand away. His anger had suddenly faded and he felt cold.

"I understand. You have people depending on you. It would be foolish not to question our loyalties."

The words tasted like sand. He understood, but it still infuriated him. Plusby was right. He'd gone over the beam end for her. She was smart and skilled and brave. And anything between them was completely impossible. He was returning to Crosspointe to confess to treason, and she was taking her people to safety somewhere on the west coast of the Inland Sea.

He stood and this time she did not stop him. "I'd

better check on Blot and get back to work. The faster
we finish the repairs, the faster we can be off after
your people." He started to walk away and then
stopped.

"We made a bargain with you. We intend to honor
that bargain. You have no reason to fear. But as I
said, I have no proof to offer. You will simply have
to wait and see."

Before he could take more than a couple of steps,
Savaiu's hand caught his arm. Her fingers were strong
and callused and sent frissions of heat whispering
through his body.

"I do know. I do believe you."

He met her topaz gaze. He could tell she wanted it
to be true, but doubt shadowed her eyes.

"Good," he said pulling away. He needed to put
distance between them. "I'm hungry. Better go get
something to eat."

Before he could move, Savaiu stepped close, sliding
her hands beneath his coat, raising her lips to press
her mouth to his. Her lips were cold, her tongue warm.
He slid his hands behind her head as her hands settled
on his hips. Thorn pulled Savaiu closer, running his
hands over her back. When she drew away, it was all
Thorn could do not to snatch her back.

She studied his face for a long moment, then
stepped away.

Thorn watched her, his stomach clenching slowly.

"I make a mistake," she said, and turned to scramble back down off the tor.

It was his turn to grab her arm. "Why?"

She stopped. She did not look at him, her profile
carved from ice.

"It is not—" She broke off, chewing her lower lip
as she sought words. "I do not like where such a
road leads."

"Where's that, exactly?"

She gave a short shake of her head. "For Devri, my
mother risked what she should have protected. I will
not walk her path."

"That isn't the only path."

She faced him. "If my mother had not so wanted Devri, if she had not kept him after Malik, if she had sent him to another *thana* . . . but she was stupid. His eyes tangled her. He knew she could keep him from danger. He petted her; he whispered in her ears and pleasured her body. She thought only of him, never the danger. Her hunger made her mind weak, robbed her of honor. This road I will *not* walk behind her."

"It is not the same."

"Is it not? I hold lives in my hands. Do I let myself—" She flattened her hands between them, stepping back. "You may intend no harm," she said slowly, sounding none too certain.

Thorn's hackles rose again.

"But even so, you make me feel—"

She stopped. Thorn wanted to shake the rest of it out of her. Instead he waited.

"I do not forget my responsibilities. That is all."

Thorn nodded reluctantly. He didn't have any choice but to agree. And if he was truthful with himself, he wanted only what they might have now, in these few days before the repairs were done. That's all he could offer.

He held out his hand. "Let us step off this rock as friends and allies and forget the rest."

Savaiu hesitated before taking his hand. "Let it be so."

He stared after her for long moments after she disappeared over the ledge. He could still taste her on his lips. He wiped the back of his hand over his mouth and drew a ragged breath.

He stared down at the *Eidolon*, a dark shadow on the river. For the first time he understood the sea god's maddened frustration to know his lover, Meris, pined after Hurn, the dark god, who neither claimed nor rejected her. The furious quarrels between the Moonsinger and Braken were the source of the storms that scoured the Inland Sea. And just at the moment, Thorn sympathized entirely with Braken. He'd never before understood how a man could want a woman so much he'd give up everything, while at the same time hating her.

Not that he hated Savaiu. Nor would he give up everything for her, any more than she would do so for him. The sea was his true lover, adored above all others. Except he was going to lose her too. He was returning to Crosspointe as a traitor. He'd be tried for treason. The best he could do was make sure his crew got away safely.

He looked up at the sky glittering with stars. He and Savaiu were kindred spirits in a way. She was willing to sacrifice everything for her village, and he was about to do the same for his crew and Crosspointe.

Chapter 26

By the end of the next day, the *Eidolon* had been completely rerigged. All that was left to be done was to bend the canvas to the yards and they could be under way. It had been thirty days since they'd sailed out of Grimsby Bay, and so very much had changed since that day.

The camp was boiling with nervous anticipation. Not a sailor among them—Jutras or Crosspointean—liked being dirtside. But they were about to sail into Jutras territory, and the Dhucala's wolves were hunting. If chance smiled upon the two ships, they'd slip in and escape with Savaiu's villagers without ever seeing a Jutras warship. If chance was in a bad mood, things could go very badly. It put everyone on edge, though a solid camaraderie had developed among the Crosspointe crew. They knew now that they could depend on one another in the worst of circumstances. They knew their captain and Pilot would not fail them.

After dinner, Halford, Plusby, and Crabbel came to sit around Thorn's fire. Fitch climbed onto Halford's lap, nuzzling and purring.

"Captain, isn't it true that cats are bad luck aboard ship?" Thorn asked with an innocent look.

"Aye, Pilot. That is true. A man would have to be Pale-blasted to take one aboard ship. Now, Pilots—they're queer folk already, so there's some as would not only bring a cat aboard, but whistle a jig on the quarterdeck, but us regular sailors have a proper respect for bad luck. Isn't that right, mate? You being a charmer, you're especially careful of not inviting bad luck on ship. Isn't that so?"

Crabbel leaned back on his elbow, settling his mug of ale on the ground and scratching his jaw. "Aye, Cap'n. Be maggoty for a charmer t' even cross paths with a cat. What say ye, Halford? You're a proper believer in th' luck. What d' ye think of a sea dog as would curse his ship by rubbin' up close to a cat?"

"Cock-sucking, goat-prodding squibs," Halford muttered, lifting Fitch so she lay across his forearm. He scratched gently at her ears with his large, blunt fingers. "We was cursed from th' grain we said aye t' this berth."

"Cat's lucky."

Every one of them froze. Halford was the first to move. He was on his feet and beside Blot in a heartbeat, Fitch clutched to his chest. Blot began to cough and Crabbel helped him sit up, offering him sips of ale.

Blot looked like a different man. His hair had gone from blond to gray. The bones of his face protruded sharply beneath his skin, and his dark eyes were like holes in his face. He trembled, unable to hold the pewter mug. He pushed it away, his breathing rough and shallow. He looked around at the men staring down at him.

"Cat's lucky," he repeated. "Never stopped that cursed purring. Just like a foghorn. Followed it back."

At this point the object of their conversation leaped lightly down onto his lap and rubbed herself beneath his chin. Even standing at the foot of the cot, Thorn could hear the rumble of her purr.

"What happened?" Blot asked, glancing blurrily about. He listed against Crabbel, who held him firmly.

"Lost th' main- and foremasts. Ye was crushed," Halford said bluntly. "Figured ye'd be feedin' th' sea."

It took a moment for that information to register. Blot looked down at his blanket-covered legs, his mouth working. No sound came out.

At last his voice came back to him. "Crushed? My legs?"

"Pretty much everything below your waist," Crabbel said cheerfully.

Blot sagged, unable to tear his eyes from his legs. "Can't feel 'em."

"It's the pain amulet. If you weren't wearing it, you'd be in agony."

Blot's eyes rose to Thorn's. "Amulet? For me?"

"And one for healing. It appears it's cured whatever internal injuries you had. I doubt it's made much headway on your legs yet, but at least you're awake. Halford, see if there's broth for him."

As the bosun trotted off, Thorn turned a fierce look on Blot. "Now listen well. I'm only going to say this once. I do not want to hear any of your tripe about how I should have saved the amulets for myself. They are mine; I get to choose how to use them, so you can just keep your mouth shut about it."

Blot said nothing, his gaze shifting uncertainly to Crabbel. His hands moved up to feel around his neck. When he touched the amulets, he yanked his hands away.

"You've got him between Chance and a lee shore," Plusby observed. "If he takes them off and throws them in your face as he feels he ought to do, he'll never get his legs back."

"He'll wear 'em," Crabbel said.

"If he doesn't, it will be mutiny," Plusby said. He glanced at Thorn. "Do you think he's more surprised that he's wearing them at all? Or that I am ordering a charmer to do so?" He looked back at Blot. "Remember that they come from *my* healing stores when you feel the need to fawn and bootlick with gratitude."

"I gave them to him. You had nothing to do with it," Thorn said.

"On the contrary. If you recall, you were wearing the amulets from *my* kit. If anyone is to be groveled at, it is me."

"There is no virtue in having lent me your amulets; as I recall, I gave you mine—you were so wretchedly pitiful after our race up the mast."

"True. But then I gave you another healing amulet." He rubbed his chin. "Very well, we both deserve his gratitude. And as I recall, we never quite finished that race," he mused.

"And ye'll not ever while I can stop ye," Halford said, returning with a steaming cup of broth. In it floated crumbled bits of hardtack.

"Nor I," Crabbel agreed.

Thorn's brows rose as he looked at Plusby. "I thought you were the captain of the *Eidolon*. Surely you can keep this rabble in hand."

The captain shook his head. "Seems the Pilot has given them uppity notions. Remind them I can bust them all down to snotties. Better yet, I can drop them over the rail into the black waters and let them swim ashore—if they can."

"And I'll be remindin' ye both that we crimped one Pilot—we can crimp another and a captain too, if we be needin'. Then we'll toss ye over th' taffrail and ye'll both be swimmin' w' the spawn," Crabbel returned.

At the mention of swimming with the spawn, both Halford and Plusby gave Thorn a worried look, like they were waiting for him to grow another head or run screaming off into the trees, or perhaps just drop into a sodden heap.

"What?" he said. "It's over. I'm fine."

Neither of the other two appeared convinced. Thorn grimaced.

"I am not glass; I am not going to shatter apart at the mention of spawn."

Crabbel looked baffled. "What be goin' on?"

Thorn crossed his arms, looking at the three men. Four—Blot was watching him, his eyes bloodshot and squinting, his head tipped against Crabbel's shoulder. He was too weak to hold it up.

Halford and Plusby said nothing. Thorn gusted an annoyed breath. These were secrets he didn't feel like keeping anymore. He didn't belong to the Pilots' Guild. He belonged to the *Eidolon* and these men. He looked at Blot.

"Among the many things you missed while you were trying to die was that Bess attached a cipher to me in order to kill me. Once we made safe harbor here, the captain, the bosun, and Savaiu took me down to the ocean." Blot couldn't know about their Jutras friends or their captain, but Crabbel and Halford could fill him in on the details later.

"I was uncomfortably close to dying. I floated out to the surf. The storm had released a splatter tide and I was hoping to find *sylveth*. I did. It healed me and now I'm fine." He glanced at Halford and Plusby. "I *am* fine."

"What our Pilot neglects to mention is that in the surf on his way out to take his *sylveth* bath, he encountered a horde of spawn. The results were . . . as might be expected. Though his body was healed, his mind was a little off its keel," Plusby said.

Halford snorted. "A *little*."

"At any rate, there were a couple of days there we thought we might yet lose him to madness."

"But you didn't and there's no need to be prancing about on eggshells around me." Thorn hesitated. "Though I wouldn't complain about a swig of brandy."

Halford handed Blot's broth to Crabbel, who was staring stupefied at Thorn and Plusby, and then went on his errand.

"*Sylveth* healed ye?" Crabbel asked.

Thorn shrugged. "Best-kept secret of the Pilots' Guild. We're all spawn."

Crabbel almost dropped the mug he held. Then his mouth clamped together and his brows furrowed. He bent over Blot, helping him drink some of the broth. The injured man swallowed perhaps a quarter of the mug, and then his eyes rolled up into his head and he slumped. Crabbel laid him back down before turning his attention back to his captain and Pilot.

"Knew they wasn't human," he muttered. "Puffed-up bastards walkin' th' decks like their asses was stuffed with dralions."

Thorn snorted. "Aye. Those are my guild fellows."

Crabbel looked up at him. "Ye was never like them."

"Much to their deepest annoyance. The guild sold me to you. Now you know why."

"I could use a drink."

Thorn nodded, sitting back down on his cot. This had been an evening of revelations and disappointments. He was exhausted.

"Where in the depths did Halford get off to?" Thorn wondered aloud.

Plusby found a seat on the ground, his back against a tree. He looked at Thorn, lifting one eyebrow. "Things did not go well with Savaiu, I take it?"

"Not particularly."

"Then it is well you can be rid of her soon."

Thorn made no reply as Halford returned and filled their cups with generous doses of brandy.

"Good thing there's a raft of this stuff in the hold," Plusby said thoughtfully, swirling his cup. "I'd hate to run out." He lifted his cup in a toast. "Here's to the Inland Sea, the lover we always return to. She's a bitch and a tease, but we are faithful to her all the same. May she smile on us fondly tomorrow and every one of our days."

He drank and the others did as well. As Thorn swallowed the last of his brandy, it was Savaiu he thought of.

Chapter 27

The next day, they emerged from the river's mouth just as the late afternoon sun was slanting down behind the Gwatney Mountains. The day was clear and cold, the wind biting. Thorn stood at the compass feeling stronger than he'd felt since the day of the mast race. Plusby stood beside him. Ahead, the *Zhala* slid out onto the waves, bobbing on the water like a child's toy, the yellow stripes on her sides glowing in the dimming light. At the helm, Thorn could see Savaiu.

It had been decided that if the two ships were set upon by warships, the *Zhala* would attempt to keep them at bay while the *Eidolon* rescued the village and made for open seas. Though he hated the idea of it, Thorn could not disagree that the plan made the best use of their resources. The *Zhala* had ballistae and a gun, and Savaiu was skilled at sea battles. The *Eidolon* was built for speed. She could easily outstrip the Jutras warships, but had no attack capability. But in running, she'd also leave the *Zhala* to the mercy of the Dhucala's wolves.

Thorn found himself brooding on the danger. If the *Zhala* was captured, the punishment would be severe for everyone aboard, especially Savaiu.

The tide was turning out and there were few dangers lurking in the nearby waters. The sea was quiescent, as if the upheaval of the storm had exhausted it. But Thorn knew it was deceptive to think so. The sea never rested. But at least the vescies had returned to

their home in the depths and would not return unless
churned up again.

The two ships clung to the coast as they sailed east.
Savaiu's people would be waiting in a secluded cove
just inside the mouth of a narrow bay—one of Savaiu's
coastal hiding places. The villagers would have jour-
neyed overland there from above the Verge, while she
and her crew captured the warship.

Soon it was dark and the *Eidolon* slipped into the
lead. With Thorn at the helm, they didn't worry about
the lack of light this close to the coastline, though the
moon was waxing and gleamed brightly from behind
a gauzy wisp of cloud.

The wind was coming from the southeast and they
were sailing close-hauled. They went as silently as possible, giving orders in quiet voices and relaying them
on. The *Zhala* carried full sail, while the *Eidolon*
sliced quickly and easily through the water under re-
duced sail.

They made good time. It was approaching dawn
when they reached their destination. It was off the
coast of the former Relsea, and just east of the Goa
Maru—a large peninsula forming the eastern headland
of Kutranil Bay, the gateway to Bokal-Dur, the Jutras
capital city.

The coastline was broken and pitted with hundreds
of inlets, large and small. The two ships found the one
they were searching for, sliding inside a tongue-shaped
waterway that licked a long channel into the high-
lands. Coming about in the narrowly slotted bay was
difficult. Currents swirled in a baffling churn. The high
cliffs on either side twisted the winds, and as soon as
their sails caught the wind, they fell off it again.

The *Zhala* was far more maneuverable here. Savaiu
had her turned about quickly, almost looking like
she'd leaped out of the water and swapped end to end.
The *Eidolon* followed far more slowly and gracelessly.

They trailed the Jutras ship into a small protected
cove. It was exactly the sort of place Thorn would
expect to find pyrates. A long, steep-sided tentacle of

tree-covered rock curled out into the water, shielding them from watchers in the bay and the Inland Sea. Anyone sailing past wouldn't know there was even a cove there.

The water inside the cove was deep and the current was soft and tender. The narrow bottlenecked entry made the inlet supremely defensible. Thorn eyed the passage. He thought it might require warping to get the ships back out. A single Jutras warship could trap them. Suddenly he felt like the walls of the cove were pressing in on them.

It was midmorning; getting turned and inside the cove had taken hours. Thorn couldn't help his wide yawn as the anchor chain rattled out of the hawse and hit the water with a splash. The crew reefed the sails, bundling them loosely to the yards.

"You should sleep," Plusby told him. "You need to be sharp when we weigh anchor."

"I don't think I can," Thorn said, leaning against the rail, watching the bustle of activity on the *Zhala* as Savaiu and her crew began to lower their longboats.

"Have you thought about where to take them?"

Plusby shook his head. "I figure to run first for the Bramble. Jutras can't follow there and we won't run into any Crosspointe ships. We'll leave the *Zhala* there with the villagers while we go lay in stores." He paused. "Lalant Uly is the best choice for that." He cast a sidelong glance at Thorn.

"I don't like it. Whoever is expecting those compasses may be looking for us there. We should have passed through Lalant Uly a sennight ago and been well on our way to Calenfor by now."

"Aye. And they may try to take them by force."

Thorn rubbed his hands over his face, bracing his elbows on the rail. "Maybe Savaiu's people have enough stores to get us south to Penrean or Lanivet."

Plusby snorted. "Not likely. They've just made a trek of fifty leagues or more, on foot. And it's the middle of winter. My guess is they've been living off turnips and beans, and precious few of those."

"What do you want to do?"

"I want not to be carrying a load of ships' compasses." Plusby drummed his fingers on the rail. "I don't think we have a choice. We can't risk going to Lalant Uly. We'll have to make a run south to Revahait."

A port city on the border between Penrean and Opiloron and sitting on Hatrine Bay, Revahait was a sprawling trading hub. It was a city of tents. Every year just before Chance began, it vanished, its denizens retreating back from the Verge. As soon as the Chance storms passed, it sprang to life again. It was a vast city entirely devoted to commerce. Even the Jutras bought and sold goods there. There wasn't anything that couldn't be found there.

"Savaiu won't like us leaving her stranded on the Bramble."

"She'd like it less if the Dhucala's wolves notice the *Zhala* in Hatrine Bay and burn it to the waterline. She and her people will be safe on the Bramble and if chance favors us, we'll be gone less than two sennights."

"She'll want to know why we don't make for Lalant Uly," Thorn pointed out.

"You will find knucklebones blocking the mouth of the Saithe River. Or Koreions or *sylveth* loose in Roche Bay. Since we can't afford to waste time—and who knows how long such dangers will continue to block our path?—we'll head for Revahait. Agreed?"

Thorn nodded. "Where do we take them after that?"

Plusby shrugged, looking grim. "Anywhere they want to go. Maybe down by Normengas or up around Orsage. That will put them far out of reach of the Jutras."

He paused. Then he said slowly, "What if she wanted you to go with her?"

Thorn smiled. "I don't belong with her."

"Why not?"

"She doesn't want me, and I—" He gave a faint

shake of his head. "I don't know if I want her enough. More than I want the compass. I can't have both. Besides, I won't walk away from this ship. And we have an appointment in Crosspointe."

"If we turn the *Eidolon* over to the Crown Shields as planned, you won't ever get a ship again. And the crown will see us both dead."

"I know."

Degby had prepared a breakfast of thin porridge mixed with chopped salt horse and scattered bits of dried fruit and nuts. Thorn ate his quickly, ignoring the shuddering feeling in his gut when he chewed the meat, and then retreated to his cabin to sleep. Despite the repairs that had been made to his bedchamber, it still reeked of smoke. Remembering Bess's body, Thorn couldn't go inside. He kept the door shut, slinging a hammock in the sitting room.

Halford was scowling when he shook Thorn awake. "Ye don't go off without someone t' watch over ye. Might be someone still as wants ye dead."

Thorn swung out of the hammock, tossing Halford a mocking salute. "Aye, aye, sir." Then, "Are you waking me up just to chastise me?"

"Cap'n wants ye on deck."

He hesitated, then pulled Thorn's Pilot's ring from his finger, holding it out. Thorn looked at it a moment, then took it, sliding it on his forefinger. It rolled around, loose. He moved it to his middle finger, where it slid back off his knuckle. He cupped it in his hand a moment, considering. The ring and matching brooch, which even now was stuck in the back of a drawer in his house in Blacksea, had been given to him upon entering the Pilots' Guild. He'd worn the ring proudly every day since, a badge of who he was and how far he'd come from his parents' home. He'd worn it every day, that is, until he'd given it over to Halford to hold.

When he looked at it now, it seemed a mere bauble. Insignificant. It no longer defined who he was. Rather, it symbolized what he didn't want to be. He sighed.

But it also opened the locks in his cabin. He looked at Halford, who glowered. The bosun wasn't taking it back.

"Fetch me some twine, then," Thorn said ungraciously.

Halford disappeared and returned with a length of it. Thorn strung the ring on it and knotted the ends before settling it over his neck. He tucked it beneath his shirt, feeling the hard lump on his chest and the rough scrape of the twine on his skin.

They went out on deck. Plusby was up on the poop deck talking with Savaiu. Thorn climbed up the companion ladder and joined them. She was tense, her mouth pinched, her eyes narrowed.

"Trouble?"

"Aye. Seems Jutras warriors attacked the village before they could flee. Only about half got away. They may have been tracked. And something else."

Plusby went to the taffrail, pointing back toward the mainland. High up on the cliffs was a pair of tall poles. They were narrow at the bottom and then widened and narrowed again, the tops ending in sharp points. Both gleamed white, with long, fluttering white banners swirling on the wind from their pointed tops.

"What are those?"

Savaiu moved up beside him. "They are called *hoskarna*. They represent the twin gods, Uniat and Cresset. These were not here before the storm season."

"What are they?"

"As Jutras flowers, extending its embrace wider, the gods must touch, must taste, must learn the new land and bind it to them. The *hoskarna* are—"

She made a sound of frustration, one hand waving as she searched for the words.

"They are placed by *kiryat* so the gods know to come. The *hoskarna* let the gods touch the land, to be one with it. These are new, but already the gods move in them, pushing down into the land, claiming it. Do you see? They will know my people have come here. They will send Dhucala's wolves to finish what they started when they crushed the village. They will come soon."

Thorn looked at Plusby. "How fast can we bring them aboard?"

"I sent all our boats to help. There are just over sixty people left. It won't take more than two turns of the glass."

"I shall take the *Zhala* out past the bay's mouth," Savaiu said. "We will keep the passage open until you can escape. Please get my people far to safety."

Plusby nodded. "May chance favor you."

Savaiu nodded soberly and then strode off the poop deck. Thorn followed her. The rail gate was already down, waiting for her departure. She turned, stepping backward onto the dangling ladder. She paused, looking up at Thorn, waiting for him to speak. But he didn't have any words. Admonitions to "be careful" were ridiculous.

Words were useless. He bent forward, kissing her hard. Abruptly he pulled away.

"Do you believe me now?" he asked, more sharply than he intended.

She nodded. "You are a man of your word."

His lips pulled into a grim smile. "Do try to remember that, would you? Fair winds. May chance favor you," he said, stepping back.

"May she smile on all of us," Savaiu said, then scuttled the rest of the way down the ladder to settle into the longboat that waited for her. She never looked up as they rowed away, back to the *Zhala*.

Thorn watched after her. After a few minutes, Plusby joined him.

"She did not gut you with her knife for kissing her," he observed. "Some would take that as encouragement."

It took several turns of the glass to ferry the villagers and their meager goods to the *Eidolon* and get them aboard. Climbing the ladders wasn't easy, and

Thorn chafed at the slow process. Rather than sleeping, he stayed at the compass, noting every slight change in the sea.

The villagers were stoic, and had clearly suffered a terrible ordeal. Many carried weeping blisters and livid burns from the fiery attack on their village. Others had taken wounds from arrows and swords and all of them were bent with weariness and hunger.

As they came aboard, they were sent down below-decks, where space had been cleared and what few comforts the *Eidolon* had to offer were distributed. The villagers stared furtively at their rescuers as they scuffled across the deck. The children clung to the legs of their parents. Despite their cowed demeanor, Thorn noticed that each carried a weapon at the ready, their hands hovering close over hilts of daggers and handles of cudgels. They were no more meek than Savaiu was, and far less trusting.

A pair of children scrambled onto the deck together. They were perhaps ten or eleven seasons old. Both were girls with shaggy brown hair cropped short. There was white scarring on both their faces. At the sight of it, fury flooded into Thorn. The girls scanned the deck and then followed after one of the Jutras sailors on loan to the *Eidolon* who was helping the boarding. As they approached the hatch leading below-decks, one caught sight of Thorn at the compass. They both froze, clutching each other's hands. The seaman gestured for them to go below, but suddenly one of them marched over to Thorn, dragging the second girl behind her. The seaman rushed to catch them, but Thorn waved him off.

The first girl stood on the other side of the compass, staring up at Thorn with an expression he could not read. Her eyes were pale blue and icy, her cheeks flushed with cold—or was it anger?

"You're the Pilot," she said in perfect Celwysh, with a hint of an accent he couldn't place.

"Aye."

"You'll take us over the black waters?"

He nodded.

She glanced back at the other girl, who was hunched up against her, ducking down and trying not to be seen. "We will be safe?"

Thorn rubbed a hand over his jaw. "Safer than staying here."

She didn't speak, pondering his answer. Then she nodded, accepting it.

"Is it true you tangle people in your eyes and steal their spirits?"

He snorted. "And what would I do with somebody's spirit?"

"You don't eat them?"

Thorn shook his head, then knelt down, leaning close. To her credit, the girl didn't back away an inch, though her companion was trembling.

"The food I crave most is—" He stopped, looking over his shoulders, then dropping his voice. "Apple-pear bread pudding with hot orange pepper sauce and roasted almonds."

She frowned at him suspiciously, her companion peeking with one eye over her friend's shoulder.

"If they aren't for stealing spirits, then why are your eyes like that?"

"So that I can see what's happening all across and below the black waters. Once my eyes were like yours and I was blind to the wonders of the sea."

"How do I get eyes like yours? How do I become a Pilot?" she demanded, rocking forward on her toes and staring at him fiercely.

Thorn recoiled a moment. Her question was not idle, but one of intense need.

"Do you hear the black waters singing to you? Do they whisper to you in your dreams? Do they call your name?"

She hesitated, then nodded once.

"Then when we reach safe harbor, I will tell you how to become a Pilot."

She did not answer, her gaze fixed on him with a kind of desperation. The pain of the summons would sharpen for her here, actually riding on the waves. She would ache to answer the call. It would become a physical hurt that demanded she leap into the waves. But her mind would tell her that was suicide. She'd go mad. Many who were called did.

He put a hand on her thin arm, squeezing gently.

"I promise you. You just have to . . . endure . . . a while longer. Can you do that?"

She nodded haughtily. "I am strong."

"I can see that. What is your name?"

"Izzataba."

Her friend giggled and Izzataba flushed, her eyes dropping. "Izzi."

"I am Thorn, Izzi. And who is your friend?"

"She is not my friend. She is my sister. Eglena."

"Welcome aboard, Izzi and Eglena. You should go below now. We will speak again later."

Izzi hesitated, looking doubtful again, but she turned and dragged her sister to the hatch, disappearing below.

Thorn pushed upright, staring after them.

"What was that about?" Plusby asked, standing beside him.

"Whether they know it or not, the Jutras have begun breeding Pilots," Thorn said slowly, reeling from the discovery. Had Izzi been born in a *thana*, the product of a careful breeding program? Or had she been taken as a slave? Thorn's stomach roiled. First Malik and now this child. If there were two, then there were more. All the Jutras needed now to overrun Crosspointe was ships' compasses. He looked at Plusby and could see the other man had drawn a similar horrifying conclusion.

As the last of the villagers went below, the boats were hoisted into their davits and those from the *Zhala* secured to the decks. Sailors spun the capstan, hauling up the anchor. Plusby returned to the helm, leaving Thorn by himself at the compass post.

The sun was dropping quickly. Thorn welcomed the

obscuring shadows. Soon they'd be clear of the coast and out of reach of the Jutras.

Getting free of the cove proved as difficult as Thorn had supposed. They set sail at low tide and could not catch a steady wind. They dropped two of the longboats, each carrying a half-dozen sailors. Drawing towing lines after them, they landed on either side of the passage and looped the lines around the trees and began to warp the ship through the passage. The time-consuming process took them nearly to dusk.

Out in the bay, they managed to pick up a steadier breeze, though it was still wobblier than not and they had to trim the sails constantly to keep from falling off the wind. They'd begun to pick up speed and Thorn could see the open sea beckoning when the first explosions shattered the air, and out beyond the headland, brilliant flashes lit up the falling night.

Chapter 28

Plusby shouted orders. Two sailors monkeyed up to the top of the mainmast, straining to see ahead. But there was nothing to see but the hulking shape of the headland.

In moments, Plusby was demanding more canvas. He wanted to be at speed when they cleared the mouth of the bay. Thorn recalled his duty and focused on the sea. There were no dangers. A storm was brewing far to the southwest, but it would be days before they saw it.

There were more explosions. They seemed farther away, as if the *Zhala* was drawing off their enemies. Thorn clenched his teeth, his body so rigid he could scarcely breathe. Everything was going exactly to plan. A plan that would inevitably end in the *Zhala*'s capture or destruction. It was an exchange Savaiu had been more than willing to make. For only the cost of one stolen warship and her pyrate crew, the villagers and the *Eidolon*'s crew escaped. A good bargain.

The *Eidolon* was picking up speed, slicing through the smooth water on an even keel. More explosions and flashes. Every thundering *boom!* made Thorn flinch.

They skimmed out of the mouth of the bay, the wind shifting to abaft the port beam. Swiftly the crew hauled the braces and trimmed the sheets. The *Eidolon* made an elegant curvet to the starboard and then straightened as her sails bellied on a broad reach. She lurched and lunged and then was flying over the waves.

Thorn shifted around so that he could see the raging battle as they fled.

There were three Jutras warships and the *Zhala*. It was obvious which was which. The *Zhala*'s red and black-striped sails contrasted sharply with the moon-bright white of the other three ships. Their sails were bleached as white as the two *hoskarna* on the cliffs above the bay. The contrast with the black and red of the pyrate ship was dramatic. The Jutras gods had marked their loyal servants, making targets of their enemies.

The *Zhala* landed a few of her agun missiles. One of the Jutras ships was in flames, the sails and masts burning brilliantly. There were more fires as the agun burned in pools on the waves, creating a dangerous maze, with the *Zhala* hemmed all around. If the seas had been higher, the burning agun would have washed up onto her decks. As it was, she couldn't easily run. Thorn didn't doubt the tactic was intentional. Now the Jutras ships could be more leisurely in their attack. If any of the agun missiles had struck the *Zhala*, her crew had managed to suffocate or chop out the fires.

With the time provided by the burning maze surrounding their prey, the two undamaged Jutras warships began to pull back, coming about to bookend the *Zhala*. Their intent was clear. They would line up on each side of her for a broadside attack. She'd be caught in the cross fire.

Thorn watched, helpless to do anything but witness. Did Savaiu know the *Eidolon* had escaped? Surely she should be trying to maneuver out of the burning agun so that she could make a run for it. But the *Zhala* only launched another attack at the nearest ship, barely missing, the agun exploding just aft of the ship.

"Why doesn't she *move*?" Thorn whispered. But he imagined what the sea must look like to those on the deck. It was on fire, with every escape avenue narrowing as the waves rose and fell and the pools of agun stretched and merged together. All the *Zhala* could do was wait until the fires burned out and she could safely escape her scorching prison.

But the warships weren't going to give her any such chance. They continued to stay beyond range of Savaiu's ballistae, splattering agun onto the waves to refresh the fires that burned low while they angled into place. They had plenty of missiles to waste, while the *Zhala* had already engaged in two firefights with the ships pursuing her out of the Bites, and had greatly depleted her supply.

Thorn was so caught up in the agony of watching and anticipating the inevitable annihilation of the *Zhala* that he didn't notice when the *Eidolon* first began to slow. The sound of the sails luffing caught his attention. He looked up. The royals, topgallants, and topsails were clewed up and the main courses fluttered empty as sailors hauled the lines to pull the main and mizzen braces hard around. Then the *Eidolon*'s prow swung lowly to the east. As she completed the turn, sailors freed the forebraces from their pins and hauled them around, pulling tight the jibs and forestays.

Plusby called out orders and the upper sails were deployed again. The *Eidolon* was sailing close against the wind. She was running due east away from the Bramble and straight toward the Bites.

After one last check of the broad sea, Thorn abandoned the compass and flung himself up onto the poop deck. Plusby was at the helm, calling out adjustments to the set of the sails.

"Steady! Mind the starboard helm! Right the helm!"

"What are you doing?" Thorn demanded. His chest was so tight he couldn't get a breath.

Plusby slanted a look at him before lifting his gaze back up to the sails. "We're going to go help."

Thorn clamped his lips together. He wanted to. By the gods, how he wanted to. He'd promised Savaiu he wouldn't abandon her. But when he'd made that vow, she'd thought he meant that he would lead her people safely across the Inland Sea; he knew what she'd want him to do now. Get her people away.

Jagged words impaled themselves in his throat. He forced them out, feeling like they were shredding him apart. "This is madness. There's nothing we can do but provide them with an alternate target. We've got a hold full of innocent people. We cannot risk it."

Plusby's lips curled in a mocking smile, his eyes never leaving the sails.

"We've got a couple of tricks that might surprise them. You do *want* to help her, don't you?"

"Don't be a buggered ass. Of course I do. But she won't be grateful for us risking her people and she'll likely carve my heart out. Yours too."

"True. But she'll still be breathing. And when it comes down to it, that's all that matters, isn't it?" Though his voice was even, the words were spoken with searing intensity.

"What about the compasses? What if we are taken?"

"We'll scuttle the ship," he said easily.

It would mean killing all aboard, more than eighty souls. And Crosspointe's enemies would only try again, funding another black ship, crimping another Pilot, and scraping together another crew, sending them off to sell ships' compasses to the highest bidder. The king needed to be warned. Thorn shook his head.

"We can't risk it. There's too much to lose."

Plusby turned, the moonlight and shadows carving his face into a gargoyle's mask. "We already have. You don't have a choice. Now get back on the compass."

For a long moment Thorn didn't move. There was a fire burning inside Plusby, one he didn't understand. Was this about his wife? Did he somehow see rescuing Savaiu as redemption for failing to keep Sherenya safe? Or was this something else? His friend's stony expression gave away nothing. But Plusby knew the consequences as well as Thorn did and he feared them just as much. So why?

He reached out and grabbed Plusby's arm, pulling

him around. The captain snarled and shoved him back, but Thorn lunged back at him, gripping his collar, determined to get answers.

"Why are you doing this?"

They stood, nose to nose, fury heating the air around them. Plusby gave in first.

"Because you won't ask. You *can't*. If this journey has taught me anything, it is that duty is a cold lover and what I would never do for that bitch, I will surely do for my friends and my crew. And thanks to you, and thanks to the help of the *Zhala*, I still have both. You told me once that the charmers would never have left my wife, not for any reason. You also said that you never abandon your own. Not ever. Can I do any less? Can I be any less a man than you and those damned charmers? So understand me. I am not going to leave the *Zhala*. We owe them. We're all they've got. So get your hands off me and go back to your cracking compass and do what you do and let me finish this."

He pushed Thorn away and strode forward a few steps. "Ready about! Station for stays!"

Thorn stood a moment, then jerked around and climbed back down to the quarterdeck. Plusby's speech had rocked him to his boots. The two of them had changed on this ship—transformed. The men they were no longer existed, and the men they'd become . . . Thorn wasn't too sure who those men were, but he knew Plusby was right. As much as he loved his country, as much as he feared the Jutras gaining access to the Inland Sea, those things paled beside the bonds formed on the water.

He returned to his post. Nothing had changed in the sea. He sucked in a frustrated breath and blew it back out. At the moment, he was as useless as a limp prick in a brothel.

His attention snagged on Crabbel and Halford, who jumped down off the forecastle and flung open the hatch where the villagers were secured. They disappeared inside, and then a few minutes later reappeared. Behind them villagers boiled out of the hatch. There were about two dozen altogether. All were able-bodied. Thorn frowned. What were they up to?

Crabbel and Halford directed them into the crew cabin beneath the forecastle. They hauled out a collection of variously shaped wooden bits. Thorn watched as they began assembling them.

It soon appeared that there were two objects under construction. Each had a thick, fifteen-foot-long post as its base. At the top was a stumpy crossbar sticking off to the side with a swivel mechanism that slid over it, flush against the main pole. The swivel was fixed in place by a flat disk with a spike in the center that was driven into the end of the crossbar. They attached another long pole to the swivel device, this one more slender than the foundation pole. It had a crossbar at one end, and a scooped-out bowl at the other end in the shape of a ladle. It was set unevenly, with the crossbar end extending only four feet or so from the bottom of the swivel device. Attached to the crossbar were eight lengths of rope.

As they stood them up, Thorn realized at last what they must be. Catapults.

These were the kind Jutras foot soldiers carried. They could be staked into the ground and loaded with ammunition. A group of warriors would yank down on the ropes attached to the lever at the bottom, flinging the missiles toward the target. They didn't have much range—perhaps two hundred yards. But they were light, easy to carry, and easy to shift around for tactical advantage.

Thorn eyed them warily. Using them aboard the *Eidolon* would be quite a feat. He didn't know if there was room anywhere where they could be launched without being fouled by a yard, a stay, a brace, or some other piece of ship's furniture.

But Halford clearly had a plan. He guided the villagers up onto the poop deck to the starboard taffrail, where they inserted the base of the first catapult into a hole cut in the deck just for this purpose. The second was placed just beside it along the poop rail. It could work, if the spanker was doused entirely and the mizzen yards were braced up.

Now Crabbel emerged from the crew cabin carrying a crate of—

Thorn stared. Agun missiles. They were made of glass and swirling inside with the explosive liquid.

As Crabbel carefully stepped up on the quarterdeck, Thorn stopped him.

"How did you get those?"

"Th' *Zhala*. Halford asked for 'em when he found out about th' 'pults. They was in th' hold, like th' ship was expectin' t' haul foot soldiers t' war afore our friends made off w' her."

The mate didn't wait for any more questions, but crossed to the companion ladder and lifted the crate up to Halford, who gingerly took it from him. Thorn had a good idea what Plusby was up to now. Swing up close beside one of the ships and hit it with agun. It would have to be very close, and they'd have to come in slowly if they hoped to hit the mark. Then they'd come around and help the *Zhala* deal with the other ship. And if their plan failed, launch agun onto their own decks and sink her.

It was a brilliant, mad plan. His stomach tightened with anticipation and even hope. Minutes ago the *Zhala*'s bleak fate had seemed inevitable. Now she might be saved.

They tacked around in a long curl to come around close to the coastline. They were running before a freshening wind on a direct heading for the embattled ships.

Plusby called for the royals and topgallants to be doused and the main course taken in. Still the *Eidolon* cut swiftly across the water. Soon they were running with only a handful of sails, their momentum slowing.

They were close now.

Ahead the burning waves made a brilliant glow. It was almost like dawn breaking. The two Jutras warships had at last managed to pinch the *Zhala* between them. Thorn gasped. They were too late.

But it appeared that the warships were in no hurry. Or perhaps they meant to take the pyrates alive. Thorn thought of the torture that had been inflicted on Savaiu's mother. The Jutras liked public punishment. They would want to carry the pyrates through the streets and show the people what happened to those who broke the laws.

The *Zhala* had ceased to launch her agun missiles and Thorn wondered if she'd run out. Would the supply Savaiu had given Halford mean the difference between freedom and capture? He swallowed, his heart pounding.

They crept closer and closer. The Jutras warships were too absorbed in their prey to notice the *Eidolon*'s arrival, though with her dark sails and black paint, she was like a ghost. The mizzen came down, the yards braced up to permit the catapults to fire without fouling. On the poop deck, agun projectiles were loaded into the bowls, the dangling ropes gripped tightly. They floated closer, coming within a hundred yards. Slowly they began to pass.

Suddenly the men and women on the launch ropes yanked down hard. The catapult rotated around, the agun globe spinning across the narrow strip of water between the *Eidolon* and the Jutras ship. It was impossible to miss. The missile struck in the upper sails and instantly bloomed into flame. The second catapult launched. Again a hit in the sails.

There was shouting from the ship, and sailors scurried to rotate their weaponry around toward the *Eidolon*. The catapults launched again. Still too high. They needed to hit the decking or the sides of the ship. Quickly they launched again. A cheer went up as the agun struck the castle deck at the fore of the ship. Fire erupted all along the prow, and screams of agony rent the air. The flames roared up the foremast, shriveling apart the stays and licking at the bottom of the topcastle.

But the Jutras ship was not helpless, nor was it going to be destroyed without first trying to kill its killer.

It's ballistae had far greater range and though the *Eidolon* had swept past the wounded Jutras ship, she was not clear of danger. The first missile whistled overhead and landed on the port side, exploding in a geyser of fire. Plusby didn't yet call for more canvas. Had the upper sails been deployed, the agun would be feasting on them. Another agun globe, this time astern. The explosion rippled outward, pushing the *Eidolon* forward.

The captain kept the clipper on a western heading, trying to present as small a target as possible to the Jutras ship. The entire front half of the warship was now engulfed in flames. Grains passed and then explosions ripped apart the castle deck as the spreading fire detonated unlaunched agun globes. The entire ship went up in a roar that was louder than one could imagine. Thorn's flesh quivered with the force of it, the flash blinding him with its brightness.

He blinked, searching for evidence of the other two ships. He feared what might have happened to the *Zhala*—she'd been all too near the destroyed ship. Burning bits of debris could have set her afire.

He could see nothing but the glow of the fires on the water and the brilliant splotches of orange and yellow dotting his vision. He held his hand up over his eyes as if it would help, then dropped his arm. He looked up into the rigging, shouting to the topmen. What did they see?

But then another blast shook the ship and sent Thorn tumbling as the *Eidolon* yawed and bucked. He leaped to his feet, running up onto the poop deck to look astern. The villagers who'd helped launch the catapults gathered at the taffrail, blocking his view. He shoved between them, leaning far over the rail and straining to see something of the *Zhala*.

Grains ticked past with no sounds but the crackle

of flames and the creak and flap of the *Eidolon* as she rose and fell over soft swells.

There was a swirl in the smoke. Thorn watched it, holding his breath. A bowsprit emerged, followed by the beak and the castle deck. He lifted his gaze. The sails were . . . striped black and red.

He sagged, watching the *Zhala* slide from the smoke and steer a clear course through the flaming waves. The villagers beside him cheered and clapped, some slapping him on the shoulders. As if he had done anything, as if they hadn't done it all.

From this distance, he couldn't tell what damage the ship had sustained. She did not appear to be on fire, which was a blessing.

Slowly Thorn straightened. His body ached as his fear drained from him. He turned and left the poop deck, returning to the compass. He felt as if he'd been put on the rack, his body pulled apart at the joints.

He reached out to the sea, feeling the comfort of its black waters, the gnawing itch of the agun burning on its waves, the twitch far to the south that indicated the birth of a weir, the swirl of *sylveth* west of the Root. It was soothing. And then suddenly he realized they were not alone.

He froze. It couldn't be. Not now. Not when they'd come so far. He'd been too engrossed in the battle to notice them. Not that the *Eidolon* could have escaped, even running ahead of the wind. Koreions were too fast.

Like a man sleepwalking, he turned away from the compass and went to the rail, scanning the waves. He should be able to see them. There were a half dozen of them and they were so close.

Suddenly silvery white spines longer than he was tall and sharper than a sword glided up out of the water, followed by an enormous head.

*Koreion*s.

Soft, lacy protrusions waved gently around its bony head. Needlelike fangs crowded its long, pointed snout, its nostrils fluttering as it sniffed the air. Feathery scales fringed its muzzle, giving it a misleadingly soft, less predatory appearance. It rose up higher out of the water, its muscular neck bending in an elegant curve, its silvery scales glittering like diamonds. Its throat was a pale, dusty blue. It gazed down at Thorn out of liquid black orbs slashed with silver in the shape of a crescent moon.

Thorn stared back, too awed to remember to be afraid. One Koreion could sink a ship with little effort. Six could rip it to splinters.

Behind him he could hear the terrified silence of the crew and passengers. Then a heavy splash as another Koreion rose up out of the water and dived back down.

The first sea dragon swam closer. Thorn gripped the rail with white-knuckled fingers. The great beast dipped its head, setting its forehead against the side of the ship. Its body wriggled powerfully and it *pushed* the *Eidolon*, turning her to port. Then it corkscrewed around itself before diving deep under the water.

Thorn gulped air, not remembering when last he'd breathed. Plusby leaped down beside him, his face pale beneath his ruddy tan.

"That was—that couldn't be—"

"Koreions," Thorn confirmed raggedly, still trying to catch his breath. "Six of them. We are surrounded."

Chapter 29

Thorn waited for the six Koreions to surge at the two
ships, rolling them over to begin feasting. No one
moved; no one spoke. Everyone watched the beautiful
horror of Koreion bodies sliding through the waves,
their enormous, muscular bodies sleek and supple.
Their bellies shaded to cobalt near the base of their
long, snaking tails, and from their muscular shoulders
protruded a pair of powerful limbs, each ending in
four clawed fingers tipped with cruelly serrated talons.

They swam beneath the ships, skirling through the
water in long, coiling strokes. Their massive bodies
gleamed in the moonlight as they scraped along the
length of *Eidolon*'s hull, sending the ship shivering
and rocking. Every one of them was longer than the
Eidolon, with a maw that could swallow a man whole.

Grains slid past, then minutes.

"What are they waiting for?" Plusby asked in a
tight voice.

"I don't know," Thorn said, sweat beading on his
neck and trickling down his spine. His nerves were
wound as tight as when he'd been waiting for the
seemingly inevitable destruction of the *Zhala*.

When half a glass had passed and the Koreions had
still not attacked, the captain began to call orders to
tack.

"We can't just sit and wait to be eaten," he said
defiantly, and climbed back up to the helm.

Thorn returned to the compass post as the normal

business of the ship resumed. As glass after glass passed with no attack, the unrelenting tension became tiresome and eventually monotonous. Thorn found his body unclenching, not because he feared any less, but because he could no longer sustain the same level of terror. The Koreions kept pace with them. The *Zhala* followed a thousand yards off the starboard quarter, though after an initial circling inspection, the beasts had focused their attention solely on the *Eidolon*.

By sunrise they'd begun to close on the Bramble. Plusby tacked, planning to come around the northern point of the island and find a cove on the other side where the villagers could go ashore until the *Eidolon* could return with supplies.

But the moment the ship shifted on a northward line, the Koreions began pushing them south. As the first had done, one swam up on the starboard bow, setting its head against the hull and giving a hard *push*. The clipper rocked over on its beam end and then back, the stern yawing to the starboard. They lost the wind, the sails sagging and luffing as they wallowed. The *Zhala* rode up on them as Plusby shouted orders and they swung the braces to catch the wind.

As the *Eidolon* began to pick up speed again, they again tacked on a northward bearing. Instantly another Koreion repeated the same trick, shoving them off the wind.

"South," Thorn muttered. "The damned things want us to go south. But why? Why in the bloody black depths would they *want* us to do anything at all?"

Stubbornly, Plusby tried again. This time after shoving them off the wind, the Koreions lumped under the keel, pushing the bow of the *Eidolon* out of the water and dropping her down again. The ship's timbers shrieked and shuddered and the decks bucked and quaked.

Taking the warning, Plusby called orders to turn them south. It was a surreal experience, the Koreions nudging them to the port or starboard as they fell off a heading only the beasts seemed to know.

Plusby joined Thorn at the compass. "Have you ever heard of anything like this?" he asked quietly. His face was set and tense. Thorn admired his composure. His own legs were shaking so hard that he had to brace them apart to keep his knees from knocking together.

"Never."

"What do they want? Surely if they were going to attack, they'd have done so by now."

Thorn shrugged. He didn't have an answer beyond the obvious. The Koreions were taking them somewhere. And he had no idea why.

The *Zhala* continued to follow them, though the Koreions paid little heed to her. Thorn was certain that if the Jutras ship headed off in another direction, the Koreions would let it go. But Savaiu would never consider it. Not with her people aboard the *Eidolon*.

By midafternoon, the Bramble had grown into a looming shadow against the lowering skies. Jagged, snow-covered peaks ran up the center of the narrow island, reminiscent of the Koreions' spines. The shoulders of those mountains were rocky and forbidding, dropping in sheer cliffs into the battering waves of the sea. The eastern coast was entirely inhospitable. On the southwestern coast was a single sandy shingle that stretched two dozen leagues. This was where the Bramble ships dropped the convicts. Here and there were coves and small bays, but these were mostly unexplored. Most sailors thought the Bramble was, if not cursed, then bad luck. They kept a respectful distance from it at all costs.

The Koreions were taking them south along the eastern shore. This time, there was no bore current trying to drive them against the rocks, only the nudging blows of the sea dragons guiding them along.

Closer and closer they came, on a heading that seemed destined to wreck them on the vicious rocks lining the shore. Waves crashed against the cliffs, sending up geysers of spume and turning the tide to a white froth.

Alarmed, Plusby tried to turn the ship, but four of the Koreions closed in on either side, preventing the ship from shifting its heading. The last two shoved from behind when Plusby ordered all the sails doused and dropped both bower anchors. When the flukes caught on the rocky bottom, there was a jerking tug. The *Eidolon*'s prow dipped and then the anchor chains snapped and they were moving forward again.

Ahead of them the mass of rocky teeth guarded a black wall of pocked and seamed granite.

Thorn could not understand. Why would the Koreions drive them onto the rocks rather than simply destroy the *Eidolon* in the open water?

He looked behind them. The *Zhala* had fallen off at last, her sails furled as she sat at anchor some thousand yards astern. Relief flooded Thorn. But then his stomach clenched. They had no Pilot.

But it was too late to worry for their fate. The *Eidolon* was about to meet hers.

The rocks were a mere fifty yards away now. Still the Koreions rushed forward, swimming with furious strength, seemingly unconcerned at their own fate. Thorn gripped the compass, bracing himself. There would be survivors, if the Koreions didn't eat them. He had to be ready. The wreck was not certain doom. But his heart ached for the *Eidolon*. She was a gallant ship and had already suffered dreadful damage in her short life. And now she was to be ignominiously shattered on the Bramble.

As they passed between a claw of toothy boulders, spume fountained up, caressing Thorn's face. He licked his lips, tasting the salt. It felt like a benediction—a kiss from Braken. He held his breath as the *Eidolon* rose on a swell and came down on a—

Thorn waited for the impact. And then he was struck by something else. Majick. It hammered against him, squeezing him in an invisible fist so that his ribs moved and his skull felt like it was going to explode. Pain seared his lungs and he was choking, unable to draw a breath. Black spots danced across his vision and his mouth tasted of blood and something else—like wood.

Then as swiftly as it had come, the majick evaporated.

Thorn held himself erect, though his legs sagged like his bones had turned to syrup. He looked up at the rigging where toppers clung dazed. One had fallen and was hanging upside down, his foot caught in the ratlines. The villagers who remained on deck were lying in slumped heaps, unconscious. Pale-blasted. The sailors had crossed too many times to be knocked unconscious by the force of the protective majick, but most civilians ended up knocked cold for a while, sometimes days.

He looked about in wonder. But how? There was only one Pale and it surrounded Crosspointe.

The *Eidolon* was bumping to a halt as the Koreions swam in front to halt her passage. The keel thudded hard against a thick body and the ship jolted. Thorn staggered to the rail, the strength seeping back into his legs.

They were in a bowl-shaped cove with only a narrow passage leading out into the sea. The water rocked with hardly a ripple. Cliffs towered on either side, gradually softening into tree-covered slopes that dropped down to a wide, flat beach.

"Thorn!"

He jerked about in answer to Plusby's sharp shout, then hurried across the deck.

"What in the holy black depths is going on?" Plusby's voice was strained. "That was a Pale. Wasn't it?"

"It was."

"How?"

Thorn shook his head, unable to make sense of anything. What kind of money and majick did it take to create a second Pale? And why on the Bramble? And what did it have to do with the ships' compasses stowed in the *Eidolon*'s hold?

Movement caught his attention. The Koreions were slipping and rolling in the water like puppies. They writhed together in a tangled knot and then slipped apart. Suddenly they came alert, their snouts turning in unison toward the shore. They remained thus for several grains; then as one, they flipped about and swam in the direction of the cove's entrance. Far beyond them, Thorn could see the *Zhala*. Her canvas was set and she was sailing in toward them.

He could imagine what it must have looked like, the Koreions dragging the *Eidolon* at the rocky cliffs. Then at the last moment, when it appeared the ship would be shattered on the rocks, she disappeared into nothingness. Savaiu wasn't going to simply accept their disappearance. She was coming to investigate. And the Koreions were going out to meet her.

The problem was, Thorn didn't know if they were going out to destroy the *Zhala* or guide her into the cove.

He climbed up on the poop deck, craning to see. It was a matter of a few minutes before the Koreions reached their prey. Relief swept through him as the sea dragons surrounded the ship and began dragging it in.

The loud clanking of another anchor dropping made him turn. The sheet anchor had been loosed, its chain rattling as it snaked through the hawsehole.

Plusby was giving orders to secure the ship and carry the unconscious villagers belowdecks. Thorn climbed down the companion ladder and joined him.

Before he could ask what they should do next, a feast appeared suddenly on the quarterdeck. There was roasted pork, beef, and poultry. There were cheeses and fruits—fresh fruits like they'd just been picked. There was hot bread, soft butter, pastries, and vegetables, flaky meat pies, gravies, and sauces, and there was hot cream tea with sugar. Against the pinwheel appeared a large cask of ale sitting on a trestle.

No one moved. The crew stared, the scents of the food drifting mouthwateringly across the deck.

"Oh, please. It's safe enough. Eat all you want. There's always more."

The woman's voice was strained and impatient. Thorn glanced about wildly, finding her standing just on the other side of the railing. *On the other side . . . ?*

Lucy Trenton stood on a slender column of black water, looking very ordinary in well-worn boots and silky loose-fitting trousers beneath a long tunic of fine green wool. She wore no cloak, despite the cold and the wind. She was plump with freckles and her long, curly red hair was caught up in a loose braid.

"Are you just going to stand there gape-mouthed?"

When still no one moved, frozen in shock and fear, she shook her head, muttering something Thorn didn't hear. Finally, she put her hands on her hips, her jaw jutting as her eyes narrowed.

"Eat or not as you will. But, Captain Plusby and Pilot Thorn, I require your attendance. Come with me now."

"I take it you're Lucy Trenton," Plusby growled, not moving.

"I am, Captain," she said, flicking a brow up at Thorn. "Please, accompany me. We have much to discuss and little time."

She gestured beside her, and water flowed up the side of the ship forming, a stair.

"It is safe enough," she assured them both when they looked at it askance. "Do tell your crew to eat. The food is not tainted, but it will soon turn cold. I will await you onshore."

With that, the water beneath her dissolved, leaving the stairway behind. When she reached the level of the sea, it firmed beneath her feet as she walked across the waves to the beach.

Thorn exchanged a glance with Plusby. Neither said anything. Then the captain turned back to the feast, grasping up a hunk of bread and filling it with pork and cheese. He bit into it, chewing and swallowing quickly. Thorn followed suit, knowing the crew wouldn't feel safe enough unless someone set an example. It could have been poisoned, but Lucy Trenton's pet Koreions could have killed them many times over and had not. She wanted them alive.

The food was heavenly after days of bland loblolly stew and porridge. He eschewed the meat in favor of cheese, then grabbed a handful of ripe plums and gobbled them. They were sweet as summer, their juice purple and delicious.

They didn't have time to truly assuage their hunger. Neither wanted to keep their host waiting. Plusby turned command over to Crabbel and then he and Thorn went to the side of the ship and climbed up on the rail. Thorn stepped out onto the watery stair first. It felt like he was standing on thin ice. But it was firm enough. He took a step down to give Plusby room.

"Have a care," Halford growled.

Thorn glanced back in surprise. He'd have expected the bosun to question his sanity. But though Halford's face was tight with fear and wonder, he didn't try to stop them.

Thorn knew exactly how he felt. Despite the razor bite of terror driving through his lungs, he was filled with amazement. To see *such* majick. To be brought here by Koreions. To walk on water. It was awe-inspiring. And more than that. There were answers here. Answers to who had financed the *Eidolon*, who was stealing ships' compasses, and who had hired Bess to murder him. And older questions. Who had killed Jordan? Was Sherenya Plusby really still alive? Was she still herself? To learn those truths, he'd have done far more than step out onto this watery stair. Beside him, Plusby nearly shook with his need.

They carefully stepped down to the bottom, the stairs dissolving behind them as they descended. When they reached the waves, a path formed in front of them, leading them to the black sand beach where Lucy Trenton waited, pacing back and forth.

"Can you explain your Jutras companions?" she demanded, the silver in her eyes swirling like *sylveth*, her mouth drawn tight. "Can you tell me why I shouldn't destroy the mother-cracking bilge suckers right now?

Thorn flicked a glance at the *Zhala*. She was nearing the cove's mouth. But the Koreions could easily thrust her against the rocks or drag her down to the depths.

"They are renegades—river pyrates. They are fleeing Jutras and if not for them, the *Eidolon* would have been sunk. There are more aboard the *Eidolon*. Sailors and the survivors of a village."

Her gaze shackled him. He couldn't look away. The color in her cheeks was high and it was clear that her hate and fury battled with her sense of justice. Finally she tossed her head and turned away, leading the way up the beach without a word.

Thorn stole a look over his shoulder, breathing a quiet sigh of relief when he saw the Koreions bringing the *Zhala* safely through the Pale. Plusby settled a hand on his shoulder, squeezing, and then they followed their hostess up the strand.

She led them up a path into the mouth of a cave. Inside it widened into a palatial manor. The rooms had high ceilings, and the walls were paneled with mottled Jasaic wood, the floors strewn with rugs from Normengas. The furniture was elegant, with curving legs in the shape of Koreions, and covered with black fabric woven with silvery patterns that reminded Thorn of the wind and the currents. Light came from everywhere and nowhere and felt like dawn.

"Please sit," she said, after leading them into a salon.

She remained standing, going to the sideboard to pour out drinks. She handed them each a glass of wine before retreating to the fire.

"Why didn't you take your cargo to Calenfor?" she asked, the color still high in her cheeks.

"Because we may be the dregs at the bottom of the sailing barrel, but even we don't sell out our own country. We're taking those compasses back to Crosspointe and turning them over to the crown," Plusby said.

Lucy's brows rose. "Dregs?" She shook her head. "Oh, no. Dregs could not have survived that storm so well. Nor the wave that came after."

"We had help with that, as you know," Thorn said.

She smiled. "It wasn't me. Marten?"

She looked past Thorn and Plusby to the door. They turned. Thorn stood up slowly, hardly know what he was doing. The man who entered was familiar, and yet entirely alien. He had sun-streaked brown hair that that he wore in the fashion of captains, the sides cut short over the ears and around the neck, the top long and caught behind his head in a tail. He was as tall as Thorn, and moved with the grace of a Koreion. But what was most startling were his eyes. They were entirely black, corner to corner. Something that looked like silvery scales ran down the back of his neck to disappear inside his loose shirt. The last time Thorn had seen Marten Thorpe had been in the company of Jordan. When he looked at him now, it hardly seemed possible he was the same man.

Marten nodded a greeting to Plusby and Thorn, going to Lucy's side. His arm circled her waist as he stood behind her and kissed her neck. It looked very domestic, but Thorn sensed that inside Marten was a very dangerous being, one held in check only by Lucy Trenton's pale hands and soft touch. Marten's expression, when he looked back at Plusby and Thorn, was deadly and cold.

"You can thank Marten for the ease of getting to shore. He has a way with water." Lucy turned to smile up at him.

"It was you all the time," Thorn said. "And with the raiders at Grimsby Bay."

Marten looked up and nodded. "I would have done more with the bore wave, but when Braken has set his mind on something, I can interfere but little."

"You saved us. If not for you, we'd be at the bottom of the sea. But who . . . what are you?"

"That is a story for another time, perhaps," Lucy said. "Right now, it is more important for you to know who *I* am."

"You're Lucy Trenton," Thorn said, frowning.

"Yes. I am also the king's majicar."

Plusby, who'd been silent all this time, spoke up now. "You'll pardon me, I'm sure," he said sardonically, "but when I knew you, Thorpe, you were a gambler and everyone knew you'd eventually end up in the iron collar or on the Bramble. Now you're spawn. So you'll have to excuse me if you don't inspire much trust in me.

"As for you"—he turned to Lucy—"there's no such thing as a king's majicar. What you are is a traitor. Both of you are. You put together this operation, and Braken only knows where you found the compasses, but we aren't going to help you deliver them. That's why you brought us here, isn't it?"

She glanced at Marten. Undisguised bitterness spread across her face. Marten took her hand and pressed it to his lips. She squeezed, not letting go as she turned back to Plusby and Thorn.

"You are correct. We want you to deliver the compasses as planned. In fact, we must insist you do so."

"Crack that," Plusby snarled. "The Jutras will end up with them eventually. They're already breeding Pilots. We've got one of their whelps on board our ship now. All they need is compasses and Crosspointe will be overrun. Do you have any idea what they will do? You can forget it, you traitorous bitch. We'll scuttle the ship first."

Marten stepped forward, his head dropping low in a way that reminded Thorn of a hunting Koreion. Lucy tightened her grip on his hand and put her other hand on his shoulder. Instantly he subsided, going very still. But he continued glaring at Plusby with deadly intent.

"You can scuttle her if you like, but Marten will easily retrieve the cargo. There is nothing within the sea he cannot find. But you will not scuttle the ship. You will help us."

"Never," Plusby said, his lip curling. "If you want it done, do it yourself and be damned!"

Thorn said nothing; Plusby spoke for them both.

She sighed. "We cannot. The reach of my majick does not extend so far from the sea. And even if we could sail them up ourselves, we cannot be known as a party to this. You must do it."

"Why? Afraid the king will find out? What do you care? What could he do to you? You can control the waves and you can create your own Pale. What does it matter what he thinks of you?"

Lucy smiled again, this time with genuine humor.

"It matters a great deal. Cousin William would tell my mother and I'd never hear the end of it. If you knew anything about my mother, you'd know that is a serious threat."

Her smile faded.

"But let us be clear on one thing. This scheme is neither mine nor Marten's. If I had my way—" Her face contorted and then smoothed. "But I don't get my way in this. We are under orders from the king himself. You will deliver the compasses because King William has decreed it."

Chapter 30

Thorn stared. Plusby was no less incredulous.

"I don't believe it. The *king* is smuggling compasses out of Crosspointe?"

Lucy scrubbed her hands over her face. "This is going to take some explaining. You must be hungry. Please, let us eat. I shall tell you all I can."

They adjourned to a dining room, where another feast was laid out. Thorn voiced his surprise at the assorted ripe fruits in the middle of the cold season, as well as the variety of foods in the banquet.

"I should not have thought the Bramble so well stocked, especially right after Chance," he said.

"It is all majick," Lucy dismissed as she sat at the end of the table. "If you want anything different, I will conjure it for you."

"Is that supposed to impress us?" Plusby said, clearly still reeling from her revelation. "Maybe you want to conjure piles of dralions and bevies of whores for us too. We don't sell ourselves so cheaply."

She did not get angry as Thorn expected, though Marten growled low in his throat and his fingernails gouged furrows from the tabletop.

"Certainly if you wished those things, I would give them to you. Not for a payment or bribe, but . . . because I can. You must understand. I have no need of money." She shook her head and pointed down the table. A pile of dralions appeared from nowhere.

"You see? Why would I smuggle for wealth if I can merely conjure it?"

The money disappeared. Lucy leaned forward, her hands clasping together. "I *am* the king's majicar, Captain Plusby. I answer directly to him, and only to him. I serve the king and I serve Crosspointe. He has asked this of me, and I must obey."

Thorn interrupted Plusby's next question. "But why? Why would he betray his people this way? He must know that the compasss will end up in the hands of the Jutras. He must know that any safety the sea provides us will be gone. He cannot want that, else he is mad."

"Sit, please. Both of you. Eat. Let me try to explain as it was explained to me."

Thorn and Plusby sat reluctantly, serving themselves and eating slowly. The food tasted of sawdust. Neither could enjoy it. Thorn pushed his plate away and Plusby followed suit. Both glared at Lucy, who traced the edge of the table with her fingers. Marten stood behind her left shoulder, the shining black of his eyes unnerving. It was impossible to tell where he was looking. His head was tilted slightly as if he were listening to something beyond the edge of sound, and his fingers rested against Lucy's neck beneath her hair. It was clear he was there to guard her, as if she needed guarding. Her majickal ability was beyond anything Thorn had ever seen. He wondered if the entire Majicars' Guild could match her. Even if they could, he doubted there would be much left of Crosspointe or the Inland Sea if they did.

She pulled her hands into her lap and looked at Thorn and Plusby. Her mouth was firm, though Thorn could see she'd not had an easy time of it. There were shadows in her eyes, and lines around her mouth that spoke of sadness and pain.

"A short time ago, just before Chance, there was a plot by the Jutras to invade Crosspointe. Do you remember the crippled ship that found its way into Blackwater Bay? Those Jutras were priests—majicars.

With the aid of traitors, they were able to escape their prison and gain entrance to the castle." Her lips clamped together and she swallowed hard. "They captured King William in the throne room."

Thorn rocked back in his seat. His jaw fell open and he exchanged a horrified look of shock with Plusby. Captured the king? He began shaking his head. It wasn't possible.

"They captured King William and slaughtered all the guards. They tortured—" Her voice cracked and she looked down, her jaw clenching, the seam of her mouth white.

Marten moved behind her, both hands on her shoulders, the black in his eyes swirling like ink in oil. After a moment Lucy looked up again. A chill slithered through Thorn's intestines. The raw emotion on her face was no deception. Hatred, rage, horror—she was not lying.

"The memory of the event has been majicked safely away from most of those who witnessed . . . what the Jutras did. Their plan was to control King William, make a puppet of him, and thereby gain control of Crosspointe. They would have conquered Crosspointe without a battle of any kind. Eventually they would have taken control of key members of the various guilds and the government—if they haven't already. It is still not known how many agents might yet remain in positions of power.

"Marten and I arrived in time to stop them from making a terrible summoning—their gods have little power on the Inland Sea, but if you sacrifice enough blood and pain to their lusts, they can take root." Her lip curled, teeth clamping together. Her chin trembled. She firmed it, touching the back of Marten's hand as it cupped her cheek. "We stopped them, but not before Queen Naren was killed. Not before we learned that raw *sylveth* can be brought across the Pale. Not before we learned that the Jutras have spies on Crosspointe. And not before one of those traitors—Marten's brother, Edgar Thorpe—murdered Jordan."

It was too much. The words fluttered around Thorn like mad, pecking birds. Nothing made sense.

"But why?" he asked finally, his voice dropping nearly to a whisper.

"Because of me," Marten said. And when the black gaze settled on Thorn, he felt it like a smothering wash of seawater. He shivered. How had he thought that it was hard to tell what Marten was looking at?

"I asked for Jordan's help when I began to discover what my brother was up to. So Edgar had him killed."

"But—"

Thorn broke off, not knowing what he wanted to say. Of all the things he imagined, that Jordan had been killed as part of a plot against the king had never crossed his mind. His eyes burned with sudden tears, the wound of Jordan's death feeling as fresh as when he'd learned of it.

"This does not explain why the king would smuggle compasses out of Crosspointe," Plusby said, sounding shaken, his anger washed away.

"There is a great deal of turmoil in Crosspointe just now. Cousin William does not know who among his advisers was working with Edgar Thorpe or the Jutras, or how many Jutras may have infiltrated the merchants' guild. He has no idea of the extent of the treason. He's assuming the worst. But he has a plan. A very dangerous, very risky plan. The first part of it is to establish a new Pale on the Root and to make compasses available to the freelanders. Yes, he does know the Jutras will end up with some eventually. But he believes they will anyway. As you say, they've already been breeding Pilots. It is only a matter of time until they reach Crosspointe again with ships.

"But if our allies have ships and compasses, they will be better equipped to help us defend the sea. More importantly, the people of Crosspointe must be shaken from their complacency. The Pale snapped and already they forget their terror. The guilds and the Majicars' Sennet must give up pecking at the crown and start looking to the real danger. If they are not stopped, the Jutras will eat up all the lands surrounding the Inland Sea. Then they will strangle us. They won't have to fight; they'll just wait for us to wither and die."

She hesitated as if deciding whether to say more.

"This must be done now. Cousin William is healthy, but there have been attempts on his life. He wants to do all he can to establish protections for Crosspointe before he can no longer do so. I have already created the Pale on the Root. It gives us a place to escape to if the Jutras come again. And it allows Cousin William to develop defenses without worrying that spies are sending that information back to the Jutras."

"If you are so strong—if Marten can control the waves, why not simply destroy their warships and use your majick to protect Crosspointe? Why not just take the *Eidolon* to Calenfor yourselves?" Thorn asked. She'd built a Pale on the Root and one on the Bramble. She spoke of it as if it were child's play, as if for the last four hundred seasons every majicar in Crosspointe hadn't been searching desperately for a way to re-create that majick. Her power was staggering. Terrifying. Marten's was equally so.

She scraped her teeth with her thumbnail and smiled. Thorn knew she saw his fear; she wanted him to be afraid. Because it would make him obey in taking the compasses? Thorn glared at her, his jaw thrusting. He wasn't going to be cowed into it.

"Those are fair questions. The answers are simple. First—we cannot sail the *Eidolon* because we must be ready to answer King William's summons at any moment. And we are forbidden to risk ourselves, to expose our power. Second—Marten and I can both be killed. We are neither impervious nor immortal. And the Jutras can build more warships nearly as fast as we destroy them. Away from the sea our power dwindles—we cannot kill them at the root. There will always be more Jutras. They control vast lands northeast of Bokal-Dur and it is said that they either come from or have expanded their empire beyond, across the White Sea. There is an endless supply of them."

She shook her head. "This is not a battle that can be won by an army of two, even as powerful as we are. In fact, King William intends to make Marten and me as incidental as possible to our defenses. Crosspointe must make its own safety. For now, yes, if the Jutras come, Marten and I will destroy them. This is why we must be ready at every moment to answer the king's call. But we cannot be everywhere. Our people must learn to protect themselves, and the king must make changes in the world to save Crosspointe's future. Far more is at stake than just Crosspointe. And King William begins this campaign with the new Pale on the Root, and the compasses in your hold."

She stopped speaking, looking from Thorn to Plusby, letting the silence blanket them as they digested her revelations. Thorn found her explanation nearly impossible not to believe. She clearly believed everything she said and her emotions were honest. No wonder she hated seeing the *Eidolon* helping the *Zhala*. He rubbed his eyes, shading his expression from her percipient gaze. If all she said was really true, would they be patriots or traitors if they obeyed the king's orders?

"We have more than sixty Jutras with us, and the *Zhala* and her crew. We promised to guide them to safety," Plusby said curtly. "If we're going to run these compasses to Calenfor, they'll need stores and whatever else you can give them to help them settle somewhere. And they'll need a Pilot to get them there."

Thorn glanced sharply at his friend. His brows drew together. Did Plusby believe Lucy's story or did he just want to find his wife? Thorn found he couldn't blame Plusby for the latter, if it was the case.

Lucy steepled her fingers together. She clearly didn't like the idea of helping any Jutras. Finally she said, "I will speak with them. If I am convinced they are no threat to Crosspointe, I will give them all they require. Will that do?"

Thorn shook his head. "No. We need to know they are safe."

Her brows lifted. She glanced up at Marten. Something passed between them, the quiet communication of lovers who are so deeply bound together that they know each other's thoughts without speaking them.

"What you do not know is that Edgar Thorpe sent my father, my two eldest brothers, and many friends to Bokal-Dur as slaves. And after what I witnessed the priests do—"

She covered her mouth with her hand. Thorn thought of all that Savaiu had told him about slaves and he flinched from the knowledge. After a moment Lucy collected herself.

"I confess that I am loath to help any Jutras. But for the sake of Crosspointe, I will set them safely wherever they wish and I will provide them with food and whatever else they need. I will be generous. You have my word."

"Thank you," Thorn said, requiring no more than her promise. "If we decide to sail, when do you want us to leave?"

"As soon as the tide turns. The compasses must be delivered to Calenfor before the beginning of Mercy. You have less than a month to get all the way up the Saithe River. You have no time to lose. You need to choose now."

"We will need to discuss it," Thorn said firmly.

She stood as if expecting the answer. "Very well. Ring the bell when you have decided." She began to walk out, then stopped. "I should not wish you to be deceived in this matter. The *Eidolon*, with or without you, *will* take those compasses to Calenfor. If you choose not to go, you will remain here until it is safe to free you. That will be King William's decision. The difference will be how quickly Marten and I are revealed to our enemies, and that we must leave Crosspointe unprotected. In Calenfor, our majick will be considerably weakened, if not entirely unavailable to us. We will be at risk. William will not thank you, I'm afraid, if we are exposed or if the Jutras attack."

"And our Jutras friends?" Plusby asked curtly, anger curling around the words like smoke from a blown candle.

She grimaced. "I will see them safely to a good home, regardless. How can I not, when their fleeing takes a few more sacrifices from the mouths of the Jutras gods? And I will tell you of your wife, Captain Plusby, and you of your brother, Pilot Thorn. This decision must be made with both your hearts as free as I can make them, though William will blister my hide for throwing away my leverage over you." She shrugged. "I have never been a politician and I have some prerogatives in this matter. Now, if you will excuse me, you have matters to discuss."

She left. Marten remained behind. Thorn watched him. He was nothing like the man he'd been, as far as he could see. Not that he'd known Marten particularly well. They'd once sailed together briefly. Thorn had replaced Thorpe's previous Pilot who'd become ill near the end of the season. But from what he remembered of him, Thorpe had been almost gregarious, with a sharp wit. Not this silent, brooding shadow figure who seemed so angry, so dangerous. But the new Marten was clearly also capable of love—deep, abiding love, the kind Plusby had for his lost wife.

"You look like you have questions for me," Marten said quietly, his disconcerting gaze fixed on Plusby.

"You are not the man you used to be."

"True."

"The Marten Thorpe I knew was not the kind to care about a woman or a king or a country. The Marten Thorpe I knew was a gambler and a rogue who devoted himself to pleasure and vice. And now you obviously have a deep attachment to Miss Trenton and to her cause. *Sylveth* may have given you majick, but it didn't do that to you."

Marten nodded, a self-deprecating grin breaking the line of his mouth. It was the first time he'd looked truly human since their arrival. Thorn felt something inside himself unclench.

"You've learned about *sylveth*, then?" he asked Plusby as he reached for a decanter on the sideboard and poured a clear drink. "I'd like to hear that story one day. Meris's Tears—want a drink?"

Both Plusby and Thorn accepted. Marten was silent as he poured the drinks and handed them out. Then he retreated to the opposite end of the table.

"You're right. But I was worse than you thought. I gambled. Heavily. I had debts. My brother Edgar used my straitened circumstances to convince me to—" He broke off. Again that grin, bitter this time. "No. Edgar dangled the bait, but I was not forced. What I did was entirely my fault. I sacrificed my honor and integrity to my stupidity. Edgar bet me enough to cover my debts that I could not steal stamped customs seals from Lucy. But I did. He then used them to frame her for theft, fraud, and treason. Jordan was furious with me. He had fists of stone."

He met Thorn's eyes unflinchingly. "I went to him to ask for help. Edgar had warned me against interference and had me followed. He murdered Jordan to keep him from helping Lucy. At the same time, he called all my gambling markers. I had not yet learned my lesson and was back in debt. He had me arrested and put an iron collar on me." Marten touched his throat. "After that . . . I realized what kind of man I wanted to be. *Sylveth* has given me the chance to be him."

"You've suddenly become a devoted servant of King William and Crosspointe? And we are to trust you because you've decided you want to repair your honor?"

Marten was shaking his head before Plusby finished. "No. Oh no. Do not be mistaken. I belong to Lucy. Everything I am, everything I will ever be, is hers. I will never make up for what I've done to her, nor repay the generosity and love she's given me. But I will try to do so, every moment for the rest of my life. I will never fail her again."

That shut Plusby's mouth. He swirled his glass of liquor, his attention fixed on the liquid inside. Marten's profession could have come from Plusby's own mouth, Thorn thought. That was how he felt about his wife. That same soul-deep devotion. He cleared his throat.

"And why should we trust Lucy?" Plusby asked softly. "What proof is there that she is telling us the truth about this being the king's mission?"

Something moved in Marten's eyes and the human part of him sank inside. Once again he turned to shadowy strangeness. But then after a moment he thawed slightly.

"Fair enough. I will tell you this. It will have to suffice. The rest you will have to take on faith. If this was not the king's mission, then Lucy and I would already be at war with the Jutras. When she was accused of treason, Lucy's friends, her father, and two of her brothers were sent to the Bramble to be exposed during Chance. But only Lucy and I were abandoned here. My brother had been selling the Bramble convicts to the Jutras as slaves for years. Her family and friends were sent to Bokal-Dur and sold."

His fingers tapped against his thighs in what? Nervousness? Frustration? Thorn couldn't be certain. This new Marten Thorpe made few outward expressions of emotion. He was very difficult to read.

"The king forbade her to rescue them. Crosspointe needed her more, he said. If you want proof, then that is all I can offer you. I have never met anyone more devoted to her country and to her family. I've never met anyone more determined to do the right thing. She made her mistakes, too, but you don't know how she suffered—" He swallowed jerkily and slugged down the rest of his drink.

"You make your decision now. I am done."

He strode toward the door, then stopped just inside

and swung back around. His gaze was narrow, his expression flat and hard. Currents of power moved through the darkness of his black eyes. Thorn shivered with visceral fear, the memory of the spawn eating him alive thrusting up into his mind. His gorge rose and it was all he could do to swallow it back down.

"If you betray her—" He broke off, his nostrils flaring. "If you do anything that risks Lucy, you will never be welcome on the sea again."

It was a warning and a threat. One that Thorn had no doubt the other man had the power to enforce.

The door slammed shut, leaving Plusby and Thorn alone. Silence fell and Thorn sipped his drink, grappling with all they'd learned.

"Well? What do you make of all this? Do you think they are telling the truth? And if so, do we follow the king or is he making a stupid mistake?"

Plusby asked the question as he went to pour himself another glass of Meris's Tears. He drank it swiftly and sloshed more in the glass before turning to look at Thorn. He was haggard. His face was pale and drawn and his eyes were holes of misery. He was walking a ragged edge. Marten had made him think about Sherenya, as if his wife were ever far from his mind.

"You have to tell me what we should do. I don't think I'm in any state to make a rational decision," he added, tossing back his drink.

"I cannot begin to tell you how much raw power it took to pull that bore wave down. And to create two new Pales . . . I have no doubt that if the king weren't keeping a leash on them, they'd go hunting for Lucy's family in Bokal-Dur," Thorn said, pushing his own glass away. "Which means she's more loyal to the king than to her father and brothers, so I'm inclined to believe her story. But as for whether or not the king is making a mistake . . ." He shook his head. "What does it matter? Our ship, our *crew*, is going to Calenfor with those compasses whether we go or no. I'm not of a mind to let them sail off without us."

"Even if it's treason?"

Thorn shrugged. "Don't be shy about it. Selling compasses *is* treason. But here's the thing. Risky as the king's plan is, it also makes sense. And King William is taking precautions with a new Pale on the Root and keeping Lucy and Marten in his hip pocket. He's devious and I'm willing to trust him—no matter what sort of bilge the Merchants' Commission has been stirring up about it, he's always been a strong hand on the helm. But even if I weren't willing to let him do his job, I'm not about to sit on scruples here while my ship and crew are scudding across the waves without me. Are you?"

"No. But I am not sure my decision is remotely rational." Plusby was looking at his glass as he spun it between his fingers. "I need to find Sherenya. She's alive. I don't want to betray my crew, but I don't trust myself at the moment."

His confession showed how great a change he'd undergone this journey. The Plusby who'd raced Thorn up the mast would not have been sane enough to know or care that he might be out of his mind. Thorn leaned forward, speaking earnestly.

"Think of it this way. Even using majick to control the crew, I don't know how Lucy and Marten will be able to manage the ship. And once they get any distance off the sea, their powers will fade. When the crew mutinies—and I have no doubt that they will—then everyone will be in trouble, especially Lucy and Marten. And given the protection that the two of them give Crosspointe right now, I don't want to risk them. If it turns out that King William is playing this game badly, Crosspointe will need them when things go wrong. And even if the crew didn't mutiny, the Saithe River between Calenfor and Lalant Uly is a dangerous, ugly stretch. You and I can get the *Eidolon* through. I don't know if they can. It's why they wanted us in the first place. Why they didn't try to just take it themselves. I think we have to go."

Plusby nodded slow agreement. "And the crew? Do we tell them what's going on?"

Thorn smiled, struck by the strangeness of the conversation. At the beginning of this journey, Plusby would rather have gouged out his own eyes than consult Thorn. They'd become a team, all of them. "Aye. Crabbel, Blot, and Halford as soon as we get under way. The rest of them . . . eventually."

"You don't think your three charmers will slit our throats and scuttle the ship when they learn we're off to sell compasses?"

"Mine? They claimed you too, as I recall. But—no. I think, strangely enough, that they have come to trust us. Both of us. Going back to help the *Zhala* won you a lot of loyalty and trust."

Plusby snorted in disbelief.

"We are their captain and Pilot," Thorn said. "We are supposed to guide them through all the dangers of the Inland Sea. It's our job to worry and plan, theirs to obey. They know that; it's the way the world works, the way things are supposed to be on a ship. They aren't going to let you kill yourself or run off chasing siren songs, and they aren't going to let me rip myself to bits anymore. I'll be lucky if I ever get into the rigging again. They'll probably wrap me in cotton wool if I so much as get a splinter. If we tell them this is the right thing to do, then they will do it."

Plusby nodded, his jaw tight. Thorn didn't know if it was agreement or mere acknowledgment. Plusby still didn't look at him.

"Then we've decided?"

"Aye," Thorn said.

"Savaiu is going rip our balls off for abandoning her to Lucy."

"She'll get over it." But Thorn knew better.

"Aye. She has no choice."

"Neither do we." But he couldn't help the guilt he felt. He'd left Jordan, and his brother had been murdered. What would happen to Savaiu?

There was nothing else to say. Plusby rang the bell. Lucy merely nodded her head when she heard their decision, though Thorn thought he saw a flash of relief in her eyes. It startled him. If anything, he'd have expected gloating. But as powerful as she was, she was not arrogant. She did not wield her majick like a club. Her demeanor strengthened his belief that they were doing the right thing. Whatever happened, she had to be kept safe against catastrophe. She and Marten were Crosspointe's last bastion of defense. Risking her to deliver the compasses would be stupid and unforgivable.

"Thank you," she said. "Now I suggest you fetch someone to speak for your Jutras companions. Bring him here so we may speak. I hope he is not Paleblasted."

"She," Thorn corrected. "Savaiu. She is the captain of the *Zhala*."

Lucy cocked her head at him, hearing something in his voice that he didn't intend. He flushed.

"Bring her here, if you will, Pilot Thorn. Marten will make you a path. In the meantime . . . Captain Plusby, I would speak with you. About your wife."

Thorn left Plusby with Lucy and returned to the beach. Marten was a silent presence beside him, though he seemed easier, less distant. Thorn's mind churned with all he'd learned. He felt queasy. He'd made his decision and he would stick with it. All the same, he couldn't help feeling torn. Crosspointe was cracking apart at the seams. Was he about to shatter it altogether? Or begin a healing?

He'd always been loyal to the king, whenever he'd considered politics, which was rare. Once he'd left his parents' house, he'd cared only about where to find his next meal, how to keep from being raped, how to keep from getting beaten to death, how to find money, how to get out of the gutter. Once he'd become a Pilot, all he'd cared about was the sea. He'd hardly spared a thought even for Jordan. But now he needed to consider the future. He couldn't just live moment to moment, his life in the hands of the winds and waves. He wasn't alone anymore.

"I had heard you and Jordan were good friends," he said to Marten as they left the cave.

"We were, as far as it went. But he was not the sort to tolerate my gambling and what it made me do," was the measured reply.

"But you miss him," Thorn guessed shrewdly.

"I do. Though had he lived, I don't know that he would ever have forgiven me for what I did to Lucy. They were very close." There was more than a little pain in Marten's voice. He said nothing more until they came to a stop on the strand. "Hurry. You don't have much time."

The path formed again in the water and Thorn was walking across the cove to the *Zhala*. He rose in the air on a column of water and leaped lightly over the rail, looking about curiously. Charring splotched the deck and gangway that served as a bridge between the poop deck and the castle deck. There were scars where the crew had hacked out chunks of wood from the bulwarks, the rails, and even the masts. But even so, there was surprisingly little fire damage.

He climbed up onto the gangway, checking the castle deck first. Two men and a woman slumped on the deck, Pale-blasted. He hurried back to the poop deck and found Savaiu sitting dazed, her back against the bulwark. Some of the other members of her crew were starting to rouse.

He crouched beside her, brushing the hair from her forehead with his fingers. Her face was smudged with smoke and smears of blood. He didn't know if it was hers. His chest contracted. He'd never met a woman he wanted as much as he wanted her. But he wanted the *Eidolon* more. He'd found a home there for the first time in his life. A home and a family, and there was no room for Savaiu among them. He let his hand fall.

"Savaiu? Are you all right? Can you walk?"

She opened her eyes, turning her head to follow his voice. Something like pain flitted across her face. "I thought the beasts killed you. Or are you a ghost?"

Unthinking, he clasped her cold hand, raising it to his lips. "Not a ghost. But something's happened. It concerns your people. Can you walk?"

She nodded and let him help her up. She staggered and lurched. Thorn steadied her.

"What happened to me?"

"You crossed a Pale. It can be unsettling, though you get used to it in time."

She snorted. "I feel like one of those beasts chewed my head."

"They're called Koreions. Come, now. This might seem strange, but it's all right."

She goggled a little as he helped her out on the water staircase. This time, however, the stairs lowered gently and carried them in to shore, where Marten waited.

The experience was enough to pull Savaiu back to her senses. When she stepped onto the beach, she was collected, eyeing Marten suspiciously.

"This is Captain Savaiu of the *Zhala*. Savaiu, this is Captain Marten Thorpe."

"Captain Savaiu," Marten said with a slight bow. "This way, if you will."

She glanced warily at Thorn, who nodded. Marten led them back inside a small salon, where Plusby stood with his back to them. He leaned against the mantle, his hands clenched, his body rigid with emotion, as he stared into the fire. When they entered, Lucy rose from a stool in the corner, her arms crossed over her stomach, her expression tight. Whatever had passed between them had not been easy on either of them. Thorn was surprised when Marten went to stand by Plusby, speaking to him in a soft, low voice, one hand resting on his shoulder. Unable to hear what he was saying, Thorn instead made introductions.

"Captain Savaiu, this is Lucy Trenton. She is a maji-car. She has agreed to guide your people to safety and provide you with stores and whatever else may be needed to make a new start."

Savaiu scowled, whirling on Thorn. "*You* promised to take us to safety."

He flinched at the accusation in her voice. "We cannot. We have business we must finish."

"What business?"

He shook his head. "I cannot say."

Her scowl deepened. "I do not know this woman. I will not put my people in her hands. You promised. You *promised* and—" She broke off, sucking in a breath and clamping her lips together. She raked Thorn with a hot stare.

Thorn flushed, recalling their argument when they'd repaired the ships. He'd resented the way she'd questioned whether he and Plusby would keep their part of the bargain . . . whether *he* would. He'd been so angry. And now she'd been proved right. Except that she and her people *would be* safe. Their bargain would be fulfilled. He took a breath to try to explain, but Lucy spoke first.

"You don't have a choice," Lucy said, though her voice lacked the venom Thorn half expected when she addressed the Jutras. "Even if Pilot Thorn and Captain Plusby wished to, they could not accompany you. My Koreions will not permit it."

"Why? Why would you help us?"

Lucy's lips tightened. "Because I made a bargain."

"What bargain?"

"All you need to know is that I will make sure you make it to safety and are well supplied for your new start. I have already sent food to your ship. Captain Plusby?"

Her voice softened on his name. He lifted his head, turning. His eyes looked bruised, and they glittered with something Thorn hoped was not insanity.

"Marten will help you and Pilot Thorn transfer Captain Savaiu's people from the *Eidolon*. You must hurry. The tide will turn in a scant two glasses; you will sail on it. I will see that you have ample stores aboard, and anything else you need."

Savaiu started to interrupt, but Lucy didn't give her the chance.

"Captain Savaiu—would you prefer your people

join you aboard your ship or be given accommodations ashore until we can set sail? I will provide all you require either way. And you will wish to clean up."

While they spoke, Marten motioned for Plusby and Thorn to follow him back outside. Thorn went reluctantly, looking over his shoulder. But it appeared that the conversation between the two women was proceeding civilly enough. Savaiu no longer looked like she was going to attack. Her arms had fallen to her sides and she was listening. He was struck with a sharp pang. She had no more need of him. She and her people would be taken to safety. He was not likely to see her again. He felt wooden as he walked away.

Outside on the beach, Thorn stopped. "One thing, Marten. There's a girl among the villagers. I think she will be a Pilot. Can you help her? Help her change before she goes mad?"

Thorpe hesitated, then nodded. Recklessly, Thorn pushed his luck. He might not see Savaiu again, but he might be able to leave her with something truly valuable. And Izzi—he knew all too well what it was like to be a Pilot without a compass. Fierce as she was, she might go mad from that.

"There is another thing. The *Zhala* would benefit from a compass. With Izzi, they will have a Pilot. Will you speak to Lucy about it? Ask her to consider it? A ship that could navigate the sea would give Savaiu's people a means to support themselves. It could mean the difference between survival and not."

This time his nod came slower. "I will speak to her." He sounded doubtful.

"You think she will not agree. Because they are Jutras?"

"And because with all her power, she cannot make a compass. I scavenged those in the *Eidolon*'s hold from wrecks. There were not many. The sea reclaims them quickly. There are none to spare; the king needs all he can get."

*   *   *

Savaiu decided to bring the villagers ashore. A wide hall appeared on the beach, full of soft beds, warm fires, and delicious food. Many of the villagers remained unconscious from passing through the Pale and were put into the beds. Thorn found Izzi in the hold, holding her sister's head on her lap, stroking her hair. She looked up when he crouched beside her.

"Eglena's alive," she stated, as if refusing to accept another verdict.

Thorn nodded agreement. "She's Pale-blasted. She'll wake up soon. Let's take her ashore. There's someone I want you to meet."

After tucking Eglena into a bed, he led Izzi to Marten. She stared into his black eyes and then held out her hand in greeting. He took it with sober dignity, then met Thorn's gaze above her head.

"You are right. A Pilot. She will be very strong, like you."

With that, he led her back inside the building, talking softly.

Thorn watched them go. The tide was nearly slack. He was out of time. For a moment he considered seeking out Savaiu to say farewell, but there was no point. She'd probably kick him in the balls anyhow. He drew an unsteady breath. Slowly he began walking down the beach, his gaze fixed on the *Eidolon*. He could see activity on the deck and faintly heard Crabbel's shouts and Blot's singing. A faint smile turned his lips. He started when Savaiu seized his arm and dragged him up the strand into the privacy of the trees. She was spitting-nails angry.

"You are leaving? Just like that?"

"Aye. We have to catch the tide."

She said something guttural in Jutras, then prodded him in the chest with a hard finger. "You said you would not abandon us."

"I am *not* abandoning you. Lucy will see you and your people to safety. You don't need me anymore."

Savaiu went still, averting her face so he couldn't see her expression. She changed the subject.

"It is dangerous, this business of yours. It is why your captain's Bess tried to kill you."

"Aye."

She made a sound in her throat and spun about, striding off. Three steps away she halted, hands on her hips, staring out on the ships at anchor in the cove. Then she spun back around.

"And after? When this business is done? What do you then?"

"I don't know."

He was now a king's Pilot, as Lucy was a king's majicar. Thorn didn't doubt that it would suit King William to have a black ship at his disposal, one that did not require paperwork or permissions, one that he could send where he wished and when he wished with no one the wiser.

"We will not again see each other."

It wasn't quite a question.

He shook his head. "I do not think so."

Suddenly he had to get away, get back aboard ship. Briskly he said, "Lucy will get you whatever you need to start over. Just tell her. If you want some advice, I'd see about settling somewhere around Orsage or Normengas. There are some decent rivers and you could earn a living running cargo between the cities. Or if you go to Tiro Pilan, there's the Pradith-Na River. It'll run you clear up into Esengaile. There'll be good trading. Even good pyrating."

She didn't respond. Thorn's mouth tightened. He nodded. "Fair winds and following seas," he said, then started down the strand.

Savaiu overtook him within a few steps. She pulled him to a halt, spinning him around and standing on tiptoe to press her cold lips to his. He slid his arms around her, kissing her deeply.

"Tide won't wait," Plusby called, coming up the beach.

Thorn broke the kiss and glared at his friend, who grinned, despite his hollow, wasted appearance. Thorn sighed, resting his forehead against Savaiu's before slowly pulling away. "I've got to go."

She captured his face between her palms, locking his gaze with hers.

"You come find me. Yes?"

Thorn hesitated. "I am not my own man anymore. And . . . I have the *Eidolon*. I cannot—"

She pressed her fingertips over his mouth. "I find I wish to follow this path after all. Even if it is short and goes nowhere. Find me."

Something cracked apart inside him. How this could work, he didn't know. But he had to see her again, if only for a few snatched moments between voyages. He pulled her hand away from his lips, his fingers weaving with hers.

"I will find you." He hesitated. "It may be a while."

"I will wait." She squeezed his hand, and then let it fall away. He turned and joined Plusby, heading for the *Eidolon*. He didn't look back. He didn't trust himself that much.

On board, they found Blot, Halford, and Crabbel waiting for them. Halford was holding a purring Fitch, and Blot looked thin but well. Lucy had come aboard and gone through the crew, healing any injuries she found, including his.

"Tide's on its way out. Hoist the anchor, mate," Plusby ordered without any ado.

As quickly as that, they were back to business. Crabbel quickly roused the crew and hauled up the anchor and catted it. The Koreions gathered around them again, pushing the *Eidolon* back through the cove's narrow mouth out into the open sea. This time, because he expected it, crossing the Pale only made Thorn's ears ring and his ribs hurt momentarily. When he looked back, all he could see was a rocky seawall where the cove had been.

He took his position at the compass, listening to the familiar noises of the ship as Plusby called out orders and Crabbel relayed them. The sails luffed and then filled with a popping sound, and soon they were skimming through the waves. The storm moving in from the southwest was turning the sea choppy. To the east near the entrance of Kutranil Bay, knucklebones unfurled in the water. A streaking tide of *sylveth* wove through the deadly weir. The *Eidolon* was too far away for any danger.

They'd been under way a glass when Plusby came to stand beside Thorn. He didn't speak. Thorn could feel him seething beneath a fragile control.

"What did she say about Sherenya?" Thorn asked finally.

"She's alive. But she doesn't want to see me. Not yet."

"Not yet?"

Plusby's face tightened. "She's . . . cursed by *sylveth*. She's not ready to let me see her. But she did want me to know she's alive."

"What aren't you saying?"

"Lucy said . . . the changes in Sherenya are substantial. I should be prepared." His face contorted. He caught himself. "I don't care. I just want her back. Whatever it takes, whatever she has become, I don't care."

They didn't speak for several minutes. Thorn did not know how to respond. It must have been the purest joy to discover his wife alive, and now to learn she didn't want to see him—it had to be tearing Plusby to shreds.

"But it's hopeful news, right?" he said finally. "She remembers who she is. She remembers you. She's just scared. She'll come to you when she's ready. You must believe that."

Plusby rubbed a hand over the back of his neck. "I hope so. But what if she is never ready?"

"Then you'll find her. I'll help you. All of us will," Thorn promised, gesturing vaguely around the ship. "Whenever you want to start looking."

Plusby smiled weakly, his blond hair lifting in the

breeze. "How did we end up here? I wanted to kill you on sight when you first came aboard."

"I often have that effect on people. I'm certain you will want to kill me again."

"I am too."

Thorn chuckled. "Will you be all right?"

"For now. But if she doesn't find me soon, we'll be going hunting. Too much time has been wasted already."

"The changes in your wife may be extraordinary," Thorn said, though whether he was warning his friend or asking a question, he didn't know.

"I know." Plusby was silent for a long minute. "I don't care," he said again.

"I didn't think you would."

There was another silence, and then Plusby spoke again, changing the subject. "I spoke to Lucy while you were finishing with the villagers."

"Oh?"

"King William is putting in shipyards on the Root. And starting to build weapons. I told her about the agun and the weaponry the Jutras carry."

"Did you?"

"I suggested that Savaiu and her people might be useful to King William's plans. It would be handy to have someone who could teach us how to build weaponry and how to use it. Plus a Jutras warship could be useful for spying. Savaiu might consider it in exchange for land and homes for her people inside the Root Pale."

Thorn turned his head, his hand clenched tight around the southern point of the compass. "What did Lucy say?"

Plusby smiled slowly. "When you go looking for Savaiu, you should start on the Root."

Glossary

agun. A weapon employed by the Jutras warrior ships, usually catapulted. A glass globe contains an oily substance, resistant to water, that burns on contact.

Bess. Steward of Captain Plusby on the *Eidolon*.

Beyoshen (bey•OH•shuhn). A member of the Pilots' Guild who contracts all the assignments and distributes them.

Bites. An area east of the Bramble. They are characterized by tall, angular cliffs and a jagged shoreline.

Black Sea. The Inland Sea.

Blacksea. A town on the notheast coast of Crosspointe. It is home to the Pilots' Guild and to many Pilots.

black ship. An illegal ship.

blood oak. A rare tree highly prized for its majickal properties.

Braken. The sea god, lover of goddess Meris.

Bramble. An island outside the protection of the Pale where Crosspointe banishes those who have been convicted of breaking the law.

celestie. A sea creature. Celesties are luminescent and translucent animals equal in size to a pony. They live primarily in the depths of the Inland Sea. Storms stir them to the surface to feed.

Chance. A month of severe storms when *sylveth* is blown into the air. Everyone and every ship must take refuge beyond the Verge or inside the Pale to be safe from the *sylveth*.

charmer. Anyone surviving three shipwrecks is made to

wear a wreck charm to warn other sailors of his or her luck. It cannot be removed. It is bad luck to kill a charmer.

Chayos. Goddess, mother of earth and all things green, the giver of life and mother of Hurn.

chinai (chee•NAHY). Sex slaves of the *picrit arrai.*

cipher. A majickal object that carries a curse or gives an ability to the wearer.

Corbies. Private police force paid by the crown to seek out any *sylveth* spawn that makes it to shore.

Cresset. A god of Jutras, paired with Uniat. One is the giver of life and the other the harvester; they change roles during the time of Seir Muta Re.

crimper. A kidnapper ("to crimp").

Dabloute (dah•BLOOT). The housing of the Pilots' Guild.

daxs (DAX). The water caste of the Jutras.

daxs maryad (DAX•MAIR•ee•ahd). Subcaste of captains with the *daxs* caste, an honored position.

Dhucala's wolves (du•KAH•la). Seafaring warriors of Jutras.

efiole (ey•fee•ohl). Priestess in training of Tapisriya.

Ekidey. An ancient dead language used by the Pilots' Guild for certain rituals.

freelanders. Those people whose countries have not been conquered by the Jutras.

glass. An estimation of time equivalent to an hour.

grain. An estimation of time equivalent to a second.

hishmali (hish•MAH•lee). The children of conquered peoples who have become Jutras through service to the Jutras Empire.

hoskarna (hohs•KAR•nah). Two tall poles that represent the twin gods of Jutras (usually one is red, the other white). The poles allow the gods to infect the land where they are placed, providing a conduit for them.

Hurn. The stranger god, son of the goddess Chayos, and lover of the goddess Meris.

Inland Sea. The Black Sea that surrounds Crosspointe.

jeras (JEE•ras). Tapisriyan divine women.

Jordan Truehelm. Sea captain, brother of Thorn, and friend of Captain Marten Thorpe, murdered in *The Cipher*.

Jutras. An enemy country of Crosspointe that is slowly invading all the countries surrounding the Inland Sea.

Ketirvan. An annual three-day meeting held by the Pilots' Guild at the end of Chance to honor the dead, discuss and vote on guild business, and hand out assignments for the next season.

kiryat (keer•yat). Priest caste of the Jutras.

kiza (KEE•zah). Purebloods who have fallen from their caste. They are usually made into breeders at a *thana* or they are made *neallonya*.

knacker shed. Storage area where majickal gear is stored for capturing and storing *sylveth* spawn.

knucklebones. A hazard of the sea. They look to be as soft as seaweed but can rip the bottom out of a ship.

Koreion (kor•EE•on). A serpentine sea monster larger than a ship with four legs and claws; also a symbol of the sea often found decorating clothing, ships, or buildings connected to a living made from the sea.

Kyries. The walking dead of Chayos.

Leighton Plusby. Captain of the *Eidolon*.

Lucy Trenton. A customs inspector who is a member of the Rampling royal family; she is a powerful majicar.

majicars. Those who can use majick.

Majicar Sennet. The ruling committee of the Majicars' Guild.

Marten Thorpe. Once a sea captain, now capable of manipulating the sea; lover of Lucy Trenton.

Merchants' Commission. A group of merchants elected from each merchants' guild. They represent all the merchants' guilds.

Meris. Goddess, aka Moonsinger, ruler of the moon and tides, lover of Braken but pines after Hurn. *Sylveth* is called "the blood of Meris."

neallonya (ney•ahl•OHN•ya). Slaves of the Jutras, mostly conquered peoples who are not used as *picrit arrai*.

Pale. A majickal fence of wards surrounding Crosspointe, protecting the collection of islands from the threat of *sylveth*. It includes two sets of wards, one above the waves, and tide wards below.

parastraya (per•uh•STRAHI•uh). Jutras eunuchs.

picrit (pee•creet). Jutras warrior caste.

picrit arrai (pee•creet•ah•RA•YI). Lowest *shaghi* of the warrior caste, made up of conquered peoples who take the opportunity rather than become slaves.

Pilot. Navigator on a ship, sensitive to the sea and majick; uses a majicked compass to read the sea.

Pirena. The head of the Pilots' Guild.

Pirena-elect. The next elected head of the Pilots' Guild.

points. Newly discovered Pilots who are still in their training phase.

Ramplings. The royal family of Crosspointe.

Relsea. Country to the northwest of Crosspointe taken over by Jutras.

river pyrates. Sailors of small vessels that run the rivers and steal from seagoing ships or the towns along the coast.

Root. The mass of tangled mountain spines north of Crosspointe. They thrust far out into the Inland Sea like a mass of roots. This is a home to spawn.

Savaiu (sav•O). Jutras pyrate captain of the *Zhala*.

Seir Muta Re (ser•MU•ta•REY). The time when the two gods of Jutras swap positions of giver of life and harvester.

shaghis (SHAH•jeez). Special skill sets within a Jutras caste.

snottie. A young boy or girl brought on board to apprentice in ship work.

splatter tide. When a storm flings *sylveth* out into the waves in blobs rather than in its usual skeins.

Squall Solution. A race up the mainmast often used to settle disputes aboard ship.

Sylbrac (Geoffrey Truehelm/Thorn). Guild Pilot, son of Lord Chancellor Truehelm, and brother of Jordan Truehelm.

sylveth. A majickal substance found as silvery skeins in the sea. It can mutate any being or thing into a hideous creature; can also be carefully harvested and used by majicars in spells.

Tapisriya (tap•is•RI•ya). A country overrun by Jutras; homeland of Captain Plusby's wife, Sherenya.

thana (THAW•nah). A Jutras farm breeding humans.

Uniat (YOO•nee•at). A god of the Jutras, paired with Cresset. One is the giver of life and the other the harvester; they change places during the time of Seir Muta Re.

vada-eels. It is a flat, bony eel, ranging from less than an inch at hatching to the length of a ship. Vada-eels live in the mid-depths of the Inland Sea and are voracious. They are mostly translucent with a black spine, black teeth, and two brillant luminescent green stripes running down their top and bottom ridges.

Verge. A broad twenty-league band of no-man's-land surrounding the Inland Sea where storms drop *sylveth* during the Chance storm season.

vescie. A sea creature that lives in the depths, rising only during storms. They are small creatures, the size of a child's hand. They are composed mostly of teeth and stomachs. Vescies hunt in swarms and lay dormant at the bottom of the sea much of the time.

White Sea. The frozen sea that runs north and east along the Jutras territory.

Zhala (ZAH•lah). A Jutras warship stolen by Jutras pyrates.

ziyada-had (zee•YAH•dah•had). The Jutras term for the Verge.

See my Web page at www.dianapfrancis.com for more terms and definitions regarding ships.

Days of the Sennight

Sylday
Moonday
Merisday
Hurnday
Seaday
Pescday
Emberday

Months of a Season

Mercy
Passion
Tragedy
Retribution
Fate
Hope
Fury
Loyalty
Justice
*Decay
Chance
Forgiveness
Malevolence

*With one day between Justice and Decay for judgment (when con-
victed prisoners are sent to the Bramble).

ABOUT THE AUTHOR

Diana Pharaoh Francis has written the fantasy novel trilogy that includes *Path of Fate*, *Path of Honor*, and *Path of Blood*. *Path of Fate* was nominated for the Mary Roberts Rinehart Award. She has also written *The Cipher*, the first Novel of Crosspointe. Diana teaches in the English department at the University of Montana Western. For a lot more information, including where to read her blog, maps of her worlds, updated news, and other odd and fun tidbits, go to www.dianapfrancis.com.